Bronzeman

The Ruach Saga Volume Three - Second Edition

Mark A. Cornelius

ISBN
978-1-959314-38-7 (Paperback)
978-1-959314-39-4 (eBook)

BRONZEMAN

THE RUACH SAGA
Volume Three – Second Edition

With Illustrations by
Shay Cavender

Introduction

"Why are you writing about what happens after the Rapture?" a friend and fellow believer asked me, the question almost an accusation. I could hear in their voice the true issue: *If you really believe in that scenario, you won't be here. Why go to the effort?*

Why indeed? After writing *The Singularity,* a preEnd Times thriller, and its sequel *Seconds,* I felt the calling to follow through with the final part of the Ruach Saga trilogy. The writers of Scripture not only wrote for the moment, but also peered beyond the horizon, preserving their work on parchment for the benefit of generations far in the future.

Not that this manuscript, or any of my writings for that matter qualify as Scripture. But this fictional representation does weave in the Word of God already recognized. The details, I pray are representations based on a long study of YHWH's message, warnings and the hope He provides us in His word.

To the point then: Why am I writing this? It has to do with something my Lord and Savior once said…

> "It is done! I am the Alpha and the Omega, the beginning and the end. To the thirsty I will give from the spring of the water of life without payment. The one who conquers will have this heritage, and I will be his God and he will be my son.

> But as for the cowardly, the faithless, the detestable, as for murderers, the sexually immoral, sorcerers, idolaters, and all liars, their portion will be in the lake that burns with fire and sulfur, which is the second death."

> —Revelation 21:6-8

It would be typical human self-centeredness to suggest that, after the rapture our responsibility to future generations—to share the gospel with those lost in hope of their salvation—will have passed. We are taught that even as we are going, we need to teach all nations what has been done for us. My hope is that *Bronzeman* will not only resonate with the world as we know it now, but also with those seeking hope when they discover they remain after the *Gathering-Up*. Of course, some may argue, such an event will never happen. Regardless, I hope you'll find this an entertaining and compelling piece of fiction.

B'rukah,
—Mark A. Cornelius

Bronzeman is a collection of letters and visions recorded during the Age of Completion—after the *Gathering-Up* when Christians vanished from Earth. Although scribed separately, these writings appear connected, not only through the language and insights of the writers, but also by their consistency related to biblical prophecy. This is remarkable in itself considering the conditions under which they were written. When *The Dark* began, immediately after the Gathering-Up, no consistent communications bridge such as the Internet, radio or television existed. Electrical and nuclear power ceased to operate at any level. Transportation reverted to horses (until they became food), bicycles, steam-driven vehicles, water travel and walking. Intercontinental exchange, even between countries, states and tribes was inconsistent and perilous, as were trust relationships.

Those who could get their message out and convince others of the truth of it held dominance. A worldwide dictatorship became the prominent form of government, supported by power hungry and self-seeking locals. These provincial rulers provided whatever food, technology, weapons and protection still existed.

In this continuation of The Ruach Saga, all Christians are gone, their character and strong ethics are no longer an influence on the Earth. It is an age of ruin and chaos in a world of intense struggle between the rulers of mankind and God's *Called-Ones*.

A new group of believers in Christ emerge called Seconds. They must survive persecution and suffering like no other generation before. This is the story of how human existence and the very planet itself will be redeemed in these extraordinary times.

"And it shall come to pass afterward, that I will pour out my Spirit on all flesh; your sons and your daughters shall prophesy, your old men shall dream dreams, and your young men shall see visions. Even on the male and female servants in those days I will pour out my Spirit."

—Joel 2:28-29

Odd these gifts we have been given. One to see, one to hear, another to *tell*: None without the other is adequate, but together—unity. We banner our gifts, both with the sigil at the front, and the proceeding credo, within the heading of this journal—all to codify the purpose of this journal. We are called *the Keepers*. What is it we keep? See. Listen. Our telling is not of our own Doing. A Greater One gives it. So great is He, that we can see and hear from afar. We can travel the globe without a walk or a cart or a ship. The Greater One we serve allows us to share what has been revealed to us and it is for His purpose, not our own.

Odd gifts yes; wonderful certainly; frightening definitely. We are watchmen on a tower that overlooks the entire world. We know the coming of the life-giving sunrise and the approach of deadly storms.

Our powers are not given for show, but for purpose. Now through our gift you will see and hear that purpose. The time is short before the last sunset. We share our eyes and ears with you, that you may know the Great One as we do and worship Him. Some will and some will refuse. All are given the blessing or the curse to choose.

See and hear. Read on if you dare and decide quickly to Do. Your fate is upon you.

Watching The Tartulians
Month 10, Year 3 After Gathering-Up (AG)

"I can't mingle you just done that!" Black Jackson stares at his companion as if he had only now arrived on the planet from some other place. The other man returns the stare without a word, then again he sticks his tongue out. He also produces a vibrating/spitting noise in the direction of the piece of paper posted on the *Do Board.*

"Küllo, Ye just Blew a Raspberry at the Mede's new Do!" Black Jackson has taken a step back from the insulter, perhaps in fear of a lightning strike or the sudden appearance of a *Peacer* or worse, a *Boss-Peacer.* "Are ye hurting to be *snuffed?*"

"Raspberry? Is that what ye call it?" Küllo does not seem afraid at all. "I've never heard it called out. No, that won't do—there is no fruitiness in it. There is no fruitiness in the world a'tal. It is not even a vegetable act—it is now *Blubbertonguing.*"

The tall, lanky Ethiopian takes another step of distance. We do not see fear in him at Küllo's telling an opinion against the most recent *Do* from the Mede and his Do Brothers of the Green Order Government, known as GOG. And in these days, that calls for hurt. The new Do on the Do Board is short and, in the terminology of the day, *fact*:

> All who live here; breathe the Supreme Mede's air here
> Ye will do for the Supreme Mede and his do brothers what
> they call ye to
> Ye will know the Supreme Mede tell the do brothers and
> the do brothers tell ye.
> Ye will do for them any ask from them. Ye will obey them
> with yer "yes" and yer "do".
>
>
> By the call of the Supreme Mede

The Signet of Artemis, god of Knowledge in the ancient Greek—signified by a capital A with the right column bowed in archer fashion—verifies that the Mede's hand blessed this decree.

The fact that tall Ethiopian cannot read the words on the Do Board carries no worth. We hear and see Küllo read the tell to him. It is the same for everyone. Readers must Do for the No-readers.

"Ye is done-done!" Black Jackson shakes his head in finality. He has seen as we have: People who don't Do the Do's, become hurt by the Peacers.

"BJ, are ye a Second? Ye say it much, ye walk as if. Are ye just a *keepsack* with no bread inside?" Küllo, the short stocky Tartulian native takes his own steps, but his stepping brings him closer to the dark man, not further away. "We are called-out and the call says shine! Don't hide under a bowl."

Shining? We Keepers are amazed he would choose that word. The boys sit in on a broken concrete bench in a gathering spot called Town Centre. It is where most public announcements in their impoverished city are conveyed. An already grey place, it seems intentionally painted over in more grey. The lack of color blends seamlessly into the dismal surroundings beyond and speaks to the condition of their lives. The ashen sky above agrees with the environment—this is just one canvas that is pathetically replicated throughout the new world.

Black Jackson makes a subtle motion with his head toward one of the pathways leading out from between the rundown buildings that frame Town Centre. He brings his friend's attention to four uniformed Peacers approaching them and Küllo immediately displays his most gracious smile.

"Mede tells," both of the young men offer as the Peacers near. Their adversaries however have other business on their mind and pass the two by with hardly a glance.

"Oh some *lit ones* are we," Black Jackson quips when the contingent has marched out of earshot. "Where went all yer Blue? Someone snuff it out?"

The shorter man reaches into his tunic pocket, pulling out a piece of cured *heeringas*—the popular local fish, to chew on. The meat is tough and takes a few tugs with his teeth to separate. As he works it, there is a subtle cracking in his mouth. Küllo promptly spits out a small piece of one of his teeth that has just broken off. His response to his friend begins with Küllo pulling off his glove to reveal his glowing blue hand. Then he speaks through his cloth mask. We hear his muffled tell beginning with a chuckle.

"It's right here, but I'm crazy mixed up about how it's my Blue to shine. The Blue is His. I'm mingling He wants me to show it elsewheres." The Tartulian sits down on the rough ground, pulls an ink bottle, quill and parchment out of his keepsack that never leaves his person. It protects his most prized possessions which he now uses, beginning to scratch a message of his own.

"Lord above, ye not be mingling ye can write a complaint to 'em?" Black Jackson is becoming more anxious by the moment and glances nervously in the direction where the Peacers had headed. He stands up and paces around like an anxious cat, looking about for other eyes and ears that might be observing them. The risk of being caught by officials in some unseen snare is a risk anywhere. Finally detecting no approaching threat, the Ethiopian sets down once more.

"Following His Do is all I be *calling-out*," Küllo says as he focuses intently on his work, unconsciously biting on his tongue which protrudes from the right side of his mouth. This makes him mumble as he speaks and the other man misunderstands him.

"Ploughing His borders? What ye tell?"

The scribe looks up from his work directly at Black Jackson. He wears the look of one who has just been given a great gift. "Ploughing His borders, I mingle that lots. Thank ye brother!" And he goes right back to his scribbling.

"I don't mingle yer meaning a'tal," the black man shakes his head in frustration.

After long minutes, Küllo looks up again from the page and addresses his friend in earnest. "Ye know me well of all who know…'cept fer Him of course. Ye know He called out fer me to lay down words, new words that people can mingle right in their hearts, not like the ol' words the Do Brothers and Boss-Peacers tell, right?"

Black Jackson responds with a nod.

"Well," continues the Tartulian native, "I be righting the writing. I'm doin' a sŏnastik…a dictionary to help tell the difference between His Do and the Mede's Do.

"Küllo, ye know I cannot mingle reading, nor yer fancy thinking. What be a dictionary?"

The writer puts down his tools of trade and, with a look of sadness in his eyes, patiently explains to his friend, "A dictionary tells what a thing be by giving it a word. If you've never heard the word *God* afore and someone speaks it at you, you can look it up in a dictionary and it will tell you, who and what God be."

Black Jackson's brilliant smile lights his face. "Like yer word *mingle* ye taught me!"

"That's one of the new ones, certain." We Keepers watch the writer turn teacher. "It be right here," he speaks and simultaneously leafs through his precious documents until he finds the word he wants. Then he says it out loud,

"Mingle: 1. Mix together, make two things one. 2. Gluing yer Calling-Out to yer Do."

"That's one I use much acause it means much,' Black Jackson interrupts. I get-rich of speakin' it, 'specially the gluin' part."

Küllo looks curiously at the other man, then retrieves his writing utensils. He dips his quill and writes something else while he speaks. "BJ, ye puzzle me much. It be from ye that I catch many of the new words."

"But I don't make 'em." The tall man looks confused. Dey be someone else's make." Then he takes a long thought and bashfully asks his companion, "Can I see yer scratch?"

"Dinner be cold if you not eat now." This is stated sternly by a slight young woman, Asian by look, who appears at the doorway of a nearby building.

"*Ye, Ye o keun, Han Ko* yes, yes oh great Han Ko," both the Ethiopian and the Tartulian sing in mock honor. The woman at the door mumbles, "Hmmph." then points a finger at Küllo and says, "Less for the one sneaking fish in pocket." Then Han Ko returns into the building.

"I mingle Han Ko being happier today than in forever long," says Black Jackson with the most serious scowl he can muster upon his face.

As one, the young men rise and turn a final time toward the Do Board, offering a blubbertongue. Then they burst out in laughter and walk together toward their waiting meal. What a picture of joy they are for us.

We will tell more of Han Ko's story later. But for the young men, she is a closed book. It is Küllo and Black Jackson's interactions we are now called-out to share. Their own stories are well mingled between the two of them. They share a common bond having grown up in slum conditions. Each had believing parents who had done their best to raise them in the ways of church, but the neighborhoods of Tartu Estonia and Adama Ethiopia provided far too many distractions and temptations. Compounding the situation, both had grown up in illiterate families.

They, like many who had obtained the age of reason, were abandoned in a single, terrible day when even the earth and elements themselves seemed eager to reject them.

How the two became mingled is in itself miraculous. Countless stories are told now of the *Bronzeman Seeings*—individuals and even whole groups who had heard and seen the Man-God. Some even claimed to have been physically touched by him and had been instantly healed of severe physical ailments, not the least of the cures included mending the hateful bug strikes that have wounded any who do not confess and claim same-said Jesus as Lord of their life.

So we begin to watch the history of Küllo. At fourteen years of age, the boy had become all frustrated with the social and physical upheaval boiling up throughout Estonia and the world. His unemployed parents and their family already suffered from a pathetic existence. The boy's angry tirades against his *ema ja isa*—mother and father—accusing them of having no value to society—told of his inner rage. He blamed them for holding him back from any possible accomplishments and accused their plight of trapping him in the mire of the surrounding poverty. One late afternoon, without hope or a plan, the naïve Tartulian finally took to the streets, rejecting all he had known. He wandered into the night finally to stand in front of an old derelict building near Town Centre. Tentatively he crept inside and picked his way through refuse, trying mostly to avoid the places where he heard the rustling of rats and other more unfamiliar disturbances. Finally, he found a relatively clear spot on the old wooden floor and collapsed into an exhausted and fitful stupor.

Küllo's timing could not have been worse, his exodus being right at the moment of the radical planetary and social shifts caused by the appearance of the V4641 Singularity. Its full effect announced itself the very next morning with a blaring sound in the atmosphere like an overly loud musical horn whose tone ripped at his ears. He bent over in acute pain at the blast and then after a few moments its attack stopped. Then, he had been sitting on the very bench where we have recently been watching his and Black Jackson's interactions. At the moment of that blowing years ago, when he raised himself back up he was stunned to realize that at least half of the people he had observed going about their daily functions in Town Centre had vanished. Driverless cars and busses began to careen into passersby. The traffic lights, electric signs and other gadgets ceased their function. The boy watched as people looked around in puzzlement, taking cell phones out of pockets or computers and pads out of cases, and punching wildly on their screens to attempt contact with others. Quickly panic ensued and a new thought came to him along with a chill that shook his being. *Minu pere—my family!*

Küllo tried to make his way back to the other side of Tartu, but the chaos of the people was violent. Trampling, looting and angry confrontations surrounded him. He finally chose to crouch in an alley until, in fading daylight the crowds seemed to thin out and he was able to make his way toward his old home. Seismic tremors, so unfamiliar to this area, shook and rattled the landscape. A hot wind blew into his face and the remaining people who he did encounter walked zombie-like passed him through the streets, no seen purpose to their amblings.

He arrived just at sunset and, since there was no elevator in the unkept building, charged up the tenement stairs to the fourth floor flat of his pere. The door was unlocked, but no-one was there to welcome him back. Küllo flipped the light switch, but no illumination appeared. He tried the telephone but it didn't function either. There was gas in the stove so he turned it on and cooked some bratwurst that had thawed in the freezer. After eating his fill, he fell into another fit of deeply disturbed dozing.

All he could see in his troubled slumber was a man shining with golden light, trying to offer the forsaken boy a bright blue ball held in his hand. In his dream, Küllo stood in a dark red room and was afraid to take the ball from the man of bronze.

Küllo waited for two days before realizing that his family would not return. He was poorly equipped for self-preservation, choosing to hide from, rather than confront his broken world. And so it was with complete horror that the nearly starved, forsaken boy exited his building one day—out into the open street—to find that everything he knew to be familiar was gone. There only seemed to be handfuls of people where before the streets had been crowded with activity.

Abandoned cars and motorbikes littered the streets and in the far distance he saw the fuselage of an airplane lodged in the crumbled structure of what used to be an old clock tower. Fires raged everywhere and the fumes of carnage insulted his senses from all directions.

He quizzed any people he did find on the streets, but no-one had any explanation for the strange disappearance of many of the townspeople. One thing he did un-puzzle on his own; the people who remained seemed to have no light in their eyes—no convictions or character of any kind. Worst of all, he had to admit his own thoughts and behavior to be no better than theirs. Küllo tried to fit in with the wandering gangs of young thugs who prowled the streets, but he had always been a loner. He felt truly forsaken and he cried out in anguish at his stupidity. To his isa, ema and his two younger *õed*—sisters, Anu and Liisa, he had not been able to say, "Goodbye". To these whom he now realized loved him and whom he cherished more than any worldly gems, yet chose to discard, he had not been able to say, "Forgive me."

A tell traveled across the continent by the lips of travelers. The few that did make it to Tartu, a remote location at best, shared what they knew with the locals.

"There was a Gathering-Up of souls. People everywhere were called-away. The planet itself was breaking," they said.

And so, self-survival became the focus. For a long-long time before, Estonia was known for its "not being known". Very few earthquakes, floods, or natural disasters of any sort happened here, and hence, little attention had visited the tiny country situated in the northern Baltic region.

Throughout recent history, any mention of the country had typically been associated with two other words—*Winter* and *Cold*. Those descriptions were certainly apt prior to influence of the *Dark Blue*; otherwise known as the V4641 Singularity. Since the appearance of the unsettling space phenomenon, the world, its axis and its climate conditions had changed drastically.

Estonia had become a rare gem hidden in the rubble of the Green Order Government, ruled by Darius Mede, whom most began to simply refer to as *the Mede*. Because of the already diminished population, the chaos elsewhere, and its un-notorious reputation, this area remained mostly invisible to the rest of the world.

Tartu particularly experienced an average seven degree annual temperature increase actually improving its appeal and capability for crop production. Its location off of the Baltic Sea also provided continued fishing trade. For Tartu in particular, flooding had not been an issue as it was far inland. When the polar ice caps reduced, the sea levels increased, suddenly redefining the city as a coastal town. Yet for some reason the tectonic forces affecting most of the rest of the planet still did not impact this region.

Everywhere there were the attacking bugs. For this people put on their *leathers*, heavy cured animal skins that the stingers and bites couldn't penetrate. They also wrapped thick cloth masks over their faces. The garb was cumbersome and overly warm, but necessary and successful for the most part in thwarting attacks. Soon, style even entered the equation with people wearing decorative hoods to distinguish one from another. Of course the larger and more bold the ornamentation, the higher the status of the individual in the area.

Ripping dust storms, other climatic irregularities, weather swings and social upheaval were the norm, but Estonia was not affected to the magnitude nor consistency that was being felt elsewhere. Regardless of the magnitude, all suffered and tried to make the best of a miserable existence.

Such were the conditions of Küllo's subsistence. For over twenty four lunar cycles he survived off the stores found by rummaging through his family's apartment complex. When conditions outside were tolerable, he scavenged for food and supplies. When the weather and other disturbances intensified, he closed himself off in the basement, staring into the darkness and many times, trying to justify a way of ending the nightmare, life had become. Frequently he would think he had heard a familiar voice of his ema, or Anu, or Liisa calling him. He even answered back, despairing at the echoes of silence that taunted him. His crying-out in the night and the memories he could not push away became intolerable. He had to escape his torment.

It was the beginning of the third year after the Gathering-Up when Küllo made his decision to search for other living quarters. The unpredictable weather changes, made it difficult to tell, but it seemed to be the approach of the warming season. Climactic chaos continued to inflict its wrath on the social order of once tranquil Tartu, but he decided it was time to search out new quarters which would not remind him so much of his family and former life. He packed up the remaining essentials he had found in his family's apartment complex and other vacated buildings nearby, loading them into a discarded wooden vegetable wagon that he found in a side alley. He waited until dark, hoping not to draw attention to his supplies or his intended destination. It was difficult maneuvering the cart through the littered streets, but finally he arrived at his newfound home, the same neglected warehouse near Town Centre that he had occupied on his first journey away from home.

During this time, some structure started creeping back into Tartu. The Mede began to post announcements about how all the people were to *Do*. The effort was futile and frustrating for any like the unread Küllo, until certain others who were literate in the community assumed authority. They became known as Mede's *Do Brothers*, interpreting the new edicts to their own purpose by means of punishment to those who disobeyed and reward to those who complied.

The boy-turned-man avoided conflict as best he could by attempting to mingle with the other Tartulians. But they seemed to fear his newfound boldness and no-one wanted to be seen as overly helpful to others—it was not the *green way*. "Do" was for each person, by each person. "Do" was not shared.

Küllo's ostracization made it necessary for him to learn another skill: fishing. He found the activity more pleasure than effort and was so productive that he was able to trade his excess catch with local farmers for vegetables. The exchange exercise was strange in that no-one would speak with him directly. He devised a method of silent agreement by placing a bag of sun baked heeringas in open common area of Town Centre. He drew a circle around the fish using a sandstone rock as his marker. He then drew another circle of equal size next to his catch. After this, he retreated to a safe, but visible distance to watch his primitive storefront.

Several times a townsman would tentatively approach the fish and Küllo watched intently. None of the initial poachers carried goods with them and so he would begin walking toward them rapidly, all the while shouting, "Kaubandus!—Trade!"

The first ones, seeing the approaching boy who all knew to be strange, retreated quickly. Then a weatherworn farmer, who Küllo recognized, cautiously neared the fish. This one carried a sack of equal size to his. The farmer gingerly set the sack within the boundaries of the void circle and quickly grabbed the fish. He ran with great stealth for an old one, back the direction he had come and Küllo had accomplished his first of many exchanges.

Most times he accepted the vegetables, but sometimes necessity demanded other goods. He would simply announce his need as he approached his circle and until another carried in what looked to be the wanted article. Küllo rejected any others' approach by again advancing toward the circle while reiterating his demand. Those with poor kaubandus quickly got the message and withdrew.

The system worked well and the new-styled entrepreneur's view of the his small universe began to expand. He spent much of his time arranging his building, exploring its refuse left from another era. Since Tartu had been relatively untouched by earthquakes and tremors, the structure of his industrial homestead was reasonably intact. But prior to his acquiring the premise, it had apparently been used to store indescribable amounts of useless office furniture; desks and, most unusable of all; table lamps, computers and other machinery. He didn't try to access the upper floors of the building because the stairway had partially collapsed due to ill-repair. The elevator was of course useless with the absence of electrical power; so why risk a foot-break or an arm-twist by an accidental fall?

The disappearance of electricity was old news, the mystery of its snuffing still never mingled to him. *What good were these plastic computer and copier boxes and who had thought them useful enough to store away?* This and many other broader questions began to puzzle Küllo thoughts. One in particular repeated itself annoyingly. *Is this all that I am to Do?*

Dreams of a life that he had tried long to forget fed the heat that rendered him inert. His mind replayed over and over the sad circumstances of his loss when suddenly, brilliant light blinded his thoughts. In his stupor he beheld the "Shining One" the apparition impossible to stare at for more than very short moments because he emitted the beautiful golden-bronze light.

Bronzeman, as Küllo would refer to him ever-after, had begun by asking a familiar question. "Is this all you are to Do?"

"No, please no," begged the tortured young man in reply.

"Do you want to live?"

An odd second question to which Küllo gave a most sincere response, "If this is life, no."

"Do you want to shine?"

Shine? What kind of shining? Bronze, like the God-man? Küllo was afraid he would burn to a cinder if he was lit-up like this one. If there was a shine that would allow him to stay with this beautiful angel, whose brilliant presence seemed to be burning with the same fire consuming Küllo's mind, then…"Yes, please, yes."

And Küllo instantly stopped breathing.

By an entirely alternative encounter with the Bronzeman, Black Jackson the Ethiopian orphan had received a different calling-out. Adama Ethiopia had been a harsh environment. Where Küllo had always been clever and adaptable, the lanky Jackson had been slow of wit and a target of taunt. Then one afternoon, one of many earthquakes in his region sent a brick toward his head. He remembered watching the object float before his eyes and a man speaking light from the brick into Jackson's eyes.

What others at the scene observed was the young Ethiopian being struck in the temple by the masonry rendering him literally dead. After making sure he was certainly killed, those who had ridiculed him were about to claim his clothing and meager possessions. That was when his eyes opened and he spoke.

"I'm very thirsty," he said simply and all within listening went immediately to find fresh water to supply him. Black Jackson, being born a natural *innocent* never seemed to realize that the bricking had somehow given him new ability. If he had a need and spoke it out, any within the hearing of his voice would comply. Because of his humble condition, he seldom had to ask for anything. And then there was his new found friend whom he called, the Bronzeman who he talked to often, though no one else could see his comrade. The Ethiopian would answer questions that the other villagers did not hear. Often he would burst out in laughter and then comment to the heavens at some amusing tale that he claimed Bronzeman had "telled" him.

The other Adamans seemed afraid of his unusual behavior, perhaps also they had become envious of his new freedom. Or perhaps his fellow villagers discerned the danger he presented to them based on his new ability to influence other's actions. Regardless of the reason, they immediately banished him from the town, but made sure he was well provisioned before he was cast out.

In the same brick-encounter, the Bronzeman had called-out Black Jackson to be ready to "walk north". So he did, leaving Adama on the day of the first new moon of the third year after the Gathering-Up. He followed the trade routes that took him first through Jerusalem. The Ethiopian arrived in the city three months into his journey and was moved by the Ruach to press toward the Armenian Quarter. He did not know it by that name, only by the intricate passageways through which he was led to that section of the old city. There the Ethiopian came upon a man who was repairing a section on the front of his dwelling and asked if he would provide the weary traveler with shelter and rest.

"I will do more than that," responded Ilbani Midehina Acdah, of Turkic origin, who was well acquainted with the language and origins of the Ethiopian. Ilbani was true to his word, inviting the traveler into his home to meet his own family, providing him clothes, supplies. That is when we who watch, met Black Jackson for the first time in the actual. It was I, Jende the Seer, Ilbani's bride, who was present. When the young man saw my dark skin, he kneeled, took my hand tenderly and placed it to his bowed forehead. Then he began to weep, calling out, "Yers be the first African smile I seen since my four months walking. It be the sun sparkling on water." We have loved his heart ever since.

"The same Bronzeman that you have met, I have met," explained Ilbani, a merchant who would later be given his own title, *Keeper of the Kin,* by the Watchman Brother Moses. Ilbani went into more detail. "The Bronzeman has a name. It is Yeshua ben Adoni and he told me you would be coming. At that point Ilbani gave me a knowing glance. I nodded in return, understanding what the moment represented. My husband excused himself from the room, moving into a secluded portion of our home. He returned with a special gift, a keepsack filled with unusual treasure and handed the bundle to the Ethiopian.

"The items in this sack are for you to give to another. You are to continue walking until you find him. Then you are to present him with the sack and thereafter protect him. He will serve you and you will be his brother. Those among us who have been given the gifts of far-sight and long-hearing through the Holy Ruach, will do our best to watch over you and help."

Black Jackson did not question, did not hesitate in his obedience to the command. He stayed with us for several weeks to regain his strength. We even introduced him to the two Watchmen who also took an immediate liking to the tall young man.

Then one morning, he came to me and said, "There be some serious God-Poking going on in me—time for Souling somewheres else."

We knew he was being called out. He explained it using another phrase, "I be walking on solid ground." So we all gathered one last time to pray over him and encourage him in the direction Yahweh was pointing him.

"I be bricked by yer loving on me," he said and hugged each of us in such an intensively genuine way that even the massive bear, Brother Moses had his breath squeezed out of him. The Brother bellowed a laugh afterwards and said, "This one is Yahweh's heart on earth!"

The Ethiopian struck out once more, trekking into old Europe and beyond. People along the way seemed to him, friendly enough, giving whatever he asked of them—food, water, clothing, shelter. Entering one such town, Bucastan, he met another with a strange gift. She could hear his past, and even current events in his life. Now his light and his salt could be located anywhere. The Seer and the Hearer grasped its presence—where he was at any given moment—from the acts of his hand and feet, by the sounds he heard, and the thoughts he mingled.

"I am listening to your path. It moves north," the Hearer explained. She even drew a map for him to follow; we know this only because we saw what she heard. She spoke more words which I confirmed in my visioning. I give site and she gives sound and Bronzeman Yeshua connected us, one to the other through the traveling of Black Jackson.

The Hearer also had ears on another young man who desperately needed friendship and so she gave the Ethiopian his charge. He was to continue his walking and would soon become Küllo's *Minder*—his called-out companion and protector.

Black Jackson journeyed until one day he saw in his inner thoughts—his mingling—the very clear Bronzeman's voice that had spoken as a light to him from the brick. The voice of light spoke in Jacksons native Amharic saying, "*Hier*…Here," and so he stopped before an old crumbling building.

Again, without hesitation he entered the confines and there found a leather clad body lying inert on an old mattress. Carefully checking beneath the protected layers to avoid any stray bugs attacking, he discovered the other to be a young man with skin as pale white as Jackson's was ebony. The lifeless body was covered in the sweat of recent fever, but now the form was cold. The eyes of the dead one were opened and stared vacantly beyond. The Ethiopian felt for a heartbeat and found none. Then, as directed by his vision, he knelt and placed his mouth over that of the dead man's. He breathed into the other's mouth one time and said, "Norä…live."

Küllo suddenly inhaled, blinked his eyes and sat up. "*Häleluya…Ta on tõusnud* —Praise

God…He has risen!"

Black Jackson was surprised that this one –knew Ethiopian words and responded in kind, "*Häleluya, T'äT'ar märet əsu honä asnäsa*— Solid ground, he be raised." Actually Küllo did not know Ethiopian, but Bronzeman mingled the two young men in such a way that each had a naturally intuitive sense about the other. What a perfect moment it was— Küllo's revival came on the same day when, in another part of the world, Brother Moses and Preacher Elijah begin to baptize on the first of the Days of Good News. It was the same day on which, thousands of years earlier in another age, the church age was born: This day of Pentecost.

It did not take long for the two to realize the blessing of communication that was now shared between them. They understood one another with little to no explaining. Both spoke some New-Roma—what had once been known as English—it was a Do Board <u>must</u>. They also bantered in each other's native tongues and that eliminated any translation challenges. But mostly, to each other they mingled in their special spiritual language to avoid the unfriendly eavesdropping of no-believers on their conversations. Both welcomed their newfound bond of brotherhood and immediately sought to meet one another's needs. "Keeping kin," Jackson called it and Küllo loved the term which he also began to use frequently.

Küllo explained his dream of fire and water to his new friend. He told how the bronze angel man—Bronzeman, had spoken to him and asked him if he wanted to shine. "Then I saw two old men, one with a long white hair and another with black bushy hair; both in robes. They smiled at me even though I was burning everything around me acause I was on fire—Blue fire. They reached out and took my hand, leading me to a square pool of water. I walked with them into the water and my fire became a song. I can't mingle it right. The song was on a piece of paper and I was reading it and singing it to everyone around me. Everyone learned the song and they sang it with me and they all caught on Blue fire too."

The Ethiopian kept his kin by first feeding the famished invalid, nursing him back to health. Then he fed Küllo something even more wonderful. One day soon after their meeting, Black Jackson simply handed the keepsack to the Tartulian and said, "Glue this to ye."

"Glue?" Küllo struggled with the word in his mind for a moment. His expression changed to the broadest of smiles and he responded. "*segunema*—mingle!"

Black Jackson also gave pause and then returned the smile, "I mingle what ye say!"

After unsnapping the keepsack, Küllo reached in and recovered *peidetud aare*—hidden treasure. He withdrew three sheaves of papers wrapped in heavy plastic storage bags for protection. Each sheaf contained neatly printed words on each page, front and back. Also stored were a bundle of quill pens, numerous bottles of ink and ten strange flat narrow sticks—each about the length of the palm of his hand. Neither boy mingled their purpose.

Unwrapping the plastic from the paper, he stared at the pages and was dumbfounded. Küllo now had full reading comprehension and began immediately reading out loud to his friend. The pages of the given gifts were titled *The Journal of Daniel Adamson. Epilogue added by Fitzgerald E. Hindeland*; *The Book of Seconds*, which seemed to be a collection of a number of people's writings; and finally, *The English Standard Version Bible—copied with honor by Fitzgerald E. Hindeland.*

As Küllo's recovery quickened, exploration of the Tartulian warehouse near Town Centre, now their shared domicile, was expanded. There seemed countless items, boxes, crates and heavy items on the first floor. Küllo had done his best to organize and dispose of refuse, but with his newfound help, he was able to make rapid work of separating the wheat from the chaff.

The two became inseparable, dividing their time between exploring the building, fishing, and their shared first-loves—Küllo reading out loud to Black Jackson and then writing the Ethiopian's responses. New discoveries abounded for both young men and they eagerly absorbed the words of the treasured texts. The Ethiopian was as eager to hear the words as the Tartulian told them from the pages. Jackson quickly memorized portions of the text, but it soon became apparent that he did not possess the gift for learning or mimicking script. His friend decided, rather than to frustrate him, it would be better to encourage the skills Black Jackson did demonstrate an ability to create new phrases. As Küllo would read passages from the Bible or the other documents, his companion would suddenly blurt out a new word that gave more relevant meaning to the text. An example of this occurred when the Tartulian was reciting Numbers 12:6:

And he (God) said, "Hear my words: If there is a prophet among you, I the LORD make myself known to him in a vision; I speak with him in a dream."

"Yahweh *bricked* 'em," Jackson interrupted.

Küllo had learned to wait silently on his kin to give him time to complete his thoughts and Black Jackson did not disappoint.

"If God wants ye to hear him, he gonna get yer attention in a big way. He gonna throw a brick. The brick hits ye and turns ye into a brick that God throws at other people."

The ideas and descriptions of Black Jackson so captivated the writer that the Tartulian began to catalogue them on blank sheets they had found in their new home. Küllo refined his craft and could not believe the words he wrote came from his hand. They appeared as he wrote them to be those of a scholar. He had no such training in the written word, his speaking skill still identified him as not much more than a street urchin. His new writing skills made him nervous, yet eager to expound his thoughts for others to absorb.

After forty days of studying together, the two came to a mutual epiphany. Soon the Tartulian proclaimed it for both of them by writing on the first story interior wall.

"KÜLLO AND JACKSON BE SECONDS!"

After announcing themselves as New Followers, Küllo & Jackson experienced several other strange new wonders. They actually did become Blue. The glowing that surrounded each of them, even on the brightest day, was evidence to *The Change* within. And what's more, the attack bugs stopped trying to pelt them. So the duo stripped off their heavy leathers and started walking around Tartu, bright and Blue, in clothing more suitable to the region. Not one insect paid attention. After observing the tall black man and the local boy, walking around unencumbered by protective hoods, both radiating blue light by day and night; all of Tartu anxiously whispered the young men's newly acquired titles: *Deemon Kaptens kota putukas*—Demon Masters of the bugs.

The more Küllo and Jackson partook in their newfound passions, the more they delved into the scripture, also Daniel's journal and the Book of Seconds. Their study convicted them to "tell out" to other Tartulians, their new *Solid Ground*—strong knowing/most true of all—of how the world was once again about to change. There was witnessing to be done and seeds to be sewed into souls—*Souling* as Black Jackson phrased it.

One morning, the boys heard a commotion outside. They were about to go out to determine the source of the noise when Black Jackson suddenly seemed to be bricked by the inner voice they were both becoming familiar with. The Ethiopian stood still and put his hand out to halt Küllo's motion toward the door. "We must leather-up," he commanded. Küllo looked puzzled, but did not argue with his friend. Both donned the bulky wear and exited the building. The noise that alerted them came from the direction of Town Centre where a crowd was gathering around a group of uniformed men. These officials had just finished erecting what looked to be a vertical panel constructed from finished wood planks. Such a thing was amazing to all because new wood was no longer easy to find. And if it was found, to use it for such a purpose seemed absolutely wasteful. Why not use it to make a shelter or for a warm fire on a cold night?

The uniformed ones then nailed one more plank to the very top of the panel. On this plank was bold letters that read "Do Board" in New-Roma script. In smaller letters underneath, "Take planks and die." Then the men nailed paper to the planks below the top. Of all the things to do! The paper also had words on it which was the strangest thing of all. Many in the town could not read and the words looked important to be mingled. One of the uniformed men, dressed up with a bright red bird feather in his head covering and in fancier leathers than the others, stood before the crowd and started speaking loudly in New-Roma.

"This is your Do Board," he pointed behind him toward the panel as if the crowd was full of idiots who didn't know what he was referring to. "It is a gift from your Supreme Mede."

At this name the other uniformed ones raised their arms in mechanical unison toward the sky and shouted, "His name do praise."

The fancier feather-man was silent, seeming to wait for something. He spoke again, "Your Supreme Mede."

The ones behind him again responded with arms raised, "His name do praise."

All the Tartulians seemed confused. The fancy uniform waited no longer. He approached the nearest townsman, pulled a pistol from a holster at his side and shot the man between the eyes. As one, the crowd jumped back several steps as the snuffed one crumpled and bled.

Fancy Feather-Man pointed his weapon at the crowd and shouted once more, "Your Supreme Mede."

The other uniforms responded in kind and this time, the message was clear to the people. Every one of them raised their arms awkwardly and echoed, "His name do praise." All would have been well then, had not the fancy uniform noticed two Tartulians at the back of the crowd, one very tall, one equally short, who did not comply.

He moved quickly toward them, the other townspeople moving aside with heads bowed, to let him through. Fancy Uniform pointed his pistol directly at Küllo's head and spoke. "I am your Boss-Peacer. I command all Peacers in this place and they command you. We serve the Supreme Mede, as do you. You will honor him and obey his servants whom you serve."

After this proclamation, Boss-Peacer extended his arm and weapon further as if about to snuff Küllo. But at that moment, Black Jackson proclaimed his own Do, "Ye don't need to."

Boss Peacer kept his aim on Küllo's chest, but his head turned to stare at the Ethiopian. "I don't need to." He repeated with an angry stare.

"Yup, ye don't," Küllo's Minder agreed.

"I don't," confirmed the man's voice. His face still revealed fury, and tears streamed down his face. Slowly and uneasily, the gun arm came down, and Boss-Peacer finally took his stare off of Black Jackson, turned and moved back to the other Peacers. He did not stop, but kept walking past the Do Board. The Peacers exchanged glanced to one another in confusion. Finally one of them turned to pursue Boss-Peacer and the others followed in rank.

As they disappeared into the distance, the Tartulians rapidly disperse, leaving Küllo and his companion alone in the square, both staring in shock at the body that still oozed dark red liquid in front of the Do Board. Both now went to the deceased and uncovered the mask.

"Lennart," Küllo identified the soul who had once occupied the now lifeless body.

We, the Keepers, look back in our knowing of the past to see Küllo and Black Jackson talking with Lennart. We hear them tell of Bronzeman's miracle work in their lives and see Lennart kneel. We hear his confession of faith and then hear the boys praying with him. We watch as Lennart turns Blue with joy at being called-out by Bronzeman.

Now we see the two standing over snuffed Lennart. It is sometimes difficult being a Keeper. We do not see well, the difference between the beginning, the now and the end. Lennart is snuffed. But his Blue is risen. He is now and ever.

Again we hear the boys praying. "He is with you, Master. May it be soon for all of us," telled Küllo. With effort, they lifted the body and placed it in a nearby cart. Then they proceeded to the town edge, to the cemetery. Long into the evening, they prepared a fresh grave, burying their Blue-brother and praying over his soul. No one else assisted. No one else observed their sweat mixed with tears. It was Black Jackson who, when they were finished, mingled out loud the joy in the moment.

"Praise be to ye, Bronzeman. Lennart be now celebrating with ye in the heavenlies."

From that day forward, the two boys have worn their leathers when they go outside. If they tell other Tartulians about Bronzeman, they are careful not to speak of their Lord when Peacers are nearby. It does not really matter—the townspeople fear the hearing of the boys' testimonies. Many no longer want anything to do with Blue and certainly nothing to do with snuffing. If the Boss-Peacer or any Peacer mentions the Supreme Mede, all Tartulians immediately raise their arms and shout, "Praise Do his name..."

—All Tartulians except Küllo and Black Jackson that is. It is not a Do for them, because if they are near any Peacers, the phrase is never spoken and the response, never requested.

Since the Do Board announces that Blue light is bad, the two have to find creative ways of souling. They invent an approach that seems to get the best results, finding blank spaces—clean walls on buildings, concrete surfaces that haven't yet been destroyed by earthquakes, even sections of undamaged roadway. On these they paint a simple question in both large Estonian and New-Roma letters:

MIS SIIS, KUI SEAL ON PAREM VALGUS?
WHAT IF THERE BE BETTER LIGHT

They then wait in some nearby protected place where they watch for others to come by. It is usually not long before a group gathers to look at the print to wonder at its come-from. Then Küllo and Black Jackson emerge, explaining to the others that the Bronzeman had breathed words of light into their eyes. One of the Mede's first Do's had forbidden possession of any book not approved by the Green Order Government—*GOG*. Although technically their new treasures, which gave them the stories to tell, were not bound books, the word *Bible* and *Journal* were two terms and specific names forbidden for common use by GOG. Hence neither Küllo nor Black Jackson mention the specific acquisitions and no-one seems particularly interested in querying him. Most of the townspeople think the two are retarded or worse yet, bedeviled. Most others refuse to acknowledge the kin's existence and give their domicile a wide birth.

The two are frustrated by their limited communications with no-believers. What can they do to better explain Bronzeman and what is happening to the world? That's when Black Jackson spies the ice cream factory. It wasn't hard to find, being that the giant popsicle hangs over the entry. That in fact, is what caused him to bolt inside, temporarily abandoning his duty of protection to Küllo. The Ethiopian emerged quickly enough, carrying four large boxes stacked in his arms. He carefully sets down the packages before Küllo as if they are chests of treasure laid before the feet of a king.

Black Jackson then tears off the tape securing the top of one box and pulls the lid back to expose hundreds of neatly packed sticks like the ones they had found in Küllo's keepsack. "Deese be our Better Light," says the Ethiopian happily.

Küllo and Jackson find it very easy to tell of Bronzeman using the popsicle sticks and the story from Daniel Adamson's journal. They show others how the assembled sticks explode out when thrown to the ground or against a hard object. They explain how any physical or spiritual object has a Creator who designed its parts to be held together for a purpose. That purpose can be turned to destruction and used to rebel angrily against the Creator. Or it can be used as an agent of love to teach others how to draw together, healing the parts of the community body to work together for the Creator's originally planned purpose—to bring His people back to Himself.

They describe how the planet itself and the people on it have come apart, like the sticks, and need to be worked…mingled back together for Bronzeman's purpose. They show them how prayer is the starting of that mingling together.

Black Jackson has each person break apart the sticks and then shows them how to knit them back into one. He explains how each stick is a Do for the mingling of the whole. He points out that there is only one way the five sticks can be wedged together, each dependent on the proper placement of the other.

But it is Küllo who relates the most important, the center two sticks. He shows how those two hold the secret for the others. It is these two that must be first for everything else to hold tight. The outside sticks are not able to mingle without connection to the inner. The inner being in the shape of a cross, was perfect, yet it would not hold together without connection to the outer sticks. Like God and Bronzeman. Like Bronzeman and people. Like Küllo and Black Jackson. Like those boys and the Tartulians.

As the boys tell it out, we can see it through them as a simple picture.

Soon there are popsicle stick puzzles carried in the hands of many in the area. At first the attempt to assemble five sticks into a pattern that locks itself together becomes a curious novelty. But as word passes through the town about the meaning that Küllo and Jackson explain is behind the sticks, we Keepers begin to see and hear more Blue becoming hidden beneath the leathers in the town of Tartu. And we know that very soon Bronzeman will begin the big change.

The Peacers have not figured out, nor do they seem to care, why more and more Tartulians are carrying the wedged stick symbols.

The water is so fresh and cool. He opens his eyes to peer up at a blurred image of two men. He can make out that one is heavily bearded and seems larger than life. The other has no hair other than a small beard. Both glow bright Blue, and Küllo knows that he loves them as he would two great fathers. Suddenly there is an even brighter light of shimmering gold behind the two and the men rise into the dark Blue sky. Küllo rises out from the water into the cold night, realizing he has just experienced another powerful vision. He looks around him to gain his bearings and sees Black Jackson snoring peacefully on a pallet nearby. They are still inside their safe haven and he is the only one disturbed by the vision. "I have been baptized!" He no sooner speaks the words when Black Jackson also sits bolt upright and exclaims, "Holy Spirit what a washing dat was!" It has been forty days since Küllo's revival from death.

The next morning, Küllo himself is bricked. He is walking outside along the front wall of the building, sorting among the many discarded wood boxes and forgotten automobiles for usable items. He is using the errand as an excuse to be alone to better unravel the strange events of the evening before. Who were the two men and how did he still feel wet from the water during his dreaming. It was a powerful image. As he is rummaging a strong voice vibrates within him, commanding:

"Look up."

Why he has never seen it before is, to him, a ridiculous question. "Acause He hadn't called out yet for me t'see," says the boy out loud for no-one but himself to hear.

But now Küllo is well prepared, and so he shifts his eyes up from the ground where he has focused all of his attention before. On the front face of the building, now considered his home, are large letters once illuminated by electricity. Though not burning now, they light his heart on fire.

TRÜKIMUUSEUM

All this time, he had been living in a museum, a place of hands-on study of history, artifacts and words. But, more than that, this place had been known to him long before he had been called-out. Memories flood his consciousness as he plays back conversations he had overheard throughout his childhood. Küllo's isa had once been a maintenance man for this very location. He recalls the sharing of stories of the duties and challenges his isa encountered each day keeping a particular group of machines in working order. Then funding was lost for the Center and that was when Küllo's family fell on hard times.

Now the called-out becomes called-in, searching every corner of the facility and his determination pays off a day later. He finds a way to climb up the badly damaged staircase and asks his kin to climb up as well to help him pry loose the boards that have denied access to the second story room titled *Töö Ruum*—Work Room. The hazy sun sifts through the factory windows there that break the light in the area into brightly colored prisms almost like cathedral stained-glass. It illuminates the most beautiful cathedral this side of heaven. The altar of this sanctuary is represented by three manual-offset movable type printing presses.

"Now what?" He asks heavenward, having no idea of how to operate the machinery. It would take him years more to manage such a task unless Bronzeman was to call-out some greater gift. Küllo decides the best strategy lay in a scripture he had just read. He pulled out the manuscript, turned to the specific text and begins to recite it aloud,

"Ask, and it will be given to ye; seek, and ye will find; knock, and it will be…"

—before the words finish spilling out of his mouth, a *know* shoots into his brain—hotter than the fever that lit his life. He is so excited that he hurriedly hands the papers to Jackson and without explanation, jumps from the damaged staircase to the first floor, racing out of the building toward the square. He has not even realized he left without putting on his boots. The rough surface of the path does not bother him, only his purpose matters.

Küllo approaches Town Centre moments later. Thanks to his initiative, it has become a burgeoning trading place with people from all around the region now standing in respective circles, shouting out their needs in order to kaubandus their goods. But in the center of the courtyard remain two empty circles, those first created by Küllo himself. Usually he would walk casually toward his appointed circle, exclaiming his need with one word repeated. Today is to be different. He continues running, almost knocking down two other vendors blocking the way to his goal. The young, socially shunned entrepreneur yells at the top of his lungs as he charges through the mass of people, "I need a printer, someone with letterpress printing skills!"

The rest of the crowd is silenced at his clamoring. As he clears the final blockade of bodies, Küllo is not puzzled to see a figure already standing in the second circle. What does interests him is the fact that this woman, like himself, is not clad in leather. The other is of small height and build, and wears a smock common to the Siberians who sometimes pass through Tartu. She is perhaps several years older than he and most certainly Asian. But her predominant traits are the Blue framing her slight form that shines as brightly as his own, and the popsicle stick puzzle held in her hand.

The crowd becomes extremely nervous at the sight of these two bright lights intersecting. Most everyone in Town Centre quickly disappear, so that Küllo and the Asian woman are soon alone at their rendezvous place. She holds him with a stern look, but says nothing until Küllo has caught his breath. Then she says in clipped impatient New-Roma, "It about time, you call-out."

The Bronzeman Seeings are evidence of The Change. Blue shows itself in more and more people every day and that causes another kind of dangerous-Do. Mede's forces have been alerted that those calling themselves Seconds, New Followers and *Remnants*—Jews, are a great threat to the wellness of any community. They have been told that these upstarts will not comply with local or world law and that they are organizing a revolt. All the Seconds are waiting for is their leader, a radical named Yeshua, to make his presence known.

An edict has gone out to round up all Seconds, but they are proving difficult to identify. The Blue makes them easy targets but that particular trait can be disguised by dawning leathers when in public. It is an inconvenience, one well worth taking in light of the alternative of being apprehended by GOG forces.

Seconds are being apprehended by Peacers, pointed out by non-believing informants who have been promised rewards. But those instances are proving rare because the New Believers have endeared themselves to many through acts of selfless kindness and servitude, so that communities tend to shelter them. And their generous grace causes curiosity that inspires many more to join their ranks.

So for their own protection, Küllo, Black Jackson and their newfound companion, Han Ko remain close to their sanctuary in Trükimuuseum and nearby Town Centre. The pleasure of going to fish or seeking treasure in other locations around town became a risk, because of the Blue, and is not easily accomplished, even in the dark of night.

Han Ko remains a living mystery to the other two—where she has come from, how she acquired her knowledge and conviction for Bronzeman, are questions hidden in her silent ways. She has followed Küllo back to the building after their initial meeting and he shows her the printing presses. Without a word, she examines the mechanics and begins combing through the maintenance and typeset drawers throughout the room. The two men watch in amazement as the lithe Korean moves quickly from section to section, servicing and oiling various levers, polishing plates, lubricating pulleys and finally walking up to them with a drawer in hand. She tilts the box toward the Tartulian and asks curtly, "New-Roma?"

Küllo does not mingle the question and shrugs his shoulders while cocking his head and fixing his facial expression to show, as best he can, that he is confused.

Han Ko sighs and elaborates, "You want message pressed New-Roma?"

"Oh!" He is bricked that she would even think to ask his advice of how to proceed in the printing process. "Yes, pressed in New-Roma is good."

The young woman turns without a reply, going to the work desk by the first press. As she nimbly begins cribbing a print frame and inserting letters into a caddy, Küllo begins to consider his answer. New-Roma has become the universal language used by traveler and local alike for familiar reference. At this thought he laughs because, up until several days ago, he had no ability to read his own language yet now he seems able to comprehend any written language placed before him. He now wonders if he can also write in any language. The very question posed to himself is astounding and before he can try to answer, Han Ko stands before him again with a printer's House Sheet in her hand. She holds it out to him and he takes the paper, reading out loud words that not so long ago were impossible for him to comprehend much less vocalize:

"The Lord your God is God."

It is Black Jackson behind him who next speaks after a long silence in the room. "Ye look like ye be baptizing dat paper."

And indeed, the Tartulian is weeping enough to cause the newly stamped inked words to run as he stares at the page in his hands. "I understand the vision now. We must Do this," is at first, all he can manage to tell. Then Küllo says something that he later will claim he could not have possibly thought of on his own. "We need to go where God is *Doing*. We must write the words of His Do…the *Bronze Word*—God's plan to mingle the world with his son. We must tell the world that the God who was, is still now much-living, and is ready to love us more than our knowing."

When Küllo calls-out his mission to his friends, they react each in their own way. Black Jackson walks over to retrieve the keepsack he had originally given to the Tartulian. The Ethiopian slings the pack over his shoulder and asks, "When do we trek?"

Küllo chuckles involuntarily and suggests that they pray and wait on the Spirit to call-out the path of their journey. Han Ko on the other hand, leaves the press room immediately and searches out wood to build a small fire in preparation for cooking. Without having to ask, Küllo mingles her Do and retrieves several dried fish from his stash. He follows the Korean, carefully climbing the damaged stairway to the rooftop of the Muuseum where he hands her his catch. Han Ko takes the fish and places them on a thick plank that she carries with her at all times in her own keepsack. She sets the board upon bricks that she has placed around the makeshift fire pit she has constructed and within moments the aroma of smoked heerring draws Jackson to join them. After this meal together, the three sit around the fire as the perpetually clouded sky darkens more into night.

"If we be looking for God, what we gone to see? He don't show hiself often." Black Jackson, as typical, is the first to articulate the question in a way everyone can understand.

"*Hananim*—YHWH God—not need to be seen, only obeyed. If obeyed, you know he is where you are." Both men demonstrate shock in their expression at the full sentence and the depth of observation just offered by their new companion.

It is several little moments before Küllo, after fully chewing and swallowing the last of his fish, shares his puzzling. "I mingle in my mind, that there are others like us in the world. They must be afraid to believe acause of the Mede's Do's and his *dark-tell* being spread around like old smelly fish that's bad to eat. They don't have scripture," he says patting the keepsack next to him. They don't know that they are part of a whole. They are all alone, none of them are hugged for loving Yeshua Bronzeman as God. We need to report. We need to…*news-tell* what is mingling in the world and how Yeshua is preparing to return as the Bronzeman King who be coming to take back what is his."

"Not sure why he need take anything back if it be his already, but I'll trek with ye anywhere ye need go." Black Jackson's faith is far greater than his knowing. We Keepers can see and hear the deep Blue love Küllo has for his friend.

Five days pass from when they made their decision. It will be a difficult departing, especially for the native of this town who has never crossed beyond its borders. The night before their journey will begin, Küllo appears sullen. Han Ko encourages his purpose. "You go to come back with a telling for others. I stay to be ready for making your story a picture. It has to be."

And that is exactly what they all agree to. Someone has to maintain and protect the treasure of the three presses. But the machines are useless without the value of the Caller-God's cause.

Han Ko once again curtly commands them into the Muuseum and upwards toward the roof where they share their last supper together. Küllo is uncharacteristically not hungry. He nibbles absently on a piece of heering, but soon withdraws a quill from his sack and begins scribing as the other two finish their portions.

The Ethiopian loves to watch Küllo scratch on the beautiful pieces of white paper with his bird feather. "Can I touch da words?" Up until now, Black Jackson had never dared to ask so much as to look at the script, so his friend highly mingles the significance of this moment.

The young scribe readily turns the page toward the Ethiopian who, after staring transfixed at the lettering, reaches out and tentatively fingers one symbol with a trembling digit of his left hand. At that moment a warm gust of ruach wind blows across the rooftop, rustling the paper. Black Jackson fearfully withdraws his finger and fortunately, Küllo has his own hand affixed to the parchment, elsewise it might fly into the night to be delivered to the heavenlies.

Jackson speaks in a hushed and reverent tone, "Bronzeman's tell makes light happen. How are we gone to take care of that light without da ones who speak the happenings having their lives be snuffed by the Mede?"

"No mingling that for others." Küllo looks into the emptiness of the night as he continues, "We ask any who want to share their happenings—them will have to decide if they want to hide their light under a bowl or live it brightly."

"You bring the words back, I make them loud on paper. God do the rest." Han Ko hands each man another piece of hot fish and continues explaining how she will print up the stories on a single sheet newspaper, "But how Bronzeman going to get words back to Han Ko, that the big question."

"The first tells should be a little easier to get back since those will not be too far from here," explains Küllo. "But to what parts of the world will YHWH lead us and how will he take us there? I can't un-puzzle that now."

Black Jackson munches on the last of his fish, shakes his head as he stares at the glowing embers of their cooking fire and replies. "Watch dat Holy Spirit fella. He liable to fly us places quick!"

Küllo and his companions have no idea how they will broadcast the editions Han Ko will print up. But they all are certain that God will somehow help them with the Do. We watch and pray over them as they spend the rest of the evening working out the small details: locations the two men would visit first, how they will seek out other Seconds for their *tells*, and their method of interviewing.

One sees
One hears
And it is written
Let us work together that the world may know!

—Keepers, for the glory of God

Letter from Ilbani Midehina Acdah, Keeper of the Kin (Yerushalayim)

> *"We wind a simple ring of iron with coils; we establish the connections to the generator, and with wonder and delight we note the effects of strange forces which we bring into play, which allow us to transform, to transmit and direct energy at will."*

—Nikola Tesla

Written to my God—through the intercession of my Savior, Yeshua. For that reason I will not date my posts for the Receiver of my thoughts and prayers will put them to His purpose in His time. Let these words then be for His purpose and to His glory.

I give thanks to You, Most High, that You would even consider in Your great plan to provide a typewriter complete with paper and ribbons to allow me and Jende to share our observations. To You it may be a small thing, but to us, the gift is great. You of course are the inspiration of all we relate, but why would I write to You, YHWH, when You know altogether my words before they ever touch my tongue or are scratched to paper? I believe that You are calling me to do this. The words are not just for You, but are to serve as markers of new things to come. You provided me with two great teachers, Brother Moses Folzman and the prophet Fitzgeral Elijah Hindeland. They taught me that there appear to be crucial times in history when You, YHWH, bring to a culmination all that You have planned for a particular age.

These age-markers—warned of through prophesies—signal the advent of difficult times, especially for those who are living in the unfolding of the changes. That generation has the most difficult time of all making sense of what will happen because their history is so firmly established. They… we perceive our outlook to be the only significant cultural vision. After all, theirs…our advancements and struggles beg to be waved as a banner well fought for. To think that You may then shift us into a new pattern of relationship with You, is truly unsettling. I attest to this as one who has approached and crossed several such thresholds into a new reality.

One of these markers was when my mentors were taken up to receive Your blessing in the heavenlies. I, and all the world are still recovering from their loss. We have struggled much to rebuild the ruins of Yerushalayim left by the *killing-quake*, as it was known to the entire world—the most cataclysmic of all earthquakes leveled much of the city to its foundations. The supposed Holy City had especially suffered when the two witnesses were Gathered-Up. During that recovery we all had to rebuild from the rubble. I also was leveled, struck down in the chaos and praise You for bringing about my rapid healing, that I might continue to serve Your will. The pain of my wounds though still reminds me, marks my memory with understanding, that life in the physical world is temporary and that spiritual life is what each should strive for.

Those who have only known the aftermath of such markers, wrestle as well with comprehension of the past age. It is like imaging the world prior to one's own birth. I would appear clumsy and foolish in my attempts to relate to the experiences of those before. An example: How can I now explain a television to someone who has never turned one on? Even that simple question is perplexing: *Turn On?* What does that phrase mean to those who have never known electricity or pressurized water? The concepts require multiple dimensions of historical texture for any hope of relevant comprehension.

I have been taught that there are not only natural markers, but spiritual lines of demarcation. The Creator of the universe has designed things to happen repetitively in the long and in the short term. When cultural routine begins to decay or becomes irrelevant to those who have maintained it so diligently, the people must become especially alert. God is signaling that a significant change is in motion. A long term example: 400 years passed between the time of the last prophets and Jesus' life on earth. In this silence, the world was thrown into a period of great chaos and emptiness. No-one at the time could adequately recall the blessings provided before and they certainly could not properly anticipate what would happen when a Galilean Jew began to heal the world with his words and his hands.

Short term examples of such changes are revealed to anyone alert to them. Observing a lady who puts her wash out each morning, I have become comfortable with the sight and anticipate its normal reoccurrence. Suddenly today I notice that neither the lady nor the wash are to be found. Has she died? Did she move? What has caused the disruption to my routine? If I am not able to reconcile her disappearance with some good explanation, my world is felt to be unpredictable and untrustworthy. Under such circumstances I begin to mistrust all things, even my own continued existence.

All of these changes, long and short are Your way of inviting hope, YHWH. Age to age, when all other things come to an end, and new things begin, You are still the Most High who never changes. I look now to You for comfort, the new age is dark without Your torch and I call on all of mankind to watch my God's light move fast! Your patience has come to an end and the markers prove it out.

Praise Do God,
ИК

Shared for the benefit of all by the hand of Ilbani the Keeper; redeemed by my Lord, Messiah Yeshua, for His purpose and honor.

The Bronzeman News

מָשִׁיחַ **WATCH AND KEEP** מָשִׁיחַ

My name be Küllo, that be all ye need to know about me. I be not the story—I be the eyes, ears and hands of these tales. The words on these pages will be news-tells from common folk. Folk like ye and me. Them will tell their story and I will copy it with as little cleaning up as possible, so that all who are left after the Gathering-Up will see what be happening: The Bronzeman be appearing and the seeings of him are much the same. What be different be what he tells each one to Do.

MINGLE IT. MAKE UP YER OWN MIND, I WILL NOT MAKE IT FOR YE.

Edition One: Slavonia
Month 12, Year 3 After the Gathering-Up

Küllo's Notes: I will try to describe the locations of our travels since all lands of the world have died and are being reborn. Due to all of YHWH's shaking-up Slavonia be on the coast of the Mediterranean Ocean (no longer a small sea). All of Spain, the southern portion of France, Italy, Croatia, all of Greece and much of the Slavic Nations are no longer. The Baltic and Black Seas are also joined into an ocean mass. I'm told that the countries of Morocco, Algeria, Tunisia, Libya and Egypt are mostly taken by the great water. It be not easy to un-puzzle.

The slummy land that we've come to walk through includes what remains of the former Austria, Hungary, Serbia and Romania. I don't want to give hint yet to our home for reasons that should be easy to mingle. We are Seconds—them that chose to believe in our Messiah after the first believers were Gathered-Up by him. Others who believe they are in charge of life mingle that we are a problem, so we are hunted. This record of travel will itself become a danger, so we must be careful in what we tell.

We have arrived at the northern limits of the country, following rumors in hopes of interviewing one who had been a witness to the recent rising up of the two Olive Trees of Jerusalem. The two Trees were known as Rabbi Moses Folzman and Fitzgerald Elijah Hindeland. They were men of Spiritual Authority who were butchered at the command of the Mede. Miraculously the Bronzeman was said to have breathed new life into them and they were Gathered-Up to the heavenlies. But the one we seek be one of the new called-out who is said to be preaching to and gathering the last strangers of Israel. He is one who carries great history in his own keepsack and we hope to hear his personal tell and see the touch of his walk with Bronzeman.

We are telled that this man, Eleazar of Jerusalem, has been captured by the Ward and Executioner of Slavonia, Serge Palmotic. There be a public demonstration at which Eleazar's case will be heard. We are going to it in hopes of hearing his defense and perhaps his story. I have low hope for his light to be kept lit—others tell that he did not obey the Do Board.

I be scripting these events in the real moment. My mingling and my heart are cut in pain by the effort. There be blood covering most of the floor of the stainless steel pit. The man crouching naked in the far corner of the putrid chamber will not look up as his attacker approaches him; nor need he. Eleazar must understand what comes next. His snuffing will be a welcomed thing, not a surprise—the attacker, Serge Palmotic, had telled it from the very beginning.

"You serve no purpose other than entertainment for the hungry of this place." Them are his words to Eleazar. This show-time was hammered on the Do Board but it be different when ye hear and see a beating to the death.

"No one Does a food hunt without my permission," tells Palmotic. I mingle that Eleazar must have broke that Do. This location be what is not undone of an old milk-making factory. Most large animals used to harvest the sacred liquid are now *gone-things* or poison to us. The big steel vats were damaged from continuing earthquakes and non-doing. Now they are for another Do. *Un-lits*, them that don't know or don't want to know Bronzeman, mingle that nothing lives on this planet without a Do. The vats are good Do's for beer making. I be told the place be also fixed to get heat from thermal vents cleverly tapped in the earth below. We onlookers above must bundle to survive. But, the two inside the vat need no winter gear. Their comfort however, comes at a price. The workers and revelers, with which I sit and watch, are shouting that they deserve reward beyond their shabby wage.

"Give sport. Give sport," be the chant throughout the makeshift vat-stadium. Torches flicker in rising wind, telling of another blizzard soon-coming. The crowds, in their heavy leathers and other weather gear, want a quick Do, so they can warm fast. They cheer the executioner on and he complies by taunting his victim.

"Have you no words with which to gift us before I send you to your God?" He shouts his question so that the crowd may also tell-back.

"Send him, send him."

A strange new thing Do's. The man, Eleazar who many tell as a prophet, continues to bow his head, but raises one manacled arm from the puddled floor. Extending a trembling finger he paints on the surface of the vat wall near to his right. The effort draws the mob's silence as he struggles to re-dip his finger into his own leaking fluid, raising his arm again and again to Do his crimson message. First he makes a large V and next spreads two horizontal lines to span just below the upper tips of the letter. Finally he bisects his work with a single vertical stroke down the middle.

I be puzzled big at his pained Do and immediately mingle the mark. It be the stick craft described by the prophet Daniel Adamson in his journal. The knowing causes me to reach into my pocket to finger the five smooth sticks I always carry with me as a demonstration tool for telling of Bronzeman to New Followers.

But below, I can see that Palmotic be boiling with his own heat, having watched in frozen fascination as Eleazar managed to finish the symbol. He must also mingle its meaning. Them I have spoken to who are not "eyes-open", them that say "No" to God in this changed time, fear the emblem as a symbol of the Seconds. They mingle we who are called-out by Bronzeman, to be a rebel band, stubborn holders-on to the old ways of the *No-mores*. They mingle us to be bent on grabbing back Un-lit ones for our so called god-man, whose proper name they will not allow to be spoken in public.

Others in the stadium mingle Eleazar's picture too, and now weigh in. "End him. "End him. End him," they shout with increased bloodlust raising their passion. Pathetic as he looks, I be joyed by the wounded man's Do. He must know he be soon snuffed, yet he still blood-boldly makes tell of his God.

The end-tell of this show must be soon. We all mingle it. The chorus from above be hungry for it. The executioner reaches out and behind him to his servant who protects his weapons. Keeping his eyes on his prey, Serge Palmotic waits to receive the beheading axe. More time passes than seems normal, but finally, the broad handle meets his palm and he confidently grasps its weight, preparing to pull it in for the killing swing.

And now a new puzzle, another thing be in the hand of the servant and be placed on Palmotic's outstretched arm. He turns his attention fully to the servant who has clasped a chained glove-lock over Serge's appendage. Palmotic the executioner stands stunned as his servant signals for two others to pull its attached chain through an iron port at the pinnacle of the extended beam welded to the gantry high above. Their motions takes the newly captured one by surprise and the pulling motion tears him further away from the conquest of Eleazar, drawing him painfully to a point where he be literally hanging by his arm, two meters from the ground.

The crowd laughs, seeming to mingle this be part of an act—that the skilled attacker should somehow break free to complete his task. But it be not so. There he dangles as his supposed loyal bondsman gives him an almost apologetic look, then passes by with the others to quickly gather the wounded prophet and spirit him out through the Warrior's entry door.

The mob no longer laughs. Now screams of insult circulate, demanding Serge free himself and avenge. Somehow the thieves' plan has included locking the bleacher gates so that the bystanders are also imprisoned as the escape be made.

Eventually the crowd, including me and my Minder breaks out of our stadium prison. I be not able to interview Eleazar, nor does that seem Bronzeman's Do. I be here to see the courage of belief and the willingness to die for God's purpose; sharing His Message of Hope.

I also now realize that my news-tells cannot be written without favoritism. Sharing the increased flood of belief in Bronzeman cannot be scratched out in political politeness and I cannot apologize for telling the passion of what I mingle happening around me.

The true danger of our journey be made clear to us after we have broken out of the stadium. The Ward and Executioner has also somehow broken his bonds and now stands afore the freezing crowd. He yells in competition with the howling wind.

"This is the third time that the rebel Eleazar and his cohorts have escaped me. It will be his last success. I, Serge Palmotic, will not wait again for a staged opportunity to eliminate him. When we next meet, I will make sure that his snuffing is very personal and very agonizing."

The shivering crowd be quick to disband, including their leader. But to the side I notice a small group who remains huddled against the wall of an out building. They appear to use the structure as a guard against the blowing weather. As we walk by them, a word be carried on that bitter wind to my ears.

"Remnants."

It be not relevant to anyone but a Second. Not even someone searching out New Followers for persecution would be alerted by the mention. It be simply a reference to either Jews who try to scratch out a life in a world that hates their existence, or to Remnant Seconds, Jewish believers who know Bronzeman by heart, who are gathering in quiet places, preparing for the appearance of their King-coming.

I am not a Remnant Second, but in my travels I hear tell of this group's existence, growth and impact on towns and villages. They are told of and mingled much in Scripture: There has always been a remnant of God's people in the afterwards of the bad days. But during these Final Times the Remnant People of God are actually numbered. 144,000 are mentioned as the last group of Hebrew witnesses to be gathered by Bronzeman. The Book of Zechariah tells that they are to be at least a part of the force of testimonial soldiers who will fight alongside Bronzeman on the earth at a battle telled as Armageddon.

Few would mingle this without the words spoken by the Prophet John at the end of the Sacred Book. I certainly do not have complete knowing of how they are being gathered. I don't even mingle half of the Do's God calls me out for much less what Do's he be telling into others. This moment be a good example of one of the crazy Do's I mingle somehow to be right. I tell BJ to stay where he be and walk back toward the small group we had just passed by. They look more nervous and get quick-quiet as I come closer. I be also silent, walking up to the one who seemed to have been doing most of the low-talking. It be a safe bet that the chattiest would be their leader. Without any introduction, I grab from my pocket one of the five sticks I carry. I hand it to the leader and turn again to walk away.

Acause this one had telled a recognized cipher does not guarantee him or his gang to be Seconds. I continue walking away from them, but as I do

I tell a prayer out loud. "Lord, ye are with me. Keep me walking, without injury or attack if it be yer will."

"Wait." The leader speaks. "You forgot something." He comes at me and it be my turn for nervousness. The man who be a head taller than I, holds out his opened hand and a pungent musky smell wafts from a small sprig of a plant laid out in his palm. "Hyssop," the leader tells in explanation. "It still grows around here even in the difficult environment. It is an excellent healing agent and if you would like some more to take with you, I will show you where we keep it."

There be nothing bad-sounding or bad-meaning in his voice, nor be there tell of his motives. He stands, holding out his hand in front of him and I realize he wants me to take the plant. As I reach for it, he grasps my hand within his, the plant oozing sticky liquid that drips from our handshake.

"Latik," he whispers his name, staring me in the eye. I have given him a new name, the one just quoted, acause of the risk that the Mede's minions might use my news-telling to track down this man of God. There be a warm, but questioning smile on his bushy-bearded face. "The shalom of Adonai be on you."

I mingle a connection by his statement only acause of my reading of scripture. Shalom be the wellbeing telled-out by them devoted to YHWH. Adonai being the term for someone's master or honored king. They are words of a story picture not often told outside the Jewish faith. I even know the right telling-back.

"And also on ye. I be Küllo."

"And I be freezing cold," says a familiar voice behind me. It be BJ, who did not follow my ask, who be rubbing his hands back and forth to warm them up. I make him known to Latik and tell how my friend travels with me as my Minder. Obviously he minds me not well at all.

Latik's smile brightens. He surveys the area with a cautious glance, signals to his group with a nod of his head and tells, "Quickly, please follow."

I be only telling these happenings acause this brave group of Messianic Seconds are more concerned with sharing the Word of YHWH than they are about their own lives. They hurry us to a secluded building, all the while explaining the spiritual, practical and symbolic significance of hyssop. "It is a medicinal and healing balm. It cleanses as soap and reminds us that YHWH is still the God of active creation in this world," Latik tells. "The plant should not grow in this climate, for that matter in any climate today. Yet you hold it in your hand. It is a tell of His power and mercy for a fallen world."

What faith and hope the *Hyssops*—my new word for these Seconds—share. They will surely be persecuted for aiding and mingling with me, but they beg me to news-tell their story. Four years ago, on the first full moon of the Jewish calendar, seven months after the Feast of Trumpets (when the Gathering-Up was done) this community of Hebrews dared to celebrate Passover. The Mede tells it to be a Do-Not. The Hyssops did not realize what would happen by their Do's.

At that Passover meal when the third cup of wine was shared, the cup of salvation by Jewish tradition, all in the room heard a voice.

"I am the way, the truth and the life. By me, you may know the Father."

In that long moment, many in the room telled of seeing a brilliantly lit man whose skin and clothing shown like…bronze.

This was their first mingling with Yeshua the Messiah—Bronzeman. Their Savior called-out each to believe in him and all in the room did that Do right away. Bronzeman then held in his hand a small plant which he passed to Latik. "This is a gift which you will share with the nations." It was the first piece of fresh hyssop ever seen in the area. They planted the seedling and it quickly spread. By great earth-caring, they were able to harvest and barter this wonderful gift, allowing them to spread their influence to the nearby communities in all directions.

I, Küllo, be a teller of this group's love for YHWH, for faith in their king, Bronzeman and for them with whom they want to share their healing tell. I write these pages with sadness acause I heard, soon after our mingling, that many of the Hyssops were found and snuffed by a Do, telled from the Mede. Them that survive do so as wanderers who plant the hyssop seeds of hope as they seek sanctuary in Jewish homes throughout old Europe and Asia. All the while they tell-teach their brother and sister Jews the new knowing of redemption promised by the Bronzeman.

Call-out and Do: I call-out to the readers of this news-tell. Please pray for all people, most-so for the Hyssops and even for them that still refuse to be eyes-open to the solid ground of Bronzeman. Pray their hearts hear the knowing of God. Help them mingle their belief and their Do to the Lion who be the soon-returning King and Priest.

To Darius Mede by the hand of Serge Palmotic—

To the Honorable Mede; Supreme Premier and ruler of Occupied Jerusalem in New Palestine: I bid you well and bow to your request for a detailed report of the unpleasant happenings of recent past. Since you are familiar by visitation with our location and our cultural nuances, I will simply begin with the contest in question. Rather than make this a fairy tale of some sort, my explanation will be brief and efficient.

The renegade Eleazar has escaped and is at large. This is a small matter as my men are on the trail and will have him recaptured in short order. I assure you that I will take quick and personal charge of his ending. Meanwhile I have set in motion plans to make examples of others who we are fairly certain are sympathizers with his cause. I will supply further details once the task is completed.

Your servant in the honor of your rule,
Serge Palmotic—Ward and Esquire of the Noreastern Provinces

Darius Mede—Chronicle III: 7-2-4 AE

I, Darius Mede, creator of the Green Order Government, Supreme Counselor over the World Council, and benefactor to the masses, have a confession to make within the privacy of this personal journal: I have struggled with a proper way to measure the history of time. Men throughout the course of events have tried to associate time to their moment. An excellent example was the cult that grew from the followers of a vagrant in the wilds of what is now Philistia. The followers of this so called messiah somehow wrestled power from the establishment of that era. To validate their power, they had a calendar created that centered the emphasis of all moments, before and after on the death of their leader. It was an absurd measurement and we were well to be rid of it along with those who trusted in it.

I on the other hand have taken the most rational of approaches. Geological evidence places the Earth's existence at approximately four and a half billion years old. Since this is not an exact measurement, I have deemed it appropriate to divide the planet's history into manageable categories using terminology simple enough for the common person to comprehend.

Since mankind is such a special breed that has risen up, evolving to control its own destiny, I think it logical to divide our time into the categories of Before the Age of Humankind (BAH) and The Age of Humankind (TAH). Again the exact date when mankind became self-aware is beyond my knowing. I can only assume, but not scientifically confirm, that it occurred with the dawn of reasoning ushered in by the great and most ancient Babylonian Empire. Regardless of the time spans for these ages, they can both be understood to have existed. According to my studies, there can be no argument. The problem is that such measurements are still much too vague

Is there any place in the march of history when we can be certain of measurement? The answer is of course, yes. It happened several years back when we did away with superstition and envy, eliminating those who claimed to have some special relationship with a fictitious ruler of the universe. When that group of primitives was dispelled, a new time of culture and civility began. It also conveniently coincided with the elimination of electrical capability. What better time to begin a new method of measurement than when the old method ceased to function? We shall recognize that moment as a new age unto itself: The Age of Enlightenment (AE).

With these factors in mind, my form of measurement is so simple that even the slowest thinker who lives can make sense of it. So I reach down and offer this calendar as a gift to the lowly and to all who struggle to make sense of the new environment in which we find ourselves.

And thus, one of the pieces of these writings that I will carve out to share is my pronouncement that this day is hereby proclaimed the Fourth Day of the First lunar cycle in the Fourth year of The Age of Enlightenment. In short 4-1-4 AE.

Palmotic, the pompous animal! He has the nerve to write his observations as if his clumsy antics are not already known to me? As if he thinks his sloppy dramatics are excusable just because he now claims he is capable of revenge against my escaped brother? I will teach him revenge and a new thing he does not know: submission!

But not now, there is small time for small things. Greater accomplishments have been made and will be made. At my laboratories here in Jerusalem, I have been busy indeed. The perfection of my Flexsteel product has already allowed worldwide construction of housing and businesses. Earthquakes be dammed. My material is nearly indestructible even during the worst instances of seismic upheaval. There is that stupid nuisance in the fact that the compound absorbs all light rendering it undetectable to the eye. At first I thought what a splendid defensive weapon it will be. But there is no way to reveal it to its providers and surrounding inhabitants once completed. Those who stand within the building must have some artificial source of light or a window built into the structure to be able to see at all. Those standing outside the building typically have to feel around with hands or feet as a blind man would do to search out the building.

After the initial construction of test facilities worldwide, I have had to blend in a special silver paint to force visibility. The problem persists though in that the paint formula eventually breaks down rendering the building once again, almost completely light-reflective—invisible in essence from the outside. People have become creative, applying their own form of markers to their domiciles in order to make them discoverable.

What I did not anticipate is my own invention being used against my plans. The upstarts calling themselves Seconds, have been acquiring Flexsteel and building hideaways. I have been searching them out for their radical views—contrary to my good social order. I am determined to end their rebelliousness, but for all I know they might be living anyplace, all places, perhaps even here within the walls of Jerusalem and I cannot detect them!

I am sure a solution will present itself. Meanwhile I busy myself with other advancements. Ironically, though my Flexsteel is imperceptible, my chemical lighting systems are letting people see again in the dark.

The process for these lights is not complex, but the assembly of the light tubes requires definite science. Separating muon electrons from atoms and trapping them, along with gasses in a plastic tube, to produce a constant glow is action that would take far too long to explain in this record. I will keep those formulas separate. For now, I will say that I am at least grateful that magnetism has not also been interrupted. Without that force, neither my lighting system, the Flexsteel formula, nor for that matter anything on the planet, would be able to still survive.

Still the *lowers*, what we have come to call the uneducated masses, complain. "Can't you make them glow in different colors?" I hear the grumblings through my sources. How ungrateful and petty they are. Gas exchange is what it is and in this case, red is the color produced! Are they not satisfied that illumination has returned?

It is ironic to me that my enemies have somehow found a way to manifest a blue hue. How they carry this with them, we have yet to discover—once terminated, their glow leaves them, making autopsies and experimentation impractical. They claim no special ability other than their belief in a god. Ridiculous and vexing, but whatever their source of light, it is obviously limited and simply makes them easier targets—when they do not disguise themselves in leathers—for elimination verses illumination. HA! Share that little joke with your supposed supreme being. I do better than one who once said he was the light of the world. Perhaps you do have inner light, but I am now the light-maker of the world and will share it with all who honor my purpose. As for those who do not bow to my authority? To them…let there be darkness!

As my systems are being deployed to strategic areas, work production of the masses is increasing significantly. Still, I must continue to find ways to employ and occupy as many individuals as possible with the mundane, but satisfactory tasks of daily living. Keeping them active, will keep them unthinking. At least now I can safely lodge the people of the world indoors to avoid the elements and the pervasive attacks of the bugs.

Ah yes, for the record, an interesting development. If I were superstitious, as those pathetic Seconds, I might pin the word miracle on the happening. What a quaint notion. Perhaps I'll use that in swaying the weaker ones to my way of thinking.

It seems that my most faithful supporter and confidant has reappeared after a very long absence. I had sent him on an errand, several years back to be specific. He was conveniently located in the area formerly called Atlanta of Georgia in that despicable country to the west. It took me enormous time and resources after the collapse to signal him and direct him to my secretly constructed facility in the mountains to his northeast. He and his followers were able to locate the facility only to find it inhabited by a group led by a minion of none other than Fitzgerald Hindeland. It is no small irony that this same upstart refused the ground to my appointed official. This one called Jason Ballard even had the audacity, and somehow the prowess, to lure away all the others and brainwash them into a belief in the sorcery of his religion. My man stayed true to the end, but was abandoned without protection to be singularly tortured by the elements and the strange beetles that plague this wretched planet.

I say it was ironic for Ballard and his ragtag group of survivors eventually found a way to join his mentor Hindeland here in Jerusalem. It was with delight that I eventually overcame Hindeland's influence on the crowds and had him sent to his just reward. But the lessor one escaped my plan for punishment and apparently has escaped the country. It is of little consequence. If he reappears, he will be dealt with.

It was soon after my victory over the Christ-cult; after Hindeland's demise, that my guards brought before me a disheveled and quite maniacal vagabond who claimed he had come from the western lands and who supposedly knew me. He was in such poor condition and disarray that I at first did not recognize him. The repetitive stings of the flying mini-monsters and his continuous exposure to the environmental elements during his journey across the Atlantic to my domain, rendered him hideous to behold and nearly impossible to communicate with.

But the familiarity was still there on his part and he muttered in his new and strangely affected voice. "Don't know your best friend, Darius? Won't greet your long lost buddy boy, Jonathan?"

With effort I saw it. Before me was the pitiful vestige of one who was once considered the undisputed ruler of the media world. He had indeed been one I referred to as an ally and now Jonathan Trimble will be used to a far greater purpose than even he would consider possible. For humor's sake, we <u>will</u> call it a miracle, that he has survived for this moment. As soon as his recovery is assured, I will give him the title I had always planned to bestow. As Deputy Premier and head of my public relations and media for my government, he will wield great influence on the attitudes of all populations. His abilities at swaying the masses are second to none. Together we will have no issue imparting our truth to all that I rule.

Regardless of Trimble's resurfacing, time does rush on. My exhaustive experiments have finally produced two great benefits. First is such a deep secret that I almost hesitate to write the words, yet the historical significance must somehow be captured. Until this moment only myself and a few carefully controlled others were aware of the conditions at Dimona. Even as I pen these words I am reminded that hardly anyone outside of Israel and within the backrooms of state departments throughout the world were ever aware of the Jewish State's highly secure and incredibly advanced nuclear facility. So ahead of its time was this facility that even the scientists of the former United States could not replicate its abilities…that is to generate nuclear energy through solar powered electric support of the centrifuge therein.

What few knew was that, even after the breakdown of electrical activity on the planet, Dimona continued to function! Yes, yes, there were leaks in the reactor core and there was the challenge of getting inside to repair damage to the facility without succumbing to radiation poisoning. I had to compensate great amounts of gold to the families of volunteers willing to pay the ultimate price in order to proceed with the reconditioning. It is still not complete, the work and cost of life is terrible.

What a great gift I can bring to the world if I am able to stay consistent in my scientific endeavors along with the recording of my experiments and these events. The solution is available, there is no doubt. The time of discovery is soon. I continue to research chemical solutions to the population issues presented by the disappearance of so many on the planet. How can we rebuild without an adequate number of willing and fully compliant workers?

For we are his workmanship, created in Christ Jesus for good works, which God prepared beforehand, that we should walk in them.

—Ephesians 2:10

Watching the Printmaker
Month 1, Year 4 After Gathering-Up (AG)

Han Ko is the patient one. She must wait for Küllo's news-tells to reach her and this is a questionable process. Pigeons fly in short messages, traveling friends risk their lives to bring her more elaborate pages. Pieces of paper folded into old containers and boxes appear mysteriously at the doorway of the Muuseum. She must determine the legitimacy of each—there are those who attempt to insert their own ideas. But she knows Küllo by heart and we also join in to help her keep sight of the truth.

All of this sounds very dramatic, but there is another part of the truth that is difficult to accept. She is alone in her work. Our visioning of her character may imprecisely portray a strong woman who has survived quite well on her own. There is more to her story, things about Han Ko that she has not yet shared with others, but that we see and hear from her beginnings.

Four years ago, the Korean born woman worked in Atlanta, Georgia at a well-known newspaper known as The Word, owned by none other than Jonathan Trimble's conglomerate, Network HeadQuarters Broadcasting Corporation. She had come to the United States with her parents who were devout Tongbulgyo Buddhists. To protect their daughter from the controversies that had begun to resurface in their native land regarding Zen sexual conduct, they made a difficult decision to immigrate to Atlanta. There they lived and worked with Han Ko's uncle.

Without much of a chance to settle in, the Koreans, along with the rest of the city began to experience and be affected by the strange physical phenomena made globally manifest by the appearance of the Singularity. Economic upheaval then required Han Ko's uncle to recruit her help into his janitorial company. One day, the print editor of a newspaper building they serviced found her helping set type for some of the older equipment after her duties were done. Her newly realized aptitude for spatial relations and mechanical systems, plus her nimble fingers and the newspaper's need to minimize cost increases by maintaining antiquated presses, assured her a job with the rag.

On her 18th birthday she received a unique gift from her new employer. Jonathan Trimble himself had announced that he would be visiting the paper and wanted to shake the hands of the 'outstanding' performers of the organization. The event was slated as an evening cocktail affair and though Han Ko's parents had not been invited, they made sure their daughter was dressed and coiffed elegantly to match the occasion. Although honored to be in attendance, the young Korean girl felt very much out of her element. She mostly stood by herself in a muted corner, under a schefflera plant that dwarfed her in size. Han Ko sipped timidly on a glass of water until her boss came over, took her hands and proudly led his prodigy to the tuxedoed Trimble. Being introduced, Jonathan eyed her in an uncomfortable way, seeming to evaluate her through some personal filter that had little to do with her printing acumen. Still the media mogul was charming, politely commenting on her demure beauty. He moved on to talk about her skills with the presses and encouraged her to study more about the older presses. He told her that the primitive types and methods would be essential with the unpredictable nature of electronics since the advent of V4641. Han Ko excitedly shared her printing passion with the man and neither seemed at all bothered by the amount of time their conversation was consuming.

"I am forming a special project team that I would like you to consider being a part of," Trimble finally offered.

The girl was stunned by the offer and said she would be honored to consider the opportunity. She explained that she would want to involve her parents in such an important decision and Trimble was quite understanding. "You do that," he replied with his champagne glass raised toward her. "But for the moment, stick around if you don't mind. I have a rather unique interview I must see to and then I'd like to return so that the two of us can become better aquainted."

Trimble's inflection and nuanced smile caused Han Ko to shudder and she was too innocent to comprehend her reaction. Her host excused himself and headed for a makeshift broadcasting booth made of plexiglass. The Korean girl watched as several attendants started applying makeup to his face and a camera was brought into position for some kind of televised event.

"He's quite a tall order, don't ya think?"

Han Ko jumped and then turned to look behind her to discover the unknown source of the voice. There stood a beautiful tall girl dressed perfectly in a black sequined evening dress with a very low cut bodice and matching stiletto heels. She could not be much older than the Korean herself, but this one was distinctive in several ways besides her sultry Southern American accent. Her deeply tanned skin, from her netted stocking-clad legs and, just to the crest of her shoulders was covered in colorful and intricate tattoos. Han Ko was sure somehow that each symbol had some story related to its application. The taller girl smiled in a way that warned Han Ko of hidden danger mixed with a friendly charm she found confusing.

"Just a friendly alert, sugar. Mr Trimble always gets what he wants. It's making sure ya get what you want that's important." The last part was said without the smile that had first greeted Han Ko. The girl seemed to have a strange gift of conveying her true emotions with a glance and her countenance briefly betrayed profound personal sadness. Then the smile returned and the branded southern girl held out her right hand which Han Ko took tentatively with her own, in mutual greeting. "My name's Roxanne. I'll do what I can for ya."

Without another word, Roxanne released her grip and glided toward the broadcast booth where she blew an exaggerated kiss to the busily preparing Jonathan Trimble. The gesture caught his attention and the man could be seen to flush beneath his powdered face, even from a distance. He

smiled, puppy like as the belle breezed by and Han Ko tried desperately with her innocent mind to decipher, not only what had just happened, but how she was involved.

At that moment the television monitors in the banquet area all blinked on and the familiar face of a Trimble flashed before them. He informed the public that he was reporting from a temporary broadcasting center since the actual NHQ complex had been destroyed by a suspicious fire. He then went on to explain that none other than the former Nobel Prize co-recipient for advances in Physics and Chemistry, Darius Mede had asked him to take on a task unparalleled in history. Trimble outlined that he would now begin a live interview with Spencer Lynd, then director of the Hubble Telescope Monitoring System in Rochester, New York. They would both offer commentary on the astounding events transpiring behind them on three view screens. One of the screens offered a caption that read *Enhanced Image of V4641 via DRRAGEN-One.* Another screen read, Dome of the Rock—al-Haram ash Sharif mosque. The third screen was most unusual of all, just showing what appeared to be a large family group sitting around a dinner table and its subheading read, *Area of Sympathetic Potential.*

Han Ko, like all the people in the world, was very attentive to news about the strange spatial anomaly now destabilizing many familiar comforts throughout the planet. But at this particular moment informing her parents about the great new opportunity that had been laid at her feet seemed to outweigh other current events unfolding. While everyone else was distracted by the live newscast, she slid back over by the schefflera and called her father and mother to share the exciting news. It was at the moment of her calling that she realized, by her cell phone clock that it was quite late into the evening. When they answered the phone, she apologized for not being home yet and went on to explain, in her native tongue, the extraordinary circumstances that kept her at the newspaper's offices. They too became animated and then her mother revealed a shock that Han Ko would remember forever.

"Your Uncle Chul has been sharing some very interesting things with us about faith. We have been reading from the Christian Bible with him and have come to believe in Jesus as our Savior."

Han Ko could say nothing for a very long time. She had always obeyed her parents in matters of religion, but had never understood their intense devotion to rituals. This news of recognizing a foreign god seemed to go against everything she knew. She asked both of her parents for more explanation, but everything they said sounded like jibberish. Her father especially seemed overly emotional and was anxious to have her come home so they could share their joy in person.

"Papa, Mamma, I love you both, please don't make the heavens angry," the girl begged her elders.

It was at that moment that Han Ko looked up at the nearest TV screen and saw the headline change to *DRRAGEN-One initiating matter/antimatter reaction within V4641.* The phone line began to crackle and Han Ko's parents could barely be heard crying out, "Do you smell that? Daughter, please love Jesu." These were the last words she ever heard them speak.

We watched as the lights in Atlanta went cold. We watched as the Blue streamed up into the evening sky. We heard a Korean girl drop her useless cell phone, groping her way to the stairwell, exit along with all in the room who had lost the light. We saw her make her way tentatively, the twenty blocks to her Uncle's high-rise apartment, crawling up to the 10th floor with nothing but her delicate hands to guide her in the pitch black gloom. We felt the protruding carpenters nail on the stairway puncturing her tender foot. We smelled her fear mixed with her dripping blood, blending with the odor of untended meals still burning in neglected pots on gas stoves in the building. We heard her anguished cries calling for her mother and father as she found the door to the apartment, fumbling blindly with her key, finally opening the door to silence darker than the night. And we felt her body convulsing in sorrow as she called out again and again into the nothingness, "Who are you Jesu? Why did you steal my *gajog*—my family?"

The delicate flower that was Han Ko, had to learn to be a strong tree and the lesson was harsh. Making her way back to The Word offices, she was received by Jonathan Trimble along with a number of his "chosen ones," as he called them, whom he was planning to evacuate from the city. "Atlanta will eventually crash in upon itself and we need to prepare as a team for a greater, better life together," he said, sounding and behaving like an evangelist of the highest order.

Han Ko needed hope and she found it in Trimble's enthusiastic teachings, along with the encouragement of Roxanne who seemed to develop a special interest in her. The latter did not associate with the Korean in public, but would wait until times when they could be more private in their discussions. "I know Jonathan's words sound all soft and warm, but I'm gonna warn ya, he has other designs. Go along with what he preaches for now, but be ready to run when I say."

It was difficult for the younger girl to grasp how Trimble might harm her. He was encouraging and introduced her as an equal to all in the party. "First you have to be self-reliant because no one else can help you if you can't help yourself," he counselled her. "Once you've found strength in taking care of yourself, group yourself with others who are strong in taking care of themselves. Then you'll be able to save one another." His enthusiasm was infectious and soon Han Ko became a devout disciple of Jonathan Trimble. Months of preparation for the group's flight from Atlanta included sessions where Trimble would teach the fundamentals of his philosophy and approach to life. It was a hodgepodge of positive thinking proverbs he had cobbled together through the instruction of his various mentors and also wisdom gathered in his rise to the top of the media kingdom.

If nothing else he was charismatic and inspired loyalty. But Han Ko did notice some strange things she could not reconcile. All the appointed leaders in Trimble's inner circle were men—not an unusual thing in Asian culture, but here it seemed odd. On the other hand everyone, including women, were given great freedoms and everyone was expected to share in duties equally, no matter the gender. All of Trimble's disciples were solid physical specimens, each with obviously higher than normal aptitudes. Early in their tutelage, Han Ko observed one of Jonathan's inner circle members introduce to him a young man nicknamed Flash whom the Korean girl recognized. He too, had worked in the print room and was very bright, appearing able to quickly take on difficult challenges and find unique circumstances. The English adage, "quick on his feet" would have been apt she thought, except he had no feet or legs at all. He was bound to a wheel chair that he himself had fashioned from spare parts when his motorized version lost its power. His new version was versatile and allowed him flexibility of movement almost equal to any of Trimble's crew. "Almost", was the issue for their leader, who smiled at the innovator, patted him on the head in what seemed a condescending manner and told him he was better suited to associate with the other employee survivors who had been given marginal space and supplies in the basement of The Word building.

Han Ko carefully scrutinized Roxanne and the other women disciples. She watched as Trimble would engage in conversation with one of them and casually invite over one of his inner circle men. A private conversation between the three would ensue and then, after they all nodded their heads in what appeared to be agreement, the inner circle man and the woman would go off together, usually not to be seen for several days. When the woman did reappear, she seemed…changed. Not quite as outspoken, not readily associating the other females in group, keeping close proximity to the inner circle man she had been paired with. Han Ko saw this happen on multiple occasions with multiple pairs and she wondered if Roxanne's warning had something to do with the pairings.

Her trust in Trimble became stronger each day he instructed them, but reconciling that instinct with what she saw in the "side show" as she came to think of it was becoming more difficult. One day she was walking down the hall and watched Roxanne come round the corner—a deep purple bruise displayed across her left eye and cheek. Roxanne passed by Han Ko without meeting her glance, but speaking in a low tone, the bruised belle said, "This won't happen to you. I'll be there to help, do the best you can."

Besides the chill of this new warning, something odd struck Han Ko. Roxanne had lost her southern accent entirely. She now realized that when they had spoken in confidence, sometimes the accent was there, sometimes not, as if it were an affect.

"Darling Roxanne, I hope you're better. Give me a hug and let me make it a better day." Han Ko was now further down the hallway. Still Jonathan Trimble's voice far behind her startled the girl. She glanced over her shoulder toward the direction Roxanne had continued and there the leader was stroking the hair of his favorite lady, giving her soft words of encouragement.

"Ah'm better now that you're here, sweet luv." Roxanne's accent had returned, even more feigned than before. She was also stroking Trimble's hair and wore a beatific smile as they stared into each other's eyes, then kissed passionately. Han Ko quickly rounded the corner of the hallway, the two lustful lovers seemingly oblivious to her passing. But she glanced over her shoulder one last time to see Trimble eyeing her while still fondling Roxanne whose back was turned to the Korean. Han Ko moved quickly to the print room to be alone. Now she understood what more would be expected of her and she wanted no part of it. But even we wondered how she would avoid the inevitable?

All of the disciples were required to go out on search and recovery sorties to find food and supplies. These junkets usually involved groups of four or five individuals in order to protect one another. The day after she had witnessed his exchange with Roxanne however, Trimble and an inner circle man named Don approached Han Ko and she knew what was coming. She remembered Roxanne's words and just nodded her head when Jonathan explained that he needed her to help his new man with a special recovery mission. They needed to go out together without support of others because of the delicacy of their purpose.

Trimble detailed that there was a storehouse full of environmental suits which he felt their group might need sometime in the future. He did not know what the equipment needed in order to function. If batteries were necessary, then the suits would be useless, but if it could be determined that the suits would work independent of electrical current, then they might become invaluable to the group.

We could see by her expression that Han Ko was not sure why the suits might ever be necessary, but Trimble spoke confidently about the need and that, if anyone could find a way to recover them for use, it would be her. He emphasized that Don would protect her from any outside threats. Their leader also justified that the reason he didn't want others involved was to not dash anyone's hopes were her mission to prove unsuccessful. It was to be a secret attempt.

Han Ko could not be pleased with this request. She had to know its true objective—to allow Don to be alone with her, away from the crowd, that he might have his way with her. Still she went along with the request and followed Don into the streets of Atlanta, knowing that somehow Roxanne would help her escape her fate.

Roxanne was nowhere to be found, with blood running down her face and stinging welts covering her body, Han Ko shouted out loud for the tattooed girl, exclaiming she was soon to die. "Why did you promise help, then send me into *Naraka*—Hell?" The Korean girl had not been taught much about rage and visceral fear from her parents or Jonathan Trimble, but she was learning much about it now.

We were there in spirit to see her nightmare unfold. After an uneventful five block walk from the newspaper building to the storehouse harboring the environmental suits, Don and she found the location already burgled and ransacked. As they combed the premises for anything worth saving, they suspected that their quest was in vain and would have to return empty handed. That is when they found a storage area on one of the upper floors. It had been broken into like every other place, but the contents of the room, fifty yellow environmental suits, complete with protective facemasks and hoods, remained relatively intact. Several of the rubberized suits had been stripped off of their hanging posts. Some of the masks appeared to have been experimented with by some curious vandals, but from the looks of it, the inquisitive ones quickly grew bored with the novelties and went on in search of more useful items.

Han Ko went right to work and tested one of the outfits as best she could, zipping it up, placing the mask over her face and securing the hood. The suit worked perfectly and was simple in design. The problem was the sense of claustrophobia it produced and the inability for the heat of her body to be totally vented. After only a few moments she was sweating profusely and eagerly climbed out of the rubber tomb.

Then she said to Don in her still imperfect English, "I not understand need for these. They keep everything away. Me too. I not want that much safety."

Her companion, who had stood guard the whole time making sure she had all the time she needed to evaluate the suits, now chuckled at her comment and came close to her. He put his hand to her cheek and replied, "I think it's time we both got more comfortable." Don then tried to pull her face to his in an attempt to kiss her, but Han Ko stepped back.

"Not good now," she reacted.

What happened next was a blur. In a second, the back of his open hand was flying across her face. The force of the strike caused her to fall backwards, painfully to the floor. "I'll decide when good is." His inflection suggested he was mocking her Korean accent and his leering smile told her of his want.

Han Ko crab-walked away from him as best she could, but the debris on the floor caused her to slide and shimmy more than anything. The room was small and soon she was trapped against a wall. Don, who was all polish and poise in Jonathan's Power Sessions, was more concerned here with blocking his prey from escape and loosening his pants. Han Ko had a strange sentiment. She felt the urge to gather the blood dripping into her mouth from his attack and spit it into his eyes hoping somehow it would blind him.

The imagery was interrupted by something striking the right side of Don's head. "What the...," were the words he got out before he was hit from behind. "Owh," he screamed and then the buzzing began. From seemingly nowhere, golden beetles the size of small birds flew about his head and torso. The bugs seemed capable of biting and stinging at the same time and did so with relish. The man's voice rose to a screech and he crumpled into a ball trying to protect himself from the onslaught. We watched with Han Ko in morbid fascination as the beasts continued to punish him relentlessly.

The Korean girl also cried out and we realized the things were not coming to her defense, but now systematically charging her as well. Han Ko's body twitched in rhythm with her own screams and it seemed she would experience even more torture than Don. That is when she surprised us with her amazing clarity of mind in the midst of terrible times. She somehow forced herself to her feet, climbing back into one of the suffocating suits, painfully managing to push away the insects long enough to insulate herself completely from their aggression. As they pelted against her costume, she compelled herself to climb down the stairs and run as best she could back through the streets toward The Word. The bugs were everywhere now and she was not the only target. People ran in every direction, yelling at the top of their lungs, colliding with lamp posts and other objects. Someone ran into her a block from the newspaper building and knocked her down again. She was about to push herself back up when a hand of someone also dressed in an environmental suit offered itself. Han Ko was lifted back up and then heard the voice of her rescuer. "Quickly, follow me to the back of the building, there's a way to get in without letting in the bugs." It was Roxanne.

Han Ko pulled away and yelled, "Why you leave me!" Her voice could barely be heard over the bugs' grating racket.

"No time to explain now, either trust me or don't, but we have to go now."

Han Ko hesitated, but then Roxanne turned and started running for the rear entrance of the newspaper building. The Korean decided she had little choice but to follow or be swallowed up in agony.

"Jonathan knew about the bugs coming. He communicates with other towns using carrier pigeons and they warned an attack was on its way." Roxanne dressed Han Ko's wounds and explained her previous actions. They were huddled in the corner of the basement of The Word. Besides the pathetic amount of light filtering in from the thick hopper windows encompassing the basement, only a single candle illuminated their discussion. To us, the scent of the wick was oddly welcoming…bayberry.

The Korean winced as her rescuer nurse applied alcohol to her wounds. "Why you leave me," and tears started flooding down her face.

Roxanne offered her own watershed as she defended herself. "I was being watched and I had limited chances to help you." With this she stroked Han Ko's hair and offered, "I'm so sorry. I actually did follow you and Don to the storehouse. The problem was getting there without being seen. You see, Trimble had you both followed by others. He gave you the duty as a test of loyalty and also to give Dom his claimed reward…you."

Reward? We were as offended as Han Ko appeared to be, judging by the expression on her face. Roxanne continued, "Here's what you didn't know. We already have a number of the protective suits stored here."

At this confession, Han Ko tried to stand up, but Roxanne restrained her and kept talking, "It was his way of testing you. He already had what he wanted. Remember what I said about you getting what you wanted?"

A strange new look appeared on the Korean's face. "What you think I want?"

"Freedom," came the answer. "It's what we all want."

Han Ko's expression then changed to puzzlement. We could see her working through the issue, but we could not hear her inner thoughts. Perhaps she never considered herself a prisoner. Perhaps she had not considered that she had a greater choice to make. What we did see was her face gradually change, showing resolve which was confirmed as she nodded at Roxanne and uttered her next words.

"I forgive you, but I not trust you," The statement came out in cold calculated precision, as if Han Ko had figured out how to make a damaged machine work efficiently again.

"I'll take forgiveness for now. Somehow I'll re-earn your trust." Roxanne offered a relieved smile which then turned to a look of grim determination. "So now there's the matter of the other thing. We need to get ready for the storm."

Han Ko learned from her rescuer, that Roxanne had pulled her down to the basement of the newspaper building. It was the area where the other, "non-disciples" were allowed to exist away in minimalist comfort. The tattooed girl seemed to know all eleven of the people down here aside from the Korean, as if she had been in frequent communication with them—as if she had been planning Han Ko's rescue and other things for a while. Roxanne would disappear for hours, sometimes days, apparently going topside to continue her dual life with Trimble.

Don had explained that Han Ko had run off when the bugs attacked. Going out, even with a suit was a risk. Bugs might enter the building; injuries were possible to Trimble's precious ones, so no-one was asked to search for the Korean. It was simply assumed that the attack had consumed her.

And then came the storm Roxanne had warned about. It was not a weather system like anyone was used to. It was an unnatural holocaust that leveled much of Atlanta and lasted for seven or eight months, depending on who was calculating. Add to this, the increasing ground tremors and sometimes outright earthquakes, along with the close quarters and meager supplies.

Roxanne provided partial relief from the dark monotony. She smuggled in extra rations and gave frequent reports of what was going on topside. In some cases she defended Jonathan Trimble. He used his resources wisely, even having his crew work to bolster the building in preparation before the storm. The old establishment had great bones and seemed well suited for surviving the onslaught. They had discovered early on that the air outside was poisoned and so the doors and windows had to be quickly sealed and the pneumatic storage tanks that had driven some of the ancient equipment now became their air supply. Water was carefully rationed for those above and graciously as well for the ones below, who were not allowed to co-mingle with the disciples. It was Trimble's Rule Number One. The upper class was literally that. Roxanne put herself at great risk when she secretly visited the twelve.

Han Ko healed fairly quickly, thanks to the attention of Flash. He continued to dress her wounds and share talk-time with her. The ongoing storm veiled the lighting in the basement even more and so the people below gathered as close to the hoppers as possible. Candles were available, but everyone was afraid of starting a fire with them or burning up too much of their precious oxygen.

Cabin fever was as big of a challenge as anything. It would be easy under such circumstances to imagine riots erupting within. Miraculously, such events typically fizzled quickly thanks to the character of Flash. He seemed to have gift for quickly settling even the most heated disputes and for calming the bottom dwellers.

One day Roxanne brought down a wonderful, strange gift. It was a long flexible tube, containing some kind of chemical compound which produced red light. The tubing could be stretched out and gave at least a limited amount of light for moving about. "The light can't be turned off and every once in a while I'll have to take it up to be recharged, but it's better than nothing," she explained. Everyone in the basement took turns hugging their provider. Han Ko observed that this crowd was peculiar. Outside the building, the attitude of survivors she had seen was one of vacant distain for others. Within these walls existed a comradery that would have rivaled any church prior to the Gathering-Up.

It was the wheelchair bound Flash who seemed the glue and who also tended Han Ko during her healing. Early on, Flash pulled out a book to read to her and others to pass the time. But when he mentioned the name of the book, the Korean resisted. "My parents came to believe in Jesu. Somehow he stole them away. I want no Bible talk."

"He didn't steal your family away, Han Ko. You could have gone with him too and still can." The young man actually sounded excited about this prospect.

"Why you no go with him?" she asked bitterly.

"I pretended to believe in Jesus as my Savior. I went to church and played the part well—I even know lots of hymns I can teach you. But I never gave him my heart…my full love, my true confession. I was a fake. But I'm a fake no more."

"You make no sense. You say you now love someone who left you in a bad place." Han Ko continued to resist.

Others wanted to hear about Jesus though and she could not help but listen. There wasn't much else to do and Flash was a wonderful teacher, explaining the story of creation and how it was man, not God who turned away. He shared Biblical stories with examples of how God kept trying to love mankind, but was repeatedly rejected. One day he explained how God had a plan all along to offer His son as a sacrifice.

"It stupid," who would die for all humans? Too many bad ones" The Korean flatly stated.

"Did your parents sacrifice for you?" Flash asked.

"They brought me to this country, telling me that I would be safer here. But then they left me," she spit these words out in frustrated tones.

"You told me they were sharing all about their love for Jesus during your last phone call with them. If there had been more time, do you think they would have invited you to go with them? Would you have said yes?" The young man in the wheelchair was relentless in his questions.

Han Ko did not answer that day or the next. In fact she became silent for a week. It was obvious that she was working through something and so she was left alone. One evening Flash was reading out loud from the book of Acts, about a guy named Saul who helped execute a believer named Stephan. Saul also rounded up and had other believers imprisoned and worse. Then Jesus encountered Saul on a road and asked why he was persecuting Jesus. Flash commented that this was incredible because Jesus had already been crucified and resurrected. More incredible is that Saul then recognized Jesus and bowed to him as Lord of his life. Everyone in the room was captivated at the tale of the man who would become the greatest letter writer and evangelist of all time. Everyone was captivated, that is, except for Han Ko.

"That more stupid than anything else. God should have made him blow up," the Korean blurted out. These were her first words to anyone since Flash's last question.

"But that's the beauty of the message, Han Ko," said Flash. "Anyone still residing on the topside of the turf can still ask forgiveness of God. He desperately wants a relationship with each one of us."

"Some can't be fixed," argued the girl.

"At the risk of you shutting me down again, I want an answer to one question," Flash asked Han Ko. "If one of your favorite printing presses stopped working, would you just leave it and work only the ones that were in great shape?"

The Korean eyed him suspiciously, but went ahead an answered, "I try to fix, but if no good, I throw it out."

"But you do try," encouraged Flash. "And I've seen your character. I know you would work long and hard, far more than most people, trying any and everything to salvage your invalid."

How odd he had used that word. Han Ko stared at the man in the wheelchair for a long moment before she responded quietly, "Person not machine."

"No. Person more valuable; person worth everything to save." Was he mocking her? The answer came immediately. "You are worth everything to God, Han Ko. He will try everything and anything, even offering His son in trade for your broken parts. But even then at some point, if you refuse His efforts to fix you, then He will gather His other fixed-ones and move on."

Flash did not mention Han Ko's parents. He did not mention the missing ones of any in the basement. He didn't have to. Each in the basement could be heard weeping, some outright sobbing. In the red light, streams could be seen trickling down the Korean's face too, but she said nothing. All the others cried out in confession and soon, each asked for a relationship with their Savior—Each, except for the silent one.

The night was filled with the songs that Flash had said he would teach them, interlaced with readings from the book Han Ko refused to accept.

Once everyone had fallen to sleep, one individual moved quietly over to the book by Flash's bedside. A delicate hand first touched the cover, then opened and flipped to a specific page. She read silently, but we could see the words formed on her lips:

"You search the Scriptures because you think that in them you have eternal life; and it is they that bear witness about me, yet you refuse to come to me that you may have life."

The book was quietly closed. The figure went back to her own corner. She did not sleep, but tried something foreign for her. The Korean mouthed other muted words. Inwardly we knew her to be lifting up her voice in a new direction:

> "*Yesu*—Jesus, please help. I am alone, I need you to walk
> with me.
> Geolughan Aabeoji—Holy Father, I am sorry for my
> angriness.
> Forgive me, let Your will be my will;
> In this place as it is in Your place…"

—Han Ko prayed.

In the morning Flash awoke to a face peering at him from above. He blinked his eyes and focused on Han Ko's familiar stern look. "You sleep too long. I confess to Jesu, now have questions," she stated.

From then on, the Printmaker turned student and would not stop asking questions. She wanted to know everything about how not just to preach Jesus, but to be like Jesus. The other bottom dwellers became just as enthusiastic, sharing personal testimonies with one another, becoming something they all thought they had lost forever—family.

When Roxanne visited, she was shocked at the transformative energy of the beleaguered crew. "Trimble's got nothing on you," she exclaimed after several encounters where everyone insisted she stay and share her own history. She excused herself each time, saying that she must get back so as not to arouse suspicion. And oddly, from that point forward, they saw less and less of the tattooed belle. As the twelve grew closer, she became strangely distant.

Then during a midday prayer, they heard a peculiar sound from outside—Silence. The light from the potters seemed to increase and not too long after, Roxanne came down to announce. "It's over. The storm is over, and we're leaving."

By "we", Roxanne meant Trimble's topsiders and that seemed to include her. The news confused them in many ways. Through Roxanne's explanation, they learned there had been a plan all along for Trimble's group to travel to another undisclosed location once conditions improved. The air had cleared, was breathable, and so the command to move had been given. There were still the bugs to contend with, but the environmental suits would keep the disciples safe. That sounded like good news until the rest of the details came out. There were only enough suits for Trimble and his gang.

Roxanne appeared embarrassed and offered an apology. "I'll make sure Y'all are left as much food and water as possible and I'm sure you can figure out some way to protect yourselves.

"Why you go?" Han Ko's eyes bore into those of the one she had once considered her only friend. Roxanne looked down and away as she answered. "I'm just not…ready yet. I…God is great and all that, but…I'm just not ready." With that she turned and climbed out of the basement for the last time.

Han Ko wiped the dirt from her hands, knelt for a long prayer and then achingly pushed herself up and began a slow determined walk away from the graves. So much had happened in the last three weeks.

Trimble and his crew didn't just leave, they snuck out! There had been much banging and clomping above their basement tabernacle, then as with the storm outside, all quieted above them.

It was an hour before anyone thought to try the door at the top of the stairs which was usually well secured. Han Ko herself climbed up to find the door unlocked.

They all tentatively rose from their tomb, several assisting Flash make the ascent. What they found above was astounding. In the middle of the main foyer of The Word was a tarped mass approximately six feet high. The tarp was pulled back to reveal a stack of crates—food, water, traveling supplies, a few packs and pull carts—most everything they would need for their survival.

One of the other women noticed a smaller package wrapped in newspaper print with a name neatly written over top with a black marker:

HAN KO

When the Korean opened the bundle, she found a note written in Roxanne's familiar script:

My sweet friend,

> I know you don't trust me and I can't blame you. But I have tried to do everything I can to protect and hide you from those in my group who, if they knew you had survived, would have changed you terribly. I could not have beard that happening and so was willing to sacrifice even our friendship to keep you from harm.
> I hope someday we will meet again under better conditions. Then maybe, I can win back your trust. I long for that day.
> Meanwhile, accept this gift as my pledge to always think warmly of you. Who knows, maybe it will help remind you of me warmly also.
> I still struggle to pray to the God that would let this all happen. You seem to have overcome that hurdle and I admire that in you. For now I'll ask you to please pray for me; that someday I'll learn to trust God enough to offer the same for you.

> Your friend, no matter what,
> —Roxanne

Han Ko stared at the note for long moments and then forced her eyes to focus on the other object that was contained in the package. It was what the her ancestral country would call a *panja*, a hardened wooden plank to be used as a cooking surface. It would come in very handy for grilling vegetables and meat when traveling in the wild. She noticed that her initials had been carefully carved into one of the corners of the rectangle and we saw the flicker of a smile briefly capture her lips. Then without a word Han Ko rewrapped the paper around the plank and packed it in her keepsack.

As we shared earlier, most everything for the bottom dwellers needs had been included in the stack. Everything but for one thing—survival suits. It didn't matter, they all were so focused on the provision that no one had noticed—in their rush to exit, Trimble's crew had left the doors to the building entrance wide open. Flash was the first to discover the danger and began wheeling madly toward the gateway, hoping to close them off before the bugs flew in.

But at the doorway he paused, then instead of resealing the entrance, he wheeled outward into the open air. No insect attacked. Not one. Oh, they were there for sure, making a terrible noise as they patrolled. Yet they left Flash alone. Slowly, each of the bottom dwellers emerged into the clouded outdoors and they too were left unharmed. There was no explaining it, other than by the grace of God.

Quickly a decision was made. Atlanta was in ruins. It was not a place to stay, so they packed up everything they could carry and, after a prayer for safe journey, they left.

It took them two days just to exit the urban plight. They had decided on a direction toward the eastern seaboard. Why? No-one could think of a better plan other than to avoid the mountains they knew to be to the north. Crumpled concrete, earthquake damage, collapsed bridges and more seemed the work of demons determined to block their way out. Thankfully they did not encounter other groups of scavenging people, just the occasional individual whom they would invite to join them but who seemed too suspicious or weak to accept the invitation. To the latter, they offered food and drink at the risk of their own weakening, and then they moved on.

Finally they managed to break through, into more rural regions. Flash's wheelchair and their own unfamiliarity with the wild required them to keep mainly to man-made pathways. Fatigue, the heat of nature, and uncertainty slowed them to a crawl, but crawl they did, singing and praying out loud, asking God to lead them on.

In the third week, they knew that they were in dire straits. Food was running low and more so, water. All the stream beds they had encountered were either dry or smelled of something poisonous. Towns they passed through were abandoned and completely void of supplies. They had to find resources soon or...

—Han Ko heard it first. Late in the day, the sound of running water! It was off a ways to the right from the highway they were maneuvering and she immediately volunteered to investigate. Everyone else was so exhausted from the day's travel that no-one even volunteered to join her. They pulled off to the side of the road and Flash smiled at her before she left. "Be careful," he advised as if any of them knew what that required.

Han Ko was thoughtful enough to carry her keepsack with her, along with a few empty plastic jugs perchance the water was drinkable. She hoped to port enough back to the group for a quick resupply and then they could return for more. She found the stream less than a quarter mile off the road, down in a ravine, but reachable. Amazingly the water smelled fresh and the trickling liquid looked clear. She cautiously tasted it and it was deliciously fresh. Rapidly she filled the jugs and tied them to her pack, then awkwardly began climbing back up the ravine wall. When she was just at the top she glanced through the meager brush to see other journeyers coming down the road from the direction her group had been traveling. She held back and watched as Flash waved a friendly greeting and started wheeling on the blacktop toward those approaching.

"We're glad to see you!" she could hear his loud greeting.

That is when a crazy thing happened. Han Ko's eyes and ears...and ours, had trouble making immediate sense of it. Flash's head seemed to jerk back and then forward violently and he slumped to the ground. Then there was a loud cracking sound, like a gun being fired. The Korean had never heard the report of a rifle before. Her group had no weapons and her family had never exposed her to such things other than in movies she had watched. Now she watched a new, strange show with the new sound becoming too familiar, along with a color—red.

One by one her other companions dropped as if life had been yanked from their insides. The cracking sound followed each slumping. And that was it. The new journeyers came into the camp, picked up all they could find of value, one of them firing another shot into each inert body as the party rummaged. Then casually, they walked on down the highway laughing and joking as they went.

The sound of their banter soon faded as did the dim sunlight. Han Ko squatted, frozen in shock into the early evening and then very slowly rose up and walked toward her camp. Her stiff legs carried her first to Flash, then to each of the others. She had no words, she displayed no emotions. All of that had been shot away with these lives. Mechanically, the Korean began to fix things. One of the provisions she had carried with her was a latrine shovel. This was to be its first use on the trip. Han Ko began digging in the loose dirt of the field. These would be shallow trenches, twelve in all—the ground was crusty and unforgiving, as was the Korean's heart at that moment.

It was early into the dark morning before her task was finished. There was plenty of broken wood about. So with twine she had brought along 'just in case of something,' she crafted crosses that were then hammered at the head of each grave.

Her prayer over her friends was shouted aloud in English to the muted sky. "I angry at You! You take everyone away and leave me! What You want from me?"

What she did not expect was an answer, but that is what she heard. It was as clear as the voice of any she had loved in her futile life and its tone was a soft breeze of peace that blew into her soul as a freshly washed blanket, to cover her shivering spirit. "I want your love."

Han Ko screamed back, "I do love!"

"Love Me then," answered the blanket.

"You take anyway, why I need to give?" Her tears punctuated the question.

"I have taken nothing, the others who loved me, who loved you, were willing. Are you willing?"

Han Ko wept uncontrollably, then whispered. "I know You love. I do not know how to fix anger. I want to love. You take me, You fix me?"

"I will send you."

The blanket whispered a mission to her. We were not allowed to hear it completely. As the blanket spoke and directed, we were only given partial sight of its unfolding. Some things are too personal. Some things require faith with no eyes or ears.

What we were given is this: Somehow Han Ko would make her way to the coast. Somehow she would sail to a faraway land called Estonia and there, somehow she would meet a young man named Küllo. She was assured of it and that was enough. As she walked away from the great pain in that field, the Korean was changed. The Ruach blanket wiped away all her tears.

One sees
One hears
And it is written
Let us work together that the world may know!

—Keepers, for the glory of God

The Bronzeman News

WATCH AND KEEP מָשִׁיחַ מָשִׁיחַ

My name be Küllo, that be all ye need to know about me. I be not the story—I be the eyes, ears and hands of these tales. The words on these pages will be news-tells from common folk. Folk like ye and me. Them will tell their story and I will copy it with as little cleaning up as possible, so that all who are left after the Gathering-Up will see what be happening: The Bronzeman be appearing and the seeings of him are much the same. What be different be what he tells each one to Do.

MINGLE IT. MAKE UP YER OWN MIND, I WILL NOT MAKE IT FOR YE.

**Edition Two: The Edinburghs of Fraspania
Month 2, Year 4 After the Gathering-Up**

Küllo's Notes: The Edinburghs be regions once called Scotland and Ireland: Two completely separate lands, but with a common history of independence and strong mingling. What would be called a *House* or feudal family in my culture; here be telled with a beautiful word: Clan. The population of The Edinburghs be sparse after the Gathering-Up. Clan be everything.

We be invited—after learning of our sticks—to mingle with a family in the Highlands and it has taken almost two months to trek here from Slavonia. Thieves on the roads, angry weather and other spiritual plagues would tell us "no", but Bronzeman be a King of "yes". So we have made it safely to the dwelling of Luther & Rachel Hine. They seem unafraid of publicly living out their belief even though some of their clan are not Seconds. There be respect for this family. They and their children Do nothing but bright Blue things for anyone around them. The tells of their travels and ways have created superstitious awe and legend about them in the view of the folk nearby. And when we meet, I am telled another surprise. In their house rests Eleazar, the same who was rescued away from the hate of Serge Palmotic. The Hine place be safe and undiscovered up to this moment. But the risk here be much and these people give up much to survive here.

Now that we are here thanks to Bronzeman, the dark world tries to say "no" again and wild things begin. There be no telling it well. The shaking of the earth be not the common kind. It be all moments with no stopping. The wind attacks bringing sand that scours the skin of anything outside our walls. The flying beast-beetles slam, and slam again, against the outer doorway demanding entry. They cannot injure any in this house, but the weather makes them angry and they argue with the barrier that denies them the freedom to fly wherever they please.

Heat as I have never mingled afore bakes the air while giant hail stones rocket into the ground outside. This place be strong-built, but against such attacks? It be a wonder any house can still stand.

"They can't break us down," offers Angie, the Hine's young niece. Luther Hine's brother and his wife were snuffed not long past, and so their orphaned children have been called into this family. Angie holds her hands over her ears trying to shut out the crazy noise that started several long moments earlier. The rope clock used by this family to keep-track days, continues to mark nature's wrath with the slow burning of its hemp threads. Its nose burning odor tempts me to crack a door or window to offer new air inside. BJ, my Minder, places his hand on my chest, knowing my want, but reminding me by his glance to hold fast. The moments slowly smolder away by the rope's count.

I do not even dare approach the boards barricading the windows. What if one took a direct hit from one of the ice missiles? As I peer through the dim light that sneaks in through the cracks in the barriers, a flash of light from outside briefly lights the room and then an explosion.

"Bombs, Unka," cries out the nephew, Elijah.

"No," responds Luther with a curious look on his face as he gentle cradles his own son, Jender, in his arms. "Something far stranger and more rare in these times—lightning and thunder."

Another flash and shaking, further away this time echoes against our stronghold. Then something stranger, everywhere around us, causes all the children and many of the adults to shriek. The ground beneath pitches. I believe the mouth of the earth will open to swallow us but then the storm-sounds begin moving on and we all start offering prayers of thanks to Bronzeman for this protected place. Will my terror move away also? To help clear my brain, I ask the Hine's if they will tell us the story of how their special home came to be.

"While on missionary journey, we was assaulted by forces of Western-Province," tells Rachel Hine. She told afore that she be a Hebrew from Israel and I mingle her to be a strong partner for her husband.

"Unka Luther, tell us again, the story!" Elijah pleads with just a pinch of fear for the moment in his voice. The story will be a distraction for the boy who clings to the leg of Eleazar BenMadai. It was Eleazar we searched out in Slavonia. That man was the one being beaten in front of the crowd and who somehow escaped. We were not able to interview him afore he disappeared and our new friends, the Hyssops suggested we seek our next tell here in The Edinburghs. Did they know that Eleazar also was coming this way to reunite with his family? The Hyssops never said. But here we found him recovering and sharing protection with the Hine's.

"I believe the angels of YHWH have massed to protect us," Luther proclaims, inviting the young boy to his lap. Eleazar nods in approval from his chair, not yet able to move about without assistance. Ayita, who be of Native American tribal decent, applies some kind of plant goo to her husband's bruises. I recognize the smell. It be hyssop. Around her neck be draped a cloth sling which holds her infant daughter Fizina, and after caring for her husband's wounds, she begins to nurse the baby as Luther continues.

"We had no weapons other than our prayers, swift feet and stealth. Our capture was soon to be fact. Yet them that were overtaking us suddenly began to choke in their protective suits. Their natural reaction was to rip off their helmets and that was when the beetle-beasts—as Angie has named them—buzzed in for vengeance."

"Praise YHWH for the beetle-beasts," cheer the children, Angie shouting the loudest.

Now Ayita speaks in her beautiful calming voice as she ministers to Eleazar. "We, as New Followers of Yeshua, are somehow protected from the nightmare-flyers, but our enemies are not. Still we must pray for them! The torment from the bites and stings of the bugs drive their prey to near insanity. If we can somehow touch their souls with our tell of love and salvation through Yeshua, they too can know joy, even in these terrible times."

Another close lightning strike and thunder clap reminds us that the danger outside be not yet finished. It be so close that the smell of sulfur chokes me. The children borough into the arms of loved ones and I force my hand to steady-down so to righty script the Hine's saga.

"After our enemies ran from area of beetles, we searched for caves in hills or some hiding place." This be Rachel Hine taking up the tale. "It was accident…"

"…There are no accidents in our new world!" The children and adults all sing the well-rehearsed declaration in loud chorus. I smile afore the sound of another giant hail stone crashing outside encourages Luther to tell with some humor.

"I, the famous Luther Hine," here he stands up, pounding his chest with pretended pride—all the children and his beautiful bride Rachel, boo comic-book style at him.

"Alright, it was completely by Yahweh's hand that we came upon our new home. Yahweh caused his bumbling fool, Luther Hine, to collide into an invisible wall."

All in the room shouted, "Whomp," on queue. Still standing, Luther twirls in pretended dizziness and falls dramatically to the floor. Even as more thunder and lightning plays outside, all laugh at his play-tell.

"I had discovered Flexsteel," he groans. "Actually the Pretender, Darius Mede" (more vicious boos from the audience; the name Mede be bad-sung among us, for many reasons). "The Pretender indeed invented this stuff we call Flexsteel. That is one of the very few good Do's we give to his credit. But what even Pretender Mede did not tell anyone was that, if not painted, Flexsteel acts like a camouflage. I bumped into my new home because my new home was hiding right out in the open."

"Ooo Ahhh," everyone replies.

Documents stored here suggest that this be an abandoned place deemed too far removed from trade routes to serve any continued Do. So, as best as we can, we hide and are protected in a place made by our enemy.

"Thank you Pretender Mede." everyone cheers.

The storm has moved off and I am just invited to call-out from Daniel Anderson's journal, when another lesser pounding be heard outside… different somehow. Angie announces in the hush of curious fear, what we all now realize, "That's somebody knocking at the door."

Two puzzles shout in my brain. *Who outside these walls could have survived the attack of nature that we had just passed through and how did they find this invisible Flexsteel hideaway?*

The first question be answered soon enough as a voice from the other side announces. "By the authority of the Supreme Mede, make your door open."

Within, I watch the response of most to be puzzling. Instead of panic and anxiety—natural Do's when hearing such a demand—I watch most heads bow in peaceful prayer. Even the children smile in their spiritual mingling, as if they are making ready for a family meal.

After looking to his wife, who nods as one who mingles-well her partner, Luther begins to move to the door. I mingle too—*what other choice do we have?* But in midstride, he be halted by my Minder, who steps ahead of our host, to the portal. I have never seen him so purposed in any Do and none of us have time to stop him afore he speaks through the door to them on the other side.

"Be going back to yer master. Be hopping fast, he needs to hear ye say this be a no-place."

Instantly we hear scuffling and much movement outside. Now I bow my own head knowing this to be my final moment on this earth. By his Do, my friend has just made our snuffing a fact. Surely the Mede's army be readying to level our fortress. The waiting seems a forever moment and I puzzle if, somehow, I missed the moment of my gathering-up. Will I open my eyes to meet Bronzeman face to face?

Instead I look to see Luther has followed BJ to the door. Together they open it and we are met with…silence. All of us rise and walk to the outside. The field surrounding the house be a carpet of uniformed bodies. Countless more are snuffed in the bouldered landscape beyond. Pieces of hail the size of oranges, and even melons, lay melting into the heads and corpses of many. Others looked bricked by flying stones or toasted by lightning (judging by the burn marks everywhere around). Some have been crushed by great shifting gouges in the ground that must have opened and closed like hungry jaws. I mingle thousands are Snuffed—who knows how many more are outside of our seeing? There be a bad smell all over, like burnt rubber, rotten garbage and poo mixed together.

In the distance toward the mainland, we can make out the dusty retreat of survivors, the leftovers of a greater force, given leave to flee by a voice behind an invisible door. Well, not so invisible any more. Now I can see how they found us. Twigs, branches and rocks seem suspended, embedded in the air, outlining the form of the house. The wind must have shot them at great speed to cause the stuff to stick.

"Jender Hine, back here come!" Rachel Hine pursues her nephew who be marching around in the field. He mingles he be the cause of the retreat and so has picked up a weapon from one of the fallen. Rachel comes from behind, expertly removes the rifle from her son's hands and walks him back to the clan.

"They arrived before the storm and were prepared to capture or destroy us." Ayita, tells in her native American fashion, moving among the dead, crouching in one place, studying the dirt in another, with a well-honed tracker's eye. She strokes the soil and surveys the moment reading it all aloud as a familiar tell. "They came from the south, with stealth, not like their escape to the east. There was no negotiation or intent to capture in their plans." Here she picks up and inspects another of the many weapons, like the bodies, carelessly strewn across the landscape. "These are not meant for intimidation. They are killing things."

Rachel also reviews the gun she relieved from Jender. "Is nothing like I see before. It be made of Flexsteel; air driven; made very good." Without hesitation, the Israeli sabra turns, takes aim at one of the dead bodies and fires. The sound that comes out from the device be a high pitched whine which turns to a rumbling. I *re-know* it in my bones from long ago when I was near a jet airplane taking off. The body of the soldier vibrates and suddenly explodes out in all directions. A piece of the hand and an ear, land by my foot.

We are all shocked into no-talk for a moment and then Rachel and Ayita clap and point all the children back into the house. The men begin to gather up the weapons in the near vicinity as a precaution.

"Why so many? What kind of resistance were they expecting to find?" Eleazar has limped out with the aid of a crutch and scans the carnage with disbelief.

"They didn't know. No-one sends out a mobilized army of this size, this far into a wilderness unless they fear the unknown. Whatever and whoever they expected to find, they wanted to snuff them completely." Ayita turns over several of the bodies and becomes interested in the helmets worn by each of Mede's minions. She removes the gear and examines the faces of our adversaries. "Odd," be her next word after ten such examinations.

Luther goes over and looks at the faces. "These two, have the same face. And these three, no, five, are like one another, exactly alike as I can tell. Twins and quintuplets on a battlefield?"

Ayita and Eleazar move to other bodies. "These are alike too but not the same as those over there. Here's a set of ten!"

I cannot mingle the carnage much less the bizarre sets of identicals. My mind finally gives up trying to make sense of it all and I vomit for several very bad minutes. I look up to see the sky darkening even more than be regular in the middle of these dreary days and realize it be I who am darkening into a hellish dream...

—I walk onto a stage with red velvet curtains drawn back. Why be it so dark here? The only light I have to see by be my own Blue. I fear falling off the stage. The Un-lit crowd below have long teeth and they seem hungry for me. Then a light of warmth wraps me up. I be in...part of... love. The Un-lit in front of me cry in pain and then melt when the golden glow touches them. Bronzeman takes my hand and tells me he be the love. "Do with me," he smiles and we fly together.

My eyes open and BJ's face greets me. "Ye flopped and slumped like one of yer fish out from water," he laughs to me. I do feel like some sort of dead sea creature and catch an odor in my nose that says I smell much like one too. Immediately rising from a reclining position off the floor, I search for my paper and writing pen to capture the moment. My attention be caught by all the goings-on in the house. How did I get inside? Was I carried?

Each person, even the children are searching for items, I am not sure what they are seeking out, but as each finds an item they methodically place it in a bag, a keepsack, or carrying box.

"Eleazar and his family, they is leaving," Rachel tells as she helps me gain my balance. I am still woozy and so I repeat the words I thought I heard her say through her crunchy Jewish accent.

"Leaving? Where are they going?"

"—Where is you going, they is going," Rachel tells me back.

So now my Minder and I have a whole family of traveling companions. Eleazar has a strong knowing acause of the moments surrounding the failed attack, that he was the true target. He will not be unmingled of the thinking. Rachel Hine received a vision that suggested there would be repeated attempts to hunt us down. Eleazar, who I learn be a former Hebrew priest, tells that we must be mobile. Since I was planning on going anyway, it seems right that going be all our Do. Where are we going? Let that be a secret tell for now, between us and the Spirit Ruach who lights our way.

> Call-out and Do: I call-out to the readers of this news-tell. Please pray for all people, even for them that still refuse to be eyes-open to the solid ground. Also ask to yer own self, "What am I doing for others? What be my call-out each day from Bronzeman, our King and Priest?" Listen and he will tell.

> **Special Do:** Ready yer traveling plans. Soon, it will be time to begin the trek to Jerusalem. Ye will know the when by the telling of the trumpet sound.

Letter from Ilbani Midehina Acdah, Keeper of the Kin (Yerushalayim)

"God has two eternal thoughts:

First, that His faith in His creation is relational
The second is that what His creation has faith in
is consequential

With the breath of these two thoughts, God loves."

—Moshe Folzman

Written to my God—through the intercession of my Savior, Yeshua. For that reason I will not date my posts for the Receiver of my thoughts and prayers will put them to His purpose in His time. Let these words then be for His purpose and to His glory.

Gravity, one force that exists in a relationship of attraction between all things in the universe. Larger objects have more gravity, smaller have less. The closer two objects exist to one another, the greater the gravitational attraction. These are facts supported by evidence, indisputable. There is Law involved with Gravity.

The Laws of Gravity are good ones—some of the best. People support gravity. Gravity is easy to believe in, Master, because gravity holds us accountable. Without gravity, we would float away, nothing to anchor our purpose. Gravitational laws are sound and provable. How does gravitational law impact us?

ON THIS PLANET: WHAT GOES UP MUST COME DOWN...

—unless the force of escape is greater than the force of attraction.

I'm fine with Gravitational laws. But to You, Creator, I pose a question. Where is gravity? How does it function? I can measure it and obey its constraints, yet I cannot put a piece of gravity under a microscope to watch it work. I cannot peer at gravity through a telescope. All I can do is observe its results. So Lord, I confess being a little sketchy on gravitational theory.

Theories are not laws. Laws require only obedience:

IF I WALK OFF THE ROOF OF A BUILDING, I WILL FALL LIKE AN ANVIL TO THE GROUND.

But regarding gravitational theory, I have to demonstrate great confidence in something unseen:

BECAUSE OF GRAVITY, I DO NOT NEED TO WEAR MY ANVIL OUTSIDE TODAY.

It seems that gravity is much like…well, like You God…

—but not exactly.

You are the force that created relationships of attraction between all things in the universe. You are the greatest attractor of all. The closer any object comes toward You, the greater the Godly attraction. This is a fact supported by evidence; indisputable. There is law involved with God.

The Laws of God are good ones—the best. But in this new age, people do not support Godly laws. It's a paradox, Master, because You hold us accountable. Without You, we would float away, nothing to anchor our purpose. Godly laws are sound and provable. How does gravitational law impact us?

ON THIS PLANET: WE HAVE FALLEN…

—unsuccessful in our attempt to escape the force of Your attraction.

I am fine with Godly Laws. But to You, Creator, I pose more pressing questions. Where are You? How do You function? I can measure and obey Your constraints, yet I cannot put a piece of You under a microscope to watch You work. I can't peer at You through a telescope. All I can do is observe Your results. So, Lord, I confess to being a little sketchy on Godly theory. I even call it by another name: Faith.

Faith is not a law. Laws require only obedience:

**IF I REJECT YOUR LOVE AND DESIRE FOR MY WELLBEING,
I WILL FALL LIKE AN ANVIL INTO DARKNESS.**

But regarding Godly Faith, I have to demonstrate great confidence in something unseen:

**BECAUSE OF YOU, I DO NOT NEED TO FEAR
THE ANVIL OF SPIRITUAL DEATH...**

—not today or any day. Not ever.

Why do I offer this weighty subject, Lord? I came across a theory posed long ago by a well-known physicist who suggested the data necessary to define a black-hole is trapped gravitationally inside the black-hole itself. So the hidden data cannot be used to define the black-hole, thus by evidence of the unobtainable information within, the black-hole is by definition... defined (My paraphrase).

Pardon me Savior, but that is one of the stupidest things I have ever heard posed by someone who was purported to have been one of the smartest beings trapped by gravity on this earth. The theory behind that theory is unprovable, unsupportable, appearing to be based on weak theory and seemingly weaker faith. I suspect that Darius Mede would now hold that physicist in high regard.

As for me, I would have been a supporter of such mush as well had I not met my beautiful wife and had my eyes opened to You through her generous spirit. I confess Lord, that before that encounter, I believed something else to be truth—that You did not exist. I set out to prove my theory and discovered that to do so, required me to build upon my unbelief with more and more unbelief. Theory supported only by more theory. There was no evidence I could find that validated my theories. The data I needed to prove my point, I found to be non-existent or totally unprovable, seemingly hidden within the black-hole of my flimsy justification and reasoning.

It took quite a while for me to realize I had never tried to test the strength of my theory by honestly pursuing the opposite position, that You <u>do</u> exist. Then came the real surprise.

When I started seeking You as a reality, I found more and more light shone on the possibility. There was, and is ample evidence of who You are and how You make Yourself known. You even made Yourself tangible in the form of Your son's earthly presence and sacrifice. I began to see You (No, I have not met You in physical form, but by the increasing gravity of Your Spiritual presence). In addition to the influence of my wife, You inspired me through special mentors: Brother Moses Folzman and Fitzgerald Elijah Hindeland. Through these people and Your desire for a relationship of attraction, I was drawn closer and closer to You. My understanding of Your purpose for me increased. And so my old theory collapsed upon itself and was replaced by a very old law of life, newly and patiently revealed by the greatest Spiritual Physicist of all. You revealed that each individual that responds with obedience to Your love will then, by a Spiritual reaction become a part of Your eternal light.

I understand that some people choose to focus, speculate on, and question of the darkness. In the chaos of this age, it is so easy to make up one's own answers; no law is necessary, no results are required. But by that approach, where is the gravity? There is no purpose.

Lord, why would I or anyone choose to theorize on that which does not exist, when You offer anyone who chooses to believe in You, such a clear and non-theoretical relationship? I would love to hear any theories on that!

Praise Do God,
ИК

Shared for the benefit of all by the hand of Ilbani the Keeper; redeemed by my Lord, Messiah Yeshua, for His purpose and honor.

PS: To those who do not believe that the God of Creation exists, I pose
one last set of questions and one answer:

> *If there were only one object in the universe, and not more,*
> *would gravity or faith exist? Is such a concept provable? Why*
> *speculate on the unknowable?*

> *Might the question only be important in pointing to a greater*
> *truth, that we live in a universe of relationships, one to another,*
> *greater to lesser? Is the evidence disputable and if so, how?*

All this is in order that no trees by the waters may grow to towering height or
set their tops among the clouds, and that no trees that drink water may reach
up to them in height. For they are all given over to death, to the world below,
among the children of man, with those who go down to the pit.

—Ezekiel 31:14

Watching the Chaos
Month 3, Year 4 After Gathering-Up (AG)

Look at them, they roam the roads and pathways of the world, entering towns as if innocent travelers. But by their fruit you will know them! These are the Scam Artists of old, the Carpet Baggers, the bounders and scoundrels that prey on the hapless in every age.

And today they have a champion in Darius Mede. Their needs are mutual. He seeks to control and administer his justice in every corner of the globe. They desire profit and authority in a local environment. And the justification for their harsh methods seems justified in many cases. People are not organized. Most towns and villages barely cling to civilized ways. The chaotic actions of outlaws demand rigid law and vicious enforcement. Who is willing to administrate such rules? Who will stand as the punishers of those who refuse to line up with the will of the government?

Mede has found them. He has recruited many and rewards them with titles and his blessing. If they obey his wishes and control the populace and enforce his Do's, regardless of their methods, they are paid handsomely and given great liberties. These ones are the Peacers. They are the eyes, the ears and the whip of the world's master. He is proud of their abilities.

We watch them grow bold, killing and maiming without reason. They have the law behind them and this legality is not polite. So why stop at legal issues? If the Peacers have a want, who is to stop them? Certainly not the younger women they rape. Such actions are encouraged, hoping that the population will increase by the children produced through such involuntary passion. The farmers and merchants dare not complain, they may find their crops burned and their merchandise confiscated.

Snuffing is not only administered to those who abuse the system, it is used to end complaint and encourage unquestioning compliancy. This is the threat that we Blue must face each day. By our very color, we are targeted, for our beliefs we are challenged. The very thing that brings us life, assures our death. Our testing is harsh and so, our faith must be swift and calculated. We serve others as we are called to do, sharing the story of our salvation, but in so doing knowing the action could be our last.

We therefore are most often on the move, for if we serve long in a town, we are sure to bring attention. That is the irony. Those who choose to believe with us must leave their families and their lives in order to survive and also share.

That would seem the worst, but not so. At least we have joy in our testimony and hope in the coming of our King. I watch in my mind, as a mother and a father plead with a Boss-Peacer. Their young son is feeble and of little help to the community. They are not Blue. They exist only for the moment. They claim that the child is an asset to them in the field, but even we can see that the abilities of the one legged child with a body coated in sores cannot be great. There is no love in the argument made by the parents to the Peacer. The young soul they produced by their sexual activity is only a by-product, who they have taught to submit to their bidding, for their own selfish benefit.

Yes, in these days any worker willing to lift, or pull or dig is a help. But sometimes the food and support necessary to sustain a weak one has to be considered. The Peacer is impatient and suspects the parents are lazy, letting the boy Do what they want not to Do. Soon the official grows tired of the negotiations. He removes a short pike from his belt and thrusts it into the invalid's chest. The child comes home to Bronzeman.

Now the couple is incensed. More labor will now be required of them to meet their community requirement. In the heat of their frustration, they make yet another error. They complain to the Boss-Peacer. As the body of their offspring lays neglected on the ground beside them, the father demands restitution. This is his final trespass. The pike strikes swiftly before the man can dodge and his blood makes covenant with his son's as they mingle lifelessly together on the ground.

But the price is not totally paid yet for their insolence. The Peacer too has needs and grabs the new widow by her hair, pulling and dragging her into the hovel she knows as home. Inside, restitution is made, another child is conceived into this earthly hell. And Mede's justice is once more equitably served.

Beware, Lit and Un-lit. There is but one God and we are not Him. Seek His love before it is too late.

One sees
One hears
And it is written
Let us work together that the world may know!

—**Keepers, for the glory of God**

Darius Mede—Chronicle IV: 7-3-4 AE

Although I have been diligent in my scientific and governmental documentation, I am more proud of my efforts to give a personal viewpoint through this chronical of events. After all, once I have re-established a library system and taught the poor masses again how to read, they will need to know the truth about my accomplishments and how humankind has benefited from the efforts I have put forth. Otherwise, the interpretation of our new history will be left up to those who would claim this period's narrative for their gods or their false teachings. Of course, the time is not yet proper to reveal this private record. The peril of sharing such great wisdom, without the capacity of readers to comprehend, has proven itself destructive throughout history.

Look at what happened to China, Greece and Rome when the masses were given free access to knowledge without proper rule. Even the archaic stories of the Muslims and Jews, who wove common tales about stealing knowledge from their gods in the form of forbidden fruit proves it out. And there is my own recent experience where my personal writings were stolen and then broadcast without permission. Who knows yet what damage my insights might inspire because the unlearned population has not the proper filter by which to consume it?

Therefore I must carefully dispense the truth and help all to understand how we have overcome the bonds of religion and individual selfish greed to become a world of cooperative social unity. This would not be such a priority but for the nuisance of that religious rag proclaiming the physical return of a very dead and very outdate Jew. And the reports that somehow keep slipping out of Jerusalem are the most frustrating of all. They come from that converted muslim who somehow absconded with my earlier journals and now warps their content and leaks falsified portions to the jury of world opinion to encourage resistance to my benevolent ways.

One cannot believe everything one reads on the written page. The populace needs my wisdom as its social filter to bring order to our disordered condition. I have come up with at least one method to control journalistic fiction. The world knows it as the language New-Roma. I recognize it as my language bestowed on the uninformed. How better to set the tone and advance the narrative than to subtly infuse specially selected words to do so? In this way I can redefine the thoughts of my fold and trigger preferred responses with the text of my choosing.

Simply creating language does not do the trick however. The written symbols must be received and embraced by the readers. To this remedy, I have begun providing my own source of high quality reporting. Jonathan Trimble could not have reappeared at a more opportune moment, but his recovery goes slow. Perhaps I can somehow help him with treatment similar to that I have found to resurrect my dead-ones, what do the new Germanic tribes call them, my *Bose-Spooks*— Wicked-Ghosts? Of course I must be careful not to risk him losing his mental capacity. How does one save from death, a servant he desires and yet keep that saved subject fully alive? An ancient question to be sure.

I am honestly annoyed at having to waste time on such trivialities as the reestablishment of my good reputation. It must be done to encourage trust in the short-term. But soon, because of my science, the idea of personal identity and self-desire will fade away. The need for trust will be eliminated, being replaced by the collective soul by which all will be equal and all will be served. Do not doubt that this can and will happen; it is happening now, it is being witnessed by others and I am its creator.

I know this because of my continuing work on the Genome Project I detailed earlier. I am proud to disclose that I have discovered a method of cloning the recombinant DNA of volunteer test subjects. By my hand and my extensive knowledge of chemical processes, I have found a way to stimulate gene material, regenerating, even replicating human cells that were formerly diseased or terminally injured. What's more, I have successfully cloned entire human subjects by these means.

And so a new creation has emerged. Those who were dying, defective or unproductive can now be revived, not as their old selves, but as fresh, new though lesser beings. These clones share no character with the host who provided the DNA for replication. Instead, they seem void of emotion and are basic in their function. They follow commands perfectly, loyal to their Master Engineer and to those whom I give authority to order them.

The trick was in causing the genes to replicate quickly and fully. So far, even with improved patterning techniques, the higher brain functions of these subjects remain minimized. Also their fear receptors appear to be marginalized: They will never be academics, but certainly they are a perfect army of committed workers or soldiers, without the psychiatric inconvenience of a conscience.

Perhaps the most significant benefit my workers offer is their acquiescence. They will perform under any circumstance and that is when I realized they would be the perfect detail to enter Dimona for the purpose of restarting the reactor and running the facility. Yes, they die quickly, but that is the beauty of their condition. They are nothing more than drones with no emotional ties. I can efficiently replace and train any who fall and so our progress in re-harnessing the energy of the atom draws near!

Think of the potential and the great welfare to the world with such a nominal expense. Soon I will be able to turn my attention to greater issues than these. When I do so, I will have more than just unlimited energy to share with the world. I will have the gratefulness, dare I say worship, of the world's people! At that point I will be able to begin afresh the plan always desired, to create a compliant and highly functional world society ready to do my bidding to the good of all mankind.

But for now, I am satisfied with this breakthrough. I had been particularly concerned about the problems related to the radiation leak at Dimona. How would we be able to contain and repair the damage? How could we harvest the nuclear activity and make the system productive once more? All those issues have been solved by this seemingly vast crop of willing beings. They show no hesitation in entering or working within that hostile environment. Once they are damaged beyond the capacity to work, they are simply disposed of and another replaces them. It is an elegant solution.

Post Script: As another test of their usefulness, I recently sent my newly created legions on a special errand to retrieve a person of interest—indeed my brother whom I have learned has fled to the northern regions of Old Europe. It will be very pleasurable when he is brought before me in reunion. I will be amused to hear his reaction to my new abilities. On the other hand, he may resist capture and be killed. So be it. Even families must sacrifice in these challenging times.

The Bronzeman News

מָשִׁיחַ **WATCH AND KEEP** מָשִׁיחַ

My name be Küllo, that be all ye need to know about me. I be not the story—I be the eyes, ears and hands of these tales. The words on these pages will be news-tells from common folk. Folk like ye and me. Them will tell their story and I will copy it with as little cleaning up as possible, so that all who are left after the Gathering-Up will see what be happening: The Bronzeman be appearing and the seeings of him are much the same. What be different be what he tells each one to Do.

MINGLE IT. MAKE UP YER OWN MIND, I WILL NOT MAKE IT FOR YE.

**Edition Three: Bucastan *Turkiyya* /Assyira
Month 5, Year 4 After the Gathering-Up**

Küllo's Notes: Bucastan be the saddest of lands that we have walked into. There be little food and less hope. Once a place of plenty: Now death dares Bucastan folk to survive one moment at a time. Death be the common victor.

I grew up in what I thought was a dark place, but now I feel myself to be one of the best off among these. Most here have no sense of family, no desire for clan. Where there are groups, even small ones, more than likely, there be one plotting to take from another. It be their Do: the stronger Doing stronger by unDoing the weak.

Sadder be the history of this place. Once a beautiful country, now it be chaos. Fumes vent up from the earth making breathing a hurtful thing and there be no escape from the constant hot wind which sucks the life out of the hardiest of us.

We fear for the children with us and Do this visit only acause we believe we have been told to Do here. We put our trust in our King who be calling us out and we press on.

Our much grown group arrives to find a barricaded gate as our welcome. "No one enters without the fee," be the shouted greeting from a tall tower filled with ready archers. Eleazar be familiar with this place so he has entered the gate to negotiate our entry. I be honestly not sure that entry be the best Do. Maybe hopping the corner, as BJ calls skirting a town— avoiding our enemies, might be a better thing.

"I can't see no solid ground in dis place," BJ tells as we wait on our permission. He means this be not a place of faith or honor. Eleazar has been gone for half of the day and we are starting to mingle he might have been taken captive, or worse.

I'm trying to mingle what worse would be. The stink of sickness and disease chokes like a thick cloud over the whole area. People who exit the city gate in this direction pass us by with their heads hung and goggled eye's looking down. I hear most of them wheezing and coughing persistently, spitting out phlegm as they shuffle past. I look for telltale signs, a faint bluish glow hidden by their leathers, but their behavior, the vacant way they stare back at us, tells me they are Un-lit, or worse, *Red-lit*—them that want most to follow the Mede instead of Bronzeman. I suddenly want badly to Do quick and get away from here.

Yet we have heard tales of Blue-lits behind the walls of Bucastan. They must be amazing bright ones and they are the reason we must enter. They are hope and hope must be chased. While we wait, we pray, while we pray, we speak out loud about the Bronze Word and we pray extra that our public tell about Bronzeman will not make-mad the leaders of this place.

The children, actually all of us, are showing reactions to the poisonous air. I am having problems even holding a thought. It may also be due to weariness. On our way here, we were careful to hop the corner around Pretender Mede's Pounder armies. Luther calls them by another name: Bose-Spooks—Wicked Ghosts. We spotted many of them on the main roads so we have kept to the more difficult paths and that drained us more. Thanks be Do Bronzeman, for at every turn, we were able to hide in time to be un-bright to them dark squads.

And that be the head-scratcher of it. What are them man-things made of? From our hiding place we caught a small see of them. They appear human, but not. They are dimmer than Red-lit—there be a machine march to them and no talk between them. We puzzle if these are alive versions of the snuffed identicals we puzzled in the Edinburghs. We watched them pound into a town with no care, only killing in their Do. BJ wanted to tell them to stop, but the Ruach Spirit called-out, "No," and so we had to stay in hiding and watch the ugly act. It be as if they are lit only enough to snuff others. Tucked away on a hillside of boulders, we became watchmen of the *Pounder train*, like they be on tracks, not stopped by anything, marching below us toward the small village we had earlier planned to enter. We watched as the Pounders trampled everything and every person in their path. Besides the crushing, the only sounds were the screaming of their victims. I still hear them in my now-dreams.

There were some sickly goats alongside the road. The Pounder train slaughtered each while passing; not even bothering to gather the meat for their own meal. Soon all was silent except for the sound of their boots fading to the west. There was no purpose to their attack and no pause for plunder. They simply killed through the village and continued on. As quickly as we thought it safe to Do, we ran into the field of death to search for survivors. There were none, and no Pounder had been snuffed so we could not un-puzzle them.

That seeing has learned us to listen loudly for the distant thumping of boots and to hold our breaths during their passing, so that we are not the next to be pounded. As I re-know these things with my inside eye, the gate opens and Eleazar walks toward us. "We are being permitted to visit the Seconds within the walls," he tells. "We need to hurry. They are not in good shape and conditions for everyone are worsening."

And that be what mingled in our brains as we all stand up to enter the city. That be when we hear something faintly familiar. Still distant, it be still terribly re-knowed—Boots marching. "Hurry," urges Eleazar. "Inside."

I only mingle that I might choke to death on the smell-rot outside the gate. Within, the air be…not air at all, more like a foul soup that struggles to be swallowed. I am dizzy and want to faint just so I don't have to mingle about what ugly stuff be floating around inside me. A hand pulls at mine and a voice in the darkness orders my steps. "Quicken your feet, Norther, lest they be cut from you."

It be a female voice, more girl than woman, but it comes from the unseen in front of me. I be in some sort of tunnel within the city walls and no light penetrates. The talking around me echoes, so the covering must be stones or brick, or some other hard surface. It be all a puzzle in the dark. I be led from nowhere to nowhere, but the hand holds firm and will not let me stop. I have to trust that I be not lead into a wall or worse, into some lost dungeon. My body scrapes against the narrow stone passageway on both sides of me. The only thing that keeps me from passing out be several bumps of my head against one of the rocks, waking me with a rude mingle to keep low and force my seeing forward.

Brightness ahead…better breathing, the echoing tunnel be no more. Now I be in an open space of foggish light. Heaven? No, the air be still sour tasting, but compared to the tunnel, it be honey. My head starts to clear and a face un-blurs to focus over top of mine. I must be lying down acause above the face I see buildings angled upwards. The light I see is sky beyond the buildings, but I cannot mingle the portion of the day. Other people are in a circle, bending over looking downwards at me. Yes, it be coming back. I had collapsed and now can barely move. The face above me be fuzzy and full of red pillows. No, that cannot be right. They are crayon drawings of canals and craters, like a movie I once saw of the planet Mars. Then I gather my mingling. It be the girl that was at the gate. I mingle it was not my dreaming.

I use my inside eye to re-know how it all played afore. Ayita Blueroad and I had been the last ones of our clan to near the iron-gate for entry into the city of Bucastan. I was on her right side and felt something quickly tug at my pants, so I looked down. There I saw what had to be the most hideous creature I had ever come upon. Its body was bent almost impossibly to the side and the arms and the appendages were gnarled and colored to look more like tree limbs. The face was festered with living boils that appeared to erupt even as I starred in my shock. One eye was replaced with a dark gouge, plunging like a pit into its skull. But then the most grisly of things happened. The thing spoke in perfect New-Roma.

"I'm having kind of a bad day, do you mind giving me a lift?"

I confess to no Doing at all in that moment. My mind was trying to un-puzzle how this lump on the road could be human. It was a *she*, not a beast. And, still grasping my trousers, she spoke again to remind me.

"Trust me Norther, those Pounders will be here quick, we ain't got a multitude of moments."

Her mouth was not moving, but I heard her. Then she coughed up and spit out blood that smelled of rot-stuff.

It was Ayita who made my decision for me. "Bring her in. She is a Second," instructed the Native American. How did I miss the Blue?! How sad that I had let the ravaged body, rather than the redeemed spirit first catch my mingling. But there was no time for sorrys. I could hear every boot pounding close.

The body of the (*what do I even call her?*) girl came up easily to my lift and she expertly swung to my back, using her arms to hold on. *Her grasp be strong!* That had been my last thought afore we entered the next tunnel; afore the fumes of the foul place mushed my re-knowing.

It be taking a long moment for my mingling and knowing to clear up. I watch people running around the inner court and try to re-know why we are being so afraid. Now it all comes fresh—the Pounders are coming. I try to sit up, but I am not used to the world spinning so quickly around me. A strange re-know comes to me. *How did the girl mingle the word "Pounder". Would not these folk have their own name for the Bose-Spooks?*

"They call me Kirik."

I struggle to turn my dizzy head toward the sound of the voice floating over me. It be that of the girl I had carried into this place. Her face be still moving, reshaping. It be the boils floating on her skin that never stop moving. What happened to cause her strangeness?

Kirik has been placed on a step that be high enough to set her over me, holding something in her hand. I mingle, *it be a wet cloth.* That be why my hair and forehead feel moist. She has been caring for me, cooling my burning fever. For some reason, my own name seems unimportant at the moment. I can only mingle one reply to her statement. "They call ye Kirik? What do ye call yerself?"

Her sudden smile does much more than the water to cool down my sweat. She does not tell for a long moment and I puzzle if anyone has ever afore asked her the question. A drop of water trickles from her eyeless socket.

"Ki. Call me Ki," she tells.

We don't have time to learn much about our new Blue sister, nor the other residents of Bucastan. An arrow from somewhere outside sails over the ramparts and somehow finds its mark in the leg of a man, whose scream of agony tells the assault be on. There must be more to the arrow than just its vicious point for in a short moment, the wounded one vomits and slumps to his death.

No one seems worried by the man's snuffing, they are too busy hunting shelter. Apparently this be not the first strike and most here are well mingled in the art of self-preservation. Ki seems calm and places her molted hand on mine, speaking words of calm waves on sunset waters.

"You're laying in a good place. Best not to move."

The gloomy sky darkens more than usual and I look over to see thousands of arrows strike the inner court. There be a clatter as more arrows imbed the heavy timbered roof above us. Several of the deadly points ricochet or glance into them that have not found the best protection and they too drop in their own spew. The smell of poo, blood and fear seeks to suffocate us. I had not mingled it could get any worse, I vomit more, not from a strike, but in reaction to the vapor strangling the place. I hear the twanging response of bow strings from the archers of Bucastan and pray they are good at their jobs. My ears strain to know the sound of injury outside the walls, but no cries measure the damage.

Then a thunderous sound signals the next phase of the battle. "*The Big Pounder* knocking at the door," Ki tells, though not to me. Her face and mingling be now nervously turned in the direction of the tunnel we entered through. If not a regular Do, this be familiar to the Bucastan folk and all wear looks of panic. "I hope we have enough powder," again Ki speaks toward the tunnel and there be doubt in her eye.

A man wearing poor-fitting armor runs up to another man standing near us who has soldier medals pinned to his chest. The runner be out of breath and answers Ki's question by telling the other man, "We only have enough powder for once blow."

I have no idea what having or not having enough powder means, but by the reaction of the medal man, this must be very sour-milk news. He screams back at the soldier. "That's not possible. We stole plenty!"

"We stole plenty enough for three moons, but it's been five moons now," the soldier argues. "We'll do what we can with what we can." And he runs off not waiting for a response. Medal man slumps into a sitting position on the ground and stares vacantly. It be enough for me to mingle, *we may die here*. The Big Pounder, as Ki calls it, hammers unstopping at the door. I mingle it to be a large tree trunk or some other big weight being struck against the gates of the city.

"The Big Pounder hasn't ever broken the door, no matter their trying."

Does Ki read minds? I puzzle. The success of previous attacks be exactly the question in my brain.

"We took all their powder when they weren't looking." She tells me in my brain. "If they found more, then prayer is our only Do."

The silent thought-talk be almost as crazy-braining as the battering at the gates. But all be interrupted when the earth drops and lifts beneath us. Ki be tossed like a doll onto my chest and I wrap my arms around her as an explosion rips at my ears. Rocks and rubble fly about and I'm sure the attackers have entered to snuff our lights.

"Lord forgive them, for they know not what they do." Ki whispers.

Maybe she didn't whisper, maybe my hearing has left me. It has been replaced by a ringing in my ears and a stinging in my left leg. I open my eyes to see only dust and fog. Then the face of BJ, my Minder, be over me. He seems to be speaking from the far off land where we met and his words are long to reach me.

"Yer walker got stabbed." He holds up a bloodied splinter of wood that must have hit my calf. The pain turns from sting to throb. He casts the sliver away and cradles both Ki and me, lifting us as if we were bags of feathers, "Best to be downside."

I do not mingle downside, but BJ seems to and carries us to an archway descending into a dark room. "Don't mind the nothing here," he tells while laying us on a dirt floor. "Better nothing than something right now," And he leaves us.

"Your friend loves you more than life," Ki speaks into my head. **and I mingle that I hear her in my native tongue.** I be suddenly sad. Might BJ die and I cannot help or be with him? My leg hurts too much to move and the ringing in my ears competes with every other sound for my mingling. There be only one thing to do. I hold Ki in the emptiness and begin to tell in prayer:

"Father in heaven
Yer name be holy to us
Yer kingdom, Yer will be all we want to Do.
As it be in the Heavenlies, let it be in this place
Give us now bread for tomorrow
Forgive us for the bads we Do to others, like we be forgiving
them, the bads they Do to us.
Steer us to Ye, not away
Protect us from the darkness that wants to snuff us."

As I finish the words, I mingle that Ki be praying prayer-song with me, still in my tongue. We retell the ask and dwell in the wellness of our kinship with the Master who loves all things. There be no good counting of the long moments until another voice mingles with ours. It be the voice of BJ. He lives! Scooping us back into his arms, he carries us up and out to the open court where survivors are now caring for the snuffed and wounded. We do not stop our praying, and one by one, all in the place are in song with us, one-being-all.

Ki be lifted from my arms by someone and I am helped to my wobbly feet. That be when I notice the Blue that has spread, not just to some, but to every dweller of Bucastan. The prayer-song now tells, with tender and beautiful harmonies, our thanks to Bronzeman who saved us. We sing into the night with many solos giving praise for their life and for the God who has hugged this place in His arms. Slowly each be sung into peaceful snoozing. I don't mingle much when I drift off into sleep, only that in my dreams there are uncountable blue stars surrounding a throne from which one brilliant golden light shines. The brighter light somehow smiles, the blue stars sing forever, and I cannot re-know what darkness looks like any more.

I wake to dim sunlight and the sound of BJ's voice. In his unusual Ethiopian lilt, he be telling Ki and others what had happened to stop the Pounder attack…

> "—We would only need da bugs in here for a short moment, dat what Bronzeman told me and ah just mingled it to be solid ground. He let me see His Blowing Blaze coming about dis place and ah mingled that da bugs was needed elsewheres. He spoke me up to da tower and used my mouth for His. Ah just called-out what He telled me to tell, 'Leave forever'.
>
> "Dat's when da powder blew lots of da Pounders to nothingness and shook us up big. Den all da bugs from

here and all about here, dey went for the leftover Pounders. Ah never seen so many of da critters afore.

"Strange enough, da Pounders never said a sound, even during da stinging. Dey was swarmed to where all ah could see was bugs, but no crying came. Da bug-Pounder swarm just marched away, twitching and bleeding all da time."

I am handed a piece of bread by a new Bucastan believer. As I gratefully chew on my first meal in this place, Medal Man tells his name—Rughert—and more.

"The Pounders had found more powder, enough ready to blow our door. But we snuck in and lit our own powder, throwing it on top of theirs afore they could bring it to the gate. We done them loud damage with lots of Pounder snuffing. But we lost lots of our folk."

Then Rughert looked awful sad. His eyes tried to cry, but he turned away to hide the water. Still he kept telling. "Pounders don't sound, they don't feel. We poured arrows and bricks and blew them down, but more of them just kept coming. That's when your friend called the bugs at them. If it hadn't happened, we wouldn't be happening now. Praise Do to God."

"Praise Do to God," Came the shout in response from all in the big open area. I could hear clearly now and the shouts traveled away through all the streets and alleys within the walls of Bucastan. The Bluing of souls had not been a dream. This was now a place lived-in by the Ruach of the Creator.

We stay within Bucastan for over one full moon cycle helping to mourn for and bury the snuffed, teaching the lit ones that still live, helping them copy all the Bronze Word scriptures and history I had been called-out to carry with me in my keepsack.

The walls and the people are being repaired, the smell-rot be gone. Also gone be the need within Bucastan to wear leathers. There be hope in the air and in the eyes of our kin here. Yet we all know there be bad outside the Bucastan gates and others out there that need our love, so we must go. We Do this not wanting to leave, but Bronzeman tells it be a big Do for us. He wants us and them to be better, to go out and make new Seconds so that there is more Bronze-telling too Do by us all. The Un-lit will want to kill our telling, the Pounders will come again. Pretender Mede and his minions are bent on snuffing our lights and so we tell our Bucastan kin, as we are going, to be cunning as foxes and meek as lambs.

Our travel group moves on, capturing other news-tells of Seconds throughout the world. The telling needs to be shared. Now we also teach the song we have learned together in Bucastan, to the rest of the world. There be one additional journeyer with us. Ki has become special to me and to our whole clan. The children cannot have enough of her and we are amazed at her power given by Bronzeman.

She not only seems to be able to hear our thoughts but also to foresee things and places we are journeying to. She also tunes in to words we use. I had been puzzling about the Pounders when we first met and so she started using the word to help her mingle more to me.

A special harness has been sown by Rachel Hine that allows BJ to carry Ki on his back. The work of it be crafty and lets Ki turn and see easily from her perch. Her skill will be great good for us, especially at our next destination (which I will not tell now to protect our journey and our Do) where we will need to be unseen and unexpected.

> Call-out: One Do I ask to ye readers of this tell: pray for us much and pray for all other Seconds mingling these words. But more, find yer widows and orphans and take care of them. Bronzeman did it and asks us to do it too.

> **Special Do:** Ready yer traveling plans. Soon, it will be time to begin the trek to Jerusalem. Ye will know the when by the telling of the trumpet sound.

Darius Mede—Chronicle V: 9-6-4 AE

By my new calendar, it is the Ninth day of the Sixth lunar cycle in the Fourth year of the Age of Enlightenment or 9-4-4 AE. I am constantly insulted by how, even the simplest of concepts, such as my very rudimentary calendar program, is either not understood, or ignored in preference to some other less accurate and overtly religious measurement.

The pesky Jews and reformed steeple people (HA! I cannot resist my own humor) continue to appear with annoying regularity; the more of them that I eliminate, the more they seem to increase. They are a fungus to be sure. Their stubborn ways will not interfere with my greater good but it is a pity they do not realize how they slow the progress of mankind by their efforts. One day I will be rid of them once and for all.

To the good news: The Deputy Premier, Jonathan Trimble, is recovered enough and has assumed his duties as my administrator of Media Affiliation for the Green Order Government. True, my treatments for his healing have somewhat contributed to his madness and unpredictability, but I prefer him that way and his strangeness suits his mission. Who else can understand how to revise the reality that others perceive they endure in the physical world? Who else, being given the highest authority by me can produce and overlay a new world vision that the hopeless masses will readily accept and embrace? Very soon, using the platform of MAGOG and Jonathan's skills, my greater reality will be imbedded unquestionably into the minds of all. They may be pricked painfully by the thorns of life but they will only appreciate the rose of my provision.

Trimble's assistance is critical to my efforts. Perhaps he adores my plan even more than I. Ironic is it not? Such was the desire of the imaginary god of the Hebrews. They tried to write into their fiction a master who doled out suffering and guilt while asking all to envision joy and happiness. They even had the accidentally brilliant plan of causing their creator to be an invisible being so that they could define him without proof of existence.

I, on the other hand, will provide a better thing. I will give the world a very tangible god and Jonathan Trimble will make me appear all-mighty in the doing.

Yet I hope to not lose my own sanity at the hands of other clumsy cohorts. I am receiving reports now of failings by my clone subjects. Simple tasks I give them such as "retrieve my brother" or "kill anyone who appears blue". I would think these would be basic enough concepts for them. But do they? Can they? I am at a loss as to how the upstarts in the northern realms escaped. They are a small crew but very bold and unafraid. History has proven such fundamentalists not so easy to engage and to neuter. But still the task is achievable if I persevere.

Even more puzzling however are the events in Bucastan. Certainly they had walls of defense and had cleverly absconded with the explosives my troops would have used against them. They too were canny enough to turn those very weapons against us. I had even anticipated that move and sent plenty of reserves. I did not plan on the bugs somehow developing a massing strategy. That does not fit their typical attack behavior. This is new and also must be explored along with the report that, as our attack commenced, my troops heard shrill singing that angered their ears so much they could not focus on the attack. This rabble has somehow developed some type of sonic device capable of great damage during a battle.

Fortunately I can equip my armies with noise suppressing earphones for such instances. The only problem will be then hearing the orders to battle. On a brighter note, my chemical concoction that is now coated on the arrows of my warriors' quivers has proven most effective. One prick of the skin and the enemy is immediately killed. As long as I can get the stupid clone archers to march close enough to a targeted location before striking, all is well. Again, the problem is my not being close enough to the action.

Regrettably, the only dependable general I have found to see my orders carried out precisely is the ass Serge Palmotic. I have found that as long as I stroke his frail ego enough, he complies adequately. I must watch him though. The danger of his thinking he is an equal, or of his starting to believe his thoughts are higher than mine, is great.

As an aside, I admit to the oddness that blue people even exist. I know that once Fitzgerald Hindeland, though a renowned scientific associate, barbarically experimented on subjects to somehow infect them with tau neutrinos. I now wonder if his work was more damaging than anticipated. I must find a way to investigate his work and perhaps use it to my great purpose.

I am optimistic because of the progress at Dimona. We have completed the initial tests for connecting the damaged nuclear reactor core to a chemically charged power grid. It demonstrates that we can utilize charged muon particles and send them through conventional wiring systems, to any location. The damage done by earthquakes and weather phenomena will easily be fixed by utilizing Flexsteel to repair the facility and construct a new wiring infrastructure. I may soon even devise a method for shooting the beams through the air without the use of towers or wires. Think of the power of such technology. We thought ourselves so debilitated without electrical power. Now I say, who needs it!

A small concern continues to be the radioactive energy that is inherent to the technology and that unavoidably bonds with the hydrogen electrons. I cannot seem to counteract the damage of prolonged use. It will be a continued quest of mine to provide clean energy but meanwhile shortened life spans will be a small price to pay for light, air conditioning and other critical utility resources. I will direct the Deputy Premier to begin a campaign of encouragement along these lines; something to the effect that there are troubles enough in this world. Why not live a limited life of greater luxury rather than a prolonged existence of suffering? My goodness, sometimes I amaze even myself. Why didn't I pursue this idea far earlier?

I realize that world conditions have changed dramatically, and that it is these events which have helped consolidate my power. But the slowness of economic and social recovery is unacceptable. I have developed the necessary solutions to counter the seismic and environmental conditions. Now safe shelter and amenities are available for all. Filtered water is also available although porting it throughout the world is costly. I am appalled by the fact that some regions refuse to honor me with allegiance and total loyalty in return for their supplies—why would some refuse such a small price for such precious resources?

Food is still an issue, but that too is being dealt with. The technology and resources to develop and build hydroponic greenhouse gardens is readily available. Recycled fecal matter for fertilizer is gathered easily enough so that all those still remaining may live a manageable if paltry existence. For such technology to be supplied to a community, I have asked in trade, that worldwide communities submit to a rigid program of restricted procreation until such time as we can manage greater population numbers. To that end, I have designated that only one child, regardless of sex, may be born into any family. Any others will be dedicated to research. It may sound harsh, but is demanded by the greater good. Of course there will be exceptions. Those families who have demonstrated exceptional gene history will be encouraged to bear more children. Those who conceive or bear defective specimens will be allowed a one-time exchange. They will be permitted to offer the unviable material as a donation to scientific study in exchange for one additional try at producing good stock. If the second effort is faulty as well, the parents will be sterilized as to not risk further contamination of the world's gene pool.

As I think of it, the eradication of those individuals encumbered by old age, who can no longer contribute to their communities, should also be handled in the same way. They of course will be easier to terminate for they, I'm sure, already realize what a burden they pose to society.

It is a simple and efficient way to cleanse the world of defective human refuse. Of course we will honor the sacrifices appropriately and will make sure each is memorialized with a plaque of recognition. It is the least we can do.

All this being said, there is much more to be done to revitalize civilization. Ours is a rare moment. At no other time in recorded history has mankind rebounded so quickly. We are even surpassing the achievements of the past age, quickly advancing after the worldwide cataclysm. We shall overcome!

Note to self: I must use that last paragraph on my speaking tour.

The Bronzeman News

מָשִׁיחַ **WATCH AND KEEP** מָשִׁיחַ

My name be Küllo, that be all ye need to know about me. I be not the story—I be the eyes, ears and hands of these tales. The words on these pages will be news-tells from common folk. Folk like ye and me. Them will tell their story and I will copy it with as little cleaning up as possible, so that all who are left after the Gathering-Up will see what be happening: The Bronzeman be appearing and the seeings of him are much the same. What be different be what he tells each one to Do.

MINGLE IT. MAKE UP YER OWN MIND, I WILL NOT MAKE IT FOR YE.

Edition Four: Jerusalem in Israel / New Palestine
Month 7, Year 4 After the Gathering-Up

Küllo's note: I still recover from our mingling in Bucastan. I confess that I dreaded the dismal fortress upon arrival, but after the conversion of thousands of souls with whom we became quick-kin, I had even more difficulty leaving. The thing that drove me on was the mingling of our next destination.

And here we are, in Jerusalem, in the season of *Pasach*—Passover. I had not mingled what a sad-enough place it be. How can that be? The streets are perfectly clean. There be order and plenty for every person. In the middle of it all, I be told, be the new Temple, more beautifully built than any afore it. Something called alabaster covers the building and gold trim shimmers even in the murky daylight. Yet as we enter through the newly renovated Dung Gate on the western side, near the ancient city of David, the sense of evil be in every corner. The residents are nice enough, but in that superficial way of people who keep secrets.

I've been here afore. Not in the real, but in the unreal—the land I know by my inside eye, where Bronzeman sometimes takes me. In a mind view, he had me meet his two Watchmen—Brother Moses and Preacher Elijah. They explained things to me and turned my fire into a song, then my song into food that people can take in. That food be what ye are reading at this moment.

In my dream, Jerusalem looked as it does now, but it was all Blue and Bronze, a place of perfect mingling. In the real it be a dingy place and there are bugs here so leather be everywhere which helps us hide our blue. We are told that in the recent past, the creatures avoided the place, but they invaded after the last *Great Cleansing;* the time when the Mede decided his Do was to snuff the lights of all Seconds.

Every story can be told two ways and heard two ways. The Jerusalem dwellers we meet speak of the event proudly, as if it was a fantastic Do to butcher hundreds of thousands of Seconds in the time of Brother Moses and Prophet Elijah, afore them saints were Gathered-Up in a big way.

We Seconds understand the telling of the happening differently. We had been warned of the attitude and conditions here and wear our leathers to be secret Seconds. Most important of all, we must not let these people recognize Eleazar, Rachel or Luther Hine, for we hear that them families have bounties placed on their lives. Word be also spreading out about my news-telling, so I too must be careful to hide my Blue. It be a dangerous game we play coming here.

Thank Bronzeman, no one seems much interested in mingling us. As we move deeper into the heart of the restricted areas and cross between occupied quarters, we are more watched and instructed, just as are all in-travelers. There are many who seek shelter in the once holy city and all are welcomed in the same way. There appears to be a desire to acquire a work-force: We are politely questioned; mostly about our skills, our willingness to contribute labor, and then pointed toward the next Do-point. Everything be smooth and nervously quite.

They have animals here, large ones. It be a miracle to see a donkey carrying a load for its master. A cow…A COW…protectively quartered in an old stone storage building. An old woman milks the animal while well-equipped guards stand on each side, telling the curious to move along. They use that professional army-tone that tells not moving along could be sour-milk for one's good-being.

Within the city walls, we are led by my Minder. Although Eleazar, Ayita, Rachel and Luther had lived in the city for a time, BJ has been here more recently. He mingles the safe places where other Seconds still hide and provide for one another. On our way, we are stopped at yet another Do-point. This one has more Peacers than the others. We stand in line waiting for whatever request that will be made of our group. As we near the tables where guards and administrators stand with stern looks on their faces, we begin to make out the command being made of each.

"Show your service ID."

At this, many will pull back their leather hoods to reveal something on their foreheads. But others shrug and I hear-tell their answer, that this be their first in-travel to the city. These are shuttled to a booth off to the side where several men and women have some kind of device which looks to be a combination of stamper and chemical tubes. The thing includes a rubber bladder like an old suction cup. The cup be placed upon the foreheads of the in-travelers. Then one of the Boss-Peacers push a plunger and there be the sound of hissing as something be injected through the tubes. I watch as someone ahead of us gets the treatment. He scrunches his face as if in minor pain and then the bladder be removed. When the man again turns toward us, his forehead be smoking from some kind of vapor, but clearly visible be a marking.

We are to be found out, my inside voice tells in panic and I begin to pray for a quick ending to my light. But somewhere outside of me, yet specifically to me, another voice speaks in soothing tones.

"You are safe. Trust in YAHWEH."

I see around and the others in our party also at first look alarmed, then seem to nod to themselves. Do they hear what I hear?

"You are safe. Trust in YAHWEH."

The voice be clear and I now recognize it as Ki's! She be still in her special carrier on the back of BJ and I look at her now. Her swollen eyes are closed and her misshapen lips are moving silently. I can't tell if she be praying or somehow sending out messages to us or both. I try to do my best to see what she be saying in private, but what I mingle she be speaking makes no sense. It looks like she be repeating over and over in English.

"Move on." And I hear it in my thoughts as well.

The line we are all in begins to move faster. I focus again on the processors and I hear an incredible command from them.

"Move on."

And we all do. Even them afore us and them behind are herded on past the Do-point and we are free beyond. As a child, there was a movie I remember watching where an old man waved his hand in front of someone guarding a place and the old man said something about the robots he had with him were not the ones the guard was told to look for. The guard just let them through and this be just like that. I see toward Ki and she opens her eyes again to greet me with her most beautiful smile ever. She still does not speak out loud, but I clearly hear her voice.

"You are safe. Trust in YAHWEH."

Our spiritual communication be interrupted when, from behind us in the distance, we hear a single voice from the processing line.

"You let all them go, you don't need to check me either." It was a young woman who was holding up the system. "I'm just like them, I don't need no number."

She must have once been very pretty, but now has a scar across the front of her face from her left forehead to her lower right cheek. It makes her look like she now has two faces in one. I guess her to be about 20 years and she be surrounded by the Peacers and Boss-Peacers. She cries out. "I will not." There be scuffling and I make out the woman's hood being removed by the Peacers. She be a no-believer, not a Red-lit or a Second. There be no forehead mark and no Blue about her. She continues her complaint.

"I serve no one. You can't tell me who I belong to."

One processor walks up to her as the others hold her. Her attempts at resistance end with a hypodermic needle injected into her neck. She convulses twice and I see a spew of reddish orange vomit spew from her mouth. She slumps in silence and a large burlap bag be drawn over her body. As we watch in horror, the bag be then hefted by two large Peacers and dropped onto a waiting cart which be then wheeled off to the side and set down. The bag moves not at all.

"Show your service ID," be the renewed command shouted by the lead Boss-Peacer and there be no other protests by them in line. We decide that it be best to put much more distance between us and them, double-quick.

BJ brings us to what used to be called the Essene Quarter and then to a particular door. How he mingles this to be a right place, I puzzle. There are no numbers, signs or anything that tells to me that this be a place of Seconds. My Minder knocks loudly and unafraid he announces, "I brung dem."

It be more long moments. Much noise of latches and bolts and such are undone from inside. The portal opens and another man with rich olive skin and who be lesser tall than BJ, lets out a great laugh and says, "Shalom brothers and sisters."

He glows very Blue.

When we are all inside and the door re-latched, Eleazar, Luther and their families fast-crowd the man. He double-quick brings us all into a large open room, lit by small clay oil lamps, not the strange reddish chemical lights we have seen more and more used in towns we have in-traveled. The place best way to tell the room be to say it be a warm-spirit place. There are long sobbing greetings spoken. Apparently our host be well known by most. Even Ki, with her strange powers seems to already mingle the spirt of this man. He be only a stranger to me. Then I hear his name and he changes in an instant for me. He be no longer just a Jerusalem-liver, but one of the great surviving faith-men. This be Ilbani the Keeper, the God-letter writer whose work has so flamed my own light. I suddenly cannot stand. Dropping to my knees I cry out my own gratefulness to Bronzeman for this blessing.

"B'rakah Haberim kol bet Kulanu." Ilbani pronounces as we eagerly shed our leathers. I be truly in the most foreign of lands I have encountered yet. I only understand one of his words "B'rakah", a greeting that offers blessing on the one being greeted. Ilbani sees the question on most of our faces and explains.

"Here, we are trying to speak more and more of the ancient Hebrew tongue. It allows several advantages and a few difficulties as well. First, no other dwellers in this place seem to mingle or even desire to learn the language. This affords us a way to converse without full disclosure of our communications. As well, it is a way of reaching out to the *Remnant*—Jewish survivors who yet cling to God, waiting ironically for their Messiah who we know to have already come. We protect many of these here in Yerushalayim and throughout New Israel. Daily, many of them come to recognize Yeshua. I hope you will have the opportunity to celebrate when one of them receives their Savior. It is like nothing I have experienced before."

At this moment, the most beautiful woman I have ever gazed enters the room. She be midnight dark like BJ, but graceful in unexplainable ways. Behind her are two children and she shows the signs of another birth soon to happen. The children run to Ilbani and hug his legs. There be a stop to his explanations as he introduces his wife Jende and their children to me. Everyone else in the room greets her with hugs and Jende purposefully goes to Ki who remains on the back of BJ. Ilbani's children pull at the hands of the BenMadai and Hine young-ones, inviting them to another where they play together freely.

Jende gives Ki a long kiss on the forehead and they seem to communicate without words. Then the gracious lady turns and walks toward me. I cannot explain the peace inside me when she nears. And how can I describe what mingles in my head? Instead of hearing thoughts, as I do with Ki, images, like a picture book…and sometimes moving flashes, almost like old time television, replace my normal sight. I fall back onto the floor pillow behind me, dizzy and confused by the happenings.

"Ki has explained so much about you," Jende tells. "I and my husband are honored by your presence in our house."

What has Ki telled in their moments together? What does the small girl really know about me? I have not shared much of my past, or my purpose with her. Apparently, this lady as well has a gift of knowing the thoughts of others. No, it be more like she sees the lives of others, a movie of important parts of my past plays afore me.

It be incredible. Countless strange memories, not my own, I don't know how to mingle it, flood my mind. They are from places and people I have never known. All I do know be that they are living in our time, pleading to be seen. It makes me feel smarter and tell better.

"I have been saving them for you," Jende says to my inner ear." They are now yours and mine to share." I see relief on her face. I puzzle what must be the look on my own face. The pictures come with a great weight. I want to give them to someone else, but Jende's hand be on my shoulder and she tells out loud. "Don't worry, Bronzeman will help us all," and the unexplainable peace comes back. Still, there are tears in my eyes for the pain I watch as echoes from the other's experiences.

BJ brings Ki over who gently touches my forehead and speaks inside me. What she tells be the voice of each picture I see. It be as if the two, Jende and Ki complete the stories together.

Finally they release me and I know somehow that I must sleep. Nothing surrounds me.

I wake up with no memory of any dreams, but am more relaxed than I re-know ever being afore. It be impossible to mingle how long I have been sleeping, the windows have been boarded so there be now telling night from day. Everyone be still in the room and I guess that it has not too long since I blacked out, for at this moment, Ilbani remembers he has not completed his explanation about the Hebrew language and so chooses to continue his tell as if never interrupted.

"The difficulty with using Hebrew to communicate is the suspicion it draws from non-believers. Particularly from the Palisti and the Peacers.

Most of those loyal to Mede are bent on discovering and destroying anything connected to Judaism or Christianity. That is why a special greeting has been determined to help identify friend from foe. It's not foolproof, but at least it sets the tone of any discussion that might be sensitive to our interests."

Ilbani approaches me, grasps my hand firmly within his and pulls me close to him, then kissing me on both cheeks and exclaiming warmly, "Kulanu."

"Kulanu," The Keeper tells, "is Hebrew for 'all of us', a better translation might be 'we live as one'. Your response to me would be 'Shalom Haber' which means 'Peace to you my God-kin.'"

The Turk's command of Hebrew be big-know. I feel myself hungry for more and Ilbani mingles the interest. "The term Haber be an expression of individual endearment, but the plural term, Haberim holds a new and special meaning of unification for Remnants and Seconds alike. We are much more the same than different and all Seconds in New Palistia—what all of us still refer to as Israel—embrace the greeting as a means of showing compassion for our Jewish kin.

Jende comes alongside her husband and now tells out loud while mingling her hand in his. "My husband loves to share his language skills, but sometimes forgets where the conversation began. When you entered our home he exclaimed, 'B'rakah Haberim kol bet Kulanu' which means *Blessing kin who fear God to this house of all.*" The beautiful lady smiles whimsically and then adds, "I have learned that the Spanish have a similar way of expressing the sentiment, 'Mi casa, su casa,' *My house is your house.* And since this is your house too, you'd all better get ready for dinner. There is enough for all and all can help clean up after."

Everyone laughs. I un-puzzle that this be a special place glued by special people. Suddenly I feel small, not understanding why Bronzeman would honor me to even be mingling with these *brainers*. I must be like a no-learned peasant from a bad-sung land to them.

"You Küllo, have also been given a great gift and duty," Jende shows within me privately. "My husband shares it. Others do not mingle, but I do. Ki does. You both see and hear and can share your mingling in a way that will bring many lives to Yeshua. You do not mingle yet what this means, but it will be un-puzzled for you soon."

The children rush to me and grab both my hands, leading me to a large floor pillow at the head of the table. The meal afore us be simple, made up mostly of vegetables, bread fish and something I have not seen since the Gathering-Up. Cheese! We all recline and I find myself salivating, but afore any of us begin, Ilbani makes a request.

"Küllo, will you please recognize God's provision by leading us in prayer?"

I don't know if they can mingle my words, acause of my thick accent and the tears I shed, but Bronzeman must be telling to each of them—with each phrase I finish, they respond with "Amen".

Today I had a strange re-knowing. Walking through one of the narrow alleys of this old place, I sniffed some folk cooking. I mingled it to be much like Han Ko's sizzlings on her wooden plank and I could taste heeringas in my mouth. I reached into my pocket as if to pull out some of my cured fish and there was emptiness there, like wanting back my sisters. This moment I badly miss Anu and Liisa teasing me. It be a sad-enough thing to tell.

I mingle strongly I am not the only one who has a heart-pain for family and friends Gathered-Up. There be no easy fixing of it, I hurt with ye much. All I can tell be what I Do now and hope ye mingle the same—pray to Bronzeman for a new home and family. I mingle he now be making one for me and he will for ye too if ye let him.

Over the long moments of the next several days we mingle more with the Seconds of Jerusalem, about our travels and new-knowings. We tell of our seeing; slaughtered towns— innocent people who Mede's minions killed while searching out information of Eleazar's whereabouts. We tell of the Seconds we discovered in our travels and how bravely they hold on to their faith. Ki be living testimony to our telling, but she stays mostly quiet, letting our tell be her tell.

From others who have been to destinations we have yet to visit, we hear similar tales; how the division between the spiritual forces of Light and Darkness seems to be widening more each day. We discuss the increasing presence of the Pounders and the *Mede-Mark* that followers must display. There be no denying now his Do and his place in Biblical prophecy, nor our own. In this time he will continue to gain power while we will be persecuted and martyred. Somehow, the knowing of this fact, brings more peace than fear to my soul.

Four days into our visit, Pretender Mede puts out an announcement that a special day of celebration will be held at the new Temple court. The Do tells that all them that inhabit Jerusalem are to attend. We mingle that any who are found not attending will be dealt with severely.

Eleazar be the first to comment on the date. "*Reshit Katzir*—Feast of First Fruits, when Yeshua rose from the dead, three days after Passover. Mede does nothing by accident. What be he going to reveal this time?

No one responds. I mingle that, like me, they are puzzling the risk of this Do. Being found out as a practicing Second or Remnant while mingled with the crowds will be an excuse for snuffing. Many have died or been injured when it was discovered they do not bear the Mede-Mark. We pray together and then make the best course. To reduce the risk of all believers being somehow discovered in one area, it be better to separate so escape of some be possible. All Seconds and their known Remnant kin will split up into three groups. One of the groups will be led by Jende, one by BJ and one by Ki. Why let these three lead? Each has displayed an unusual ability to move the minds of the Un-lit. Their gift looks to be Bronzeman's way of protecting his surviving people in this place.

All three of the appointed protectors are reluctant, each voicing in their own way, the same concern:

"I am not worthy of this calling."

Their humility tells all the more that the Body has chosen with spiritual wisdom.

The day arrives when we are to Do the show-time at the Temple court. This place can only be described with one word. Evil. It be sad-enough that the building of this structure brought such hope for them that hoped for its construction throughout Bible history. The book of Ezekiel, Daniel and Revelation tell its importance. Even Bronzeman himself speaks of its coming. The scriptures tell that the place would be a Remnant sanctuary and solid ground, that be how its rebuild began. Many martyrs were even honored with burial beneath the altar stone.

Then came the Second Gathering-Up. The Mede waited for his moment and struck during the Days of Good News—the Pentecost of Seconds. Brother Moses and Prophet Elijah—the Great Ones—were baptizing thousands of New Believers. The Palisti Peacers stormed the assembly and butchered almost all involved, including the Two Great Ones. Miraculously some escaped and were hidden. It was then that Seconds and Remnants formed a strong bond of protection for one another. Some, including Luther and Rachel fled to the hills to live in caves. But the greater number stayed within the walls of the city. The Spirit's call for evangelism was strong on them and put them in great danger.

Ilbani had been anointed as Keeper of the Kin by Brother Moses and Prophet Elijah prior to their deaths. They recognized his gifts of leadership and chronicling so they appointed him as the Keeper of the Records and of the Faithful in Israel. He and his family have had to move several times by dark of night to avoid finding by of the Peacers. It be amazing to hear what they sacrifice to assure Seconds and Remnants are protected.

Snuffing and persecution are still daily happenings in our ranks and we must Do with stealth even in the gathering of supplies, which the Palisti Boss-Peacers claim to be free and available to all. We have un-puzzled that the food be bait to lure in the innocent for punishment or worse.

Such are the conditions under which we approach the abomination which be the Third Temple. We have disguised ourselves in our leathers and pray that there will not be random checks of foreheads. The throngs of people will discourage that kind of security. There are just too many moving to the Teaching Steps and the crowd be anxious for whatever new surprise the Mede has in store—no use in frustrating their hunger.

Once we arrive at the Outer Court, we see hands raised in every direction and for good reason. Peacers stationed on the parapets of the Temple walls are throwing bread out to the crowds below. Every loaf that hits the sea of people causes a surge. We hear cries of pain as someone be either crushed or maimed by the uncaring populace, more eager to grab the precious food then to watch out for their more feeble neighbors.

"Leavened bread during the week of Passover, he is definitely trying to goad the Remnants," tells Ilbani, who has joined us.

BJ, my **Minder,** also mingles the danger and tells the word throughout our group to protect one another. I mingle a similar message be told through the ranks of Jende's and Ki's group. All at once there be another wave made by tossed bread and our group sways dangerously in reaction to the other hungry participants. Just as I begin to pray against injury, bass drums hammer rhythmically to tell some important announcement and the crowd stills.

To make-big the news, the Mede shows himself at the top of the Teaching Steps. We know it to be him acause he be closed-up in some kind of clear box. It must be made of Flexteel. The bugs attack it but then they stop flying and start flopping as if something be biting them back. The box must be special-made to protect the Mede who stands, confidently surveying the courtyard and beyond. He be dressed handsomely in a three piece business suit, complete with the symbol of the Archer's Bow he uses as his logo on the breast pocket. He be wearing the shiniest red tie I have ever seen with a matching handkerchief folded and placed tidy-like in the breast pocket. There are many of us now pressing in to hear his words, but afore he speaks, another man joins the Mede on the Steps, but be not in a special box. He walks to a large megaphone that be set on a stand. It be hard to see the man behind the amplifying device. It be so large, it blocks most of him to the people furthest away. What can be seen when he moves just right, be that his face be in bad shape. I mean ugly sour-milk bad and I know this acause he does not wear any leathers. *A Second?* I puzzle. No, there be no Blue.

The man's booming voice projects out to us now, his first words coming as an ecstatic command.

"Praise Do the mighty Mede who brings us bread and water for life."

The crowd roars in reply, "Praise Do Mede" and suddenly I fear the prompter will suggest we bow down. By the power of Bronzeman it does not happen. Instead, the command and response repeat multiple times, each response bringing the crowd to a higher frenzy, probably due to the fact that the louder they shout, the more loaves and bottles of water are cast out to them.

"Oh no." Someone gasps loudly behind me. I turn to see Roxanne, one of the Seconds who has been in hiding with Ilbani the Keeper's clan. It be her strange Southern-American accent by which I mingle the girl. We met through Ilbani and I remember how strange she seemed, all covered in tattoos. Also Ilbani the Keeper told us she had escaped slaughter during the Days of Conversion and Baptism. With both hands she be holding tightly the arm of Rachel Hine and a look of horror fixes her face as she stares past me toward the Teaching Steps.

I see out over the raised hands of the masses, trying to get a better see at the man with the megaphone. His voice sounds already-heard to me and I try to go back in my re-knowing to un-puzzle him. Even from this far away, I can see that his face be not his only hurt. The bugs fly about him, but seem uninterested in any attack.

Ilbani asks to no one, "Why would the Mede allow him such prestige, addressing the crowd and occupying the same stage as the Premier?"

Megaphone Man begins a puzzled introduction: "You may recall that several years ago, the religious zealots once called Christians, diabolically altered the plans of our great sainted one, Darius Mede."

"Praise Do Mede," the people offer in chanting fashion.

Holding up his arms in a friendly gesture to avoid another rant, I can see that his hands, like his face are mangled. He be at ease and comfortable as a speaker and he be dressed almost exactly as the Mede, but he does not bear the Archer's Crest. The crowd be again quiet enough for him to continue his tell.

"We have yet to determine how the rebels managed to cause a misfire of the Dragon-One rocket ingeniously designed by our leader. It had been meant to destroy the approaching Singularity, but due to their sabotage the phenomena somehow reacted causing great destruction and loss of life on our once fair planet.

"Curse the Christians, Curse the Christians," comes the mass response and this time the man does not try to stop the repetitions.

I don't mingle what bricks me; maybe the inflection of his voice, maybe a gesture by his gnarled hand: Whatever it be, I see another face in my mind. It comes in the image of a news-telling I saw on television not long afore the Gathering-Up. It was a show by the National HeadQuarters Broadcast Corporation, an interview actually between the scientists planning for the launch of the Dragon-One and the actual owner of NHQ. He was a good teller, very familiar, handsome and a popular face in them days. His name still hides from my knowing until Roxanne tells it out. She spits it like a curse, "Jonathan Trimble."

Prayer—I have never mingled such prayer. I thought my conversations with Bronzeman were special, but late into the evening after we mingled at the Temple show, as I sit on the floor of Ilbani and Jende's home, I un-puzzle that I mingle too much of myself. There are at least thirty Seconds and Remnants here, most lying flat on the floor, strong in their pleas for forgiveness and reconciliation. Most pray to Bronzeman, some to YHWH. As the praying goes on special knocks are heard at the door and more beckon to join us. I be puzzled by the fitting of all in here. We have been in this condition for at least four hours. Several times a Remnant will cry out something amazing. The name Yeshua…Messiah and then suddenly he or she be Blue.

Ilbani rises from his position on the floor and begins to pray over us. "Father YHWH, son Yeshua we are moved by Your *Ruach HaKodesh*— Your Holy Spirit in this place. This day has been difficult for us for we have met evil once again. Its presence was so strong that we felt retreat to this place necessary. Lord, we ask for strength and light to turn back the darkness, to light the Un-lit and to face our advisories with courage and Your wisdom."

The Keeper now asks us to share in the tell about the day's happenings. The appearance of Jonathan Trimble at the Mede's side be sour-milk. As deformed as he was, the man was very real to the crowds, telling in a convincing way how we Kin, have been the trouble and will be the trouble unless we are snuffed. He seemed to know our ways and the ways of the crowd, touching nerves and reminding that the Kin seem to be doing fine and the Un-lit suffer, so it must be the Kin's Doing.

I could hear and see the anger heating up and so could our leaders who pulled us quietly away back to the safety of Ilbani's house. The return of Jonathan Trimble also makes our hearts heavy, especially after together reading Jason Ballard's confessions including great detail about the man.

"You have no real mingling how dangerous he is," says Roxanne. The tattooed redhead seems really frightened. She tells some of her own personal experiences with Trimble and I can see why she wants to avoid the man. As she be telling, I suddenly see a flash afore my eyes. It be usually a warning that Jende has something to share with my vision, but this flash burns my brain. Jende cries out in pain and through red-hot light, I can make out Ilbani putting his hands to his head as if he too be suffering. Now I can hear Ki in my mind, praying in a very strained voice, *Spirit, what is this? Please protect us.*

A dark image grows in my head. Two omen walk toward me. But it be not toward me, they are in another place and seem unknowing of my being. I turn my head and realize that beside me are Jende, Ilbani and Ki—all of us invisible to the men. The image clears some and, to my horror, I realize we are watching the Mede and Jonathan Trimble sitting down at a table. Right away, Pounders dressed in white server coats (from old age fancy restaurants) tromp into the room. The servers cannot seem to avoid bumping into one another as they try to place tattered napkins on the laps of their masters and chipped platters of food on table. The men try to ignore the stumbling, but their faces show anger and frustration.

Now words start to come to me, Mede's and Trimble's words, meant only for one another…

—"I'm telling you I saw her out there," Trimble be telling the Mede. "There's no doubt. If it hadn't been so crucial we keep the crowd's attention, I would have dealt with her."

"Relax my friend. All is coming together. Of course she is in Jerusalem. We will acquire her." The Mede seems calm and pleased.

"But the others have her. They're putting things in her head. How can you…"

—The Mede glances at the other man with a look that gives me a bigger headache. It be both a look of warning and correction and Jonathan Trimble reacts by wincing. At the same time a server-Pounder spills a bowl of soup on the floor. It be the color of fresh blood mixed with yellowish clumps of fat—sickening to look at, even in a vision—what be it made of? Trimble tries to ignore the accident and begs…

"—I'm so sorry Lord. I meant; how can I be patient when every day, every minute she is being negatively influenced by those, those cultists! I know she must be suffering and I can't tolerate her absence any more, I…"

—another warning look from the Mede silences the ranting Trimble. Still he quivers like the still-live fish being offered on a plate to each of them by another of the clumsy house helpers. The Mede tells him…

"Remember well, that before she was yours, she was mine. I have already sent out Peacers to rescue her. I will make sure she is brought back to you and in the meantime, remember also who you serve. Do it well and do not remain distracted."

Trimble nods and forces himself into an upright up-right position. He puts on a serious look that mostly hides his simpering, but a slight twitching of random body parts still betrays his thoughts. We notice now that the Pounder-servers have small markings on their skin, like the marks of measles or chicken pox. As they bump about, they are seen scratching the blisters, opening lesions of yellowish liquid, much like that seen in the soup.

It takes the laying of hands on the four of us by Ayita to bring us back to full mingling in the room. We tell our strange joint vision, and for a long moment the room be silent, each person trying to un-puzzle what we have telled. Roxanne speaks first, begging to us to leave and to take her with us. It does not take a brainer to un-puzzle that the woman being referred to by the two men be the girl we have all come to honor for her strong belief. She has no desire to be close to the madman Trimble. I cannot un-puzzle how he mingles she be in danger from any of the Seconds or Remnants. Roxanne, like all of us, be free to go and come as she pleases. She tells that she does not please to go to the Mede, but does please to get away from him and Trimble as soon as possible.

"We have kept you too long in Yerushalayim," Jende tells us now and I can see her thoughts as a jumble of light and dark colors on a stormy ocean. I have learned this to be her way of sharing anxiousness. If there are Peacers searching house to house, based on the vision we have just shared, then it would be a dark time to be discovered as a large group. I mingle it be even more dark for my traveling companions and also Roxanne to stay. But afore anyone be willing to pack up, Luther asks if any are willing to pray until the dawn.

Everyone agrees to the ask, and afore the pale sun tries to light the day, all mingled in the room have come to be Blue.

> Call-out and Do: I call-out to the readers of this news-tell: Please pray for all people, even for them that still refuse to be eyes-open to the solid ground. See to the horizon, watch with hope in the direction of the rising sun for the change, each day. It be coming, the clouds will go and Bronzeman will come. Be ready in yer heart.

> **Special Do:** Some of ye are trying to get to Jerusalem right now. Ready yer traveling plans. Don't go yet. We have been there and it be not a place to go until Bronzeman says so. Soon it will be time. Don't worry. Ye will know the when by the telling of the trumpet sound.

"Therefore, when you see the abomination of desolation, spoken of by Daniel the prophet, standing in the holy place then let those who are in Judea flee to the mountains For then there will be great tribulation, such as has not been since the beginning of the world until this time, no, nor ever shall be".

—Matthew 24:15-21

Watching The Beasts
Month 8, Year 4 After Gathering-Up (AG)

Television, the box of moving pictures, no longer exists. But the enemy exists, as do we. Two sets of Keepers, two channels as we used to watch on the box, two choices:

> One choice is light reflected from a bright and shining source, difficult to look at because of its brilliance. But if the light is chosen, then greater gifts await.

> The other choice is darkness. The enemy reflects nothing. Beasts do not give, but only consume. Still people are drawn to the power of dangerous things. They hope to gain favor, that they might share in the consumption as smaller animals are prone to do, living in the fearful shadow of a benefactor who at any time might determine the smaller one's value is done.

The Keepers offer spiritual witnessing of things the world must learn; things hopeful and things disturbing. Keepers of light warn but do not command. They do not order that a channel must or must not be watched. The Un-lit watch the channels and choose for themselves.

The Keepers of light have been given one great gift. At times, we can see out into the world, beyond the sight and sound of the common. We can even see and hear the Keepers of darkness from afar, but the viewing comes at a great price. Bronzeman has given us strength, but as with any physical or mental contest, endurance is limited. The darkness burns the flesh and pains the brain. It tries to snuff the light. It cannot, but in the trying, there is pain to the light. Only the strongest of lights dare to watch the darkness, that we may guard the horizon.

The Keepers of darkness? By the very description, they have no eyes or ears to watch us from afar. Their skill is in the darkening of others, believing they can command and overpower the Red-lit, and those who choose blindness to any light whatsoever—these are the prey and the slaves of the dark-Keepers.

So now we watch. There is a rumor that Jonathan Trimble, a beast of great talent, is planning to produce a publication to compete with the reports of our beloved Küllo. The mad man's production will surely be of great physical quality. His ability to distribute the information is vast. We are told he is even trying to reinvent the still-camera, to capture pictures to share. The difficulty is in the chemicals used for developing the images. They are difficult now to find in this cursed world, thought to exist only in places that humans cannot. The beasts use their soulless Bose-Spooks for the seeking, but they have apparently not succeeded. No pictures have yet surfaced.

Knowing Trimble's skill, the news within their paper must be all fragrance and no flower. The Mede will tell of great strides and improving conditions, but the earthquakes and foul weather increase rather than subside. Their gift of chemical lighting and durable housing do nothing to quell death and despair. The Mede therefore will blame the Blue for these problems and his beast Trimble will charm his readers (they look to be charmed!) into believing we mean them harm.

Once we secure a copy of the paper, we will share only small parts of the dark text. There is little benefit to its disclosure. We will note specific concerns as examples of their treachery. The enemy is already circulating that certain of us, in particular, are criminals: Ilbani the Keeper, Jason Ballard (who is for the meantime safe in a faraway location), Eleazar and Luther, and most certainly Küllo and his clan. All of these willingly accept the danger of being discovered in order to tell more loudly of Bronzeman's soon-return.

There are others who the beasts of the dark news are eager to influence. They even chase them. Roxanne is one and we protect her. As much as they pursue her, we will make her light invisible to them.

It is a blessing that the Keepers of darkness cannot locate the Keepers of light. It is not permitted by Bronzeman and we are protected by His Ruach. But in the blessing, we are sad. We watch others near and far, suffering, being tortured. We see the spiritual forces of evil gathering in the weak, and we are all the more anxious for Bronzeman's appearance. Meanwhile, we watch and warn—it is our Do. Let Bronzeman be praised by all.

One sees
One hears
And it is written
Let us work together that the world may know!

—Keepers, for the glory of God

The World Standard

Editor in Chief—Jonathan Trimble
Edition I
29-8-4 AE

Look at what the Supreme Mede offers to all
who want and desire greatness for themselves.

PRISONER OF TERRORISTS SOUGHT TO BE SAVED

I am myself resurrected by him! The cult-criminals tried their best to undo me, but the Supreme Mede intervened. There is nothing he cannot control, no one he cannot repair to his purpose.

As for those who resist? Let them try, but they are the ones who have lost the greatest prize of all. Imagine a world where all people from all walks of life were to join together in cooperation. Anyone who would resist such a perfect unity must be the crazy ones. They claim they want such a world, but they point to a leader that cannot be found—does not exist except in works of fiction. There is only one leader, one great man who can build the great reality and he is very much visible!

It is his great need that causes me to publish this next request. There is an unfortunate one, a young woman who has been captured by the cult-criminals. At this moment she is being abused in ways we can only guess—it would be the same with any of us if captured by the perverts, so report any suspicious religious activity! The Supreme Mede desires that this example be discouraged so he offers a generous reward to help find and secure the safety of poor Roxanne.

You will recognize her by her natural red hair and the many distinctive painted markings on her arms, face and legs. We hope soon to be able to present you with photographic materials in this publication, but for now, let that description stand. If we can rescue our sister to the cause of a better world, she will surely help us in convincing the other that we serve all mankind, even them, in our tireless efforts to build the most beautiful of societies where all might live together in perfect tolerance of one another.

Praise be to the Supreme Mede by whose hand all good happens.

Community Do: *As always, we ask your cooperation by alerting us if the whereabouts of the following people are made known to you.*

Ilabani Midehina Acdah (alias The Keeper)	**Jason Ballard**
Eleazar BenMadai	**Küllo (last name unknown)**

The hunt for these fugitives is worldwide and so assisting in finding them will be rewarded generously. The Premier's is notorious for his benevolence to those who live his cause.

Watching the 144
Month 8, Year 4 After the Gathering-Up (AG)

New prophesy has revealed itself on the horizon, as the sun bringing warmth on to the coming day. But in the warmth there is sadness we foretell, a great burden that we know must come. It is a continuing of YHWH's Do, passed on to a special one. The special one will soon understand the meaning of sacrifice, he will have Bronzeman's love within him, and he will count it as joy.

And there is more to happen. Before all of you, a gleaming light, brighter than any other will arrive. It is the Bronze Man, come to claim the Remnant of Israel that remains. He will show them the place where he is to come. Let all 144,000 of them be counted, kneeling before him. We Keepers have been blessed with the honor of continuously praying for each of them by name. You, YWHW have gifted us with a picture of each one in our eyes and ears. They have become a tenderly loved portion of our clan. We refer to them fondly as, "the 144". They and the martyrs will be Yeshua's army. They are all that will be necessary. Bronzeman will finish the victory that was won long ago. These words will no longer be a riddle to the world and our kin's new calling will be a clear path.

As for the other wrath that has been prophesied, it is written of, not to condemn, but to warn. The stiff-necked will of mankind is foreseen by the Eternal who was and is, and is to come. Babylon be aware; Jerusalem tremble. Your rulers will try. They will fail. But in the meantime, the servants and the saints must hope in their Messiah.

One sees
One hears
And it is written
Let us work together that the world may know!

—Keepers, for the glory of God

The Bronzeman News

מָשִׁיחַ Watch and Keep מָשִׁיחַ

My name be Küllo, that be all ye need to know about me. I be not the story—I be the eyes, ears and hands of these tales. The words on these pages will be news-tells from common folk. Folk like ye and me. Them will tell their story and I will copy it with as little cleaning up as possible, so that all who are left after the Gathering-Up will see what be happening: The Bronzeman be appearing and the seeings of him are much the same. What be different be what he tells each one to Do.

MINGLE IT. MAKE UP YER OWN MIND, I WILL NOT MAKE IT FOR YE.

Edition Five: Babylon
Month 9, Year 4 After the Gathering-Up

Küllo's Notes: Our clan be safe now. I mingle that to be a strange, but true tell. We nearly did not escape Jerusalem for the Mede and his mangled servant Trimble put a high price on our heads. We were prepared to travel out by night and left our hiding place just as we heard the Peacers busting doors close by. Ilbani and his family had to flee as well to avoid capture, so we traveled as one large group—dangerous when being chased, a pack of hunters can more easily catch a slow herd.

Thanks be to Bronzeman, our company has had experience with these streets and their secrets. There be a door known only to a few, which we searching out. We were nearly there, but round a corner came Peacers along with some Pounders under their control. The Peacers ordered us to halt. There seemed no escape and the Pounders began to shove us to our knees. We did not know if we would be snuffed on the spot or presented to the Mede as some sort of trophy. Ilbani set the great example, beginning to pray out loud, not for our comfort, but for shalom to cover even our enemies and for the Ruach HaKodesh to reveal the glory of God to our capturers.

We all began to pray even as the Peacers laughed and joked about our pathetic efforts. I mingled for sure that BJ would Do his telling to them. But then I started seeing bright images afore me and hearing beautiful chords in the air, a sign that Jende and Ki were *visioning* as we'd come to call it. All the hairs on my body danced and then Ki, in barely a whisper spoke, "Sleep."

Two things happened right then. The ground beneath us woke up and the Peacers went to snoozing. The earthquake caused new cracks in the ancient walls that framed the street. Like tree roots they spread. One building close by seemed ready to collapse and we watched as people poured out its main entrance. Some jumped to the street from windows above. I realized it must have been a house of sex-want for everyone jumping was naked and they had the merchant mark on them that labeled them as property to a slaver. Men, women, even children scattered in all direction, last the slaver his-self after making sure all his precious stuff was out, hobbled out the door and down an alley. The building seemed to burp and then fell to pieces.

The earth stopped shaking and, besides our clan, the only ones on the street were the still-snoozing Peacers. I cannot mingle how we and they had not been snuffed by flying stone but there we were. Praise Bronzeman. As we left the scene, one of the Pounders twitched nervously on the ground. I don't know what called me to stop and puzzle the withering figure, but I did, and here be my tell of it.

The Pounder along with two others were identical and I recognized the face as that of a young girl with a scar across the front of her face from her left forehead to her lower right cheek. Each of the Pounders shared the trait on the otherwise beautiful face of the girl that was behind us at the Jerusalem Do-point—was that only three moon cycles ago? The result of her resistance was now afore us. Though it seemed a hopeless Do, I knelt and told a prayer of healing over the bodies, asking Bronzeman to find a way to use this poor soul's lost life to YHWH's glory. He be the God of miracles and so I mingled, this was as good a miracle to ask for as any. Afore re-standing, I looked once more at the girl's face. I mingled her greatly, but could not un-puzzle why I felt so close to this one.

Leaving our chasers to try to find us in their dreams, we took the path toward our wanted passageway. What puzzled us most was the after. Leaving the street where the Peacers found us, there was no damage to be seen anywhere. It was like God put his finger in one place to fix it and left the rest for another day. There will be much telling of this happening after we flee Jerusalem.

In a safe place outside the city, we said our goodbyes to Ilbani and his family who Bronzeman has called to set up camp in the wilderness for their own Do—to prepare for Bronzeman's soon-returning. We cannot un-puzzle when, but mingle we will see and hear their needs and successes when the Spirit tells us to.

Babylon be four months walk north and east from Jerusalem. Between the towns be a wilderness puzzle bigger than the foot traveling. It be a Dark Land of Dark Dwellers. Broken buildings, bones of gone-things, and leftovers of snuffed folk be all about. There be a nasty sniff in the nose to all of it, like what used to be the smell of old eggs when them still were. The living here be a sad-enough tell, the Dark Dwellers be so terribly un-lit. I watched one who was squatting on the side of the road we trekked—a ragged wrinkled man of very few teeth, who smelled of blood and pee. He had an old carpenter's hammer and swung it machine-like onto the armored head of a recently snuffed Pounder. The clanking noise made by the hammerer scratched my nerves and I saw no look of feeling in the ragged man's eyes. Ayita tried to offer the sick soul some food, but when she came near, he would back pedal, snarling like a scared animal. Only when we were all past him did he crawl back to his hammering job, ignoring the bag of dried vegetables we left for him.

Others who looked much the same peered at us from behind rocks or from within caves. They would not attack, even when their groups were greater than ours. The Dark Dwellers are hope-lost, even the hope of thieving a travel party. But as a caution we still lit large fires at night and watched always in case they got somehow brave enough for snuffing us.

Dark Dwellers were not the biggest head-scratcher in that strange place. We would turn a corner to see beautiful Blue kin! In the hardest of places to be lit, and not so far from the Dark Dwellers, we found whole villages of Bronzeman followers. But the big tell was how they be called. No-one came skipping in from Jerusalem to share—this be a hopping the corner place to skip around. So Bronzeman came and bricked them himself! They all telled of their seeings and mingling with the King. I felt special kinship with them acause of this. I have been sore lonely for others who mingle him like BJ and I mingle him.

I wanted to have them leave the Dark Regions to come with us, but Bronzeman said to them and me that they was called-out to here and so here they stay. Our "so longs" were hard and I now pray for them maybe more than any I have mingled with.

And now we have walked straight into New Babylon. This be a city that does not puzzle well in my brain, as we mingle its streets. Passage throughout the town be open and free, there are no Do-points to check through, as there are in Jerusalem and the population be all calm and about business. Everything be a *buy*. If ye want to walk, ye barter to carry a load to help another. If ye want to sit, ye must trade food for a seat. If ye want to enter a place, ye must offer a hand-over of goods. Even intercourse be handled as a casual transaction. "Want a woman? Prefer a man? We have a buy for all—children too—your pleasure be our pleasure." It be all done clean and easy…but it be done.

Many strange things are here, but stranger be what be not here—bugs. We have shed our leathers acause we are telled by the Babylonians that they are not needed. At first we were very worried. Without the leathers, our Blue shines, but we are assured there be no punishment for our color or our creed. Still I do not see other Blues on the streets and puzzle what the locals mingle about us. My other puzzling be how the bugs are not in this place?

All here be Flexsteel, painted pretty in many colors to be seen-good. All be clean…like people have never touched it. There be food to be had, again at some worked-out price, and it has the taste of freshness. It be not dried and preserved like the mess we have brought in from our desert journey.

Ki rides in her harness on the back of BJ and the Babylonians find her a *want*—something for a buy. They ask if they might offer trade to examine her, touch her with a finger, speak with her. She be willing and her strangeness gives us credit to use in barter for passage to the Sector of the Remnants. I had no mingling that this place would have such a large Jewish population—the Remnants seem well treated and active in the community. We are learning that all are free and respected here as long as they trade well.

Eleazar be our leader here. He knows this place and mingles how to get us fast to our place of want. When we turn an alley to find it, I be puzzled again. All the Flexsteel stops and it be like we are back in Jerusalem. Stone and plaster houses all well done and kept. The street be full of kaubandus, people trading—like me. The smell of cooked meat and new vegetables tells my stomach it has a need. One house has a very large double door and Eleazar moves us right to it. He does not knock, but instead tells loudly in Hebrew, *"Awb, bane chay.*—Father, your son has life."

There be much moving and words on the other side of the doors and then they are opened to us. There be a large courtyard with green plants everywhere and something in its center that I re-know from being a boy. It bricks me acause I have seen the things many times, but had forgot the Do of them. It be a rock carving of people looking up to the sky. They are reaching with hands and look almost…rock-real. Most of these I have seen on our travels are in pieces or cracked bad. But this one be wonderfully made, like new and out of the mouths of the rock-people sprout water. I can now see in my brain, another of these from my home, in Town Centre. I smell the life in the liquid and my ears want nothing more than the trickle-sound of water meeting water in the pool around the thing. I re-know the name of it now—fountain.

I be not the only bricked-one. Our whole clan stands afore the fountain—all except Ki who be as quiet as I have ever heard and Ayita who falls to her knees and sings one of her tribe-songs that dances with the water:

> Lord of earth and sky,
> Your spirit rains blessings
> It blossoms fruit
> And overflows in living water
> Your stream fills us
> And spills over in our song of joy

It be another oven-hot day and I feel a strange puzzling inside of me. My throat burns for the water but the beauty of the moment makes me not want to move, as if staying will stop time and keep us here forever.

An old grey bearded man moves time for me. He glows Blue and I realize that blue shines from all of them that have greeted us inside the gates of this place. Why did I not notice afore? He rushes into the courtyard amazingly fast for someone of many years and embraces Eleazar, who weeps and falls to his knees when he catches sight of the running man. The elder cries, "*Bane, bane*—My son, my son," and smothers his prodical in a long embrace. Without letting go of Eleazar, Amos BenMadai looks us over and realizes our poor condition. He encourages all, "come to the fountain, there is fresh water and food for all."

Afore anyone else makes a move, Eleazar releases himself from his father's arms and comes into our clan. He grasps the hand of Roxanne and leads her to the greybeard. There be a long and awkward silence as the old man surveys the young tattooed woman. She in turn does not look at the man but keeps her head lowered as if she be ashamed. Amos BenMadai turns to his son who nods at an unspoken question. Then Amos gives his full attention back to Roxanne, speaking gently to her.

"You have nothing to fear within these walls and we love your presence here. I am perhaps more acquainted with your circumstances than you are aware. Eleazar and I have been in correspondence but I do not think he has given you the full benefit of my sad story. Let me connect a few of the puzzle pieces to help. You know Eleazar to be my beloved son in whom I am well pleased. And I am sure it has been widely shared that Eleazar has a brother whose name I have difficulty now speaking except in my prayers to YHWH. You see, that man's position and behavior are sadly a result of my poor efforts of upbringing."

Here he puts a finger of his wrinkled hand under Roxanne's chin. He pushes softly up, so that her head lifts and their eyes meet. "That man, my other son is now the self-proclaimed ruler of the world, and if I am not mistaken, your father. The reality of his condition shames me, but it should not shame you. Your Savior has redeemed you and in doing so, has redeemed me as well, my beautiful and courageous granddaughter."

Amos smiles gently and Roxanne cannot keep her tears within. She cries out, "Oh Grandfather!" The two embrace and someone mingles it be time to break-out in song.

> Make a joyful noise to the LORD, all the earth!
> Serve the LORD with gladness! Come into his presence with singing.!
> Know that the LORD, he is God! It is he who made us, and we are his; we are his people, and the sheep of his pasture.
> Enter his gates with thanksgiving, and his courts with praise! Give thanks to him; bless his name.
> For the LORD is good; his steadfast love endures forever, and his faithfulness to all generations.

I be puzzled acause, as I sing, I cannot stop crying, though I mingle this be a happy time. Jende comes beside me and places her hand on my shoulder. I be bricked with an image of my parents and sisters, Anna and Lina, hugging me and I mingle that I too want the love and forgiveness I have just seen shared. Jende steps me to BenMadai's side and places her other hand on his shoulder. The greybeard looks suddenly puzzled, but then a new brightness shines from his eyes. Jende must have shared my story with him, for he puts an arm around my shoulder and tells, "Of course they forgive you. And since they are in a perfect new place, your family will not mind if I take you to be my grandson for a bit."

Bronzeman, I know that ye have given grace in this moment and I praise you. The blueness of the Amos BenMadai's house shines brightly into the night and mending tears bathe the hearts of all in the house.

In BenMadai's house, there be no bartering or want. Here there be only serve and Do. The old father teaches us much of New Babylon. We already mingle Dame Brenda Anders, the self-appointed benefactor of the place. Ilbani the Keeper, Ayita and Rachel have met her and I have read of her in the Book of Seconds, as have the others.

"What you have not yet heard of be the increase of tensions between Darius Mede and the Dame," tells the greybeard. "Because of her ecological and business stewardship of this place, Babylon has flourished beyond all possible expectations. And what I would want to know is why are you all so anxious to meet the Dame?"

Roxanne, who be seated by her grandfather on a pillow tells next, "I have…information for my mother that, if shared may help us all. It has to do with Jonathan Trimble.

"Can you explain why we should risk our family and our lives for this quest?" BenMadai asks.

Roxanne looks around the room. Most of the faces are smiling back at her, as if to encourage her in her tell. But she seems, for the only time since I have mingled her, to be with no words. I watch as she bows her head and mouths a silent prayer, then she looks up and tells loudly. "I was the mistress of Jonathan Trimble. He shared…very personal thoughts and ideas with me and considers me his property. Bronzeman has called me to share all of this with my mother, and…to offer her Bronzeman's last chance of love.

We have all heard her tell afore, but now we wait for BenMadai's reaction, which be immediate. He bursts out in a loud laugh, rises from his pillow and goes to a cabinet in the wall to pull out a document. It looks to be the same type of paper we use for the printing of the Bronzeman News, but this has the symbol of the Mede on the banner. He passes the paper around and I read that Roxanne be the headline, telled to be a captive and in grave danger. There be an offer of reward for her rescue.

BenMadai comes back to his pillow and strokes the head of his granddaughter. As fiery as Roxanne's confession be, what Eleazar's father tells next stops our hearts. "Praise Adonai, young lady, that you have come to know your Savior considering the extraordinary burden you have had to carry. Your wanting to reconcile with your mother is noble. But it is the danger this places you in with your father that concerns me."

Danger from her father? The greybeard had mentioned Brenda Anders as the mother of Roxanne—that woman I have been telled be trouble enough. But no one has mentioned to me the name of her father, Eleazar's brother, BenMadai's problem child. Again them in the room who do not have the total tell seek understanding of the family and what danger they speak of. And then in a flash, the un-puzzling bricks me. Can it be, dear Bronzeman? Can Roxanne's father be that darkest of dark ones?

I wake from a fit of sleep, something stirs in my stomach and I doubt bad food to be the cause. The re-knowing comes to me that it has only been one day and a night since we arrived in Babylon. And as the fog leaves my brain, I realize that I be listening to old BenMadai and his son Eleazar in conversation. They sit cross legged in a corner of the room, too dark to know which man be which, except by their voice. The elder tells the younger, "John's vision was great, but perplexing. It be as if he be dancing back and forth in time. In the 14th chapter of God's revelation, the disciple appears to be having a vision within a vision."

"I agree, father," responds Eleazar. "But how can we properly prepare for what is to come unless Bronzeman shines more light on current happenings?"

"I believe the confusing text is intentional, describing a future time when our Savior will appear. He has not made the time or moment precise so that we must yet trust only in him. You must have missed the release of the false-herald Trimble while on your journey from Jerusalem to New Babylon. The beast is on the move, I believe to seek out my granddaughter and to eliminate the threat to his power in this place. I believe strange alliances of our own may be necessary. If we are to walk alongside the Wh...Dame Anders, we must also be as quick, cautious as the serpent. And after that, I suspect none of us will be safe in this place."

Eleazar be silent for a long moment and then tells his father, "I have even trusted him with my dreams, and he has given me one."

I sneeze, it comes from nowhere! I try to stop the next, but it too flies out just as loud.

"Küllo," I hear the old BenMadai call. "Come sit with us. I believe my son is about to share a great story. We know you to be skilled with a pen, but now we will explore your ability to keep secrets."

A treacherous dust storm postpones our audience with Dame Anders for two weeks, but the delay gives us all good planning time. BenMadai has sent a secret message to the leader of the city, but he be careful not to let her know of Roxanne's presence. We know that once this word be mingled out, there be a good chance that the Mede will insist on a trade of some sort for the return of his daughter to his man, Trimble. So we have prepared to leave New Babylon quickly if the threat plays out.

We all mingle in a large room during the dusting and I have the privilege to be invited to listen as Eleazar and Ayita talk about a peculiar object they have brought along on the journey and now examine, it be a piece of rock shale, about the size of two large dinner plates. On its surface, scratched symbols of an unfamiliar language. The husband and wife, along with Ilbani, discuss the importance of this tablet.

"Preacher Elijah gifted me with this during our travels from South-South to Jerusalem," tells Ayita. "He found it in a stream and you will soon see why he considered its message as strong spiritual medicine, important enough to guard with our lives."

I puzzle the scripting on the slab. Not as Preacher Elijah had puzzled— He had written smartly about the runes. My questions are not smart, but confused. Much of the language looks to be old Hebrew as I have seen many times. But there are other symbols I do not mingle easily. Ayita tells us more of the strange stone. "Yes, some of the etchings look to be Hebrew, but with very slight differences. And these images," she points to a grouping, "are quite different. They resemble, but are not exactly, symbols of the Cherokee nation."

As we puzzle over the message, I sense Ki near me and lift her up to also gaze at the slate. She reaches out and touches the symbols, tracing each one with a stubby finger. Suddenly all my senses come alive, like fire cooking a frog, my brain jumps.

"There are no participles," I tell. "The first portion be a derivative language created by the sharing of Dikaneisdi with Hebrew." I point to the tablet…

—DᏞᏅᎣᏛᎩ ᏱhᎥᏋᎠᏞᎵ…
"—would best translate as…
Fruitful Tribe"

The words have just popped out of my mouth without control. I be bricked as to how I mingle these things. And I be not done. The un-puzzling in my brain pours out more…

"The next phrase, as Preacher Elijah had already told, be not a mixing, but pure Hebrew, as if the words are a holy tell, not to be changed…

—בשנה הבאה בירושלים…
"—would mean…
Next year Jerusalem"

I hear none of the others talking, so I look up from my study and see them all staring at me. Have I blundered? I be not brained enough to know. Eleazar comes to my side and points to the other symbols scattered on the slate. "What do you make of these random symbols?"

I look and know. That be the only way to explain. "It be like a…a card. My ema…mamma bought them in the store. We would write our names around the phrase…Happy Birthday, We Are Sorry, Get Well, We Miss Ye…things like that. And then we would give the card to a person we cared for. I do not mingle if ye understand…"

"Greeting cards," Roxanne puts a tell on it and then asks as she points to the slate. "So these…outside symbols; are they names? Can you read them?"

I can and I Do, out loud for all to hear: "Asher, Dan, Gad, Issachar, Manasseh, Naphtali, Reuben, Simeon, and Zebulun."

The silence in the room be long moments. Amos BenMadai be the first to speak out, "The lost tribes!"

Then Rachel asks, "Küllo, you says the word in middle am Fruitful. What tribe be Fruitful?"

Eleazar laughs and tells for us all. "The word for Fruitful in the old scriptures is Ephraim, one of the half-tribes. Holy scripture often refers to all of the Northern Kingdom as Ephraim."

I be awed by the clean-up after the storm. The organization of this city tells much of its leaders. Hearing that the storm was approaching, massive tarps were pulled over all the crops in the area. And all the water wells were sealed tightly. The people of New Babylon seem to have a practiced way of dealing with crisis and it has paid off. There be small damage to the buildings and, unlike what I mingled in Jerusalem after such an attack of nature, this place moved forward in a short moment.

Our clan now mingles that there be great tension between the cities of Jerusalem and Babylon. Ilbani tells us, by pigeon, that the favor of YHWH on the Holy City has evaporated. Food has become scarce, earthquakes and plagues have increased dramatically. Seconds and Remnants share what they can, but are still accused of hoarding and of trying to wrestle control from the Mede and his minions.

BenMadai tells a different story of Babylon. Dame Anders seems well suited to inspiring all in the city to overcome community obstacles. She first set in place a commerce and trade system to reward hard work and also sought out them that appeared to be sacrificing their own good to help others.

To these *Do-gooders*, she gives special privileges, recognition and position within her administration. The results are a big tell and so the city is a get-rich place. Botanical gardens and water wells have been constructed, Flexsteel is the wellbeing of all and more building Do's go on. The sad part of the tell be the missing morals of the place. Almost nothing be a Do-Not in Babylon as long as the Doer registers and pays a Do-Fee to Anders. If the Doer wants to sell children or put on a show that has people performing sex with large rodents: no problem. Commerce be the rule of law as long as the government makes a good profit.

Amos tells of his sources, close to the Dame, who warns that a bitter rivalry between the Premier and his wife causes both locations to suffer. The Mede denies any problems with Jerusalem, claiming that all people on earth have been improved by his rule. He speaks in generalities of global betterment, but seldom be he specific about his own Do, other than an occasional poster-child, some individual who has seemed to overcome adversity and now prospers. Jonathan Trimble be very busy telling how the Green Order Government has been responsible for these successes though we have difficulty determining exactly how.

Dame Anders be self-absorbed in the bettering of New Babylon. The folk of the city and many leaders have approached her to share her methods with Jerusalem and beyond, to improve conditions for all. She has yet to do so and it be hinted that she awaits an invitation from the Mede to ply her skills. Old BenMadai mingles no such request will ever be forthcoming.

And this be where Roxanne fits the puzzle. She tells that she knows things about Pretender Mede, Anders and Trimble what might help get everyone working together again, instead of ignoring the bigger Do. Ilbani, BenMadai, and all the leaders are very concerned for the young woman. No matter how strong her faith and how blessed her calling, we can't mingle how the daughter of the most powerful Red-lit and the highest Un-lit of this world will be affected by meeting and mingling with either of her parents again.

A picture starts playing in my brain. I don't know if it be Jende playing it, or if it be just a re-knowing. I see the girl who had been stopped at the checkpoint in Jerusalem—the one turned to a Pounder. At the top of her head where the scar splits her face, a bright blue light starts shining out and the girl's head parts in two. The pieces fall off and inside be another face, that of Roxanne. She be bright-lit. It be a strange picture—the two seem very much the same, but different. And it warms me and I know that Bronzeman has just told me a puzzle through Ki, using her inside whispering. The clones have never been soul-filled. But all true living beings, not the copied ones, are soul-filled. The scar-faced girl and

Roxanne both have their own souls. One has not found hers but the other has. You need to follow the found one to help the lost one.

No other person in the room seems to hear Ki speak. They are busy trying to make their own tell, but now I know what we must Do, so I stand up and tell loudly, "Roxanne goes to see her mother and so I go with her. Who else will go with us?"

I'm having trouble seeing and everyone else in the room be squinting too, the Blue be terrible-bright. Now I realize, the Blue be me, the Bluest I have ever been. There be no doubt in our mingling that Bronzeman will be with us in our Do.

I be seeing another strange picture in my head, through the spiritual eyes and ears of Jende and Ki. They say the sharing of it brings them both great mind pains but they want badly that I tell it. So I Do, even if ye choose not to believe…

"—What in the world are you saying?" Brendan Anders be struggling out of sleep and her bodyguard/assistant, Claymore tries to explain again, this time more loudly and slowly.

"The old Jew is at the gate with a group of people he says you must see."

The Dame still suffers from the hearing loss she experienced when she witnessed the ascension of Brother Moses & Preacher Elijah in Jerusalem after *Yom Tov Shmuah*—The days of Good News. How can I news-tell what I be not standing in? I can tell this acause I be seeing it through the spiritual eyes and ears of Jende and Ki.

Brenda Anders shakes her head, like I used to see horses do, to throw off her sleep. It takes her a moment to mingle the spoken words but then she nods and tells, "The old Jew. I told him not to bother me again or face removal of his privileges. He is intelligent enough to know the power I hold over his sector, so his being here must be for something very pressing."

She speaks all this as she climbs from her bed, enters her changing room and draws the curtain closed to separate herself from her assistant. "Let them into the Aviary, but do not offer them anything, not a chair or food, not even a word. Let them wonder about my reaction."

Claymore, standing outside the changing room, nods his head—a reaction that cannot possibly be seen by the Dame—and leaves the room. The Dame continues to speak in an overly loud voice as she dresses in one of her official New Babylon green uniforms, specially made to set her apart. It be difficult to know if she mingles she still has an audience or if she be telling to herself. "This should be interesting. If BenMadai has something to share of value that implicates Darius, I may be able to use it as a bargaining chip to finally sever the relationship between Jerusalem and Babylon!"

As I see and hear this happening, the gates to the Dame's palace are pulled open by her guard and we are herded in.

True to her ordering, not a thing be told to us and we are pointed through the main entry, and to the left, into a large dome shaped room of clear Flexsteel. It be very light, warm and humid in this place and we are surrounded by giant green plants. It be what I mingle a jungle to look like. We step up a brick walkway into an indoor courtyard, a clearing with bricks on the ground, surrounded by more kinds of growth with flowers of every color—I cannot mingle it all. I be puzzling the size of this place. The jungle hides its border. There are flowers of every color, the smell be… sweet and also…there be no other word…green. There are…birds! They are small, but chirp and fly from tall branches above us. One actually swoops down and lands on Ayita's shoulder. She smiles and does nothing to discourage the perch.

Another large door opens and Brenda Anders enters without introduction. When seeing Ayita, she lets out a large laugh and tells, "Oh my dear, it has been too long, come with me and tell me what you have been up to."

Ignoring the rest of us, the Dame lays her arms about the Cherokee and leads her away toward a private part of the dome, but a stream of water that seems to come from nowhere, much like BenMadai's fountain, only it flows on the ground. How can so much water be in one inside place? The bird on Ayita's shoulder remains there, I mingle it be unconcerned and unafraid of all the goings-on. Attendants immediately appear with a table and two chairs. The two women are seated and served food and drink while the rest of us are left to stand where we are, four guards positioned around us as a suggestion that we are to stay put.

I watch as Anders waves her hands around the air in front of her, laughing and seeming to explain things to her guest, over-much. I see Ayita take a sip from a porcelain cup and nod her head. She does not appear to speak, but listens as the Dame blabs on. The birdsong in the chamber be beautiful, but makes it impossible to hear the conversation. I ask in my brain if we should be listening with our spiritual ears, but Ki tells me, with a gentle note of her own, to relax and listen to the birds instead. I do and then something in the air disturbs my ears. It be the racket of a bug! I have been puzzled by their absence—and now more so. Where have they been? Why do they not attack the un-blue in this place?

Out of the corner of my eye, I catch site of a small white and brown bird that darts toward a larger object also flying about. There's no mistaking its metallic shine – a bug for sure. I puzzle to myself, *why be the bird chasing a creature twice its size, especially a creature with a stinger and sharp teeth!* But the bird does not attack. Instead it circles the bug and…sings! I cannot mingle the melody, but it conjures images in my brain of flowing water and forests from the old days. It makes me want to sing too, but that be not my gift—I'm told to let others sing for me to avoid people crying out in pain at the sound of my voice!

What I do not expect be what the bug does next. It matches the bird's path and its ugly buzz turns to a soothing bass drone that compliments the birdsong. The bird leads the bug toward a passageway and out they both go.

"House Sparrows," I flinch and turn at the same time to see one of the Dame's guard standing next to me, looking in the direction I had seen the two exit. He continues to stare, but speaks to me and our clan, all who observed the aerial dance, "The sparrows are native to this area. They have been here since the first man. When the bugs came, we suffered like all suffered, but then the birds gathered and sang their song. Now only a few attack, but right away, one of our feathered friends will lure it away, we don't know to where. Now there is no need of protection and we also benefit by the beautiful music."

"His eye is on the sparrow." It be Ki who tells this and I do not mingle her meaning. Then she breaks out into her own song, perfect and pure:

> **Why should I feel discouraged and why should the**
> **shadows come?**
> **Why should my heart be lonely and long for heaven**
> **and home?**
> **When Jesus is my portion, a constant friend is He,**
> **His eye is on the sparrow and I know He watches me.**
> **His eye is on the sparrow and I know He watches me.**
> **I sing because I'm happy;**
> **I sing because I'm free;**
> **His eye is on the sparrow.**
> **And I know He watches me.**

In the time I have traveled with Ki, she has shared her singing, but never with the deep love I hear in this melody. She be the birdsong and the voice of God in one. It rips at my heart and I see the music on the faces of all the others in the chamber. Even Brenda Anders be hushed. She rises from her chair and slowly walks toward us. Her eyes are blurred with tears, and Ayita has to guide her to the center of the courtyard.

"I can hear you," tells the Dame to Ki.

Ayita explains to us that Anders has had difficulty hearing ever since the day of the Prophets' ascension. I have heard the story telled. Many Unlit and Red-lit who were at the ascension were affected. Some lost hearing, others sight, many more gave their lives to Bronzeman.

The Cherokee leads the leader of Babylon over to Ki in her sling. Brenda reaches out with a trembling hand to touch the girl, but afore it happens, Ki asks a question in her mind-voice, her lips do not move. "What do you want?" I can hear her clearly and so can Brenda Anders who tells, "I want to hear again…like I used to."

"What happened that you can't hear now?" Ki wears a frown on her face. The beauty in her voice has changed to a boiling hiss.

"Nothing…I…there was a wind that burned me. I didn't do anything wrong…I…"

"—You did nothing wrong, you did nothing right. You did nothing," tells the small girl to the tall mistress.

Anders falls to her knees and now covers her ears as if the noise inside her head be painful. She yells out, "I have tried so hard to be a steward of the planet! You can't tell me I haven't tried."

"It's not that you can't hear, it's that you are not listening." Ki now reaches out and grabs one of the Dame's hands in hers. "What do you feel?"

An agonizing sound erupts from the mouth of the Babylonian and her guards try to respond. But they suddenly can't see and most fall to their knees, the same sound of pain coming from their throat. Only one, Claymore, crawls toward the sound of his mistress' distress. He manages to tell, "Please have mercy. It is my fault."

All the moaning in the chamber stops and Ki asks, "What is your fault?"

"I…have not confessed," Claymore responds between labored breaths. "I saw a vision of Jesus and he…told me to share my sight with Dame Anders. I was afraid I would be dismissed or…worse. I…did not confess my Lord. Jesus, forgive me. The pain in this room is mine. Please take it from the others and place it on me where it belongs."

Claymore be weeping like a child now. Our clan has seen it happen many times in many places, but it be still a puzzle to see such a giant man in so low a place. Anders be crying too and keeps repeating. "I can hear him! I can hear him!" She stumbles over to Claymore, bends down and puts her arms around him. They lay there and Ki speaks again, this time in a soothing, voice.

"I have words from the past for both of you. Belief is something you must wrestle with of your own volition, no one else can be involved in your grappling."

Both Anders and her bodyguard are jolted to look up at the speaker. The Dame reacts with words of her own. "Fitzgerald Hindeland said those words to me. Claymore was there too."

The big man nods his head and also tells, "His words burned into me, I hear them whenever I sleep, no matter how hard I try to push them out."

"The dreams!" Apparently Brenda Anders has un-puzzled something. She looks from Claymore up to Ki. "But you were not there. How could you know?"

Ki does not explain, but tells more. "Preacher Elijah and Brother Moses spoke other words to you that day." In my mind, Jende shows the day of the New Pentecost when the two Watchmen shared their message with the world. Everyone in the aviary can see it played out. Even the blind ones raise their heads in wonder at how the pictures in their heads have shown up.

Ki speaks again and as she tells, Brenda Anders, Claymore and the other guards who had been at the event, also chant the words in perfect unison, "As for what I expect, all I have left is my faith. Everything else of value has been stripped away and nothing I see now proves my faith misplaced."

Brenda Anders cries out alone, "What then am I to believe in?"

All respond "Believe in God. Believe in His plan."

The Dame cries out something that no mingling could prepare me for. "I have done nothing wrong, only good. That should be enough."

Ki's voice be thunder and rushes like the water that runs on the ground but in angry waves. "Only Jesus has the power to forgive. Ask him."

"I tried to become a protector of nature; he should know my love for the planet. Why should I be ashamed of that?" Anders shouts upward to the pinnacle of the dome. The birds scatter.

Ayita takes her hand and pleads, "Brenda, we all love this world, but it needs more repair than we alone can give it. Jesus can take your work and complete it. Ask him."

The other guards and Claymore raise their hands and shout. "Jesus, Lord, forgive us."

The Blue in this place sparkles and I have trouble seeing the people. Instead, each be a shimmering flame. The flame I mingle to be Ayita encourages us to help the blind ones, along with Claymore into a close circle around her. She then tells…"

—Adonai bless and keep you

Adonai make his face shine upon you and be gracious to you

Adonai lift up his countenance upon you and give you shalom."

Ki asks to be placed on the floor at the knees of the Babylonians. She touches Claymore and the others successively, with a stubby hand, praying over each and then asks, "Whom do you serve?"

Claymore responds first, "I am nothing. There is no other, but you, my King and Savior, Jesus."

The others call out together, "Jesus, my Lord."

Ayita touches the eyes of the new Seconds and tells, "Your faith has healed you." And one by one they rise up with new sight.

In the room there be only one Un-lit that remains. The Cherokee comes to Anders, she whispers into the woman's ear, "You wanted Fitzgerald and Moses to remember that you tried to save them. At the time, you did not realize that it was you who needed redemption. God did know and saw your heart at that moment. He remembers and now wants your belief."

But the Dame laughs out loud and pushes Ayita away. "You sad creatures, you don't need a god to do your good. Your good is already in you."

Another Blue flame comes up to stand by the two. A hand reaches out to softly touch the face of Anders and asks, "Mother?"

A gasp escapes the Dame's mouth. She turns to the new flame and with the palm of her hand, touches the face in return. For an instant, there be an astonished smile on the Ander's face and she asks questions in return, "Rox…Roxanne? You're alive? You're here?" Quickly this smile turns to a look of fear and she backs away from her daughter. "You must leave here. All of you, now! There is nothing for you in Babylon." She reaches out and strokes her daughter's face again, then Brenda Anders turns and flees from the aviary.

The power of the moment in the aviary be still with us. I can see better now and recognize each flame and mingle who they are. We have also mingled that Red-lit and Un-lit ones cannot see the flame, but Remnants can. Most of the Remnants are now fearfully curious about their Second kin. They wonder if the flame be a work of YHWH or of something sinister. The good news be that their questions allow us to tell them more about the love of Bronzeman. Conversions continue almost daily. One or two Remnants will come to us requesting to know the Son of God and the blue flame spreads throughout Babylon.

It has been a week and Roxanne still be struggling with the rejection of her mother. She does not go out, but sits with Amos BenMadai who teaches her about their Jewish roots. Others are drawn into the conversation, including me. We had not considered ourselves Jewish until the wise old greybeard explained things.

"What makes one a Hebrew?" he asks of his granddaughter.

Roxanne squirms on her floor pillow. "I don't know. Does a Hebrew have to speak with a funny accent?"

Everyone, even BenMadai, laughs at the reply. Roxanne's Texas-American drawl be foreign to us, as be my Estonian tongue. I mingle we all have funny accents. BenMadai tells, "The word Hebrew—*Ibri* in Hebrew—simply means stranger, traveler or *One from the other side*. We are all in this world strangers of a sort, are we not? But then YHWH spoke directly to one traveler, Abraham, who chose to have faith in this one God, and so YHWH made him the father of nations. Then Abraham's grandson, Jacob, YHWH blessed. He did not deserve it other than as the inheritance promised. His Maker had a far reaching plan, not just for Jacob, but for his growing family, a nation and anyone who would call on YHWH as God in all time. That same Creator renamed Jacob, Yisrael—God Strives, and a nation was born. Not just a nation of land, but a spiritual community that could not be destroyed by the conquering of a place or the scattering of clan. Those actions would only make YHWH's people strive in response to their God striving for them. The Hebrews would only become stronger and more vibrant when they were cast out…made to be 'strangers' by the world."

I see many others asking a question with their eyes, which BenMadai mingles and answers. "Though it is important to understand that the scriptures identify Jews as those carrying the bloodline of Jacob, each Second is understood to have a special privilege, a bonded relationship to their Savior, not by bloodline, but spiritually. He was fully Jewish, of the tribe of Judah and so his followers are grafted into Judaism as our kin."

We have been in New Babylon for nearly four moon cycles and have mingled no warnings or signs of an attack from Jerusalem. Amos and Eleazar BenMadai are pouring weight on my shoulders by passing on to me a personal "secret mission" for a soon-moment. The Do has been validated by Ki and Jende who still talk to my inside eye by pictures and sounds. They warn that doom be coming and the moment to leave be almost at the door. I cannot and will not argue.

I am sure I am not the best person for the duty but others believe differently. BJ, Ayita, Roxanne and Ki herself have telled in strong language that they will follow and protect me in my travels.

But what about them that believe they are called to stay in this place? The BenMadai's and the Hine's are especially in danger. Should I not stay to support them? Claymore and Anders' other guards pledge to watch over Eleazar, his father and his family as they also follow through with their calling-out. There be solid ground in all of these people, so the decision now becomes clear and that be how we come to be boarding the steamer to our next destinations. I will not say where or why we are going, but there be new purpose and passion in our hearts. I pray to Bronzeman that he watch over us for the most dangerous part of our journey be about to begin.

Call-out and Do: I call-out to the readers of this news-tell: Please pray for all people. Give forgiveness to them that confess to ye—the ones who Do mingle solid ground. Ye will mingle who they are when it happens, acause ye mingled the Change when ye confessed yer own self. If ye don't mingle it yet, confess now, all that ye are, and ask forgiveness from the True One who be soon-returning: Bronzeman, our King and Priest.

Special Do: It's still not time to trek to Jerusalem. Wait, wait and the going will be easy when Bronzeman says so.

Letter from Ilbani Midehina Acdah, Keeper of the Kin (in exile)

**"Violence does not and cannot exist by itself:
it is invariably intertwined with *the lie.*"**

—Alexander Solzhenitsyn

Written to my God—through the intercession of my Savior, Yeshua. For that reason I will not date my posts for the Receiver of my thoughts and prayers will put them to His purpose in His time. Let these words then be for His purpose and to His glory.

In my mind, I replay the writing of my notes, late into the previous evening before I slumped over my desk into an exhausted slumber. I remember scribbling this day's significance, *Yom Teruah, the 3rd anniversary of the Second Exodus*, or as most call it now, the Gathering-Up. At lease, I believe it to be the morning of that day—the clouded sunlight through the eastern window tells me as much, I have been shaken awake by the other Keepers, Ki and my beautiful Jende. "We must go," they simply tell. Lord Yeshua, I'm confused. What am I doing with these two? Ki has been traveling with Küllo, Jende be on a mission of mercy elsewhere in the city. I look around to orient and find this place familiar. It is the house of BenMadai that I have visited on many occasions in Babylon. You have me visioning from afar, my God, with the assistance of my kin, Your Keepers. It is nearly as real to me, as the prick of a pin.

Claymore has come to assist in our Babylon clan's escape. He explains that Brenda Anders refused to warn people of the invasion she knew to be coming. She was confident that her own military was incentivized properly and would stem any assault. As a demonstration of her resolve, she refused to leave her palace or sound the alarm even when the stealth attack began in the dark of the night. Babylon has slept through its own defeat and the Dame has been captured by GOG forces. By not ordering the city's evacuation she has condemned the population.

People are now taking matters into their own hands, fighting hand to hand with the Pounders, setting off explosive devices that bring down even the strongest Flexsteel structures. The beautiful garden city is now in ruins. The explosions and background flashes support the immediacy of our urgency. I hear screams that seem to grow nearer with every delay. Claymore and his troops are no strangers to conflict. He signals each of his captains to react and they do. Our clan is ushered to multiple steam-mobiles and driven to the docks where ships, planned for such an event, await our arrival.

Too much, too fast! The Seconds are taken on-board, and BenMadai protests, refusing to stay on board without first finding Roxanne. His fears are unwarranted. Küllo has already located Amos' granddaughter and now I see her, climbing the gangway to be at our side: Thank You Father YHWH for your mercies and protection.

We watch from the deck of the ship as workers struggle to load equipment and supplies. The weak sunlight has been covered by the thickening smoke, so that only by the light of the many fires throughout the city do we watch the approaching fight. The smell of death and suffering is the first to assault us from the heights of the city. Then descends the sound—screams and orders, pleas and protests. Finally, the bombs and bullets near us, people drop or fly as the weapons find their mark. Pounders emerge from the distant smoke. They trample upon the injured and continue to pursue the docks in an attempt to board our vessels.

The Babylonian army now comes to our defense, flanking the aggressors and meeting them in hand to hand combat. Now, something strange…

—From our distant vantage point, I witness a group of Pounders being held at bay. Suddenly there is an explosion in their ranks and a wash of chemicals sprays the area. Screams follow and I watch in horror while both attackers and defenders melt as if the very bones within them have turned to soup. Their flesh bubbles and other fighters on the perimeters of the destruction begin to collapse epileptically. Another detonation in the street illuminates other disintegrating and convulsing bodies. We had received premonitions that this treacherous warfare style was coming, but to see it in reality is gruesome beyond the imagining.

None too soon, our twelve boats launch. As we creep away from the docks I glance once more at the carnage and a new sense of terror engulfs me. I am looking directly into the eyes of one of the Pounders who has managed somehow to pass through the chemical gauntlet. He looks directly at me, still a respectable distance away, raises his rifle and aims. I see the puff of smoke and know there is no time to duck. The bullet passes right through me and into the chest of Claymore. He then looks at me, as if he can actually see my spiritual image and says, "I go to Bronzeman." He slumps to the deck with Ayita, Küllo and others trying to ease his passage. Another martyr has gone before us.

We gain precious distance from the onslaught unfolding before our eyes and, at my side, I suddenly sense weeping. Ayita is comforting her frightened children. Their father Eleazar, along with Luther and Rachel Hine are not on the vessel. Those warriors left by other means, at the first warning of the attack, to assemble the Remnants of Babylon and lead them away by land. Their families long for company in this present danger and they all begin to sing:

> **O soul, are you weary and troubled?**
> **No light in the darkness you see?**
> **There's a light for a look at the Savior,**
> **And life more abundant and free!**
>
> **Turn your eyes upon Jesus,**
> **Look full in His wonderful face,**
> **And the things of earth will grow strangely dim,**
> **In the light of His glory and grace.**

Amos BenMadai stands stoically watching the fall of city from the bow of the ship. We all gaze as the fleet sails, an aerial bombardment displays before us.

New Babylon crumbles in slow motion with each flash of light. Eerily, the attack plays out. The former servants of Brenda Anders attend those on deck and even pour wine into cups, handed to us, as some kind of intended comfort. BenMadai looks from the devastation to the cup in his hands. He pours the liquid into the churning sea and looks up to the heavens, crying out, "Alas! Alas! You great city, you mighty city, Babylon! For in a single hour your judgment has come."

Too soon, the enfilade diminishes to a smoldering relic. There are no words among us as we helplessly experience the fall of great Babylon, split apart to commit her demons and beasts of old, to destruction.

"Even so, YHWH saves his people," tells Ayita.

"Even so, Bronzeman comes," mourns BenMadai.

I am startled from the waking vision by my own Jende, who has stood with me through the whole ordeal. She clings to me and sobs aloud, "The prophecy is completed, Babylon, the great, is no more."

Praise Do God,\
ИК

Shared for the benefit of all by the hand of Ilbani the Keeper; redeemed by my Lord, Messiah Yeshua, for His purpose and honor.

The World Standard

Editor in Chief—Jonathan Trimble
Edition II
10-12-4 AE

*Look at what the Supreme Mede offers to all
who want and desire greatness for themselves.*

BABYLON IS TOPPLED

It is a sad and tragic day for those in New Babylon as the Peace Keepers of the Supreme Mede attempted to rescue those suffering under the domination of the Whore. Our military and policy experts had been monitoring the conditions of the noble city, and it became evident that conditions for the beautiful Babylonians had become oppressive. Under the Whore's rule, there were heavy restrictions on trade. People were forced to transact as opposed to allowing the needs of one to be served by the abundance of another. A separation of the wealthy and the poor was clear and no equality could be negotiated.

When these conditions were brought before the Supreme Mede, he wept for the underprivileged. Then, being the great man he is, developed a plan to right the wrong. First the Whore was sternly warned that her methods were not tolerable. It was also discovered that she was concealing some of the cult-criminals we pursue. When no response to our pleas of cooperation were forthcoming, it was reluctantly decided that a physical presence of the Supreme Mede's Peace Keepers would be necessary to ensure equality of all.

Our hard working heroes were sent and were met with resistance, rather than embraced for their mission of mercy, and so the unfortunate battle erupted. Many of our best people were lost in the conflict, but we were victorious. As to the condition of fair Babylon: the destruction was unavoidable, much of it caused before the Whore and her cowardly militia finally surrendered in defeat to the Supreme Mede.

So there is great news that justifies the unfortunate circumstances. The capture of the Whore is especially wonderful, for information can now be extracted from her regarding the Jew and Christ-cults.

One of the sad losses of our victory relates to the Supreme Mede himself. In our last issue, we mentioned the innocent girl known as Roxanne, but kept from you (only for reasons of her security and wellbeing at the time) was that she is the daughter of our beloved leader. It is now thought that she was in Babylon at the time of our peace keeping efforts and is now the captive of the criminal Jews known as Eleazar and Amos BenMadai.

As previously mentioned, anyone who might have knowledge of Roxanne's whereabouts will be richly rewarded. You will recognize her by her natural red hair and the many distinctive painted markings on her arms, face and legs. We are still unable to produce photographs, but your individual reports are of immense help. It was one of these reports of her that made us aware of the terrible conditions in Babylon. The person who made the find now is considered a prince and lives in great wealth.

Efforts to rebuild will be attempted, but resources are limited. We will be assigning work details and the cooperation of all is appreciated in advance as some conscription of laborers will be necessary. The loss of so many of our brave ones offers a new honor to a privileged group of you. We will be recruiting new members to our 666 Ground Force Unit. There is no higher duty and so it is as a lifetime commitment. The opportunity to protect our families by the efforts of this group is not taken lightly and your families in particular will be well compensated for your dedication.

Praise be to the Supreme Mede by whose hand all good happens.

Community Do: *Offer your sympathies to the families of our fallen heroes. Begin preparations to reduce your monthly supplies for it will be necessary to share more with these suffering ones. New volunteers for the 666 Ground Troop Unit will be granted exclusions from these reductions.*

Welcome the Supreme Mede's representatives when they enter your homes. Their duty to redistribute our shared bounty equitably is to the betterment of us all.

As always, we ask your cooperation by alerting us if the whereabouts of the following people are made known to you. Please note that the list has grown larger

Ilabani Midehina Acdah   **Jason Ballard**
(alias The Keeper)
Luther Hine   **Küllo (last name unknown)**
Eleazar BenMadai   **Ki (known as the Freak)**
Amos BenMadai

The hunt for these fugitives is worldwide and so assisting in finding them will be rewarded generously. The Premier's is notorious for his benevolence to those who live his cause.

Letter from Ilbani Midehina Acdah, Keeper of the Kin (in exile)

"The Promised Land always lies on the other side of a wilderness."

—Havelock Ellis

Written to my God—through the intercession of my Savior, Yeshua. For that reason I will not date my posts for the Receiver of my thoughts and prayers will put them to His purpose in His time. Let these words then be for His purpose and to His glory.

We survive well in our new dwelling place; well-hidden caves along the Nahal Arbel near ancient Migdal in the Galilee. God of protection, You suggest to me that there is no reason for me to disguise this information. The letters I write are not meant for the now, but for the later. If we are apprehended, then Mede will obviously already know where we are! And let them come if they dare to try. Your foresight in providing this place is perfect as always.

What day, what time, what season is this? Who is to tell? The shrouded sky, the absence of city schedules, the paceless silence beyond the droning of the wind, no wonder the Patriarchs heard You better out here. What else is there? I am done with keeping time. Others may try, but You, the Greater Being, mock us in our attempt to measure Your plan. Calendars and counting of events is for historians. These define the past, not the future. What I will do instead is listen and, when You beckon, I will obey.

We try not to travel. The paths are absolutely treacherous to hike. When dry, there is always a chance of a rock avalanche, when wet, mudslides come from nowhere. The ground is not to be trusted, and has managed to protect itself with a rarity, vegetation, if you can call it that. These spikey nuisances resemble what used to be called the Spiny Alkanet. These however produce painful welts at just the touch of one of their barbs along the skin. If left untreated, serious infection drains the life of the victim. Ironically, the treatment is within the plant itself.

Prior to her journey to the far-lands, my dear friend, Ayita Blueroad BenMadai mentioned similar plant-life in the frontier of America. She encouraged us to test the medicinal properties of all remaining flora. Lo and behold, this one, though difficult to harvest produces a fluid that reduces fevers and cures many ailments of our new times. It even reverses the effects of the worrisome bacterial infection that has crippled the globe.

And yet, many throughout history have perished from ignorance of this flora's curative properties. We have sent word through discrete channels to Mede, but sadly, he still refuses any discovery, not of his own creation. We have done what we can to distribute the remedy through trusted merchants I know, but as again, the footing even to carry it out of here is unreliable and the risk of capture increases with every contact. You Lord, command to help however we can, so it is a risk we take and pray the results for the afflicted are timely.

Speaking of history, I suppose for those of you who do not know (because you are not from the heavenly realm!), I should document how we came to be in this place. Although the visions through myself, Jende, Ki and others have been recent things, others had been seeing long before us. Omniscient YHWH, You have made it possible. We honor greatly the foresight of those amazing prescients now known as the prophets of scripture; but between the ancient times and now, there have been others. During the 1900s and into the 21st century of the previous age, there were men and women to whom You spoke, warning them of these days, soon coming. Some of them, including of all people, the parents of Fitzgerald E. Hindeland, knew that safe harbors had to be prepared when the need for refuge came. They quietly searched out habitats in nature, knowing that the best hiding places are most often right out in the open.

In the country of Israel, there are two things which set it apart from most other places on the planet. And You, Master of Design, know the first of these things are rocks. There seem to be more rocks in this land than in the rest of the world combined! I joke of course, but one would think the same if they ever had to trek the pathways of Your promised provision to Abraham.

The other unique feature here are its caves. I suspect YHWH, that You took the rocks from the caves to train Your people how to avoid stumbling and also to clear out living spaces for the early settlers and for us now.

The cave system of Eretz Israel is so complex and intertwined, that even the most skilled spelunkers might become lost in them if not careful. Two of those spelunkers, I learned from Fitzgerald, now referred to as the honored Preacher Elijah, were in fact his parents. Being the accomplished scientists and nurturers they were, these two would venture throughout the entirety of the land, taking their son from their home town of Haifa, out on geological camping adventures into the cliff areas. Young Fitzgerald also became quiet adept at surveying the honeycombed corridors and, being gifted with an endemic memory, mapped out his favorite hideaways in his head.

He shared this information with me several years back, before his transformation. When pressure was being placed on the Watchmen to turn over all of the provisions carefully gathered for these hard times, Preacher Elijah and Brother Moses thought it prudent to find a storage location more protected from Mede's GOG goons. Because of my merchant history, I was the natural choice to help in moving the supplies covertly. We actually had to transport the goods in the middle of the night over several weeks' time, and to multiple locations, in order to assure that if one location was discovered, the other might remain secure.

During this procedure, I too became familiar with the cliff-lands and found this canyon place, with its ample supply of food, water and supplies, and its challenging terrain, to be our best chance of remaining undiscovered by the searching eyes of GOG.

I am surprised, Adonai Eloheinu who made the heaven and the earth, that this area remains relatively unscathed. The earthquake activity that continues to jolt the rest of *Tselem Yisrael*—Israel in His image has not been as severe. Thanks be to You, it allows us opportunity for farming and training. In preparation for the anticipated confrontation at Jezreel Megiddo, we have sent spies—perhaps operatives is a better word—into that land 60 kilometers from here to scope out the terrain. But more than spies, by the council of Your Ruach HaKodesh, we have made them historians so they may learn from the many battles of that theater. More wars have been waged at Megiddo throughout history, than at any other place known on the planet. Victor and vanquished, they all suffered great losses. Even armies of great strength collapsed there, being handed defeat by a lesser foe. Why and how did it happen? We study the past to benefit from its lessons.

Our operatives carry with them, certain tools that will also prepare us and them for what lies ahead. It is sly work they perform, and we must be sly for our numbers are so very small compared to our foes.

Of course there is our true advantage—this engagement will not be ours or theirs. Its outcome is already decided by You, the God of the Universe. Your will be done. Bold for me to say? It is my belief, based on my faith in His son who died and rose again for my salvation. If that faith is bold, then so be it! We will obey our King's direction to the death and beyond to new life.

I confess to missing Yerushalayim and its intricacies, but I have had much time here to help with and coordinate plans for the escape of Seconds and Remnants from the clutches of the GOG. And yet in the silence that often covers the night, the Ruach of YHWH whispers to me. *You must return.*

It would be a futile exercise to question Your reasons. Still I pray to understand why we have done all we can, by Your guidance, to escape and avoid the ancient city, only to reinsert ourselves. It will be made clear, no doubt. But what a ticklish thing is waiting and listening to the tease of Your plans.

Praise Do God,
ИК

Shared for the benefit of all by the hand of Ilbani the Keeper; redeemed by my Lord, Messiah Yeshua, for His purpose and honor.

For where jealousy and selfish ambition exist, there will be disorder and every vile practice.

—James 3:16

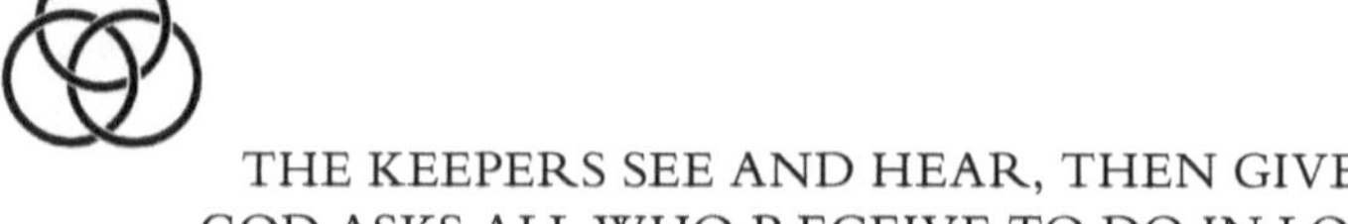

Watching the Un-lit
Month 1, Year Five After Gathering-Up (AG)

Is it that you do not want to see? Or more sadly, could it be that you desire the world to be exactly as it is now? We can offer the warnings. We can provide the evidence of dark things invading. But do you care?

Could it be that you are so removed from holiness that perfect love is a foul thing to be cursed? Do you even understand these words? Are you desperate to consider yourself as good, but fear the mirror that begs the true question…

—Have you become your own enemy?

One sees
One hears
And it is written
Let us work together that the world may know!

—Keepers, for the glory of God

Darius Mede—Chronicle VI: 2-1-5 AE

My charming bitch-wife has been returned to me, and what perfect timing. I have become the hero, rescuing the world from the plight that was that foul city to the east. And now the pressure is off of me somewhat, so that I can focus on the biggest concern at hand. There has been a worldwide outbreak of the same resistant bacterial strain which is causing catastrophic sickness in the Ethiopian and Middle Eastern sectors. I would accept losses of life as inevitable, but this pestilence is not so polite or convenient as to offer death as a solution. The victims are plagued with boils and open sores over their entire body. Even the eyes and mouth are affected and the sense of touch becomes searing pain. The condition is indiscriminate, attacking even those who are highly cautious of their hygiene. How do I know this? Because, I too have become infected; as crucial, my right-hand man, Jonathan Trimble— already severely disfigured after his personal battle with the demon bugs— has also become a walking fester. He (and others, even myself at weakened moments) scream to the touch or when performing simple tasks. It takes all of my higher willpower to even write these words, no drugs dampen the discomfort. The productivity of all peoples is feeble. Food and material production is virtually nil. Thus, global starvation and decay of the great work which I have built, is at hand unless something is done.

Another minor inconvenience is that the infection plagues my clone army. Although replaceable, the time for replication is wasteful when more important matters are at hand. Though they do not seem to suffer as we do, they might be infectors of the population. As a matter of fact, I am beginning to think they may be the original carriers of the problem.

So far there is no cure and so I work through the anguish to seek a solution by the only means I know: a chemical remedy combined with DNA alteration to eradicate the ill effects. I have been in desperate need of subjects who have shown resistance. So what does this have to do with the Green Witch?

It seems the population of the once proud Babylon, for whatever reason: diet, environment, genetics or some secret cure, demonstrated no signs of the infection! I had to discover their invincibility. The non-compliance of their leaders to my rule of government made for a convenient excuse to invade and subdue. I've been needing a test subject for my vaccination trials and who would have known that the Whore would be the perfect one!

Of course I did not want other provinces to think I was playing the cruel dictator so I had Trimble, in the midst of his own pain, conceive a media campaign that impressed the notion of our motives being strictly humanitarian in nature. His finely written newsletters, posted worldwide on the Do Boards in the now common and required New-Roma language (all instituted by my own clever devising), have resulted in changing opinions. Subtly, but swiftly, the populations of most provinces are responding to our Do commands. And so my power over the masses and my eyes searching for, and rubbing out the rebellious ones ever increases. The next step then is to seal my authority by perfecting a cure to permanently eradicate the curse of the bacterial plague. Let us see how the Steeple People react to that miracle!

I might end the conflict with the Jewish and Christian conspirators so quickly, if only I can locate and sequester their stores of food and supplies. As with any hidden gang, they cannot last long without provisions and I have set my mind on starving them out.

But out of where? After our campaign at Babylon, the escapees from there were reported to have come this direction—how bold to advance on your enemy in your retreat! And I waited covertly for them, watching without appearing to have ill intent even announcing our mercy and willingness to offer clemency to those poor, poor souls (thank you Jonathan for your clever ploy).

Was I too clever? I think not, yet they did not arrive as predicted. Somewhere in the dessert region, between Babylon and Jerusalem, they disappeared from my sight. In fact, while I had my eyes trained on the east, small groups of those same sects that I had been monitoring here in the capital, also slipped away. Several of my administrative lackeys lost more than a little skin due to their ineptitude in that slip-up.

Now they are all gone and I must pull the rope very tight indeed to gather them in. I am convinced that in their quick flight, they could not have moved the vast stores and food they had accumulated early on by the conniving efforts of Moses Folzman and Fitzgerald Hindeland. They had worked in proxy with the local agrarians to rob the land of its produce. I had rightfully commanded the goods to be shared with all of society and I had been more than willing to be the magnanimous distributor of the cache.

"No, no," they said. They had the gall to refuse me and to claim that they had the better methods of provision. Now those two are done for good and their secret stash seems to have floated up with them to some puffy cloud, for I have not been able to locate it here.

I know it is within the city walls. It has to be. And my Palisti Police will tear into every ancient alleyway and cove to find it. The world deserves those resources and I will be their benefactor. Doubt me not on this.

As for the rag-tag army of refugees that must now be wanting that same food for their survival? Let them eat sand. I will locate them as well and they will have wished they had starved when we meet again.

We have succeeded! The magistrates of the world are placated and we have found hope for eliminating the pathogen. I have been working diligently on the solution which involves injecting a small amount of the bacteria, combined with blood from the involuntary subject, into an infected individual. The results are promising, but there is still a hurdle to overcome. Most of the victims become worse because the bacteria seem to strengthen in their bodies, developing a defensive reaction. Much like the condition of leprosy, their body appendages; arms, legs, ears…even eyes and lips and tongues; begin a melting process. What is left is not pleasant; worse than the original malady if that can be imagined.

I struggle to focus, but I must, if for no other reason than for my own suffering. The people of the world need a strong leader and I am that man. I must not disappoint my own purpose.

For now I must rest from this writing, the effort takes away from the time spent on the cure.

Bucastan is but one example of the niggling Christian cultist problem which continues to interfere with my plans. They refuse to bow down to progress and somehow, the word of their counter-culture ideas is spreading. Other towns and villages, not only in Old Europe, but also Eurasia, the Middle East, China, even the Americas (what is left of them), report growing numbers of the blue-plight. Their beliefs tell them that there is only one hope and it is not me. The stupidity of it continues to vex me. After all, my desire is only to restore order to the world and improve its condition. Why do they resist my kindness? I might even allow them to continue their whimsical religious practices, at least for a time, if it would lead to a compromise whereby we can all work toward the same goal. Surely they would listen to that reasoning.

But they will not! I have tried and they have failed to acquiesce, the fools. Now I must take even more drastic action. I am dedicating more resources toward the apprehension of their leaders; particularly, the writer, Küllo. Not that he is anything special, except that his work is seemingly everywhere. My loyal subjects and spies report that the pathetic news rag he produces is more vastly distributed than Trimble's marvelous bulletins. I am told that the drivel is often times posted over top of my Do commands and communications on our own Do Boards. Insolence! It must be stopped.

And so it shall be. As I research methods for combating the biological pestilence continuing to spread through the world, I have come upon interesting compounds that affect stone, wood and metal all alike, dissolving them, like heat applied to chocolate (Oh how I miss that delicacy!). This would render any barrier, even my own FlexSteel, defenseless against my force's entry.

And how do I know Flexsteel to be destroyable by my new prescription? Intense laboratory time, even while I suffer from my maladies. Hydrofluoric Acid is of course, the building block for my weaponry. It not only eats through most other substances, but it is also highly toxic to the eyes and lungs of anyone who comes near it. There lies one of its challenges. Upon dispersal, a wise person would be a far distant observer.

For that matter, how can HA be safely stored and transported? It is extremely unstable. I have found the simple answer: a protective inner coating of polyethylene inside the canisters, carry it safely to the point of release. Where can such quantities of this polymer be acquired? Ha! It is so simple. The landfills from the previous age contain vast amounts. Simply put, the plastic baggies once used in every household are the perfect protectors for my lethal mix.

Then came the true paradox which resulted from the question, *how to release the weapon?* The answer was so twisted that I could not stop laughing when I discovered it. The very bacteria that attacks us internally, also reacts destructively with plastic. One dose of the pathogen, injected into a canister of Hydrofluoric Acid, protected by the polyethylene, results in a complete melting of the container and anything within a two meter radius.

But this process would be ineffective on a battlefield where one must hurt the enemy from a distance. I found the way. The bacteria that harms us, appears to be born from microbes that thrive in a volcanic environment. As a side note, I believe that the planet's seismic destabilization and resulting lava flows has become the very breeding ground of our biotic nemesis. This hardy germ which I have named Acholeplama Magnumus is amazingly resistant to alcohol and petroleum compounds. Therefore, after many trials and errors, I have successfully infused equal portions of methanol and the AM bacilli.

Introducing a small portion of this compound into a FlexSteel chamber containing one of my plastic pouches of Hydrofluoric Acid causes a healthy explosive reaction that sends the deadly mix out in a much broader radius. I have not yet developed a cannon or rifle with the complexity necessary to combine and shoot the stuff reliably, but I have come up with a reasonable distribution solution for the time being and have tested it. Part of my victory in Babylon was due to the testing of this method and it will soon be improved due to that experiment.

More research remains in order to expand my plan. Babylon was only a minimal trial. How do I produce the necessary volume of these compounds, the storage and triggering devices? The time and materials required to concoct the acid alone are significant.

These are simply formulas to be solved and calculations to be figured. Such is life—production and application have always been worthy contests for the human brain to tackle.

Once all the intricacies have been solved, I must decide on a place to test my theory—it must be a location that will serve as both an example and that will provide a strategic victory. I believe I have just the place in mind, however there is much more to do prior to implementation.

All this is to say that I have once again proven science to be the perfect god whose results do not deceive. Let that be the lesson to those who oppose my methods. I dare them to withstand such truth.

I would rather focus on the positive than the negative. Jonathan Trimble encourages me in this practice daily and, as drained as I am by disease, I will prevail in that attitude.

I have found the fault and why the effort, using the Whore's blood for a vaccine, failed! I should have thought of it before. It is not a matter of harvesting blood, but letting the host fight the battle. Instead of drawing plasma, I injected the bacteria directly into her blood stream. The reaction was violent to be sure, her screams being louder than any others, but after a relatively short time, her struggling stopped and the precious fluid was drawn. I almost feel sorry for her, but then again, she has always been driven to save the planet and here she is, doing just that.

I tried the new serum on a number of infected individuals. Several became worse, but after adjustments in the amount of serum injected, I found the balance. The true test would come when I had to choose a valued colleague to save. Jonathan Trimble, loyal subject that he is, immediately volunteered and was rid of the bacterial attack. Unfortunately, there was nothing to be done for his already hideous appearance, but at least now he functions without pain.

There was only one more thing to do. I risked self-injection and, though I too am now physically misshapen, the disease is defeated in me! I have begun trials on other captured Babylon inhabitants and their blood appears just as effective.

Another delicious irony: I have been deliberating over how to share my blessing of the bacteria cure with the world's population. How can we provide the means to transport and keep the product fresh and then, most important, provide the means of injection into the blood stream? Transportation has been handled fairly well because the ships captains and overland merchants are more than eager to get the cure out. They cannot sell to those too sick to buy.

I have developed a way, using small Flexsteel ampules to seal each dose air tight. Something about the composition of Flexsteel allows it to maintain a constant temperature even in extreme conditions. A happy accident to be sure, though my loyal subjects are eager to pay me tribute for the benefit.

I must admit it was Jonathan Trimble though, who solved the greatest problem. He and I were out monitoring a vaccination facility. We were discussing the potential of reusing injection needles with syringes, even though neither had been properly re-sterilized. Would another worse infection be born of such clumsy actions? Finally, in his crazy impatient way, Trimble walked up to the injection table, grabbed a vile of vaccine and walked over to one random man in the long line waiting for relief. Trimble opened the vile and handed it to the man saying, "Drink this."

The man looked extremely puzzled, but then looked over and saw my emblem on my leathers. He suddenly realized he was in the presence of royalty and immediately kneeled. He tore off his mask, even at the risk of a bug attack and quickly downed the bloody concoction.

He choked a few times, but recovered and was about to replace his mask when I noticed the skin changing on his face. A large festering welt was on his right cheek. The eye on the same side of his face was a milky green color. But within moments, the welt started to change color and I could see clearing in his eye. The man knew something was happening too. He looked directly at me and smiled, then shouted, "It works! I am freed by drinking the blood of Mede!

The crowd reacted immediately by starting to charge the tables, but Trimble saved the day by raising his own still strong voice. "Stop and be orderly. You do not want to anger the Supreme Mede and risk that he will cause some other plague to consume you!

The crowd hesitated and then reformed a line with not much effort. The medical people acted quickly as well, making sure the ampules were distributed rapidly to the impatient crowd. All were careful as they passed to acknowledge my presence—I confess to a certain satisfaction at their idolization. After all, I have worked hard to produce this result for them. What is wrong with a little worship presented to one who is deserving of it? And now the Do can begin. It is simply a matter really when thought through, and the masses will worship as they choose.

And if this record of my accomplishments is ever released to be written into history, let me expound my ironic delight mentioned at the beginning of this entry. Thousands of years ago, a radical cult leader actually led people to a belief that his blood was a healing agent that would save them spiritually. He even encouraged his followers to drink wine as a symbol of that blood on a regular basis. Some even came to believe the wine turned into blood, if properly blessed!

I, on the other hand, actually do offer blood that will heal in the physical world— A real tangible healing of an immediate nature.

I leave it to the reader to decide who is the real savior!

The World Standard

Editor in Chief—Jonathan Trimble
Edition III
2-4-5 AE

*Look at what the Supreme Mede offers to all who
want and desire greatness for themselves.*

YOU ARE BETTER!

The Hunt Continues for those responsible for the insurrection against our fair Father Mede. They continue to disrupt and run as cowards do. But they do little damage and we do much good for the world even as they try to disrupt communities.

We have heard they are trying to spread their lies inviting themselves into communities and offering to do favors. It is a ploy only. If they win over a group they immediately begin relations with the women in hopes of producing children that will further their cause. It is a despicable practice and our leader urges you to resist and report the rascals.

Meanwhile, food and shelter for all is promised to continue. The medical issues, the draughts, strange weather and geological conditions continue to be worked out and soon you should see relief.

Therefore do you see how your Ruler is acting on your behalf? Serve him in gratitude!

Praise be to the Supreme Mede by whose hand all good happens.

Community Do: *Continue to share your monthly supplies as we all must. New volunteers for the 666 Ground Troop Unit continue to be granted exclusions from these reductions.*

Make sure to provide for Supreme Mede's representatives when they enter your homes, anything that they ask of you. They are your protectors and you should honor them with all you have.

As always, we ask your cooperation by alerting us if the whereabouts of the following people are made known to you. Please note that the list has grown larger.

Ilabani Midehina Acdah (alias The Keeper)	**Jason Ballard**
Luther Hine	**Küllo (last name unknown)**
Eleazar BenMadai	**Ki (known as the Freak)**
Amos BenMadai	

The Bronzeman News

מָשִׁיחַ WATCH AND KEEP מָשִׁיחַ

My name be Küllo, that be all ye need to know about me. I be not the story—I be the eyes, ears and hands of these tales. The words on these pages will be news-tells from common folk. Folk like ye and me. Them will tell their story and I will copy it with as little cleaning up as possible, so that all who are left after the Gathering-Up will see what be happening: The Bronzeman be appearing and the seeings of him are much the same. What be different be what he tells each one to Do.

MINGLE IT. MAKE UP YER OWN MIND, I WILL NOT MAKE IT FOR YE.

Edition Six: Rio de Janeiro
Month 10, Year 5 After the Gathering-Up

Küllo's Notes: The journey from Babylon has been harsh and has covered incredible distance. Yet we have mingled with great believers. Our Do destination be still guarded, but in preparing for that greater place, we have passed through many incredible locations. Of course Egypt had to be reached first. With Tehran destroyed by volcanic bombardment, there was no safe overland route to the east and our hasty escape made the city Aswan, the closest place by ship. There, provisions and known Seconds who might help us would be found. We learned that, afore the great spreading out of the Mediterranean Sea, the Coptic Seconds of Alexandria were warned by dreams from Bronzeman to run south, and they obeyed. They followed the great river to its dessert point in the land once known as Sheba. When the waters rose, they found themselves again on the coast, and in a good place to trade and provide. I mingle it as Bronzeman's Do that they now dwell here in a land long ago famous for its merchants and wealth.

The Coptic Seconds are like all of us. Many of their family members were Gathered-Up, but there are a good number who had been so mingled in defining and Doing the law of their beliefs, that they failed to hear the need for tight mingling with Bronzeman. I cry inside and out for these un-gathered. They now all appear to understand the desire of their Savior to be more than a pretty picture figure to each one of them. I saw the same happen in my home place and now live with that same sadness for my birth-town. Praise to Bronzeman that he be the God of Second chances. We can all still be saved by his grace.

Our Coptic kin gave us all that we needed for our extended journey, including maps. They are mighty sailors in the treacherous waters of the world. They have carefully noted the changes of geography that have reshaped all we knew to be and have helped us avoid many perils. For example, we hoped to travel first to BJ's home in Ethiopia, then to Southern Africa, especially Zimbabwe, the birthplace of Keeper Jende, and then over the ocean to India. But we were warned that Africa, the great continent admired by all for her vast and wild beauty, be reduced by over half its size. Its southern places are no more and what be left be mostly a smoking crater. What be more, India and the East Asian islands still suffer from atmospheric poisoning brought on by the meteors that smashed them places.

We spend days mourning the losses, and comfort our clan whose families disappeared in the destruction. I mingle I no longer need to keep the secret of my Minder's origin or identity. There are none of his people left to protect. I proudly consider him my family, my best brother who be now safely called Black Jackson. Still, "BJ" be a fun way to call him.

No-one dare sail the Pacific ocean, renamed *Infernos*. We are telled that lava erupts in the middle of the sea and that waves of red hot water promise no return for most who have tried. Australia and New Zealand are nothing but volcanic pumps spewing their own poisonous fumes — refugees who escaped early on have shown up in Aswan and prove the point. Their look be like Trimble or worse.

Our attempt to deliver supplies to these areas was simply not God's Do for us. Along the way, we hear tell of more and more seeings of Bronzeman and we meet newly testified Seconds on almost a daily basis. I hesitate to tell how we know one another as Seconds. It should remain a secret to protect our kin. But we do know, even when fully covered in leathers; that be solid ground. The struggle be still to stay ahead of the Pounders who always seem to chase our Blue.

As we increase the distance from Jerusalem I have become more and more involved in Ki's and Jende's visions. I watch and hear things that puzzle me much. The brain-pictures and sounds are from strange lands with stranger people. All of them look to be Remnants, but the banners on their leathers tell that they are from elsewhere. Their language be unfamiliar to me and they seem to be searching for me, pleading with me to find them.

In the real, I pace the ship, the pictures of my inside eye are almost better, there be nothing but waves and dark grey clouds to watch. But I should be careful in complaining. Bronzeman listens to that too.

I am alone on my walk and begin to turn a corner on the deck, but hesitate, hearing weeping of a known voice. Ayita! She be the strong one on board, I do not mingle well with the sound of her sadness. My heart be ripped by it. She enters into conversation with, I don't mingle who…

> "—It's been so long. I can't look at your faces or touch your hands. There is no laughter, not real laughter without you. Why does God need me here when I should be wife and mother there, with you? I know His purpose is most important, but I can't stop longing for all of you, for each of you. Remember when we would all gather under covers on a cold night, making up silly stories that would make sweet Fizina giggle with that special tiny trill of hers. I can almost smell the breath of her joy and taste your kiss to my lips. God, please help me to see my family again if it is Your will."

I un-puzzle who she be talking of now and feel like I have stepped into a secret that I should not be sharing. I would not write it, but Bronzeman says, "Do," and tells why. He says that all of us have purpose greater than our own mingling. He says he will take these tears away someday, but they are the water of the now, to grow a more beautiful garden later, so the tears must come and we must share them.

I want to love my sister Ayita, I want to help her in the now, but in what way? And the answer tells loud in me. Jende gives us a picture and Ki opens our ears. I see and hear it, and without doubt, Ayita sees and hears it too for I hear her gasp, "Oh!"

There in front of me be young Fizina playing with the other children of our clan-in-hiding. There are giggling noises and shouts of excitement as they run in a game of tag. Sabra Rachel Hine supervises the activity and it be with pleasure that I notice her belly, which suggests she be with child again. Luther has been busy during our travels and his wife's smile tells their happiness. I am smiling too, just by the seeing. I reach out with a hand to touch the untouchable.

To the side Eleazar sits cross-legged on a rock ledge, watching and smiling. In his hand be a piece of paper that looks worn from folding and unfolding, many times. On the paper be the hand-scripting of Ayita, I have seen it and mingled it afore. The note be simple, full of love,

> I left this note in your pocket before we were separated, knowing you might want to stop me from this traveling if you first read it. We both knew and chose these missions, but that does not make them easy. My love for you will deepen with every mile that separates us and every one that I pray will bring us back together. You must love Fizina, both as father and as mother—I know it will not be easy, you are so strong, but you must learn gentleness also, for her…for me.
>
> I touch you now in my heart and I feel you touching me. I am warmed by it, even in this chilled world without your presence. Do not lose hope and know that He will complete His work in us.
>
> —Ayita

From our inside eye, by the kindness of YHWH and the gift of Jende, Ayita and I see Eleazar refold the parchment and return it safely to the pocket over his heart. We see him gaze over at his daughter and we watch as new water from the husband's eyes water the garden which Bronzeman be preparing for us all. Then the man stands and walks over with open arms to receive his girl who runs to the love. Eleazar speaks words that cause Ayita and me to also water the garden. "I have heard from your mother, she misses you and will return as soon as she is able. She loves you so much. Can we say a prayer together for her? And then let me teach you another game that she taught to me."

With that, the father takes the daughter's hand and they sit. The man pulls a pouch of glass stones from another pocket and shows each to her. "These are called marbles. There is a way to throw them into a circle that we can draw on the ground. They can teach you how other people think and do things—by how they throw their marbles…"

—I do not need to see Ayita's comfort, it be my comfort, our joy, mingled in this special way. I turn and walk back the direction for which I came, no longer looking to the waves and the sky, but to the horizon that connects us all.

After giving images and voices, Ki and Jende are head-sick for days. In a selfish way I be glad when the visions are paused. My whole body aches when the pictures play. But when they are gone, I find that I miss them. It makes no sense.

And then comes the worst image of all. Babylon in flames, a smoldering ruin. Even the smell of death be given, but praise Bronzeman, for the see and hear of our kin's narrow escape. We know that the Pounders will track us to these parts for certain. We cannot risk the lives of these beautiful people, so we make a loud tell of our leaving, even sending rumors out by pigeon that we are being chased away. We pray this will convince the Pretender's forces that we were not staying but moving.

As we set sail for our next destination I be given a comforting brain-picture—Han Ko, from my home. She be cooking on her wood plank grill and she speaks words that kindle my fire. "You are scripting good. The Word grows and Bronzeman is smiling at you."

My friend who prints the precious papers for me looks well from the view of my inside eye. I still worry for her safety, but I know she has chosen this Do and be risk-willing. On our ship, I stare into the ocean and realize how many kilometers I have traveled, how many kilometers separate us and I ask Bronzeman to find a way to someday take me back to my birthplace once more when he be done with me.

A cool breeze touches my face and I know it be his whisper, telling me, "I love you and will not fail you." What a puzzle. I had just been mingling that I was the one who desired not to fail him.

It has taken over a month to steam the Atlantic, water and more water, storms from nowhere going to nowhere. It makes me mingle the stories I have been reading in Preacher Elijah's Bible. Jesus was on the water with his disciples and the waves are tossing them. He be sleeping! They have to wake him up to tell the danger and he reacts strangely, saying in his own way, "What trouble? There be no trouble here." Then he tells the wind and the waves to behave—and they Do! I knew we might have been drowned-down on our journey, but even with that fear I had a powerful thought that Bronzeman would Do what was needed to get us here.

Where be here? Brazilia, a place I always thought of as a jungle. But it now be cold—Slavonia cold. The captain of our ship warned us that the world was crazy mixed up in weather and that we would need winter coverings. He was right and BJ calls our parkas a "big-shout blessing".

Somehow after months at sea, the captain of this ship has found Rio. We steam to port, but discover that we have to anchor offshore due to ice buildup. I have never walked on the ocean afore and I can say it be not something I mingle to do again. We are greeted by locals who lead us inland. They explain that the land once known as Peru, Bolivia, and parts of Chile and Argentina sank into the ocean during numerous earthquakes. To the north, Venezuela and Guyana were bombarded by a combination of large meteors and a strange type of fungus that floats through the air. It be highly poisonous to breathe in and no word comes from that region any longer. Most of once was called Central America; Columbia, Panama, Nicaragua and Guatemala exist, it be a sure thing. Merchants from them areas sail around the poisonous areas, arriving here to barter much needed supplies in trade for the great mineral treasures found in this place—gold, copper, zinc and other metals readily dug out by them that are brave enough and know the locations.

I had been told of the magnificent statue of Jesus on earth, afore he became Bronzeman. I be blown that it be still standing. It be afore me now on the only mountain in the land, still to be found. I stare at it for long moments. I puzzle at how it can continue with all the changes of nature. There be ice and snow surrounding it, but the statue be unfrosted. It stays white as it has always been and that makes me puzzle. In my brain, Bronzeman be golden and fiery, ready to lead us against an enemy. This monument seems calm and inviting with arms reached out in love. Both images are good, each solid ground. Who but God, could be both?

Brazilia: The streets are empty. The ship's crew, who have been here afore warn us to stay together. This be an unpredictable place we have come to. I puzzle if any place besides Jerusalem can be mingled as friendly, and even there…the Mede wants to snuff our lights.

What craziness be this? Cold, but with the bugs, the Un-lits and Red-lits wear leathers and though many kilometers separate us from the Pounders, we are still encouraged to wear coverings to hide our Blue. There be a price on our heads and there be no reason to attract attention.

Ilbani the Keeper told of one who was called here. He says the man be one of the original Seconds and has traveled the world to tell of Bronzeman. I can't mingle him by the Keeper's description and look forward to meeting him to hear his tell. The Keeper warned me though, that though this one speaks New-Roma, he has an accent that makes him sound like he was popped out on this planet from some crazier place. "Worse than Roxanne's drawl?" I asked.

"Oh yes," he laughed. The ship's crew tells of meeting the man too, and they say he be "All Bronze News", but that we should be all "ears careful" when trying to mingle his tongue.

The knowing that there are no Pounders here be very Bronze news and so our alertness can be focused toward our quest. Here we have been approached by a remarkable thing. People will walk up to us and pull from their keepsacks, five wooden sticks. In front of us, they assemble the sticks as I had done many times myself. The news has spread, and this has become the kin-greeting of Seconds. It also allows all Seconds, a simple way to explain the message of Bronzeman to them that have not heard.

We are talking with a Second who has just *made the five* when another man walks out of a near building, taking off his head covering as he approaches us. He be one of the Bluest I have ever seen.

"Well there y'all are, praise Jasus."

I have no mingling of what the stranger just said, but Ayita and Roxanne grab onto him and hug him while yelling, "Jason, we've missed you so much."

This can be no other—Jason Ballard, the warrior.

Now that we are inside, we take off our parkas and Jason builds a bigger fire, using wood he has stored in another room. "Ah share as much 'o this as Ah can, but if'n Ah don't hide some of it, the whole town would be banging the door down."

I'm mingling his accent better and can follow what he says. It be a chuckle though, I have noticed that, since reuniting with Jason, Roxanne, also from the South-South region of the old United States, has increased her accent.

"What's happened to your clan from afar?" She drawls.

Jason puzzles for a moment afore he tells, "As most of y'all know, Ah had to scurry out of Scandinavia when Crazy Trimble got back in cahoots with Duffus Darius. Mede's weird-goon army had already caught Baby Ben, Fielder and Pavoli 'fore we could rescue them…"

The muscled man can't help but start watering the garden with his eyes. Ayita, Roxanne, all of us also start watering too, acause these names and their amazing tells are known well to us. Another woman who holds a young child starts singing one of the saddest, yet sweetest songs I have ever mingled:

> Be still, my soul: the Lord is on thy side;
> Bear patiently the cross of grief for pain;
> Leave to thy God to order and provide;
> In every change He faithful will remain.
> Be still, my soul; thy best, thy heavenly, Friend
> Through thorny ways leads to a joyful end.

Ayita leans over to me and whispers, "LaShandra, Pavoli's widow." Then the Cherokee goes over to the mother and holds her as only another mother can. We all offer prayers of remembering and then Jason be settled enough to tell on.

"—Ah had to try to protect the rest of the clan and Ilbani suggested we skedaddle on over here to set things up for ya."

When he said, "ya," Jason looked right at me. I be most puzzled acause we have not mingled, and at the time he was telling about, I had not even surrendered to Bronzeman. How could he and Ilbani have mingled that I would come here?

It be Ki who speaks in my head. "Just because you're stuck in time, Norther, doesn't mean that Bronzeman is."

And she be right. My God was, be and be coming. He be God and can be anywhere He wants. Any time He wants. Of course He would know today would come and would have planned perfectly for it.

"Ah think ya might want to be careful how much ya write about what ya came here for. " Jason tells me. "Let's make it a surprise ending, in case anyone who thinks they might be important is actually reading your paper."

I mingle his words as being solid ground and so we start making plans to contact the ones we have come to talk to. Jason says he knows of many locations we must trek to. The ones we seek don't mingle well with outsiders and tend to stay to themselves in small isolated groups.

"We'd best be careful when we go out. Ah know we got protection, but there's more Un-lit and Red-lit than there are of us." Jason has been chewing on something in his mouth and now spits it into a copper bowl on the floor. It would not be tobacco, that would not grow here—then what? Tree bark? They be rare. Animal hide? I'm very distracted by the action, but his words brick me. I don't often feel comfortable mingling my thoughts out loud around others, especially in a language that be not mine from birth. But something nags at me and I have to speak it out.

"Didn't Elijah once say to not be afraid acause them that are with us are greater than them that are with our enemies? I mingle that 'greater' means stronger in spirit, so should we not Do that way?"

I be not used to people staring at me, but they are staring now and I want to be somewhere else. Then a picture comes to me from Jende, far away. It be a simple picture of her smiling. Again Ki speaks into my head. "Well, you have their attention, now what?"

Looking around the room, I see everyone smiling now and nodding What happens next puzzles me more than most all things afore. Jason gets up off the floor and comes to me. He holds his hand down to me, inviting me to grasp it. I do and he pulls me up like a lion nudging a lamb to stand. Once I be on my feet, he keeps my hand in his and says, "Sorry bro, you're absotively right. I spoke words of fear and yours are words of right. Ya lead and we'll follow."

I struggle to get my mouth working. One of the greatest new age Seconds has just put me in charge…of something. But, what? I blurt out, "I be not the leader. Bronzeman be our leader. He tells and I go, that be all. If ye want to follow him, I will follow with ye."

"Best answer ever, Norther," says Ki in my head, and everybody nods.

The next months are spent seeking out the *Others*, I have to call this group something, without telling our purpose. We have sent out coded letters to leaders of these people and Ayita has helped me with suggested words they will respond to. We are told that there are clans of the Others that are spread from the most south parts of this land, up to what be left of the once Great North. My hand be cramped from all of the special scribbling I have had to do. This large family prefers to be private, and like our clan, guard their whereabouts. We have started visiting the local groups and many times, the meeting locations we are sent to are just tests to make sure we have not been followed.

As this be happening, the world comes apart around us. We hear tell of awful things. The bacteria had stopped spreading when people started drinking Mede's blood, but then something happened inside the stomachs of the victims that now will not let food stay. People eat and eat, but they cannot keep anything from passing right through. How can people be starving with a full belly? It happens afore our eyes. I have seen Brazilians gorging themselves as they trudge down the cold streets and suddenly, fall to the ground, never to stand again. Other diseases steal the minds of the sick and death takes more out of the world than life can bring in.

Fire rains from the sky in some places, the earth still swallows whole towns and villages and the bugs have become even more vicious. I would mingle the stories impossible to believe, if survivors from other places did not continue to stream here displaying injuries that testify to their truth.

As careful as we are, the agents of Pretender Mede still hunt us. Not Pounders or Peacers, these bounty hunters want profit for our skins. A group, including, my own self, Black Jackson, Jason and two of the Others are heading for a secret place when BJ stops in the middle of the road.

"I can't stop them," he tells, looking back where we have come from. My Minder has a special gift, not like Ki's voice, Jende's eyes or Ayita's healing touch; but as powerful. As we have traveled, I've seen him use it many times, although it be not easily understood. He can know when no-believers are chasing Blue and…there be no better way to tell it…he can change their minds. In Bucastan and Jerusalem, I saw him do this much. A Peacer or a Pounder would somehow find out one of us was a Second and would start walking our way. Black Jackson would stop, as he be doing now, and he would cause them to walk by with a look of confusion on their face. Sometimes he might say something as they walked by, like, "They got away," but mostly he would just let them keep walking until they were out of our sight and then he would rush our group to a hiding place.

Only one other time have I known him to say he could not stop the hunters. It was when we were escaping through the alley roads Jerusalem. We did not know then, and we don't know now how these ones are able to shut out his mind changing, but they can. In Jerusalem, the problem was solved by the strange voice that came out of Ki—strange acause it was not her voice. The voice in Jerusalem only said one thing…

"—Sleep."

Wait, that was spoken just now, and not in a whisper. It was a command from someone in our group. Not just any someone, it be Jason.! I look beyond where BJ be staring, and two bodies slump to the ground. They had been tracking us from a distance and had not been seen until right now. The voice be the same, the results happening be the same, but how can that be? Jason was nowhere close to us in Jerusalem when the sleep was put on our chasers. I'm try to un-puzzle this as Black Jackson and Jason hurry us down another street and into a safe place. The Others come with us, but afore they come inside, they take off their ponchos and use them to sweep the street to disguise our footprints in the snow.

Soon enough, they are in, the door be closed, and it be a good thing, for we hear footsteps a moment later. The bounty-chasers run on past without stopping to check the door. We listen as their footfalls grow quite with distance. Then I can't help but ask Jason the question. "How?"

"It started happening, when Ah lost my wife, Betty—when Crazy Trimble shot her. That was the first time I spoke commands into people and it has come in a might handy since. I don't know how it works and it doesn't always work, just when the Voice says, 'this time,' Ah guess. I have to be real careful with it 'cause a word of power can be real permanent. Ah don't like the thought of doing something that messes someone up permanently.

"Sometimes it happens right in front of me and sometimes Ah get a message…a picture in my head or a voice like what happened with Ki. I just knew y'all needed help in Jerusalem, so Ah just spoke, or speak like now. God does the rest."

With the protection of both BJ and Jason, we are able to safely contact all the Others and share our plan. It fits right in with their ideas and so they agree to travel with us. That part will be the challenge acause, according to their clan leaders, there are over 12,000 of them in this area and we will be walking for long-long moments, months and more. It will be hard to move fast, and easy for chasers to track us.

"We gotta believe God's got our backs on this one," Jason tells.

Call-out and Do: I call-out to the readers of this news-tell: Please pray for all people, even for them that still refuse to be eyes-open to Bronzeman's solid ground. We ask a special praying from ye to our own selves—walk in yer hearts with us. Do what ye are called-out to and we will be praying for ye also—mingling the will of YHWH be done. In the name of the Soon-Returning: Bronzeman, our King and Priest.

Special Do: It be dangerous everywhere for ye, but running somewhere else will not help. Stay put on yer knees. Yer house will be ready for ye when Bronzeman says it be ready. Wait on the trumpet.

Letter from Ilbani Midehina Acdah, Keeper of the Kin (Nahal Arbel)

"While there is life, there is hope."

—Marcus Tullius Cicero

Written to my God—through the intercession of my Savior, Yeshua. For that reason I will not date my posts for the Receiver of my thoughts and prayers will put them to His purpose in His time. Let these words then be for His purpose and to His glory.

I am still reeling from my most recent dream, Comforter. I was reminded how small I am when, in the night, a frightening being stood at the foot of my bed. Jende was away, providing comfort to a friend, so I was the only witness to the event. It is best—I do not know that I would want to subject anyone else to the encounter. The being was huge in the room. Our apartment has ceilings nearly four meters in height and my visitor's head was just below its threshold. I say head, but to explain that creature in human terms is not adequate. The eyes of it seemed to move about the whole face and to the back of the head. It must have amazing visual abilities. Six wings, two nearer the head, two additional on its back and two closer to what I would call legs (though they were more inverted so the knees bent backwards, like a bird's!).

The creature was blindingly bright, not bronze in color as many now describe you Lord Yeshua, not blue like our Seconds. This shimmering is more silver, like armor. I felt I dare not speak in its presence, but it held no such reservation.

"Prepare," it thundered and every bone in my body vibrated. "Your kin must ready for the battle ahead to join with the Remnant, once they choose obedience."

I wonder why all of the other people in our home; my children and friends, had not rushed in to see about the explosive nature of the noise. Perhaps they had been taken to the next life…perhaps I was in the next life. A panicked question suddenly formed in my brain. I am not sure if I spoke it, but I could hear my voice daring to address the creature. "Lord, how is it that you want me to prepare?"

"I am not your Lord! There is one far greater that I serve; that you also serve." The reply was more powerful and does nothing to help my urge to urinate my fears out. "I am called Michael. You will gather the Remnant and your kin will teach them."

The archangel was gone as quickly as it appeared. I knew it to be an angel because of my study of the scriptures. What I had not known, until the explanation, was that I had been addressed by the one known in the Bible as the spiritual dragon slayer in the Book of Revelation. What is now more unsettling is that I am to somehow teach the Remnant that are gathering to Eleazar. What am I to say to them, Master? What instruction can I offer?

But offer I will. You, my Lord, have been faithful in all things, so I do not doubt you will provide me with the answers I will need to serve your purpose. And so I must leave this safe, if shaky asylum to find the gathering place of the Remnants and guide them back again. YHWH, give me eyes to see! Then again, how hard can it possibly be to camouflage a clan of nearly 120,000 Hebrew servants?

The Keepers will help guide me in my coming travels and, as well, they currently inform me of the progress in the Americas. Küllo and Jason have done an amazing thing! Over the course of 10 moon cycles, under the harshest conditions, they have already identified and met with over 12,000 of the Others and have cleverly escaped a dragnet of bounty hunters sent to…what is the crude term now used by Mede's minions…"snuff them out". Imagine trying to move so many people undetected, especially in a frozen wilderness with limited provisions and shelter.

Oh and Lord, let me not fail to affirm that I have received the vision of Ayita, who has also done an amazing thing! The picture of it that Jende and Ki have played in my mind, must be shared. I know You have no need of hearing the story, but I believe You desire to hear how it has impacted me. So, I share its power in this letter:

Seven months into their Rio mission, several of our America journeyers can hear the familiar peaceful chanting of our Cherokee princess. She is in the room that Jason kindly set up for her and Ki to share privacy and to be prepared for when Ayita's moment came. Küllo, Jason, and BJ are in the main living area of their shared quarters when a pounding on the front door is heard over the bitterly cold storm that rages outside.

The men are all confused by the racket, trying to reconcile why there would be anyone at the door during a blizzard such as this. Küllo is the one to rise from the floor and go to the portal. When he cracks it open, flurries fly into the room along with a blast of frigid air. I watch in my mind as Küllo first reaches out beyond the door and then pulls in a parka clad individual. He immediately helps the poor soul peel off, first the icicles, then the frozen outer garment. It is LaShandra who shivers off her wet gear. Küllo helps our Blue sister toward the fire where she stands only briefly to catch a hint of its warmth. Then she says matter-of-factly, "I have been called here for Ayita."

At first the three stare at her dumbly, then all hear the rising crescendo of Ayita's song. Even I, being a dense man about such things, understand the moment, but how LaShandra knew of the need? That is a secret of the Spirit. BJ leads her to Ayita's door and tentatively raps on the wood surface. Once more, Ayita's song grows in volume and the other woman nudges BJ aside with another terse statement. "I'll handle things from here."

With that she cracks the door and briefly, BJ in the hallway, and I from afar, catch a glimpse of the Ki, on the floor, praying by the mother in active labor. LaShandra passes through and immediately shuts the door again.

BJ is left with nothing to do but return to his friends and they all reposition themselves on the floor, beginning a prayer chain of their own for madonna and child. Whenever Ayita increases her volume, the three glance in the direction of her room and their prayer volume nervously rises in unison.

It is not many moments before they hear a new song. The squalls of a healthy crying infant. The three men all jump up at once, sharing man-hugs and congratulatory handshakes, as if they had much to do with the effort at all.

Long moments after that, LaShandra comes out of the labor room and curtly, but kindly announces, "Ayita has asked for you to help her welcome her baby."

There is another pause before the men realize they are to enter Ayita's private space—a terrifying thought for each of them, none having ever been involved in such an enterprise. Single file, LaShandra leading the way, they each enter shyly to behold the wonder.

On her pallet, Ayita is sitting, while Ki manages to wipe the sheen from the mother's forehead. Swaddled in her arms, her newborn comfortably suckles at her breast. Ayita wears the most beatific smile that any of the men have ever beheld. But they are immediately shaken by the site of the nursing even and Ki lets out a belly laugh. Then chuckles out loud, "You boys need to get used to this, one of these days, you may have to help your own wife with such things."

Küllo falls to the floor in a dead faint.

Lord, thank you for my bride, Jende, and for sharing through her, more visions relating to Black Jackson. And great Yeshua, I even hear his thoughts loudly because Ki is his almost constant companion. The incredibly faithful and protective Minder of Küllo's clan is sent on a mission that he accepts eagerly. He takes with him fifty of the Others and they begin to journey north from Rio, through the Brazilian winter frontier toward the Islands of Mexico.

Yes, I said Islands of Mexico! As much as the geography has been dramatically altered here, the landscape of the Americas has been reshaped even more so, and Mexico has become more of an archipelago and tangle of atolls than an actual land mass. Much is submerged due to the great earthquakes. Boiling hot seas and swamps rise and fall without warning. California, Wyoming, Colorado, much of the mid-west and the entire eastern seaboard of the former United States have suffered the same if not worse fates. New York, Pennsylvania, Virginia—they are simply gone. I would not care to be the cartographer of this new world.

And so, in what was once call the Southern Americas, despite conflicting climates of blistering heat and killing cold, people survive. These are the geography and conditions through which Black Jackson and his crew travel loudly and clumsily. They actually desire to be followed, and followed they are. Their group is just large enough that it attracts the attention of all the chasers in that region. The savvy Jackson travels only fast enough to stay safely ahead of their nemeses, but slow enough to invite dedicated pursuit. For two full days this continues and then Jackson's group reaches a preplanned location, known to the Others. It is an area of caves in the warmer section of northern Brazilia that now is crisscrossed with canyons and canals that confuse the best of navigators. Black Jackson makes sure they are followed into the alleyways and leads the chasers on a grand journey. Deep into the gulches, our kin suddenly turn about and wait.

When the chasers arrive, Black Jackson causes their minds to become confused and befuddled. He nudges their thoughts toward wandering into a particularly perplexing set of channels. How You have enabled him and others with this gift I am clueless and it causes my awe for You to grow even stronger.

The chasers commence to chase themselves while the group of Others (who have fully familiarized themselves with these hideaways) and Jackson's clan, negotiate their passage more westward.

Why this complex ruse? The distraction of Black Jackson's exodus left no-one observing the assembling and exiting of another much larger group—this one made up of Küllo's clan and a much larger contingent of the Others. Their journey takes them into a more risky area, also well explored by the Others, aiming toward what remains of the Peruvian plains. Once known as the great Andes mountain range, it is now a vast graveyard of enormous boulders where those who are unfamiliar with the terrain, would soon find no hope in any direction. This trek to the northwest takes the Küllo expedition discreetly around their pursuers, avoiding the toxic lands and navigating through what remains of Columbia and Central American passageway. They are amply supplied with the aid of burros and llamas, the stubbornly durable animals that somehow thrive in the most hostile of environments, much as the beloved camel endures in my region. The beasts carry much desired supplies and tradable goods for survival along the way and to finance their secretive quest.

On that journey they rendezvous again with Black Jackson's clan (who has been careful to scout behind to make certain there are no other trackers on their heels.).

The rejoined group now carries out two purposes. The country known as Panama still survives, if somewhat altered. In fact it has risen in elevation and so, countless hundreds of ships, once intent on passage through the once notorious canal that defined the country's commerce for so many years, float or founder. These vessels beg to be repurposed, if only shipwrights with knowledge of steam engineering might be found.

And so, You, Holy One, provides! The Others had been discretely forming alliances with related family members in the Mexicos (as the islands are now called). Prior to the Great Exodus—the term Middle Eastern Believers use for the Gathering-Up—the country of Mexico began an aggressive quest to out-commerce the mighty Estados Unidos. The land of the ancient Aztecs was determined to revitalize its past splendor and might have accomplished much more, had not the Sovereign God intervened. Since the upheaval beginning with the Age of Completion, the Others have patiently sought out equipment and surviving skilled mechanics to assemble and convert a worthy fleet.

For what purpose, YHWH? Even they did not know the whole of it. The dangers involved in sea travel had become so much more daunting: for every ten ships sent out to trade, only three returned and so the term *Fiesta de Neptuno*—Neptune's Feast—came to be the name for the Mexicos flotilla.

And then, eleven moon cycles ago, a small ship sailed into Rio de Janeiro carrying a strange group of Blues. One among them was a princess from the Tchalaquei tribes of America del Norte—in what was once called Tennessee. Her family heritage and beauty preceded her and so her clan had been welcomed. The fact that she and her father had braved the high seas to encounter Great Israel and then for her to return to the Americas to give birth to a child, was the stuff of legend. Her clan, including a humble but well-traveled page writer; were immediately embraced. When the mission of this odd group was made known, the Others became extremely receptive and eager to help see the cause through. Messengers were sent out and discrete plans began to take form that would do as much to reshape the people of the western lands as nature had done to reshape the continents.

Thousands? Is it possible? Yes by Jende's vision I see it. The Others of the Americas, some from below the equator and as many from what remains of the North, have been inspired to action by the writings and invitation of an Estonian man-child, barely able to grow his own mustache!

Now in the Mexicos, ships are loaded with supplies and prayed over in preparation for a most difficult crossing. I pray now for the voyage— so many lives at risk, and yet it is Your purpose and Your will that now prevails. Lord, are we…am I strong enough for the work You are preparing? It will only be accomplished with Your help.

Adonai, I am not strong enough to endure these images. And I now bathe my wife's forehead with a cool rag to reduce the searing fever that her pictures produce in her own head. I can only imagine how the hearing of it affects Ki. She is strong enough somehow to mask her own mental screams, holding them back from us as she shares the voiced agony of those we see in Bucastan, her once proud home.

The Pounders have returned there, but this time with weapons of a different sort—an unknown chemical that melts the very rock of their bastion. It is not shot with arrows. It is not fired from cannons. The army itself, massive in size, marches to the walls withstanding unimaginable casualties to then explode themselves. Each carries a keepsack containing canisters of the liquid bomb. When it splashes onto the base of the fortress, the foundation crumbles and the army behind the army marches in.

Once inside, they also self-destruct, taking with them, all—valiant Bucastan warriors, innocent civilians, families and merchants who have volunteered to defend against the onslaught. The Blue in this place fade fast.

I can somehow feel the anguish of Your loss, the outrage of Your Fatherly grief. It burns within me as if I too were attacked by the acid. Master, please provide us with wise council on how to combat this threat.

There are survivors. Praise the warning that came as a foretelling from other watchmen with that gift. Thus, secret tunnels were prepared and an elite military group led by Rughert had already been chosen to spirit away the majority of the population. It is now that difficult task which we strive to pray our kin through. They carry limited provisions and work desperately to make thousands of people invisible to the pursuing foe.

They are clever though, You have made available unique provisions to these stalwart ones. Many of the Pounders from the previous attack, witnessed to us by Küllo's report, succumbed to their injuries. Their leather uniforms have become camouflage for the Bucastanians. Many are dressed in the foul garb and pose as a detail leading the others as if to a work camp. The ruse is flimsy, but effective, and amazingly they pass through many areas of risk without questioning by the authorities.

We petition for their continued safe passage and have even sent out our own detail led by Eleazar and Luther to intercept them and guide them here to safety. In the meanwhile, we all suffer and mourn their casualties and indignities. Adonai, be their protection and their comfort on their journey. Help us to find them, to embrace them and to welcome them into our fold to share in whatever we can offer, to Your glory and purpose.

Another terrible and frightening vision—I can barely see in the blurred darkness. A body is strapped to a hospital bed. Tubes seem sewn into the skin of the prisoner, whose restraints prevent any attempts at removing the primitive medical equipment. The patient's haggard face looks upward, briefly. It is Dame Anders and she utters no sound, nor would she even hear her own anguish. She is now totally deaf, her blood is transfused continuously for a vaccine that is only temporarily effective. She has been examined and tested countless times, then to come to this.

And as if the terror and futility of this moment is not enough, the door to her cell opens and in walks Jonathan Trimble. He smiles a warm, wicked greeting and speaks words I cannot hear because the Dame cannot hear them.

I am suddenly so cold and alone—feeling her vast hopelessness. I am tempted to beg death for her death, but know that it will not happen any time soon.

These images cause great anguish. It is not for me that I pray, but for those who languish throughout the world. Give strength, Messiah—give sight to those who seek you. Give Blue to those who want you.

Praise Do God,
ИК

Shared for the benefit of all by the hand of Ilbani the Keeper; redeemed by my Lord, Messiah Yeshua, for His purpose and honor.

Darius Mede—Chronicle VII: 4-10-5 AE

Why am I blocked from all directions! First the struggle to find a permanent cure for the bacterial infection which continues to revisit each time with worsening agony: For reasons not even I can fathom, the only relief comes from a concoction that must include antibodies from the blood of the Whore. Who would have thought that I would hope for her continued life! But there it is. She is necessary to the cause.

Then there is my brother, who none of my legions can seem to locate, yet his presence is felt everywhere. I do not understand how he stays one step ahead and at the same time, finds novel ways to secret away vast numbers of the Jews. I suppose the happy news in that effort is that I do not need to care for that insufferable population. But what can he possible want with them and where can so many be hiding?

My legion armies do no better. I gave specific orders for them to purge only the elderly and feeble from towns. I specifically commanded that one child was to be spared in each family unit. I indicated where, in selective circumstances, there would be special allowances made for some families of higher intelligence or skill-sets to be able to keep more children. But apparently the minds of my minions are not capable of such subtleties. Whole populations of villages and even larger towns have been decimated by their blunt attacks.

I decided that, if they are so prone to clumsy destruction, I must use that to my advantage. Thus, I equipped a large contingent with my Hydrofluoric Acid tanks and sent them to end the Bucastan problem. That prideful blue-haven is annihilated, sending a clear message of my intent to any who dare call themselves Seconds.

But that is a small victory in the scheme of things. I hear reports of catastrophes around the globe—enormous meteor strikes, weather systems that change the temperature from freezing to boiling and back again in moments. There is nothing to stop it and the deaths from the effects…the bodies are too many to bury and no-one cares to try anyway. The only remedy: Let the earthquakes swallow them up.

Thankfully I have the vent of this personal account. Writing seems to help me focus my attentions on what can be done. For example:

My workers have successfully restarted Dimona! We are the first to have nuclear power back in the world. True, the electrical grid will still not function for unexplained reasons, but we can at least create nuclear stimulation in conjunction with chemical reactions to generate a primitive lighting and power system.

Nuclear power, who would have imagined we would succeed so quickly! Though I dare not have the stuff piped near to my location. Why risk the contamination and side-effects! I long for a day when we might eliminate the gruesome effects of the radiation that now must be tolerated by the masses. Someday we might even revive the glory of once beautiful Geneva. I miss that place terribly—the pristine landscape, the orderly architecture and well-kept community, the perfect climate and of course, the conveniences and luxuries that I was able to incorporate.

But that was in a life the no longer exists. My only consolation is that this miserable place is just a little less miserable than most others. The climate remains rather predictable, if just a bit warm. We are not subject to as many natural calamities and I have accumulated a good crew of workers and a defense force for protection. In fact, I have treated myself to one frivolous acquisition because of the manpower I now have access to. I have had a splendid swimming pool built for my personal pleasure. Since I have worked so long and hard to improve the conditions of others, it seems justified. The delicate issue is the value of water in this region of the world. I have made sure that few know about the amusement and fewer would be able to even see the pool. It is hidden within the confines of the Grand Temple!

I deserve the distraction in that place considering all I must do to satisfy the plebeians who insist that I appear at least once a day in the balcony above the sacrificial court. What religious drivel, yet if I do not present myself before the crowds, unrest and frustration increase. As long as I inspire them with hope and give them trivial wisdom to mull over, they seem more content and that contentment is golden. It spreads outwardly in the midst of despair, so I am obligated to run through the formalities. Who would have thought I would become a prisoner of my own worship!

In regard to the continued bacterial infestations across the globe, of one thing I'm certain: there are solutions to even the greatest hurdle and I vow to find them. Individuals indeed walk this planet who have the cure living within them already nature has proven this repeatedly throughout our history. All I need to do is locate these privileged ones and volunteer them for service to humankind.

With the elimination of Bucastan and the revitalization of Dimona, I should be a happy soul. Why do I continue to worry and focus on the negative? It stops here. Now I will look toward positive methods to my purpose. The first of these is in devising a way to track the whereabouts of the pest, Küllo and unDo him. After the elimination of their main communication method (which will also crippled them morally), I will decide on a place to lure their numbers to meet in battle. Their resistance must be ended once and for all. Only then will I reign supreme.

The boy has been clever, but my spies serve me well! All along I have been watching for some complex communications effort where the Seconds have been amassing data for distribution. How simple the discovery seems now that I have uncovered it. They have been trickling the information, small bits at a time via carrier pigeons, to a backwater in the old Black Sea region called Estonia. It is clever and practical at the same time, I must admit. With such a message the origin and destination of the news is difficult to determine. It was only by chance that the later was found. And, as I would have done myself, multiple messages can be simultaneously sent this way as a protection from information being lost due to the harm of one bird.

At first I thought to go in and crush the effort immediately, but that would not stop the bleeding. The trickster Küllo is still on the move and would simply set up his printing efforts elsewhere. No, I will let him come home, he must eventually, and when he does, I will end it all.

The words on this page comfort me. I am invigorated by my own pledge and there will be no stopping until the true ruler of this planet is recognized.

The Bronzeman News

מָשִׁיחַ **WATCH AND KEEP** מָשִׁיחַ

My name be Küllo, that be all ye need to know about me. I be not the story—I be the eyes, ears and hands of these tales. The words on these pages will be news-tells from common folk. Folk like ye and me. Them will tell their story and I will copy it with as little cleaning up as possible, so that all who are left after the Gathering-Up will see what be happening: The Bronzeman be appearing and the seeings of him are much the same. What be different be what he tells each one to Do.

MINGLE IT. MAKE UP YER OWN MIND, I WILL NOT MAKE IT FOR YE.

Edition Eight: Estonia
Month 5, Year 6 After the Gathering-Up

Küllo's Notes: Be it possible? I be home. After so much Doing, hiding and dodging in Rio, cat and mousing from there to the Mexicos. Voyaging within the cramped rusty hulls of ships that should not be able to sail, but do. Surviving storms and strange surges of water until we manage to arrive on unknown shores and somehow follow YHWH's Ruach tug toward His desired destination. How can I possibly thank Him that His will was for us to make it safely here?

I mingle it like a dream I walk into. As we walked over the southern rise that overlooks the city, I knew real tears. This be the place of my birthing and my re-birthing as a servant to Bronzeman—I have trouble mingling it.

Little has changed. Why should it? I have changed only acause of who has changed me. This place wants little of that. We must be careful for we come here hunted and who knows what people will do in these times for extra privileges or even a scrap of food? The Mede's increasing desire to see us snuffed has increased the risk to any Second who stays in one place too long and so we will sadly be here only a short time.

Why return at all? It be for a purpose. We are here to gather our clan and be gone. Simple, but my heart puzzles that Bronzeman has pulled me back here for another reason. He will tell me at the right time, but in the now, I have to trust much.

This report will not be circulated until long after we have moved on, to allow opportunity of escape for any who might be slower in their decision to leave. Once it becomes know where I am from, I am afraid this place will be punished severely—an example used by the GOG to tell what happens to them that shield Bronzeman's called ones.

Help me pray for all of His children.

"*Eungsi jungi, ol*—Stop staring and come in!" It be the voice of Han Ko. She be the amazing Korean journey-woman who appeared in our lives in Bronzeman's perfect time. Without her, none of these news reports would be possible. She has been protecting the amazing printing equipment that I found in the Muuseum and she has been printing all our stories. It be mainly for Han Ko's protection that we have Black Jackson and I wanted to return.

Our clan has approached the Trükimuuseum but I have to stop to get my brain on straight. There are so many re-knows about my parents and sister, how I survived alone after the Gathering-Up, mingling in a world where no-one else cares for anyone else; then waking up one day after a burning fever-vision to find Black Jackson watching over me.

All of these things I tried to un-puzzle as we stood outside staring at the building. Even the choice that my friends and I made thirty-eight moon cycles ago (a lifetime) to gather the tells of Seconds around the world and share them…how could we have dreamed such an idea?

We must be a strange sight, all of us Blue, standing outside an old rundown muuseum. I can't puzzle what be more strange in the world—how we look now or what we are planning to do very soon. Are we ready for what Bronzeman desires?

What I am for sure not ready for be our walk into the Muuseum. Han Ko, pulls me by the hand and all the others follow. Inside, be Blue. Lots of it. There are hundreds of people, all glowing bright and Doing. Some are cooking, others are helping sick ones. Some are taking care of children. But right in the center of everything are many Blues reading. Others sit around them, some are very blue and some more pale. I come closer and peek to see that what tell be read. The pages are printed type. I see a title, The Journal of Daniel Adamson, another be Dr. Hindeland's Bible and someone else be reading out loud, the Letters of Second's. Han Ko has not only been printing the Bronzeman News, but also she has been telling and helping people know our King by having them help her typeset, print and proofread the most valuable documents in the world.

Now I see that the ones reading are then explaining to others around them what the words mean. In the background, I hear the mechanical workings of presses. The sound comes from the 2nd floor above us and Han Ko pulls me toward the stairs which have been fixed. The tiny Korean woman eagerly leads us upstairs and as we near the print room the smell of fresh ink gives me a wonderful warm feeling. The doors open to show dozens of Seconds, setting type and working the presses. Someone brings Han Ko a page and she reads it with a serious look. A smile sneaks onto her face and she hands the page to me to look at:

"I know now what I have never known afore. A peace I cannot paraphrase, a home where I have never lived, but now know to be the sanctuary where I will dwell until I am called to heaven's gate. This is all I need to write. I have come from the bondage of worldly religious rituals to a place where I am one with a God who loves me so much, He would make Himself known to me (and anyone hungry for relationship with Him). He knows I am not able to love Him enough and so He does the loving, even loving to His death, even loving in Resurrection. Not a reincarnated life where we must keep striving for some ambiguous attainment. This is new. He makes me and all who call His name, complete in Him—a concept difficult to describe other than with the image of a marriage. I am a new being and I thank Him now for inviting me to the holiest city of all. Now only the greatest question of all remains...

Lord Jisu our Savior, what would you have us do?"

These words are close in mingling to me. They come from the journal of Pasha Sumje who discovered his deep faith during a terrible time in his life, shared his love of Jisu-Bronzeman through his scriptings and then was sadly martyred after just arriving on his pilgrimage to Jerusalem. His inspired words have help many find Blue.

It looks like Han Ko has not only been Doing but also teaching! I see everyone walking around with Danny-Sticks (here, that's what they call the five wooden strips assembled to tell the love God has for his children). The sticks are sometimes assembled and worn around the neck, tied by a string, while others keep the wood broken down, in a handy pocket, ready at any moment to pull them out and show how the pieces hold one another together when they are wedged rightly. The Spirt be here, no doubt and I am sad at the Bronze news I bring, acause it means the time has come for these people to Go Out with their Do.

Han Ko gathers everyone together and has them sit on pillows on the floor of the building's third level, which has been cleaned out and seems to be a place of worship. Crosses and Danny-Sticks are everywhere. Also I see a copy of Professor Hindeland's Bible on a table next to us. Han Ko explained to me earlier that they do not bind the pages, so that parts of the scripture can be handed out easily. Then the missing pages are simply reprinted as needed. The Korean has me stand next to her afore all them that are gathered. Jason, Ayita, Black Jackson and several of the Others-now-Seconds stand behind us. Most of the faces of them sitting, I recognize. Tartu has always been a small town, so people stay knowing each other. But I mingle that we know each other differently now. They re-know me as the strange boy yelling out "kaubandus" to trade his fish. I re-know them as frightened and unlit. But now we are all Blue and what be strange and frightening be outside, not in.

Han Ko's way be no-fooling and tells right out, "This is Küllo. You know him and his words." At this the sitters jump up and start clapping and praising Bronzeman loudly. I'm red faced embarrassed, all I Do be what I am called-out for, there be nothing special in me except my Savior who tells me my Do. I try to get the crowd to settle, but they are not hearing me.

Han Ko, mingles a better way to quiet them. She points behind me and tells, "Jason, Ki, Roxanne and Ayita." The look of startle and surprise on the Tartulians' faces be much fun to watch. All together they close their mouths and bend their knees, falling back to the floor with their heads bowed.

Jason be not for this at all. He jumps forward and tells, "Come on now, we can't have none of that. If we start a'worshiping us, then that leaves out Jasus, and he's who we ought be bowing to."

Everyone lifts their heads and look at each other with puzzling. I hear a couple of people whisper, "He speaks in tongues, what strange spiritual language does he tell in?"

I laugh acause I mingled the same thoughts when I first heard Jason's drawl. I speak out to repeat in Estonian, the South-South Man's words. Then I explain. "His be not a special language, he comes from a place far away and so his New-Roma sounds different than how we speak it. But I need to mingle with ye a new thing that Bronzeman be calling-out for me to tell. It's not a language, but a Do.

"He wants us to take the beautiful thing ye are doing here and he wants it in a new place. This will be a big Do, with much trust and travel. Bronzeman says that this be no longer *kodu*—home. He be asking us to find other the last of the kin he will call and to share all we have with them. Our words, our Do and our love."

I do not know if they are un-puzzling this tell I be saying. The look on their faces be hard to mingle, but Bronzeman has given me a strong Do to share with them, so I trust him. "Who will go Do with us?"

As one all the Seconds in the room shout, "We will Do!"

Jason then looks back to Ayita and asks, "Ah don't get it. What's so different 'bout my Anglish?"

Ayita steps forward to stand by us and the Tartulian Seconds almost instinctively start bowing again. The Cherokee Princess catches the hand of a young woman on the front row gently encouraging her and the others to remain standing, using the smile in her voice.

"Brothers and sisters, are we not all the Bronzeman's creation? Are we not all his hands and feet? We have come here to be a part of you. Not a better or greater part, just more of his Doers, following him. Please tell us your stories as well so that we may be in awe of what he has done through you!"

She now kneels with the one whose hand she captured and they start talking. Ayita listens as the girl weaves her tell. The rest of our traveling clan see her example and we all go out into the crowd and start listening to stories. The communion goes on all night and as the sun tries to make its morning rise known.

Jason speaks up, "It's time to praise Jasus for the day."

And we do. Someone begins an old Estonian folk hymn and soon everyone be singing along:

> *Kuula*—Listen…now to what the horizon says
> Listen to how far it brings
> Listen to what the wind has yet to say
> *Kuula*—Listen…now
> Look, when darkness be on the way
> Wait, there be still the light
> Listen to how yer land be breathing
> *Kuula*—Listen…now
> *Kuula*—Listen…now

The singing goes on and I feel the greatness of the Ruach in the room. Something very special that be new comes to my ears. While the song echoes in the building, I hear something underneath the notes. It be individual prayers of some gathered. Their conversations with YHWH are a murmuring that blends with and compliments the music, touching my spirit as nothing ever has. It be true fellowship in Bronzeman. I mingle love deep in my heart's beating. These prayers and this song are for me and for all Seconds. Now the Bible verses where Paul says that we are "one body" are clearly un-puzzled for me.

I write down all I can of this moment, But deeper inside, there be a calling-out. "Go," it says. "Go now."

I know the voice and I mingle very much what "now" means. From long away, Jende sends an image of the shore where I used to gather my favorite fish to dry and eat. Be there a kaubandus to Do? Bronzeman, I know ye call, and I now go.

Call-out and Do: I call-out to the readers of this news-tell: Please pray for all people, even for them that still refuse to be eyes-open to the Truth—the soon-returning Bronzeman, our King and Priest, be here. I give my love to ye by my mingling with him.

Special Do: Be ever so ready to be bricked by his love. Be ever so ready to give out his love.

I hear, and my body trembles; my lips quiver at the sound; rottenness enters into my bones; my legs tremble beneath me. Yet I will quietly wait for the day of trouble to come upon people who invade us.

Though the fig tree should not blossom, nor fruit be on the vines, the produce of the olive fail and the fields yield no food, the flock be cut off from the fold and there be no herd in the stalls, yet I will rejoice in the LORD; I will take joy in the God of my salvation.

—Habakkuk 3:16-18

Watching Küllo
Month 5, Year 6 After Gathering-Up (AG)

Black Jackson opens his eyes. He has been lost in the music and that is good. He would not have let his friend leave on his own. "Where is Küllo?" He asks of Ayita, but it is Ki who answers in his mind.

"He is no longer here."

The Ethiopian becomes very anxious. He takes Ki from her harness on his back and cradles her in his arms. "Where is he, sweet one?"

I send him a picture, for Ki's voicing would make no sense to him at this moment. The images fly into him and BJ cries out, "Küllo! Why?" The singing of the kin stop and Ayita rushes to the man.

"What is wrong my friend?" She reaches up to touch the side of his head and immediately jerks as the images are shared with her. Turning her head, but keeping the palm of her hand on Black Jackson's cheek to sooth him, Ayita calls out to everyone. "We must pack quickly and leave sooner." To Jason, she tells. "I need you and Black Jackson to come with me now. Küllo is in danger…Pounders are here."

Küllo has just finished netting a large cart of heeringas, a skill at which he still surpasses most others. It took him hardly any time at all to fill the large cart that he has brought with him. He wears no leathers. The weight shed by abandoning the cumbersome clothing seems to also shed years from his visage. He is the clever boy again unconcerned that his Blue might be seen by those who might not mean him well.

Smiling and singing to himself, Küllo totes his catch to a secluded and shambled part of Tartu. It is the sector of the farmers who struggle to eke out a living in the new environment. Something has called him to this area and soon the purpose becomes clear. He pulls his filled cart to a hovel, poorly maintained and neglected, even by the other poor ones around. He calls out in strong voice, "kaubandus," several times and finally the door to the shanty opens. There appears the farmer who first agreed to trade with a bold street urchin years ago, examines the Blue one. The old one's eyes struggle to make out what is before him, though the strong smell of the sea coming from the large cart full of fresh fish is hard to miss.

"Mu lei ole midage kaubelda—I have nothing to trade," states the impoverished man and he puts a frail arm on the door to close it.

"Palun—Please," Küllo also reaches out and puts his hand on the farmer's. "You have already given. It is my turn to share."

The old one glances suspiciously, but is too weak to argue. Küllo takes this as an opportunity and asks, "How many others in the village?"

"Not many left," replies the farmer, "seven families."

"Call-out to them, please," requests Küllo.

The farmer looks puzzled, but then shakes his head and walks past Küllo out onto the dirt pathway. *"Kohtumine*—meeting, " he shouts. It is not long before all the village creeps out onto the path. The poor are typically cautious of those offering help. They want to know first what is the cost (there always is one). But the sound of one of their own calling them is a curious thing and they respond.

Some might use the term simple folk to describe these, but they are far from that. Even after the Gathering-Up, when most family groups either disintegrated or devolved into mobs of predators, the poorest here had already learned that survival depended on small tightly knit and highly secretive groups.

By no means are these friendly toward one another. They exist only by a rigid code of law. A primitive patriarchal culture has emerged—not like the ancient desert wanderers; far more ruthless than even the strictest of those old ones. The strongest of this new class do not tolerate the smallest of infractions and so punishment for any disobedience whatsoever is ironclad—death. Fear rules all. Trust is non-existent. Little wonder that the Spirit of Bronzeman has had difficulty making its way into the hearts of these Tartulians.

One legend has worked its way in however. The story of a boy who began an honorable trading system with just one word, "Kaubandus" and a circle drawn in the common area of Town Centre. Küllo is the nearest to a savior that these destitute ones know and his Blue attracts the poorest of the poor within Tartu. The man-boy is familiar with the ways of this section of town. He wastes no time with pleasantry knowing his life may be snuffed at any moment if they become intolerant of his presence.

"My name be Küllo," he tells. "I be obviously a Blue, but ye knew me afore as the trading boy in Town Centre. I come to thank ye for being eyes-opened enough to risk Doing trade. This fish be a small give for that trust. There be no cost to it, 'cept the answer to a question."

Here, he pauses and lets the minds of this place prepare. He knows enough about this clan to understand that no-one ever bothers to ask them anything, except perhaps brief directions to the main road. For him to ask for their advice is a puzzling thing indeed.

"What if someone offered ye a new life away from this place, but it meant you had to believe someone loved ye so much that they would die for ye? If ye chose freely to believe in that love, ye would have to give up everything ye now know to go to yer new home."

This is the first test, for Küllo knows well that these people, like himself, value the history of this place above any material goods.

"Ye will have to trust in other folks and in a God ye have only heard about, but who ye never have met. I can tell ye that, once ye come to know that God and his folk, yer lives will change to shining-beautiful. Ye will become Blue, like I be Blue."

This is the second test, for the history here is one of many false prophets promising utopia, only then to enslave the ancestors of this clan. The lineage of those who trusted in feudal lords, religions and governments, only to die at the hands of their benefactors, is long and sad.

"And if ye trust enough to take these steps…"

—before Küllo can finish, another young man comes running up the path. He is dirty, ragged and looks to have run a great distance. He stops at the gathering, and takes only a moment to catch his breath before gasping, "Bose-Spooks!"

The third test comes earlier than planned. The runner describes a vast army, miles long, marching toward them. There is no doubt of the Pounders' purpose, for every house and crop they encounter is razed.

Will these peasants abandon everything they have known to seek out the unknown? The clan begins to panic, but Küllo gains their attention.

"I be not asking ye to make a choice now, but I tell you that ye must leave yer homes quick if ye want to not be snuffed. I will catch the attention of the Bose-Spook army and lead it in a different direction, but ye should warn all the folk ye can find, clan and no-clan. Ye and any who ye care for must hurry to the Trükimuuseum. Friends await ye there to help ye mingle a great journey."

There is a moment of talking by some of the elder folk and then the old farmer that Küllo first approached, comes up to him. "*me läheme, aitäh*— we will go, thank you."

Ayita and Black Jackson, with Ki on his back fly out the Muuseum door. They have directed the others to disassemble the presses and pack all provisions and gear as quickly as possible. They are told of the special carts repurposed from some of the steam ships they sailed on. Jason and the Others are to begin leading the Seconds away at sundown, regardless of whether or not Küllo's searchers return in time.

The images that I am able to give them offer little help as to where their friend has gone. It looks like countryside by the sea, but not anywhere that Black Jackson remembers Küllo sharing with him. They must guess at the best direction to begin searching for their companion. As they go through the town, they hear disturbing news of an approaching force, much larger than any army before marches toward Tartu.

Time becomes a spiritual thing and the searchers stop to pray for guidance.

There is peace all over Küllo. He is the Bluest I have ever seen him. He sits on a short embankment, dangling his feet in the cool water of a lake he loved to visit in days gone. He has lured the entire army of Pounders in a direction opposite to Tartu and he can hear their boots approach now. His misdirection has bought time for his kin, for the peasants and possible even opportunity for other Tartulians to discover their faith before the end. On a hilltop, before the lake, he glanced behind to see the attackers. It looked to be that all had followed him—their lack of brain was good. The marchers stretched from horizon to horizon and that was bad—he had nowhere to escape.

Küllo had had his own vision. He foreknew this moment and Bronzeman had shown him even more. He is unafraid. And there are two final Do's he knows must be.

"Ki, please tell Black Jackson, I be sorry. His trying to move the thoughts of this army would have been sour-milk. I had to lead them away, it was Bronzeman's greatest Do for me. Tell BJ that I mingle him as more than brother, he be my In-kin. Please tell our clan of my solid ground love. Tell Ilbani and Roxanne, the news be now all theirs to write and to teach others to write."

Then the boy-writer notices a convenient rock flat enough for him to sit comfortably upon. He takes out his quill and ink. He produces a piece of special parchment and lays it out on another rock before him. He dips the quill in the dark liquid and before beginning to write, briefly examines and sniffs the tip of the pen. "Purple, the color of kings. And what a beautiful scent. Thank you Bronzeman, for the love of writing and its elements. I pray to serve you with my tell, to the end. Mother, Father, sweet Anna and Lina. I love you and am so sorry I hurt you. If it serves the Master I serve, I will mingle with you again soon.

Then he begins to write:

> To Darius Mede,
>
> > My name be Küllo, that be all ye need to know about me. I serve the True God, YHWH and honor His son, the Messiah Jesus. He be who ye need to tremble about.

As the clatter of the approaching Pounders increases, Küllo's nose wrinkles. He must be catching their stench on the northern breeze. He does not seem alarmed but appears as if he is scribing in the comfort of a university study. And indeed that is what the world has become for him. YHWH's great gift to this humble servant was to give him the continents as a canvas on which to sketch the stories of Bronzeman's devoted followers. Küllo has telled it well with his best loving strokes and we can see in return, the true love of his Creator now gleaming in his eyes. He gazes with a smile at the shoreline before him and does not see or feel the killing blow that comes from behind.

Black Jackson stops in his tracks as if he has run into a wall. He is stunned to his knees. Ayita who had been several paces behind, trying to keep up with the Ethiopian, also senses a change in the Spirit and comes to the side of her friend. He looks over at her with anguished tears and Ki, who is still on his back and also crying, tells, "We don't need to look any more. Küllo's light is snuffed, his Blue has been gathered."

The reality of what has happen is crippling for all three of the searchers, they are unable to move for long moments. It is the knowing that the Pounders have only momentarily been distracted that motivates them to motion, heading back toward the Trükimuuseum.

On their way, they come upon a strange thing. Ahead of them a large group of Tartulians come off of another alleyway and turn onto the main boulevard toward the Muuseum. They appear to be families of one clan, very poor and with their few possessions carried in keepsacks, except for a large cart that looks like one of those fashioned from the remains of a Mexicos steamer ship. It is packed full of the local fish that the area is known for. As the group plods forward, some of them knock on doors and call out, "*Meiega liituda või hukkuvad*—join us or perish." In many cases the door opens and another family group will join the vagrants.

Ayita risks approaching these Un-lit before Black Jackson can stop her. She has a gift for languages and calls out to an older countryman who seems to be leading the mass. "miks sa tuled seda teed—why do you come this way?"

"*Kaupleja- Küllo ütles, et me leiaks sinine sõbrad seda teed*—Trader Küllo said we would find Blue friends on this path," says the elder who keeps walking forward as he replies. Then he switches to New-Roma, surprisingly comfortable with the transition. "Trader Küllo said he would die for us and so now we honor him. He said his death would give us new life.

"And so it shall," Ayita says through her tears.

"Küllo, Trader Küllo followed another who had died to give Küllo new life. Would you like to know that other?"

"If he gave life to Küllo, then we will follow him well." The old man said as they turned the last corner toward the Trükimuuseum.

One sees
One hears
And it is written
Let us work together that the world may know!

—Keepers, for the glory of God

The World Standard

Editor in Chief—Jonathan Trimble
Edition IV
6-6-6 AE

***Look at what the Supreme Mede offers to all who
want and desire greatness for themselves.***

VICTORY CELEBRATION
Küllo is eliminated

This day is particularly good because the subjects of the Supreme Mede have answered his call. Based on reports from the region of Old Estonia, his great armies were able to track down the most notorious of the terrorists who subvert the Word and the Do of our benefactor.

Küllo has been found! Unfortunately, though at the merciful request of our benevolent Father, our noble troops tried to negotiate a surrender; the angry upstart would not repent. He spewed his venom to the last moment, attempting to subvert our cause. In cowardly fashion, he would not relent and when we found him hiding, his life-source had already left him.

It is pathetic that there are still those who will not recognize the power and the benevolence of the Supreme. But enough of sad talk. Now we rejoice for we are close to capturing the rest of Küllo's ugly gang.

More good news: There is even hope that we might safely recover the poor Roxanne, whom we have all wished well and for whom we desire only comfort and protection. The Supreme Mede will not stop until she is rescued and her kidnappers have been punished.

It is by your efforts enhanced by the resources of the Supreme Mede, that we have accomplished this. Those who contributed to the whereabouts of the criminal Küllo will never again have a worry or a want—we have seen to it. And those who help us in the pursuit and subduing of the others will be rewarded as richly.

Praise be to the Supreme Mede by whose hand all good happens.

Community Do: *As always, we ask your cooperation by alerting us if the whereabouts of the following people (and their supporters) are made known to you.*

Ilabani Midehina Acdah (alias The Keeper)	**Jason Ballard**
Luther Hine	**Ki (known as the Freak)**
Eleazar BenMadai	**Amos BenMadai**

Letter from Ilbani Midehina Acdah, Keeper of the Kin (Nahal Arbel)

"Love will find a way
Through paths where wolves fear to prey."

—George Gordon Noel Byron

Written to my God—through the intercession of my Savior, Yeshua. For that reason I will not date my posts for the Receiver of my thoughts and prayers will put them to His purpose in His time. Let these words then be for His purpose and to His glory.

The vision of Küllo's death still haunts me. There is no escaping the message of Mede's intent: Submit or perish. And yet the better message is broadcast in the way our brother committed his soul. He pointed the way for others; not to his own peril, but to eternal security. And many claimed faith in you, Yeshua, by his example!

Honestly Lord, I will need your help to work through my grief. As much as I understand, my brother is now perfected, and rejoice in that. Still, I have become less complete by his loss. It will only be when I am taken, or when you come for the rest of us, that this wound will heal entirely. That is the mystery of you, is it not? As I become less, you become more.

Thank you, Yeshua, Adonai, for providing a fresh moment of joy. I am privileged to witness a most beautiful reunion, a bride to her husband. We are in our camp at Nahal Arbel when the lookouts warn of an approaching group. We are about to retreat into our precautionary hiding places when someone shouts, "they show the sticks! It's Jason and Black Jackson. They have Ayita!"

I feel a rush of wind as Eleazar flies by me at a dead run. He hops nimbly down the craggy embankment to the canyon floor near the caravan in quick time. But someone else is also running. It is the Cherokee princess who has handed her infant to LaShandra and who leaps from her camel to come with equal force toward her husband. We all watch with joy and lend our own shouts of praise to theirs as the two are reunited. They hug, repeatedly kissing each other's tears and begin a passionate dance which soon is joined by others.

Their daughter Fizina appears between the legs of some of the onlookers and I can hear Ayita's laughter rising over the others as she receives the eager child into her arms, the as the three lead us in a dance. She refuses to let go of her mate's hand or release her daughter as the celebration continues into the evening.

When the dance began, my own bride had also come to my side and joined my hand to hers, inspired by the romancing of our dear friends. And You, YHWH apparently wanted to dance with us as well, for a new vision washed over me in the beautiful moment…

—I am back in Yerushalayim, peering out from the Eastern Gate toward Mt. Olivet. There is a deafening blast and brilliant bronze light that take me to my knees. I try to glance at the origin of the light and then I hear a song voice that melts my soul, "Come my love." It is all that is sung and all that needs to be.

It is you, Yeshua my Lord, who calls and I too now leap into the valley that separates us. Before I can start climbing to reach your presence, you are before me, and before the countless others with me. You are mounted on a perfectly white stallion. Tears literally begin to flood the Kedron and I fear we will all drown in our own rejoicing. But Master, my Savior, my King, you reach down dipping your hand into the current and moving the water, somehow raising it above and beyond us, sending it toward the other side of Mt Zion. There the water cascades, crashing away the defiled Temple, washing its bones into a crystal lake fed by the spring of Gihon. From the merging of the two waters—those of the tears you have captured and those from the source of the first garden of life, a tree appears.

The people raise their voices in song as terrifyingly majestic angels hover and speak in powerful chants, "*Kadosh, Kadosh, Kadosh*—Holy, Holy, Holy." They too bow their heads in honor of you who died for all, and rose again.

"But are we too late?" I hear the words escape my mouth as I reach to touch the garment of Yeshua. I'm not even sure I understand my own question, but you do. And your melodious voice again sooths every fiber within me.

"There is no time. You cannot be late to a love that has no beginning and no end."

Something stirs within me and I am lifted, with everyone else to gaze at your magnificence.

"Our wedding is now and has been and ever will be. Take and eat, drink in the feast," you sing to us.

We join in your song. We dance. We eat and worship for eons, all believers, past present and future, have joined in the celebration. And then another sound, the shofar again gains everyone's attention. You, Yeshua have more to tell us all. "The good work has begun, now there is more to do."

"Whatever it is we must do Lord, we will obey," the body of believers, your bride, responds.

It is the twelfth night of the continued marriage dream, when you appear to claim your bride on Mount Olivet. I am exhausted and contrastingly refreshed by the experience of it. I pray for more. Please Lord Yeshua, supply me with your strength and wisdom; strength to endure the unfolding of this vision and wisdom to write it into a workable truth to share with others.

The vision is beautiful, though I confess to being depressed each night at its closure. It is just a vision—hope yet unrealized. I am contemplating my current state, when a soft palm touches my shoulder. It is Ayita who bends down and smiles at me radiantly.

"A gift my dear friend," she says as she hands me a package about the size of a small loaf of bread. I carefully peel back the brown paper and it is my nose which first hints at the surprise. I become hastier in my unwrapping which ultimately reveals what my senses already knew. During her travels, the native-American princess somehow acquired a brick of Bedouin coffee which she has bestowed upon me. Lord, I don't know what has lifted my spirits more—her effort to acquire and port the grounded treat to me, or the sensation of tasting the delicacy that You, Ruach HaKodesh, have been brewing in my mind.

Praise Do God,

ИК

Shared for the benefit of all by the hand of Ilbani the Keeper; redeemed by my Lord, Messiah Yeshua, for His purpose and honor.

Darius Mede—Chronicle VIII: 21-8-6 AE

I cannot see clearly and the air in my lungs screams to be exhaled. But I dare not. It is the only oxygen available in the strange alien environment. I fight my way through the thick fluid that surrounds me. My eyes struggle to see through the stuff, toward my ending.

And then I touch the wall, it tells me I am done and so, with my last energy, I kick my feet, aiming upward and suddenly I am free! I have surfaced from beneath the water of my private swimming domain and gladly gasp for new air.

I enjoy this game as I do my laps. It is a treat to dive down and imagine myself transported to a hostile world where I must quickly locate a solution to survive. The underworld, as I call it, wants to take me permanently. I must expend all I am to find my way or I perish. I confess I am grateful it is only a playful fantasy.

The irony is more in the location of my pool—inside yet another alien place, the Temple of Worship. How tedious the ceremonies have become. My swimming is a joyful diversion from that dark process. I find myself infusing juvenile pranks to lift the somber mood of the ridiculous pomp and circumstance. Several episodes ago, I had a temporary tattoo set on my forehead. It is the number 666. I thought, what a joke it would be, but at the next ceremony nearly all of the masses in attendance had mimicked my demonstration, only I'm certain the tribute involved permanent ink! What am I to do now? Remove the silly symbol? Of course not, I must now consider making mine permanent as well or risk their reluctance in other requests.

But on to better things—the pest is dead! Not only that, but I have been assured by my representative in Tartu, that his fledgling printing enterprise is completely disassembled and the cultists have been done away with. No longer will their false rhetoric stifle my initiatives. No longer will my word be questioned!

From here on, it is simply a matter of rounding up and disciplining the local faction, including the likes of my disinherited family. With great pleasure will I look into the eyes of my father, brother and daughter and pose to them, the last question, "who is God now?"

Once, Moses Folzman, the noisy old rabbi bear argued with me that, "There had to be One," meaning his concept of a supreme being, "for any other to exist." Such nonsense; the evolution of one to another is my truth, each creature rising above the one below by the slow but sure crawl of biochemical adaptation in this cruel competition we call life. I disputed with him then and I stand firm upon it today, "There had to be the extinction of the first, for the next to move up."

So then, because they do not measure up to the rigors of natural selection, I will be quite comfortable in rubbing my inferior family's face in the futility of their superstitions. Then I will watch in amusement as life leaves their insolent bodies.

The nerve of some. I have heard that a myth has taken on life. It stems from my continuing to struggle to eradicate the bacterial nemesis which racks the world. The more primitive folk of my kingdom have personified the plague, now perceiving it as an actual thinking entity errantly created through some accident of my own. They see it as now bent on my destruction and have even given it a name: Mede's Folly. Will the fairytale notions of lessor-minded plebeians never be purged from mankind?

And the problems never cease! Dimona continues to be a problem. Though the radiation is contained within the concrete walls, the reactor chamber will not be tamed! There must be a way and I think I know it. A chemical method, using the unique properties of the saltwater found in the Salt Sea, not far to the east of the plant. The porous nature of the saline crystals in this area, are indicative of a high absorption rate. It suggests that, if I can find a way to feed the water into the reactor and then allow the salt crystals to absorb the radiation, I can then collect the nuclear salt sponge in safe storage vessels and bury them until we can determine a way to reverse the contamination.

The trick is eliminating the water once the salt is in the reactor. If the water remains, the salt will not absorb. But how does one separate the two these days? I believe the remedy is hydrochloric acid which is a reliable separator when used in a highly cooled state. The danger is in the reactor heat – if the acid reaches normal temperatures, it will melt the structures and also release chlorine gas. Anyone or anything near the area would be instantly liquefied in an ugly manner.

If however the hydrochlorides could be kept super cooled, it would freeze the water along with it and the salt could be separated using a sonic charge at a sound frequency of approximately 376 hertz. But then, without electronic equipment, how can I generate such a sound with enough volume to create the reaction?

My solution is ingenious, although completed and strange sounding to the rational ear (ha, another great pun to one day be shared publicly). I will not share this information except through these pages because of the original source that inspired my idea. It seems that the archaic Hebrew text, called by them, the Torah, did reveal some interesting science of an accidental sort. When the renegades who attacked the fortress city of Jericho, they blew through horns fashioned from the antlers of the indigenous *ibex* of the antelope family. By happenstance I had referenced the frequency emitted by blowing on such an instrument and its average tone vibrates at 376 hertz! What a twist (there I go again, I cannot stop myself), not just of the antler but of its current day application. Much of the stone from which Jericho was constructed was rich in salt content, also because of its proximity to the Salt Sea. Now the mystery of why portions of the walls fell at the blowing of the horns, is solved; and with it, a solution for encasing the radioactive core in a salt tomb.

I must master the improvement of my clone servants. There has to be some flaw I have overlooked in the formula. They are nothing more than that, an almost perfect army of loyal subjects. But the spark is not there, no initiative or advanced level of cognitive thinking can be found in them. They are fashioned from living tissue. It should be a simple matter of duplication and therefore exact replication. Instead, the donor remains superior. It is the way of things for now, an evolutionary rule of some sort. I have not yet found the missing link, but no doubt I will.

As long as they serve a basic purpose, the replications will continue. To that end, I have also attempted to clone the genetic material of the clones themselves—disaster! Not only are they without reason, those secondary clones are nearly vegetables. The only things of use they provide are their body parts which I am allowing to be harvested to replace defective or damaged parts for the masses, clone and human alike.

Now if I can only manufacture more capable surgeons to perform the repairs. Ha! There is so much more that I must bestow to my subjects, I hope they grow in appreciation of my sacrifices to the fullest.

The Bronzeman News

מָשִׁיחַ **WATCH AND KEEP** מָשִׁיחַ

My name is Roxanne. You may have heard reports of my capture by those known as Seconds or the Blue. I'm writing to tell you the truth about these rumors.

As with my Blue Brother Küllo, I'm not the story—I'm the eyes, ears and hands of these tales—I only reflect the light of Bronzeman. The words on these pages will be reports from common people. People like you and me. They will tell their story and I'll copy it with as little cleaning up as possible, so that all who remain will see what is happening: The Bronzeman is appearing and the seeings of him are much the same. What is different is the Do he asks of each Second.

Edition Nine: Location – With My New Family
Month 9 of Year 6 AG (After Gathering-Up)

Roxanne's Notes: This reporting is going to seem different than the others because it contains a warning...

YOU'VE BEEN LIED TO!

The fraud was started by Darius Mede. He is just a man, not a god or anything like one. If you had the opportunity to know him as I have you would see it clearly. There is no humility in him, only conceit and self-importance.

How do I know these things? I am his daughter. This is not something I'm proud of. We all have things we'd rather not reveal, but it is better this way. I am done with his pathetic deceit.

And the lie has been laid at your feet in a glamorous way, by another deceiver, Jonathan Trimble. He is as dangerous as the one who now claims to rule the world. Together they conspire to tell you that your life is improving by their efforts if only you will honor them.

Don't believe it. As hopeful as you may be, look around you and ask yourself, "Am I really better off? Just because someone offers me a few basic needs and shelter in trade for my unquestioned loyalty?" Run from this thought. You will be trapped into a hell of their making.

But what choice do you have? It is the same question I had to ask myself, and the answer is in having a relationship with someone who is truly willing to sacrifice everything for your better condition. He even sacrificed his own life and then was resurrected—taken up to the heavens to be God's choice of ruler for His children. Now a miracle is about to happen. He, Bronzeman, is about to return. Doubt it? Fine, but what if you are wrong? Look what happened to your lives when you dismissed His calling a few short years ago. Imagine how much more he can offer you if you will only admit to your selfishness and give your whole dedication to him!.

I didn't used to talk like this. Maybe I even sound "preachy" to you. What should I do, lie like my father? Would that be better for you? Trying to live within a lie is like pretending fire doesn't burn when you touch it. The pain tells you differently, but you want to somehow tell yourselves the wound will make you stronger. Tell that to Mede's victims selectively slaughtered and now lost in the ashes of his failed experiment.

No one can force you to believe in anything. No one can make you loyal to them. These are choices. Choices are the only freedom we have and they define the path to our eternity.

I will honor the memory of my fallen brother Küllo whom I loved and who often shared wisdom that he was inspired to offer. I cannot say it any better. "Mingle it. Make up yer own mind, I will not make it for ye."

> Call-out and Do: I call-out to the readers of this news-tell: There is no more time. Please do more. Yes, pray for all people, even for the Mede, that they and he may all come, eyes-opened to the Truth. But also look them in the eye, hold their hand, tell them your story of Bronzeman's love, that their hearts hear the knowing of God. Help them mingle their belief and their Do to the Soon-Returning: Bronzeman, our King and Priest.

> **Special Do:** Jerusalem is almost ready for you. Look in that direction for the light.

As he sat on the Mount of Olives, the disciples came to him privately, saying, "Tell us, when will these things be, and what will be the sign of your coming and of the end of the age?" And Jesus answered them, "See that no one leads you astray. For many will come in my name, saying, 'I am the Christ,' and they will lead many astray."

—Matthew 24:3-5

Watching The Pretender
Month 10, Year 6 After Gathering-Up (AG)

How odd to observe the slow motion action, the fine cut crystal glass spinning through space; droplets of some rare vintage wine, both clinging to and then trailing off the object. The sound of its explosively angry meeting with the wall is almost dismal in comparison to the emotion coming from the man who launched the goblet.

On the floor by Darius Mede's side lays a ripped copy of The Bronzeman News. The editor's name is severed, but it is still plain to be made out by recombining the pieces in our mind...*Roxanne.*

One sees
One hears
And it is written
Let us work together that the world may know!

—Keepers, for the glory of God

Letter from Ilbani Midehina Acdah, Keeper of the Kin (Nahal Arbel, New Israel)

> ***"You don't stumble upon your heritage. It's there, just waiting to be explored and shared."***
>
> **—Robbie Robertson**

Written to my God—through the intercession of my Savior, Yeshua. For that reason I will not date my posts for the Receiver of my thoughts and prayers will put them to His purpose in His time. Let these words then be for His purpose and to His glory.

Old BenMadai strokes the hair of his granddaughter who sits on the floor in front of the stone on which he has propped himself. The others in the candlelit cave include Black Jackson, Ki, and Jason. By a small fire, Eleazar dotes on his wife, their toddling daughter Fizina, and the growing infant son. On the rock floor sit Luther and Rachel Hine, myself and my own beautiful bride Jende. Han Ko has taken all the other children to another cave and is teaching them about the printing presses which have been brought to this place and reassembled to continue the work begun by the amazing young Tartulian.

It is dangerous for the entirety of our kin to be gathered in one location. Mede has seen to it that a rich reward has been posted on each of us. Yet, we feel called by You, Sovereign God, for two reasons: First to mourn the loss of our dear one, Küllo, as a family. We share stories about our meeting him, humor regarding his unique phrasing in his speech and stories, and awe at what God was able to do with such a humble life.

None of us are naïve to the fact that Küllo's death will not be the last. We sing a favorite song together to remind us of our Savior's presence within us on our temporary walk:

> What a fellowship, what a joy divine,
> Leaning on the everlasting arms!
> What a blessedness, what a peace is mine,
> Leaning on the everlasting arms!
>
> Leaning, leaning,
> Safe and secure from all alarms;
> Leaning, leaning,
> Leaning on the everlasting arms.
>
> O how sweet to walk in this pilgrim way,
> Leaning on the everlasting arms!
> O how bright the path grows from day to day,
> Leaning on the everlasting arms!
>
> What have I to dread, what have I to fear,
> Leaning on the everlasting arms!
> I have blessed peace with my Lord so near,
> Leaning on the everlasting arms.

The second, equally important reason for our gathering is defined by the youngster in Ayita's arms. Cherokee tradition precludes the naming of a child until the personality and circumstances help define the nature of the newborn. Eleazar and his bride have bestowed a great honor on us all by having us participate in the naming ceremony. The highest honor however is given to Amos BenMadai, the boy's oldest male relative on the father's side. Amos must actually choose the name that will identify this infant onward throughout his life. Old BenMadai has a way about him. You have certainly gifted him, YHWH. At one moment he is talking to one individual in casual conversation, and then suddenly, he is speaking to the entire clan. It is the way of the ancient Rabbis and requires anyone who wants to learn his deepest teaching, to be alert at all times to his conversation.

It is no different in this moment, for the greybeard has gone from brushing his granddaughter's hair, to bouncing his new grandson on his knee and talking to him in that special way of dialogue that all parents and extended family readily recognize with a smile—baby talk.

"Do you think I can toss you up in the air and catch you quick? Catch you quick, quick, before you bounce on the ground? Do you little one?"

With this he expertly launches the infant into the air. The eyes of the boy become saucers and we all hear the expected gasp that comes from his tiny mouth. The grandfather then smoothly catches his prize and rocks him back into his lap. At this the child squeals with delight and the others in the group instantly know this will become a favorite pastime for the two.

But instead of repeating the trick, Amos holds his grandson upwards and to the side with fully outstretched arms. We marvel at the man's vitality in his advanced years and the infant stares down at the elder with a smile of wonder. BenMadai continues to chat with the child.

"Many places in the Tanakh tell of Yahweh, His name Do praise, or His representatives encouraging His people, commanding them to not be afraid in threatening circumstances. But is that so?"

It has become obvious that he is no longer playing with words, but is now speaking to us through his interaction with the youngling.

"The Hebrew phrase used most often to express this command is *yare ad*. Many translate this as *fear not*, but a better expression is *do not worship*. A healthy amount of anything can be good, but to focus your being on one thing leads to idolatry. Yahweh requires we fear…worship only Him. In fact, when He sent Joshua and the early Israelites across the Jordan into the land of milk and honey, he spoke these words:

> 'Be strong and courageous, for you shall cause this people to
> inherit the land that I swore to their fathers to give them.'"

The elder lowers his grandson and hands him gently to Ayita. Grandfather BenMadai now turns his attention fully to the rest of us.

"To the Israelites, God commanded courage seven times in Joshua's account. That same YHWH, our God, is asking for the identical courage in this moment. And so a name of courage has been inspired into me by Yahweh. It is a name, by its very speaking that offers strength to others. My grandson, Eleazar's and Ayita's precious one has, even in his short lifetime, displayed great strength and courage. He has endured the harsh environs of faraway lands and frothing seas—just as his namesake did."

Now the proud grandfather gently receives the boy back from his mother. He stands, elevating the giggling child up toward the ceiling of the cave once more, and says:

"Yahweh, Father God, King of the Universe. We give thanks for this life. We ask You to watch over and guide his growing in Your ways, by the work of Your Ruach and the dedication of his parents, his clan and all who know You as Sovereign. Let the boy discover the joy and humbling realization that Your son Yeshua lived and sacrificed his own life. Let the child become reborn eternally when he discovers and believes in Your resurrected son, as Redeemer, King of the Earth and King of his life."

Eleazar and Ayita rise to stand by their patriarch. Old BenMadai looks to the heavens and declares,

> "Adonai Eloheinu, welcome our kin to Your kingdom on earth, as
> it is in heaven. Welcome him by the name You have inspired."

The elder then pulls the infant to his chest, still framed by the mother and father and they all join in unison to pronounce to the rest of us—their kin,

> "In the name of the Father and the son and the Ruach
> HaKodesh, welcome, Küllo."

We saw it cross the sky from new-compass east to west; another massive boulder that must have landed across the waters in the Americas or Pacific realm. Wherever it hit, the force shook us here. The wind, tsunamis and the seismic reactions took apart towns and once more reshaped geography. Beyond where once proud Mount Hermon stood, in the Syrian region, a place still called the same as in ancient times, Damascus, has called out for help. We risked the journey and wept on our arrival. A city of thousands now harbored less than a hundred. Within a crumbling cave they huddled in starving despair. To reach them, we had to step our way through mounds of death and rotting flesh.

Now we have carried them to our home and shared with them whatever we have. It has been difficult, for at first they feared our Blue as much as they did the attack of nature on their home and families.

The conditions now worsen daily. Lord, how much more of this must take place until your Kingdom is revealed? YHWH, in every dire circumstance, You offer Yourself as the remedy. Once again, these unfortunate ones began to question why we would share our limited resources and why we would open our hearts to strangers who had nothing to offer us. It was not long, before the first of them took on the faint hue of azure. One by one, Your Spirit rescued them all and now we count them all, kin.

Eagerly we await your return, King Yeshua. I want to speak hope into this group, yet am strangely without the right words for this moment. But not Amos BenMadai; he continues to attend to Roxanne with his comforting hands and speaks to us all.

I look around the room and it is clear that everyone is prepared for whatever comes. But what is that? Again, I am spent. No clear wisdom comes to me in the moment…and none is necessary for Ki speaks out.

"I've not shared much of my story with any of you, other than with Küllo and BJ. But I hear from the Spirit that now is the right time. I was not always like this."

No-one asks for clarification. We all assume she is referring to her physical appearance.

"Oh, I've always been a squirt, but my parents loved me and taught me that I could do anything I chose to. And I dared to do much in the twenty years I lived prior to *that day*.

"That day, I woke up and called for my mother, and she did not call back. That day I searched for my father and could not find him. My parents taught me how to be self-sufficient and proud, but I missed the other part of their message, about being selfless for others and humble. Small as I was, I had grown a giant ego and an even larger attitude.

"God? He had done this to me, so I had little time for Him. As a matter a fact, I wanted to throw my disabilities back in His face and prove I was better than He had made me. For that, I paid a price. I was left, like Küllo was left, like BJ and most all of you were left.

The room is silent. Ki typically speaks her mind, but inside of ours. This is different. She offers her true voice, her personal story, her honest confession.

"It did not take long at all. I walked into the world, the real world, the ugly one, and the survivors in that world decided I was not ugly enough for them. So they made me into their image; a knife here, a burn there, a break to make sure I was listening. I listened very well, and I cried out, begging for death, waiting to hear my own last breath.

"Instead I heard a voice. The most beautiful voice ever to call my name. He said, "You were taught that you may choose whatever life you desire, Ki. What life will you choose now?"

"'Life?' I called out. 'I am ready for death!"

"If that is your desire, death can be yours. But what if you are wrong? What if death is not the answer?" The voice loved me; I knew it in that moment.

"'What other choice do I have?' I knew no hope."

"Will you be My voice, to others?" asked the voice. "Will you hear only for Me and speak only for Me if I give you only My ears and My words?"

At this moment, Ki reverts to her *mind voice* and tells us all. *My Lord taught me in that moment that, no matter what something looks like, or how a person is perceived, there is incredible beauty to be discovered within, if that person will simply say, "yes" when God asks to return His love.*

"And now," she adds out loud, "Bronzeman tells that the Father has a job for each one in this room. I will let you hear it, Jende will show it to you, then it is up to all of us to return His love, no matter how ugly or hopeless we might feel."

We now see and hear YHWH's plan revealed. It is shocking, it is wonderful and frightening. It will take great courage to implement and the proof of that courage rests in each of us. I am to take Roxanne, Ki and BJ back into the bowels of darkness— Yerushalayim. It means once again, separation from my beautiful Jende and my children. Yet my bride will be with us in the spiritual sense, being our eyes as Ki guides us with her ears.

I understand the frustration I saw in Eleazar's eyes when he accepted the separation from his wife at the destruction of Babylon. Her duties were as crucial then as his and YHWH was diligent to reunite them. I can only pray that is His will for Jende and me.

Soaked clothes cling and the faint halo of the oil lamp carried by Roxanne offers unsure definition of the way ahead. Hope is chilled by the murky water through which we tread. Hezekiah's tunnel has not changed since my last visit to its depths. It is still fed from the ancient Spring of Gihon and its channels are still a refuge to many unwritten things. Beyond the light of our Blue, heard through Ki's gift, there is an end approaching—an echo of wet trudging bouncing back from a wall or a door. Prayers are in favor of a door, and YHWH, You remain faithful.

There is no secret code, no clever entry, just rotted planks that when broken away, reveal an algae covered stairway leading upward, then down again in a long crooked maze of uncertain direction. Now I lead, followed by Black Jackson—who carries Ki in her sling, and Roxanne. We move painfully slow to manage the slippery stairs. Besides the dripping of water, other sounds come from unseen corners—small scurrying claws click and clatter in alarm—we climbers have disturbed the dungeons hidden below Gehinnom and its caretakers flee the intrusion. They carry with them, their precious treasure gathered from above, pieces of flesh and rot from the refuse piles that cover the land above.

Yerushalayim has been spared the worst parts of what the world now calls normal. But it has not been completely excluded, having mourned its share of human fatality and tragedy. The rock and nature of the land surrounding the city makes the burial and entombing of bodies, a high cost thing, so most who survive, have resumed the practice of casting their departed ones into the garbage pits that occupy what used to be the southeastern section outside the Old City walls. The *Valley of Death*, as it was once called, has been made afresh, and the sewage of the place wafts down deep to where our clan sloshes along, enduring its choke. Time cannot be found here, and so travelers, unfamiliar with these catacombs, lose all sense of progress. Little wonder that darkness and evil dwell happily together, life in these carrion infested recesses is greedily consumed.

Finally, another sound, one that belongs in the lower places—distant moans of human despair…and a new light, misty at first, leaking in from some unknown source. It is the red glow of Mede's tubing and it grows into strange shadows devilishly defining the dank stone stairwell through which we travel. Then a turn to the right and Black Jackson is the first to test the iron-gate separating us from freedom. On the other side a dry concrete floor—evidence of more modern construction.

How to break through? It is less of a thing than expected. "Break," commands the tall Ethiopian. The lock and chain used to prevent entry clatter to the ground. The gate complains as it is swung aside. The place is unguarded. No-one comes to investigate.

With the light, it is easier to guide our seeing. We look beyond the immediate through the gift of Jende, and she speaks into us the most direct path. Another flight of stairs—these dry—and multiple twists for no seeming reason. The moans increase in volume and timbre. Even though we are strengthened by the gift of YHWH's Ruach, our stomachs and our countenance are unsettled by the audible anguish. We can only imagine what upsets those at the source of the obscure noise.

Another turn and we are upon it—a vast Flexsteel laboratory, lit with the disquieting red tube system common to all official Mede facilities. In a far corner stands a special liquid chamber, where Brenda Anders floats with an oxygen mask covering her face and tubes attached at numerous points to her body.

In the middle of the room is a lone figure, surely one of Mede's scientific assistants. The moaning noises in the place—*where are they coming from?*—masked our clan's approach and so he seems quite surprised when he looks up from his clipboard to discover he is not alone.

Black Jackson does not offer the man an introduction, or a chance to alert others. "Sleep," BJ tells, and the lab technician slumps to the floor. Roxanne then goes to work, finding the lever that drains the tank containing the Dame while BJ carefully reaches in from the access ladder to carefully lift out the unconscious woman, progressively removing from her body, the intravenous tentacles Mede has inserted to harvest her vital fluids.

Meanwhile, I have taken Ki and the two of us search out the mystery of the moans. They still sound far removed from this chamber and the echo makes their direction difficult to discern. "To the left," Ki directs and we move stealthily down a hallway toward an unmarked door. Testing the handle, which turns unchallenged, I cautiously push the door to enter what looks to be a small warehouse, also Red-lit, which contains shelving stacked from floor to ceiling with…coffins?

The tricky lighting makes it difficult to comprehend the setup. There are at least forty containers, stacked four to a shelf, and each has a series of tubes running into their sides. These literally are coffins rather ornately decorated on the outside, and made of some kind of metal. I am hesitant to investigate the interior of one of the vessels, but that is certainly where the groaning is coming from. Finally I push myself to move to one of the boxes on a lower shelf. There is a sliding drawer underneath each coffin which enables them to be pulled outward from the shelving unit and that allows the lid of the casket to be lifted. I lift the lid and therein lays a young man, naked and covered in some sort of yellowish oily gel. Like Brenda Anders, the multiple tubes running through the coffin are attached to him and liquid can be seen traveling to and from his body by the conduits. He is alive, but seems heavily sedated and first makes a gurgling noise—a rusty red dribble of liquid leaks from his mouth. His lips part and he emits the moaning which we heard from the chamber. The other coffins all seem to moan in unison with this one—an unearthly chorus.

There is no time to decide if the attachments are life-giving or life-taking—Mede's involvement suggest neither is good for the captive and surely our invasion of the crypt will be discovered shortly. Ki prays while I busily remove the tubes. Pus trickles from each orifice and the viscus sound made by extracting each tube sickens me. Yet the gel covering seems to keep any internal leakage to a minimum and the body continues to breathe without struggle. Still, he remains immobile.

At this moment, BJ and Roxanne enter and she whispers, "My mother is slowly coming to. She's sitting in the hallway."

I motion for them to help me pull open each of the coffins, disconnecting the occupants and as quietly as possible lifting the slippery bodies, carefully carrying each out into the hallway. The work is painstakingly slow with detection expected at any moment. If too many of Mede's people appear, there will be no possibility of BJ subduing them.

Miraculously, we manage to rescue all. Now two questions arise. What can we use to dress victims, and how can they be awakened? Black Jackson solves the awakening first. He moves to the young man's body and declares with a soft kiss to his forehead, "In the name of Bronzeman who saves, up with ye."

Instantly the eyes of the victim open. With some shock, he asks, "Where am I?"

Roxanne and I, with Ki still slung to my back, decide to offer the same remedy and are successful. Roxanne whispers that one girl whom she revives, seems strangely familiar. There is a scar running across her cheek, like that of someone she remembers seeing in Yerushalayim.

But there is more to it, more that Ki tells to Roxanne. *It is you. Ask your mother when there's a better moment.* There is no time to be shocked by the words or the recognition staring Mede's daughter in the face. As Küllo would tell, the mystery must be un-puzzled later.

Soon all the sufferers are at least well enough to be moved. The question of clothing becomes moot because as we gather in the main chamber, the trampling of feet is heard overhead. The risk of being discovered is too great to remain any longer.

Ki now takes charge, speaking spiritually into the escapees and her clan as well. *If you desire life, you must now trust. Follow the light.*

Raising my oil lamp above my head, I walk toward the iron-gate leading back into the darkness. Before entering, I turn and state, "We must return the way we came. To escape hell, one must sometimes pass through its trials."

BJ leads this time, descending back into the sewer with the rest of our lambs following obediently. I stand with Ki by the exit with my light and we invite each escapee to have courage as they follow into the unknown. Roxanne and the familiar girl are the last, besides us, to exit. I am about to step downward when my ear catches another familiar sound. An obnoxious grating sound that comes from a smaller canister in the open room. In a quick trot, I go to the source, grab the container and know immediately what is within by its persistent and ugly vibrations.

Yes, it should be freed as well, Ki speaks within me. Tucking the object in my pack we flee downward into the damp darkness where even the guardians of this foul place fear to tread.

Praise Do God,
ИК

Shared for the benefit of all by the hand of Ilbani the Keeper; redeemed by my Lord, Messiah Yeshua, for His purpose and honor.

The World Standard

Editor in Chief—Jonathan Trimble
Edition V
20-2-7 AE

*Look at what the Supreme Mede offers to all who
want and desire greatness for themselves.*

ENEMIES WAGE TACTICAL WAR AGAINST OUR LIVELYHOOD

Vigilantes and terrorists! Our entire way of life is now threatened by these criminals. And you poor, you hardworking, you who strive for goodness are most affected. Of what do I report?

Yesterday at an advanced medical treatment and research center, a group of the very people we have been warning the public about, came in and kidnapped patients. Who would even consider taking innocent, suffering individuals and holding them ransom, but that is what has been done!

We suspect that the international terrorist group known as Seconds are the culprits. They snuck in at night and when leaving, were spotted and reported by dutiful subjects of the Supreme Mede. Those good citizens have already received their reward. It was even shared by the witnesses that the victims were marched through the street naked. This says much about the cowards who have boasted of their compassion in times past. According to our loyal subjects, compassion was not demonstrated in this act.

Worst of all, the highly critical serum that has allowed us to treat the bacterial attack—also initiated by the Seconds—was also stolen. What kind of people are these? Foul creatures that desire all of us to suffer.

We do not like being the providers of such sad events, but know that it is for the good of the whole. We must battle these corrupt ones together. But be careful! Their ways are crafty. I have an example of that to share. When the Seconds cult captured our precious Roxanne, they brainwashed her so that now she works on their behalf! Imagine the torture she must have endured for them to turn her against the ones who love her. Let this not happen to you. Now we must declare her a public enemy and it pains the Premier more deeply than any of us.

Needless to say, we now plead with all of you, for all our sakes, to not be fooled by the false love these villains act out. It is a ruse and it injures you. Watch for them. Point them out to your authorities and whatever you do, avoid the temptation to befriend them no matter how sweetly they portray themselves.

Praise be to the Supreme Mede by whose hand all good happens.

Community Do: *As always, we ask your cooperation by alerting us of the whereabouts if the following people are made known to you.s*

Ilabani Midehina Acdah (alias The Keeper)	**Jason Ballard**
Eleazar BenMadai	**Black Jackson the Word Demon**
Ayita the Cherokee Witch	**Roxanne the Traitor**

The hunt for these fugitives is worldwide and so assisting in finding them will be rewarded generously. The Premiers is notorious for his benevolence to those who live his cause.

The Bronzeman News

מָשִׁיחַ **WATCH AND KEEP** מָשִׁיחַ

My name is Roxanne. You may have heard reports of my capture by those known as Seconds or the Blue. I'm writing to tell you the truth about these rumors.

As with my Blue Brother Küllo, I'm not the story—I'm the eyes, ears, and hands of these tales—I only reflect the light of Bronzeman. The words on these pages will be reports from common people. People like you and me. They will tell their story and I'll copy it with as little cleaning up as possible, so that all who remain will see what is happening: The Bronzeman is appearing and the seeings of him are much the same. What is different is the Do he asks of each Second.

Edition Ten: Location – With My Old Family
Month 3 of Year 7 AG (After Gathering-Up)

Roxanne's Notes: This report will surprise all. It sure surprised me. I have just found out from the mother whose secrets have been many, that one secret in particular now changes my life almost as greatly as my acceptance of Bronzeman as my Lord. It seems that I have a twin sister of whose existence I never knew.

The following account is of a very personal nature. It is my testimony and I offer it as a challenge to all of you who think your world is clear to you. Believe more in what you cannot see rather than what is shown to you. The governmental whitewash of these times, glossy and pretty to look at, are bitter to the taste. If you want real flavor, taste, and see that the Lord is good!

I sit on the edge of my chair, staring at myself lying deeply asleep on the bed. It's so weird. I think I know what I'm dreaming and what Küllo would've said, "I don't mingle how to un-puzzle it."

She is right here before me, my sister. I have never known her but I do. She has healed slowly from her ordeal and has not yet gained consciousness. I've had a chance by physical observations only to compare our differences—contrasts really. I've decorated my body to make a statement to the world. She made a statement to the world and someone "decorated her face." Was it a price she was willing to pay, or did she even realize the cost her actions would bear?

I've found God…well, He found me, and I have chosen to be His child. Whose child has she become? So many questions for her Awakening. I'm excited, anticipating our connection. In the meantime, Lord, I pray for her healing and benefit. Teach me how to welcome her to Your loving reality.

I'm learning the deeper things about my sister. At first it was a romantic mystery to discover her existence and, though I was angry with my mother for not sharing, I understand her protective nature.

But now there are things to be concerned about. It started with a conversation we had which I will try to recreate to the best of my ability:

I sat with mother and sister Eritha, determined to be the forgiving one that God has convicted me to be. That's hard in and of itself—I'm not naturally prone to mercy. So I offered my own confession. "I know we have lots to catch up on. I wish you had known how to contact me, I think we might have helped each other through each others' stuff."

"I knew how to reach you," Was my sister's quick reply. Then she gave a glaring look at our mother. "I knew all about the family baggage. That's why I wanted no part of you."

She was right to lash out. I told her so. I admitted my dealings with dear daddy and how I too chose to run. "You were just stronger and smarter than me. It took me a while to figure it out."

"Figure it out? What was there to figure out? You either know you're doing wrong or you don't." My sister shares my struggle with mercy to others.

"I…thought I was doing good, but I had the wrong information, made wrong choices of people to trust." *I want you to trust me,* I admitted the last part to myself, but not to her. Then I remembered who I now serve and prayed. *Lord, your will be done. Let me share your love with her.* And I was about to, but my mother decided that was her job.

"Your sister has had a change of heart and now thinks God is the answer," explained the wife of the Anti-Christ. It was so painful to hear the sarcasm in her poorly phrased explanation.

"What about you, woman? What do you think is the solution for your problems?" There was hate in C's voice. She knew the answer before our mother spoke it. We all knew the answer.

"I am the reason for and the solution to my failings. If you think I've wronged you, I'd better tell you this up front: I was trying to help, not hurt, you. I can fix my mistakes, but the truth is, only you can fix yours."

An old part of me I thought was buried for good wanted to jump up and slap my mother. She sounded so self-serving, so sure that only she had control over her destiny. My Lord calmed me and lovingly reminded of his healing within me. My old desires crumbled away once more. His will be done.

"I can't believe I'm saying this, but that is exactly the way I think," responded Eritha, the girl that now was what I used to be.

My mother was up from her chair and came to kneel at the side of the pallet that her lost daughter laid on. "Maybe we can't fix each other, but at least we can fix ourselves together. Do you want to start there and see where it leads us?"

"Wait!" I heard myself shouting. "That's the whole problem. Look where trying to be self-sufficient takes us. I thought I was the one in charge of my destiny and look where that took me. I was that person you described and hated—no doubt. But that's changed!"

"…Oh yes you've found Jesus and he's changed your life," replied my alter ego. Her statement broiled with emotion venting from deep within:

hatred, anger self-doubt, sadness. The words attacked like barbs—was it my past pain that was surfacing or hers? Suddenly a scripture came to mind
—*Take up the shield of faith, which deflects all the fiery darts of the evil one*. The verse echoed strength into my reply to her.

"I believe he has. The only way I can prove it for you though is if we spend time together. It's not about me, it's about what he has done through me."

"Fine, let's meet up for coffee sometime at a nice café somewhere." Now Eritha turns to her mother and in the gesture, I had been dismissed. "Woman, (*She refuses to call her mother!*) what's your plan for salvation?"

"I'm going to end him. That ends all our problems. I know just how to do it too."

I could barely hear the Dame's reply. Though my armor is strong, it doesn't mean the attacks won't be fierce. I thought, *These people are my biological family, help me rescue them, Lord*. I was being tested. How would I be measured? "How does destroying a master whom I helped create, solve my problem? I'm still capable of allowing another equally evil tyrant to be my ruler. That tyrant might even be me!"

Both of the women stare at me. It is my mother who asks, "Are you suggesting there's no such thing as freedom? That we have to choose which slave master to serve?"

"I'm saying I do have freedom, the freedom to say yes or no to whoever or whatever I choose to believe in and follow."

"Twisted words from my dear twisted sister," Eritha laughs bitterly. "Don't take any personal responsibility and then you can blame everything on your God."

I didn't want to sound argumentative, Lord, but inviting. I remember praying for what seemed a long time before answering, "Imagine a world where we did such a thing, actually trust completely in a God that did love His people so much that He would sacrifice a part of Himself to redeem them from the mess they had made of their own lives? What if we would simply trust for one single moment that such a being existed? Can you imagine the change to the world?"

I could see them actually trying to process the concept. Were they really wrestling with, considering the "what if?"

"Nice thought for a later date," came my sister's reply. "Let's chat about that when we sit at that charming little café together. But it sounds like the woman and I have other things to discuss. Do you mind leaving us alone for a bit?"

And I knew then, I had become an orphan to this world.

Listen, all of you. I shared the moment above, not to seek pity, but to tell you, it was worth it. I have lost my relatives, but am now a child in a much bigger, more beautiful family. My eternal family in Jesus—a family I want you all to come to know through him. Now I know love and joy that my sister, mother and father cannot imagine. I want you to know that it is possible to leave behind those who refuse the new family…it's terribly painful, believe me through the sharing of my story, I know. But it's possible…and the result will save you, set you free to obey and love the God who truly does loves you as a son, or daughter.

> Call-out and Do: I call-out to the readers of this news-tell: Please pray for all people, even for them that still refuse to be eyes-open to the Truth. Pray for your clan, for my clan, and for all who claim family, that every heart hears the knowing of God. Mingle your belief and your Do, with ours. Bow in worship to the Soon-Returning: Bronzeman, our King and Priest.

> **Special Do:** Tell your clan you are traveling soon. Ask them to come along. Tell them what they have to do and tell them to do it now. Don't just tell them about Bronzeman, show them Bronzeman in you.

Letter from Ilbani Midehina Acdah, Keeper of the Kin (Nahal Arbel)

"To hear and obey God is to conquer."

-David Yoder

Adonai Yeshua! I am in your presence somehow without death to me, you are in my sight. I do not know why my hand still pens these words, you are right here, right now and I am spent! Yet I live and breathe you. I understand the purpose, I understand that things are changing and that Eleazar, Rughert of Bucastan along with his loyal ones, and the Others who make up the 144, are the remaining keys; your keys to the kingdom.

We are to go—you command us. The valley of the Jezreel beckons and there we will meet…you! The mountain of Megiddo awaits, your spiritual conquest is about to overwhelm: But how? Millions of the enemy's forces are swarming, waiting to consume. You have assured through the words of Elijah, and Hezekiah that the victory is already unfolding. And now, can it be…a part of Your design includes my participation in these forthcoming actions? *"Be of courage, for those who are with us are greater than those who are with them."*

I understand it now—why was I so dense before? It is no longer about numbers, right and wrong, light or dark or good and evil. Those were all things of the previous age. Now it is about quality—Your quality. Your supremacy and all that You are. I have no say in it, I have obeyed Your love and now I am no more…everything within is yours Yeshua, to command.

There is new energy in the air. Your Ruach is vibrant, and I gaze toward the heavenlies and witness the singularity, V4641 drawing nearer, changing in hue to a brilliant royal blue, stirring in texture and shifting in shape. Can something so distant affect us so closely? The earth now rattles to its core. There are no moments of peace. We will either shake apart or be saved.

Praise Do God,
ИК

Shared for the benefit of all by the hand of Ilbani the Keeper; redeemed by my Lord, Messiah Yeshua, for His purpose and honor.

Then I looked, and behold, on Mount Zion stood the Lamb, and with him 144,000 who had his name and his Father's name written on their foreheads. And I heard a voice from heaven like the roar of many waters and like the sound of loud thunder. The voice I heard was like the sound of harpists playing on their harps, and they were singing a new song before the throne and before the four living creatures and before the elders. No one could learn that song except the 144,000 who had been redeemed from the earth. It is these who have not defiled themselves with women, for they are virgins. It is these who follow the Lamb wherever he goes. These have been redeemed from mankind as firstfruits for God and the Lamb, and in their mouth no lie was found, for they are blameless.

—Revelation 14:1-5

THE KEEPERS SEE AND HEAR, THEN GIVE.
GOD ASKS ALL WHO RECEIVE TO DO IN LOVE

Watching Jerusalem
Month 6, Year 7 After Gathering-Up (AG)

What sewage is that? We see and we hear, but there is a smell now about this place, like something dead that continues to live by its announcement of decay. It grows, festers, punishing the nostrils as a skunk that knows it is being attacked. But are we the attackers? We see the struggle, we here the groaning, we now smell and feel the defense of the foul opponent, the one who would demand God's power to be his own. There must soon be an end to it.

A portion of the 144, have just arrived into the city. What is odd is the calmness and health of them. They display no ill effects from the bacteria, poor food, and rank water which debilitate the rest of us. Even the best of Seconds has now been weakened by the squalor and virulent conditions. We are better off, to be sure, than the Un-lit and Red-lit ones…but we are not without our own illnesses and maladies. We still exist after all, in the world.

How they knew to come here is the same way we were told. Babylon is to be rescued. To what purpose, we know not. And why would we dream that the Palisti and GOG itself would not become immediately aware of our presence? Yet the Sovereign God, YHWH, called us here and so we have come.

Our new visitors, represented by a strong shepherd called Latik whom we first met through Küllo's eyes, share with us a secret—perhaps the very remedy for victory. Who would have foreseen it? We, the Keepers have verified it by looking and listening back to a time just before the Gathering-Up…

—In a laboratory, a bushy bearded scientist, who also wears the tassels of a rabbi, views a computerized image of a microscopic event. He has taken a vile of blood from another man, the first one to exhibit Blue.

"Danny," says the Rabbi. You are changed. The laminin within you is somehow bonding with the tau neutrinos that now inhabit your body. It is much like the process of photosynthesis with plants whereby sunlight is converted to oxygen. But this is different. Yours is a conversion to pure energy, and of course, you are not a plant, you are a man.

"Moses," asks the younger man, "How is it possible?"

"Just as we still struggle to grasp the concept of sunlight converting to oxygen through an organic process, I cannot begin to explain what God is revealing in this molecular reaction. But this much is for certain. There are examples in nature of plants and animals secreting agents that change those with which they make contact. Sometimes the agents are helpful, even healing. Sometimes they destroy. Snake venom can be both curse and cure. Tea Tree Oil mends the skin, but is toxic to taste. Too much of any good thing can be deadly.

"Are you saying this could be killing me?" The young man, Danny sounds anxious.

"I suspect you would have expired already, had the Almighty desired it," muses the elder Hebrew. "So let us not fear the inevitable. Life is provided for purpose and you are simply changing…the Ruach HaKodesh is growing you from within toward a greater purpose.

We watch Brother Moses walk to a shelf of books in his lab. He scans and picks one out, leafing quickly to a specific page which he shows to Danny Adamson. "There is one plant in particular I recall studying, It is even mentioned a number of times in the Tanakh and even once in the *B'rit Chadashah*—New Testament. Its properties have never been fully understood. I think it is one you should investigate Danny, for I believe you have much in common with its unique qualities. Let me know what you think as you research hyssop."

So the Hyssops whom Küllo encountered in the northlands also share in YHWH's great purpose. Latik tells that they had to flee Slavonia and have been constantly pursued by Pretender Mede's forces. Over their long trek, they somehow managed to carry with them large quantities of the healing plant for which they were named. They were guided by the Spirit, first to find Ilbani and Eleazar's hideaway. How they connected was surely by a miracle. While safe-harbored with that group they shared the plant's benefits and even started cultivating shoots which seem to thrive in this region's soil. The 144 were strengthened in amazing ways by the properties of hyssop and we Seconds, here in Jerusalem are now also improved and invigorated.

This is YHWH's providence, readying us for the greatest act of all time which is soon to come. The earth trembles in anticipation and we tremble with it.

One sees
One hears
And it is written
Let us work together that the world may know!

—Keepers, for the glory of God

The World Standard

Editor in Chief—Jonathan Trimble
Edition VI
15-6-7 AE

*Look at what the Supreme Mede offers to all who
want and desire greatness for themselves.*

THE WORLD IS BEING BLESSED

Can you believe it? We have had horrible suffering because of the bacterial plight that has swept the whole world. The serum and research for a cure had been stolen. But our savior, Darius Mede, is rescuing us once more! By his cunning hand, he is working on a new method for helping us and we ask your for patience just a little while longer while your better life is being prepared for you. Be confident that it is coming.

But wait, if that is not enough, our Supreme Leader is performing another miracle. He is restoring clean and efficient nuclear energy. He will soon offer to us all the warmth and comforts we once knew and more! The crazy Seconds and their fanatical Jewish counterparts schemed to rob us of our pleasures forever. But they are being done away with and we are becoming stronger than ever.

Very soon, there will be ample light, running water, reliable transportation, improved communications and even media entertainment that will surpass the days of old. Do not doubt your Provider on this. He will succeed for you, and to encourage him, you need to honor him. Tell him of your support by your hard work and cooperation. Show him that he is your greatest hope by praising his name in the company of others on a daily basis. You will be rewarded!

Praise be to the Supreme Mede by whose hand all good happens.

Community Do: *As always, we ask your cooperation by alerting us if the whereabouts of the following people (and their supporters) are made known to you.*

**Ilabani Midehina Acdah   Jason Ballard
(alias The Keeper)
Eleazar BenMadai**

Letter from Ilbani Midehina Acdah, Keeper of the Kin (Yerushalayim)

***"Everything an Indian does is in a circle, and that
is because the power of the world always works in
circles, and everything tries to be round."***

—Black Elk Speaks, Being the Life Story of a Holy Man of the Oglala

Written to my God—through the intercession of my Savior, Yeshua. For that reason I will not date my posts for the Receiver of my thoughts and prayers will put them to His purpose in His time. Let these words then be for His purpose and to His glory.

It never ceases to amaze, Lord, how many ways I benefitted from the tutelage of Moses Folzman and Fitzgerald E. Hindeland. Each man held unique perspectives which they willingly shared, but also the benefit of their combined scientific and scriptural acumen proved the truest God-send. Thank You for the great gift of them.

It was Hindeland, who became Preacher Elijah the universal wizard, who suggested to me a new plague would soon appear, one that was somehow a result of the changed polarity and workings of the planet. But Folzman, known as Brother Elijah the master of things microscopic, who filled in the most important clue.

It had begun unseen by any of us, because the evolution had to take place for the path to be traced. Sadly, neither of these magnificent men survived to see the coalescence of their theories into reality. But I unfortunately, must report it now as a new observable fact.

Master, You already know how humanity had developed an awesome tool in the harnessing of electricity. It accelerated the progress of civilization and was perhaps the greatest distractor to ever compete with You, our Creator, for worship. In a matter of a few hundred years after its discovery, we considered ourselves as our own god-species. We depended on electrical current as our scientific life blood and offered sacrifices of our resources, our time and our faith to the computer brains we fashioned to interpret and rule our domain.

As has happened with countless other sophisticated organisms in Your design, we neglected to secure our sanctum from internal attacks. Only toward the end of the last age, was it discovered that electrical current was indeed a highly organic thing, attracting other organic things to feed upon it. We never took the threat seriously, but the nemesis certainly did.

The microbes, borne of volcanic soup, had flown upon the air for eons before. At one time they had attacked us, plagued us and many times reduced our numbers. With typical human resilience, we developed antibodies, natural defenses that held the threat at bay. The organisms lost the battle of dominance with us and we forgot them.

Then came electrical power: Generators of heat and light with conduits of wire and waves; perfect paths and energy highways along which the primitive volcanic vacuoles could feed. They blossomed once again from a smattering of innocent microbes into countless broods of bacteria, ever mutating, ever morphing as all life does.

It was harmless to us, lusting on sparks rather than flesh, and therefore to us, uninteresting. The incubation and life of such creatures remained inane to *we—the better beings.*

And one day, You caused what seemed a silly thing to happen. Electrical current ceased. We thought we were the only ones punished by the cruel trick, but there was another society that had become even more dependent on our voltaic vessels. The bacteria, also being clever by Your design, adapted. It rediscovered, in fact improved upon, its ability to inhabit and parasitically feed on flesh. Because of the decimation in these dark times, of most other warm blooded creatures, the spores once more tried a human occupation. And our bodies, having been ignored as host material for so long, had become wonderful targets again.

All this to divulge my understanding as my mentors taught me, that the spiritual forces of evil come in many forms, some from the heavens and some from within. And now creation suffers by those spiritual tormentors. It is the cycle of shalom to chaos to shalom again that Moses and Elijah explained to be our plight until Yeshua's return.

Wait, I left the story in chaos. Forgive me Yawheh. Is not shalom to come again before the completion of the Kingdom? It is! You love Your worshipers and have offered us respite and relief. Our friends and kinsmen, the Hyssops have brought it to us in the grains of their herbs. And now we celebrate, ingesting the cure as a new communion for this age. Your body, Your blood and Your saving salve; are received in remembrance of You who overcame all sin and disease, both natural and spiritual.

The sky comes alive in the evening hours, by the gift You, my God, have provided. The telescopic lenses and filters that once belonged to Preacher Elijah, now allow me to scan the heavens, even on cloudy night. *Yom Teruah*— The Feast of Trumpets approaches and the constellations are moving according to Your plan. 'Signs and wonders', they have been called by others.

And it appears that yet another conjunction of Jupiter with the constellation Virgo is coming into play. As well Venus, Mars, and Mercury are joining with the seven stars of Leo, combining as a crown over Virgo.

These may not herald a specific event, but You have said the alignments of planets and celestial bodies should be watched. Is this the great sign we have been instructed to wait for? Is your son's return as Messiah Conqueror eminent? Or are these things portents of something new that only You know?

There is no sure answer, only faith that Your plan is unfolding perfectly. I find myself waiting in great anticipation for the answer and that is exactly where You desire each of us to dwell: serving those in need; witnessing to any who will listen; and being eager for you, Lord Jesus, to rule.

Some may question my trust in the unseen, but in reality, it is not unseen. The trust I have now is based on Your perfect execution of past provision. No, it is not that I expect You to honor my desires. I am simply confident that Your will is best and so that is what I desire and what I then wait for. How do I know You are active in fulfilling my needs according to Your will? Again, the evidence is clear in Your past responses, what I call the *miracles behind*. Those subtle spiritual influences are visible for anyone to review in their life, if they choose to take an honest look at their history. My amazement is how many people refuse to believe even when such evidence is blatantly presented.

But that is no longer the condition of my heart, YHWH and I have You to thank for it, God of the Universe, God of the smallest particle, God of my life.

Praise Do God,
ИК

Shared for the benefit of all by the hand of Ilbani the Keeper; redeemed by my Lord, Messiah Yeshua, for His purpose and honor.

Darius Mede—Chronicle IX: 15-11-7 AE

It seemed the only reasonable course and I am amused, both by the wisdom of my choice and the spectacle before me. I have brought Jonathan Trimble along to witness and document the event. He has commented to me on the absurd irony of what we see in the valley below us where I have placed a thousand of my clones in a circle around the Dimona facility. In the hands of each, an ibex antler, fashioned into what the ancients called a shofar—a crude but effective musical instrument used for warnings, military commands and celebratory music. The later I cannot fathom, for the sound that emanated from the makeshift trumpet is as grating to the nerves as fingernails on a chalkboard.

To think that these defective beings under my command have been mute up until now: My research solved the mystery—in the cloning process, apparently their vocal chords do not replicate completely. In essence, with these horns I have finally bestowed my creation with voice to give me praise!

Unfortunately, the offering is a comic affair for the only noise I can ever remember being as repulsive is that which coincided with the Singularity Incident. I will never forget the crippling sound that screeched through the speakers of my television monitor; it was the last electronic transmission the world heard. This reminder of that revolting moment causes a struggle within me. I do not want to command my legions to blow at the greatest volume because of its irritation. On the other hand, how else do we cause this to happen?

The time is nearing and it is a good thing, for once this is completed, I desire to quickly ride up to Jezreel and oversee the final destruction of the Megiddo forces at the hand of my efficient commandos. Palmotic has of course sent multiple pleas to begin the attack, but I must be witness to the Christian cult's destruction. Nothing will give me greater pleasure.

Now my thousand man contingent is in place, performing their bizarre bugling and I must reluctantly delay the completion of this documentary until after the repairing procedure that I must attend to. I will return to this record after this greatest of all my feats, the taming of a nuclear meltdown!

And there shall be a unique day, which is known to the LORD, neither day nor night, but at evening time there shall be light.

—Zechariah 14:7

Watching Dimona
Month 11, Year 7 After Gathering-Up (AG)

We have to agree with the Pretender, for what we see is what he sees, a mechanical marching band of shofar blowers. In one sense comical, in another, pathetic. He has placed his hope in partial science, and is overconfident in his own abilities and power over others. So intent is he on his production, that after cueing the blowers to begin, he fails to see and hear the figure who walks up from behind.

Brenda Anders, weak as she is from the torturous bloodletting at her husband's hand, has recruited the help of her newly reclaimed daughter, Eritha who has also recovered well from the medical experiments involuntarily done upon her at the hand of her father. Also, she has enlisted the help of her remaining loyal bodyguards in tracking the escapades of the Premier. When it became apparent to her that Darius was planning to restore the Dimona facility, she could no longer remain idle.

Now she has convinced her protective contingent to escort her in her steam-mobile to a spot just far enough away from the nuclear plant to be undetected. Then they hiked the remainder of the way, sometimes having to carry the Dame along with all their weaponry.

Mede is completely taken by surprise by Anders and crew; the din of the shofars masking their approach. It did not even occur to him that he would need protection in this isolated spot. So now we hear the indignant arrogance of his greeting.

"Well, my dear this is a surprise, and I would have a pleasant picnic, but as you can see, I am busy with my duties. I'll be happy to chat with…"

"—There is no need for dialogue, Darius, we are passed that," Anders shouts to be heard over the strident racket. "You will cease this sick act of global terrorism. I will not allow you to bruise the planet any more than you have."

We see a look on Mede's face that suggests contempt for his bride. Then he looks curiously toward the other woman standing beside her. Close cropped, blonde hair, wounds on her arms and neck. She is healing well from her ordeal and he recognizes her with a smirk, but not a word. He seems unconcerned with, or naïve to, the danger that Ander's well-armed escort present and it seems that he is about to spit out a command when Jonathan Trimble nimbly steps between his master and the women. Mede's media mouthpiece quickly opens his own badly misshapen mouth.

"Please, please, this is such a perfect opportunity for reconciliation." Turning to the Dame, he smiles, "Brenda, I truly regret your physical discomfort. When I was informed of your circumstances, I personally ordered your release, but learned then that you had already left of your own volition. Isn't it best that we now put all our past issues behind us? This reactor problem needs our combined skills. Just like you, we want to heal, not further wound our home."

Even in his present state of decay, Trimble is calming and eloquent. The talk might have begun to mollify her, but Darius Mede chooses this unfortunate moment to form a smirk on his face that unmistakably argues his finding this whole situation to be amusing. His unreceived daughter is the first to react, sidestepping Trimble and slapping her father with a furious strike that nearly causes him to lose his footing. The Dame also caught the look and gives her own command.

"Bring the car."

Her guards had apparently been anticipating this request and one of them fires a signal flare into the air. In moments, the approach of Anders' steam vehicle is heard, even over the continued trumpeting. Once the refitted SUV arrives, Anders orders, "Tie them both in the back."

"You have no idea what you are doing," Mede blasts at his bride. "I am your solution, not your problem. Soon…"

—Brenda Anders climbs into the driver's seat and raises the throttle to drown out Darius. Eritha takes the front passenger location and the guards climb onto the running boards. The Dame aims the truck toward the entrance of Dimona, descending a healthy two kilometers down the sloping hill and literally driving through a section of the piping Pounders to stop in front of the facility. She, her daughter and the guards then exit the vehicle and move around to its tailgate, lifting it to reveal a large cache of explosives. From the rear seat, Mede cranes his neck and struggles to view Brenda's assemblage. Then he shouts, "Don't do this, you will bring on the very damage you hope to avoid!"

But Anders is not listening. She directs her crew to ready the fuses for ignition of her revenge—a blast to once and for all bury her past and her husband's destructive schemes. The fuses are long, apparently part of the plan to allow her escape, but then revenge of another sort begins. A deep throbbing is felt and heard as an undertone to the shofars. The cadence ebbs and flows with the high tones and everyone ceases their work to pinpoint the source. All stone surrounding them vibrates and hops to the tune.

There is a new look on Mede's face. It represents the inner workings of his brilliantly analytical mind. He looks around and the factoring of his cognitive skills can almost be felt, throbbing with the earth. He looks to Trimble and asks, "What is the composition of the concrete walls of Dimona?"

"The stone for the site was quarried locally, near the Salt Sea," replies his deputy, unaware that he has just defined their demise.

Mede shouts, "Stop the trumpeting, someone stop them! The frequency, it's not separating the salt and water, it is melting the concrete!" There is no smirk on his face now; his eyes betray the anguish of tragedy realized by his very human miscalculation.

Anders' guards need little encouragement, the blowing has annoyed long enough, and they fire on the blowers—too little, too late. The cinderblocks that make up the protective sphere protecting the outside world from the molten reactor core, begin to bubble and split open. When the superheated salt water is exposed to the air, it erupts skyward. Somewhere in its trajectory, a slight cooling causes the fluidic fountain to gel and by its weight, plummet back toward the ground cooling and solidifying as it rains down. The SUV containing Darius Mede and Jonathan Trimble, surrounded by Brenda and Eritha Anders, and her guards, is instantly enveloped and entombed within a radioactive crystalline cocoon. The series of actions is almost instantaneous, not allowing any of the four to offer their own voice, not even a scream of shock, to the cacophony of Dimona.

The remaining clones who have not been destroyed continue their mechanical music, inviting a further opening of the molten reactor core. The heat is so intense that the blowers, the rock and earth itself for a circumference of three kilometers, liquefy to join the fiery furnace. In the center of the lava lake, temporarily floats the sarcophagus, its composition is supernaturally strong and is not consumed by the magma, but its weight will not allow it to sail for long and ultimately it sinks out of our site. Nothing remains of Dimona or of those who called themselves rulers over the land and the oppressed. They have been cast by prophesy of their own making into the fiery lake.

The wind has been blowing exhaustively, out of the Negev wilderness from the east. Now the hot breath shifts, blowing toward the north and on the ridge above the pool that was Dimona, pages of writing flutter under a well picked rock. The rock becomes a mere pebble in comparison to the gale. It tumbles away and the final words of arrogant testimony—what mankind believed it desired to become—are swept up and carried along in the zephyr.

The heat of the boiling blast charges toward and through Jerusalem, the once holiest of manmade cities, cleansing the avenues and alleys of its ancient architecture. Already weakened structures fly apart. Even those of Flexsteel including Beit Aghion, the residence of Darius Mede, are tumbled like cardboard boxes in the storm. As the Ruach scours, we see many possessions, prized by their collectors, scattered beyond the confines of the old city and into the crumbled ruins that lead out into the Jezreel.

From the rise called Olivet, the concussive cry of a lone shofar of terrifying power signals a long tone in warning and celebration, beckon and condemnation. Our bodies shudder with the power of its calling and there is nowhere to escape it but in collapse to our knees. At its conclusion, there is another tone, in reply. This one comes from across the Kedron valley, from within the protected walls of the newly completed Temple, beneath the stone of the altar. The stone itself crumbles with an eruption of blue light that vibrates from its tomb beneath and the light fleas heavenward. The Temple is left in complete darkness and suddenly implodes upon its foundation. On Olivet, another light appears and the earth itself gasps at its golden bronze illumination. The Blue that has escaped the Temple confines, now circles the brighter glow, merges with it, and becomes a new color, unknown before and indescribable by us, the Keepers watching in this moment.

Can you see it with us, can you hear it? Who calls? Who accepts and who dares refuse the call? It is the final Yom Teruah telling us judgement is on the move.

The light begins a gradual, steady progression down the slopes of the Olivet, outward, following the Ruach toward the Jezreel. As it leaves Old Jerusalem's ruins, we spy something of particular interest, soaring overhead, reflected in the diminishing light—the final pages of the journal, penned by the Pretender at Dimona have arrived. They are as leaves from a tree purging its fall foliage and one particular post flutters, then slaps against a ruined wall. We are actually able to read it as it struggles to be freed.

"I am certain, the world is better under the rule of my hand."

A signature identifies and condemns the writer for a thousand years to come, and for an eternity beyond.

Darius Mede, Supreme.

The paper escapes the wall's grasp and chases after its companions, spiraling as insignificant refuse onto a desolate landscape. Perhaps this collection of script will somehow be salvaged for the sake of new lessons to be taught. Much is to be revealed over the new millennium which is now come.

One sees
One hears
And it is written
Let us work together that the world may know!

—Keepers, for the glory of God

The Bronzeman News

My name is Roxanne. You have no doubt seen the visions and heard the tell of a new world that has come. There is no more destruction, no more decay, no promises are needed, for our King is here. I have been at his thrown and can tell you so. You will meet him soon, but you must come to the feast, the feast will not come to you.

As with my Blue Brother Küllo, I'm not the story—I'm the eyes, ears and hands of my Lord—but instead of reflecting the light of Bronzeman, I'm now a part of His glory. The words on these pages are to invite the Last. It's His way. He loves you, but He will not make you love him, it's your choice to Do or not will be reports from common people. People like you and me. They will tell their story and I'll copy it with as little cleaning up as possible, so that all who remain will see what is happening: The Bronzeman is appearing and the seeings of him are much the same. What is different is the Do he asks of each Second.

Edition Eleven: Location – Irrelevant
Month 11 of Year 7 AG (After Gathering-Up)

This will be a short news-tell, but what has happened reshapes me and all on the planet. I've just been told that my parents and my sister are snuffed. Many of you may not care. I've discovered that outside of Blue Communities, such loss is perceived mostly as gain for those surviving.

However, my parents you know. One was Darius Mede, the self-proclaimed ruler of the planet. My sister will remain obscure in the global memory. She chose to live out her pain without hope and with no desire to heal—striking out bitterly towards any who would desire an improved relationship; striking out even against her Creator who desire her love most of all.

Editor's Post Note: I should probably mention also that Jonathan Trimble, whom many considered the master of world media, was also taken by the same tragedy. I knew this man for other reasons, very private and unflattering reasons. I confess that I willingly engaged in a sexual relationship with the man, prior to my claiming Bronzeman as my Savior. I knew at the time that I was being used by Trimble and admittedly I was using sex with him promote my own purposes. I'm sorry and repented to my Redeemer, asking forgiveness for the sick choice I made as a young girl and it should tell you much…it should tell you ALL of whom Bronzeman is, for I know without doubt that he has washed away my blemish with his sacrifice of love.

I only mention this now because I'm saddened for each: Darius Mede, Brenda and Eritha Anders and Jonathan Trimble. Each had the same opportunity as I, to abandon their selfish ambition and to learn the joy of worshiping the true King. In a quirky way, I'll miss them; for by their influence, I discovered the depravity of the world and was broken to the point of realizing, my life was no life at all.

And it was there that Bronzeman found me. It should speak great hope into you, that if Jesus of Nazareth, the son of YHWH, can love, forgive and save the likes of me; through that same act of repentant choice, it can happen for you too.

> Call-out and Do: I call-out to the readers of this news-tell: Please pray for all people, even for those who still refuse to be eyes-open to the Truth. Pray that your light is Blue and that you have a chance to explain to others what that means for them.

> **Special Do:** If you are reading this and are not Blue, ask yourself this. Why is this group of people who call themselves Seconds, so crazy in love with their God? How can they be so sure He died and came back to life for them and why would they risk their lives to worship Him? Un-puzzle it for yourself, but hurry, soon you will have no puzzles to mingle.

The LORD utters his voice before his army, for his camp is exceedingly great; he who executes his word is powerful. For the day of the LORD is great and very awesome; who can endure it?

"Yet even now," declares the LORD, "return to me with all your heart, with fasting, with weeping, and with mourning; and rend your hearts and not your garments." Return to the LORD your God, for he is gracious and merciful, slow to anger, and abounding in steadfast love; and he relents over disaster.

—Joel 2: 11-13

Watching The 144
Month 1, Year 8 After Gathering-Up (AG)

There is a humid, suffocating stillness in the waiting as we Keepers witness the massing of Mede's army on the plain of Megiddo. This is the place where the horse was introduced as a weapon of war. This is the ground on which chariots were proven battle ready. The blood in its soil runs so deep that only YHWH knows the complete cost of its spilling.

One more conflict will be fought here. One final decision is to be made for mankind. And now, one man walks proudly before his legions, using a giant Flexsteel sound-board to project his voice. He proudly challenges the unseen above him, his adversary on the mountain called Megiddo.

"It is I, Serge Palmotic, who comes now to destroy you, Eleazar. There is no place for you to run to as you have run before."

We can also hear Jason Ballard from his protected perch. He turns to Eleazar and tells, "Ah just can't imagine why he's brought so many to the party. We didn't bring near 'nuff barbeque."

Eleazar smiles at his friend's comment, but does not take his eyes from the high power binoculars he now uses to assess Palmotic and survey the legions below. As his head and arms pivot slowly from left to right to survey the assembled forces, he offers some verbal observations. We see what he sees, but his strategy is woven within his words.

"They have heavier forces near Zububa. That is what they believe to be our flank. Their reserves range toward Afula. They must know about the well tunnel on the western portion of Megiddo, I see a concentration there also. I'm not sure if they plan an assault through the tunnel, or are just making sure it is not available as an escape route."

Eleazar, the former Temple priest, has a keen sense of deployment and his next spoken decision telegraphs his skills. "Palmotic thinks we are surrounded and therefore he can take his time to plan an assault. I suspect that he has not heard about Mede's death yet, it wouldn't surprise me if he reacts brashly when that is discovered. He will think himself to be the only one experienced enough to act and so he'll want to demonstrate his power. He might even think himself ready to replace Mede as World Premier. If so he'll want to cement that authority quickly."

"That cement might be what gets his Pounders in a big heap of trouble," says Jason, who also peers through binoculars. "Where do ya think Lord Jasus will come in from?"

"But concerning that day and hour no one knows, not even the angels of heaven, nor the son, but the Father only," Eleazar laughs out Jesus's words given to his disciples. Then he adds his own comment. "All I do know is that this will be like no other battle in history. We must trust in his ability to see the much bigger picture and so be prepared to obey any command he gives instantly."

"Yup, guess it would be like trying to guess where the catapult boulders shot from up here all those years back would land," Jason muses. "We have to be ready for just about anything. All the Seconds and the 144 are ready enough. Ah think they…mingle what's going on." The American chuckles at his use of Küllo's favorite word. It captures the essence of walking in faith for those possessing like-mindedness in Bronzeman. He laughs again and says out loud. "Ah only wish that Tartulian kid could be here to mingle this."

Eleazar nods his head and smiles, still fixing his attention on the Jezreel. The camps of infantry crowded into the valley are difficult to calculate. "The number two-hundred-million is mentioned in the book of Revelation. Are they all here? Is there enough room for such a herd?" he wonders aloud. We wonder as well. It is conceivable that such a horde could be garrisoned in a 320 square kilometer area. Or is this an intimidating portion of a larger contingent that waits to converge on Jerusalem and beyond, once this chore is complete?

"Guess it's time to send our little messenger of," Jason chuckles and reaches down to pick up a glass jug.

Within the clear vibrating vessel we see an occupant who has been integral to all that has taken place in the last seven years. The moment is ripe for Abaddon, the unique leader of the warrior insects created for YHWH's purpose, to be freed once again. Preacher Elijah had been the first to harbor this aberrational brute. When that man had been slain, Mede's men captured the pernicious pet and that was what Ilbani discovered while freeing the victims of the Pretender's experiments. Ilbani gifted the beastie to Jason who had also experienced its protective nature first hand and now respects its loyalties.

The vessel's largemouth rim is covered with a thick leather seal which Jason peels off and Preacher Elijah's sidekick does not hesitate in its flight, rocketing into the night. The two men follow his raucous track as long as possible.

"Ah sure hope Ilbani's right about that critter. We could sure use the help," Jason says hopefully.

Eleazar nods once more as they watch the bug seek a course toward Jerusalem. Then the former priest focuses his attention and his field glasses back on the masses below. "Do you see those keepsacks each of the Pounders wears?" Eleazar asks Jason. "They don't look like supply packs: Any ideas?"

Jason's history as a United States Marine comes into play. "Yup, but y'ain't gonna like 'em." The lanky Second points over the cliff face and directly down. "See how the sunlight catches the packs on the Pounders closest to the cliff base? Ah seen that kind of reflection before. It's how Flexsteel reacts to light being shown on it from just the right angle. Ah'm thinking those are canisters, like they're all carrying something they're gonna spray or shoot out our way when things start a hopping."

Both men focus on the area below and seem to be trying to work through Plamotic's plan. Suddenly they look at one another as if in a joint epiphany and speak out in unison, "Bucastan."

Before Mede's demise, he had obviously produced a new weapon, one that consumed Ki's home in its entirety. The shared image of that slaughter has warned, inspired and prepared our kin for what is to come.

Eleazar and his compatriots all sit in a circle under a *sukkah*—a temporary canopy to protect them from the wind and swirling sand. "Marbles," explains Eleazar, "was an ancient contest devised in part to help its warriors prepare for engagement." At this he retrieves from his pants pocket, a small leather bag which he empties on top of a slate stone tablet set into the earth before him. Out pour a set of glass balls. He then groups the objects into a central location on the rough surface. "One of the lessons one earns early on is to not be in the way of an undesired attack. In the Old Culture, General George Custer learned this lesson the hard way and we would like to avoid the repetition of his history."

From his collection, Eleazar picks up his favorite *shooter*, positioning it upon his left thumbnail which is cocked in the first joint of his middle finger. He flicks his thumb, sending the larger marble into the air. It arcs and lands in the middle of the other marbles which ricochet in every direction.

Looking at the chaos he has created, the Hebrew reflects, "I believe our adversary thinks it that simple to eliminate us. Perhaps we can provide him with more of a challenge."

As Eleazar says this, Black Jackson comes up to the men and is greeted warmly. The Ethiopian looks at the scattered marbles and says, "Looks like ye be mingling the end-game."

Jason and BJ both squat to help their friend collect his aggies and it is the South-South native who suggests, "Ah think it's time we ask for some help in changing the rules a bit."

After regathering the marbles, they all kneel around the stone and begin to say together, very familiar words:

"We call out to the Lord, and he answers us from his holy mountain…"

The grim day begins before the dawn with a note handed to Serge Palmotic from one of his more reliable runners. He unfolds the simple parchment and reads the short announcement without emotion:

MEDE AND TRIMBLE ARE SNUFFED. DIMONA DESTROYED, AVOID AREA AT ALL COST. GOVERNMENT IS UNDONE.

The General nods while reading and then crumples the note and calls out to a group of men standing next to his yurt, "The battle starts now." There is no need for further instruction. We observe them to be practiced soldiers.

Palmotic takes his binoculars and scans to the dark heights of Megiddo. He confirms that the enemy appears to still slumber, the campfires are only embers. No-one is at his side, but his habit is to speak out his plan and so he does. "There will be sentinels, but if we can catch our adversaries in the throes of early morning disorientation, it will be a bonus. The plan does not require surprise, yet, why not hope?"

The Pounder army is slow to assemble, even with the many practice drills over the last weeks. They are stealthy however, an amazing feat for the mindless horde, and before the shrouded sunlight creeps in, Palmotic's troops are in position. They are at his beck and call and do not stir. The General climbs a stairway of a thirty-foot tall gantry that appears to have been designed specifically for him to supervise and command this moment. When he reaches the pinnacle, the dim sun now offers just enough illumination for him to survey the assembly of aggressors. He then reaches to a green flag that is polled in a special holder. He grasps the staff of the massive pennant with both hands, raises it and waves once, from right to left. The Pounders know and respond to the signal, beginning their methodical march toward the base of the fortress called Armageddon.

"Ah'd say the Pounders' front lines are about three hundred yards from the base of the mountain," comments Jason in a calm tone. "They should start slowing down about a hundred yards out."

The lines can no longer keep the secret. There are too many and their boots strike heavily on the rocks beneath them, the cadence of their approach becoming thunderous. At two hundred yards the lines fan out to begin completely surrounding the plateaued heights. There will no longer be a chance for escape.

"I think the arrows should begin now," Eleazar comments in an unusually casual tone.

And almost immediately the twang of thousands of pointed projectiles whistle upward and then arch down upon the columns. Many hit their mark, but there are too many attackers to stem the impending flood. Now the Pounders reveal an ancient Greek defensive strategy: raising and positioning sturdy handheld Flexsteel shields perpendicularly over their heads to allow most of the raining death to bounce harmlessly away.

We were hoping for, praying for this tactic. The shields protect the bodies, but also restrict their view. The front line arrives at the hundred yard mark to discover a descending grade in the terrain.

It is subtle, not something that Palmotic had considered a problem. There was no indication by his scouts' reports that any significant traps had been set in this area. The depression runs the entire circumference of the Megiddo base and it was monitored carefully, from a distance preceding the engagement. The General did not require a close up inspection of the dip, not wanting to unnecessarily sacrifice men to the arrows that surely would have come down upon them, as they now come down. He only required reports of any unusual activity in the vicinity. None was reported, other than a few of the enemy's advance scouts, from time to time running to and fro, barely out of sight below the ridge line. The leader of the GOG army had verbally dismissed the sorties as reconnaissance work and obviously a ploy to taunt Palmotic's professionals into unplanned action.

What was not observed was the stealthy work of the Seconds, who long before the arrival of the millions, planted thousands of shoots of Spiny Alkanet. The scouts' mission was to assure that all avenues of assault were well covered in the weed that imbedded itself quickly and thickly upon the rocky soil.

So when the front line begins to descend, they discover a massive tangle of thorns and barbs. The vines are thick and not easy or quick to cut. The rows behind the front cannot see or prepare for the encumbrance and they push forward mercilessly. As the front troops become caught and fall victim to their serrated wounds, their support simply climb over top of them.

It is at this point that the harsh lessons of Bucastan prepare us well. We know that the Pounders are trained to encroach until they encounter an insurmountable barrier. In the case of Bucastan, it was the fortress wall. At Har Megiddo, it is to be the cliff base. But that is still far away for these lumbering ones.

We dared to pray in preparation that the automaton attackers would consider the brambles to be their boundary and would comply to their duty accordingly.

And that is exactly what happens. Their first canisters eject spew and the melting mist sprays not onto the cliff face as intended, but over the army climbing over the army. As each layer liquefies into the other, an added surprise appears. The treacherous Alkanet is so hardy, that it is slow to succumb to the acidic destruction. As more Pounders come forward, they too find the sea of stickles unnavigable.

Plamotic can now be heard screaming in our vision of him, "Halt! Halt!" But the clashing noise of the regiments drowns out all utterances. Yet there is another sound, curiously absent in the field, the crying out and wailing glossolalia associated with the intense pain these wretches must be suffering.

Finally the hordes behind have no place to advance; the bubbling ooze that was the forward guard proves a useless objective and so the millions remaining obey their ranting leader and halt.

The stink of damage is nauseating even to these trained to endure such things. So intense is the cooked fetor that soon the entirety of surviving Pounders begin to offer up the contents of their latest supper. Even their vomiting is a noiseless affair, begging some sort of subtitle to embellish the sight. Palmotic appears furious and is about to command a regrouping when, he too doubles over, along with his officers, to expel their meals. It will be long moments before they recover and then, only to experience another surprise.

All of this time, it has been assumed that the companies of Seconds and those of the 144 are safely sequestered on the summit of Megiddo. But we have been commanded by our leader to choose another approach. Two moon cycles ago, before any watchful eyes began to spy this land for conquest, Eleazar asked for a specific number of volunteers to become a defending unit on the top of the mountain. He chose a very specific number of individuals for this group, as an inspirational echo to the story of Gideon, the warrior-judge.

These brave three-hundred have been supplied ample food, water and weapons to make an impressive show from the heights. In addition, they are provided with an overabundance of oil lamps and fuel for a very specific purpose. When Palmotic's spys began to scrutinize our encampments, they reported the size of their foe based on the incredible number of fires lit each night. Palmotic based his own numbers and methods based on an estimation of our own multimillion man establishment. In fact, only the 300 existed, their primary duty for each day and night was to, "look large."

And large they looked. Each night they would light over 1000 vats of oil to give the appearance that a much larger contingent was looking down at GOG's minions. Clever devices were also constructed to allow one man to fire multiple arrows into their foes. In this way, our meager forces appeared very formidable indeed. It also kept the attention focused on Megiddo while Eleazar and Jason assessed and coordinated responses from a completely different location.

In the Jezreel, there is another rise that is less famous but perhaps as strategic as Fortress Megiddo. The other site is known as Afula. In ancient times, it was called Ofel, known as the actual home-place of Gideon. Because of its significant elevation, Afula at one time supported a Crusader castle. In recent history it flourished as an industrial community. Even with the wild geographic upheaval of recent years, the village survives, but now is mostly in ruin. There are survivors here; rugged folk who, by the work of the Ruach HaKodesh, have become Seconds. Housing is primitive and the activity of the place is easily overlooked…because there is little activity whatsoever. Some olive trees cling tenuously to survival here, but otherwise, only a smattering of mud and stone dwellings along with a long abandoned threshing floor. This is not the highest spot, nor a lush location, but what Afula does offer, as a perfect strategical platform for us, is its cave structure. Heavily honeycombed, the summit allows countless protrusions into the earth that weave into the rock and toward a rough gorge below. Only a few hearty people still live here and stay for one other reason we also find attractive. There is a well-hidden, but principal spring that still supplies.

Eleazar chose this place because it allows multiple access points, but only to those who know its underground avenues. From here, our warriors can easily view the goings on across the valley without themselves being noticed. Palmotic seemed unconcerned with the negligible bluff and that is wonderful for us, especially at this moment.

As the panic and discord continue within the ranks of the Pounders, Palmotic is consumed with thwarting the insolent campers of Har Megiddo. What he and his watchmen fail to pay attention to are the soldiers who exit the tunnels of Afula, into the adjoining canyon which they follow far to the rear of GOG's fracas.

Here they hold-up without sound or activity. Waiting for the inevitable, Palmotic will no doubt strive to reform and attack his target again. It is hours before the damage of the first foray is assessed. And more time passes as Palmotic works with his deputies to plan a new approach. This one is determined and it appears he is willing to sacrifice as many marchers as is necessary to win the day. This time he has had the front guard strip off the canisters which caused the previous destruction. Their function now becomes obvious. In the diminishing daylight, we watch as Palmotic climbs again to the top of his tower. It is a dangerous time for us because, were he to turn and gaze behind, he might detect small unfamiliar movements, perhaps even a hint of blue haze beyond the rear formations.

The General however, is preoccupied with what is ahead of him. The upstarts on the mountain have already begun to broadcast their presence by once again lighting their fires. Palmotic wastes no time, every bit of remaining light will be needed. He waves his green banner and his troops obey, pounding ever forward toward the now known obstacle. When the first troops reach the thorns they do an incredible thing. Proceeding in as far as they are capable, the first ones simply lean forward, allowing those behind to use the writhing body before them as a plank of sorts, they then fall forward also and the ones behind them walk over. Soon, like ants, a bridge of human corpses nears completion 360 degrees around the base of Megiddo.

When completed, it will be time to call in the secondaries, who wear the killing canisters. Their mission will be to make use of the necrotic masses pounding over the macabre dome to issue their weapons as intended.

It is dark now. The sun has abandoned the invaders' efforts. And as the final covering nears completion, Palmotic's attention is unexpectedly drawn to a noise behind him. It must be a hideous attenuation to him for we watch him crouch and cover his ears, as does every living GOG soldier on the field.

What cripples that crew, to us sounds like the sweet heralding of a call to worship. Thousands of shofars, like those used by Joshua and ironically by Mede, trumpet a warning of the Seconds and the 144 who now advance. They are not many in comparison to the millions that still serve GOG, but they have undeniable advantages; the first being this surprise attack from the rear. The second being the unsettling noise and the eerie Blue shine which identifies them as a special force indeed.

The effect on Palmotic's people is instantaneous. They have been tested too much today. What is more, there is a side effect from the earlier exploit. The chemicals unleashed at the base of Megiddo included a bacterial component necessary to stabilize the mix until detonated. It must be the same, or a similar germ, to that which has been causing the whole world to break out in pustulant boils. Now dispersed, the disease is spread by the wind into the nostrils and the wounds of the survivors. This particular brew is very fast acting and we can see the rash spread mercilessly from the original explosion site outward.

We can only speculate as to why the germs are so quickly affecting our opposition. Perhaps it is an unnatural attraction to the blood cure created from the veins of Brenda Anders. Whatever has advanced the reaction, blisters and lesions are now evident on all of GOG's contingents and this last insult is intolerable to their physical stamina and to their psyches. Without order they begin to convulse, then to run away from the new threat, blindly retreating toward the base of Megiddo. This would be a good thing if performed in methodical steps, but this is far from an orderly procedure. Every Pounder appears to have a new goal now. Instead of wanting to take down the heights of Har Megiddo, their behavior shifts in the confusion and they seem now inspired to scale the cliffs, seeking somehow to acquire the advantage.

They are doing badly, of course, and another curse starts to manifest. The remaining Pounders again begin to panic and, seeing no escape, they once more react as if they have reached their objective. The explosions of the canisters are far more widespread this time, casting their mist even back toward the command tower. Palmotic is no fool. He sees the coming doom, slides down the ladder with great skill. Once on the ground, he has a choice: charge toward the panic and try to lead one more attack himself, or turn and meet his adversaries head on. Neither option bodes well, but this is a man of pride and he will not stop until either he vanquishes or is himself brought down.

Attached to his belt is a sheath containing an odd relic, a broadsword, which he now pulls and points toward the oncoming Blue. With a cry of rage he charges toward them. There is still a significant army that he commands and they are moved to the same attacking action by his example. The wave gathers courage and organized momentum this time as it readies to meet our warriors. The coming clash and the threat of the bacterial onrush to our forces would be much to GOG's advantage…but for several factors revealed now.

At the cry of Palmotic's charge, the seismic activity directly under him and his troops increases its already continuous tremors. Now the ground sways and pitches in addition to its cracking and crumbling. Boulders from the heights of Har Megiddo are dislodged by the intensity and fly down, bouncing and creating their own thunder. The rolling rocks inspire the GOG forces to pick up their pace in our direction. This is not by plan, but in panic for their lives.

Thanks to the Hyssops, we have acquired and worked into the diet of all Seconds, great quantities of the Hyssop herb itself. It has somehow made us impervious to the bacterial threat. So fear of that threat to us is not an advantage associated with GOG's charge.

Additionally we have been greeted by a long awaited response to our prayers for assistance. There is a droning noise that starts from behind our ranks. Jason peers down at his newly calibrated compass and tells, "—coming from the east, Abaddon must have found his crew: That don't bode well for the visiting team."

And that is an understatement. The drone turns into the buzzing roar of an air force that now flies over our heads. Millions of the armored insects that have caused such havoc throughout the planet have arrived to eagerly participate in the moment. They too, draw a bead on GOG's marchers and swarm with a vengeance.

As if this alone would not subdue any army; again from behind the Blue, appears another light. This glow approaches with a familiar sound from years back—Horse hooves! The illumination brightens to blinding. There is a golden bronze cast to it and even the Blue is unable to continue. The bugs are driven away by the light, but their damage is evident. All on the battlefield are on their knees. The arrival of thousands of thundering steeds carry riders that no mortal can gaze upon. We Keepers are only allowed a glimpse of the holiness and we know immediately: it is our King that believers of many centuries have begged to arrive. With him are the martyrs finally freed for this honor to ride in victory with their Redeemer.

Bronzeman's glory becomes shaded now, it does not diminish, yet somehow we are able to let it into us, to gaze and wonder at its majesty. Suddenly, in the light, there is a word that comes to us. It must be shared. It must be obeyed. To us the word is already beautiful. To Palmotic and those of GOG, it will strike terror or, we pray, offer the last chance of forgiveness.

The word is sent out, not just to those on the field, but to all of Israel, to Roma, to the far parts of the Northlands, the Ethiopians, Rio and the Mexicos and the remains of this broken orb. Above, the Singularity throbs and indescribable beings fly out and toward us, millions upon millions. There are eruptions from below and strange ethereal bodies float into focus. All forces on the field of battle, and with them all mankind everywhere on the planet, lay and kneel—not one dare stand in the moment. Now the word comes alive on our tongue and each receives it:

CONFESS

And this command presents an immediate dilemma. To confess, one must have a tongue or a heart that might seek reconciliation. The Pounders are not created with either of these things. Those that have survived the confusion, now simply evaporate. Around the globe, they cease and so ends the fear and intimidation they represented.

But that is not the astounding part. What we witness next is amazing to our eyes. It is most evident in the battlefield of Armageddon. We assumed that Mede's creatures made up almost the entirety of his army, with a select few captains, lieutenants and sergeants to lead them. But once the clones disappear, nearly half of the survivors remain—millions upon millions! Now we Keepers must also confess: We had, like many before us, wondered why our God YHWH would choose to come to power by battle when He is already all powerful? And why is such sacrifice necessary? Did not Yeshua already pay the ultimate price? In even the strongest believer's heart, such questions might cause a weakened walk.

YHWH has had a plan all along. How could we have doubted? The world and all of humanity simultaneously receive the vision of this confrontation through us. All who live and breathe now can see that, before time began, He knew the hearts of even the enemy and desired their love for Him to replace their love for their own desires. Who else, but a loving God would use a place of ugly war to draw so many to one place for a moment of spiritual wrestling—one final opportunity for salvation?

The adversary is not only brought down, but many have been convicted in this moment. They are counted, along with us who already know, and with all those around the world who, by this colossal vision, choose Bronzeman as their King. This is the greatest call to salvation that has ever occurred and the entire world is allowed to see it. Thus the very battle becomes a testimony and around the globe, the call turns hearts from stone to spiritual light.

All of these things have been made possible by grace from YAHWH, the love of His son, and the willingness of human souls made spiritually humble by what they have witnessed. All of this was necessary for what happens now. By the gift of our hearing, blessed as a tool provided through the Ruach Spirit, with one cry, in a perfect unison never heard before, all whose hearts beat with the same spiritual rhythm say:

"—Yeshua, you are my Savior, you are our God!"

And the Blue sings to the Bronze, the lights merge into a something more, that those whose hearts are not humbled cannot understand. And that is the remaining miracle: YHWH's mercy is not done. There are still the Un-lit to be dealt with.

The evidence of this is witnessed in Serge Palmotic, who bows like everyone else, but refuses to honor the King. He does speak however, but blindly to the light he cannot comprehend. He speaks for himself and for all of those like him. "I accept my defeat at your hands, and even offer gratitude for your good treatment of my company. But I chose my allegiance beforehand and will only honor you now as your prisoner, not as my chieftain.

So it was for a portion who even with all that had happened over the last seven years, refused true love. They could not fathom that this God before them had not destroyed them, but would allow them for a thousand years to serve.

They will not be considered as heirs of the kingdom, but as guests. These new residents will struggle, for they will have to watch the familiar way in which the King fellowships with his kin. They will not experience the joy of that interaction, nor receive the promises or privileges bestowed on us as adopted sons and daughters.

Why will they not be allowed citizen status? It is their choice, not their plight. They will even be given the offer of new life if ever they will recognize Yeshua as Messiah. That sounds so simple to us, but it is a chasm of lightyears for them. These are the ones on the outside to whom the entire plan of God was presented and yet they would not turn toward righteousness. With hearts that hardened, it will be only by an entirely new and unknown miracle that they will be saved. Still, all things are possible with God.

One sees
One hears
And it is written
Let us work together that the world may know!

—**Keepers, for the glory of God**

The Bronzeman News

My name is Roxanne. You have no doubt seen the visions and heard the tell of a new world that has come. There is no more destruction, no more decay, no promises are needed, for our King is here. I have been at his throne and can tell you so. You will meet him soon, but you must come to the feast, the feast will not come to you.

As with my Blue Brother Küllo, I'm not the story—I'm the eyes, ears and hands of my Lord—but instead of reflecting the light of Bronzeman, I'm now a part of His glory. The words on these pages are to invite you Last- Ones to join us. It's His way. He loves you, but He will not make you love him. It's your choice to Do or Do-Not.

MINGLE IT. MAKE UP YOUR OWN MIND, I WILL NOT MAKE IT FOR YOU.

Edition Twelve: Location - Irrelevant
Time: Irrelevant

"So why we be going out instead of staying?"

My sweet guardian, Black Jackson has just voiced the question that beats in my own heart. All of the believers, from the beginning until this moment, have assembled: those who had been sleeping and those gathered up; those who hoped before Bronzeman's sacrifice as the suffering servant; those of the church age who chose Him as their Messiah; and we Seconds who rebelled until the very day of his return. All worship at his feet. All sing. We worship as a community for (I struggle now with the concept of time) ever.

"Why must we go, when here is paradise?" BJ asks to the sky above.

All of this is beyond explanation, even as I write the words. A favorite term from my past comes to mind.

IT IS WHAT IT IS.

Before, I had trouble hearing His voice within me. Before this Age of Completion, it was the nature of all humans, even devout believers, to doubt God's dwelling within them. In my case, His voice sounded like my own inner voice, and I could not, would not completely trust that voice deep in my spirit. So, in grace, He spoke through His scripture, affirming it through other believers, to confirm what was stirring within. It was His perfect way of communicating with someone who still wrestled to be in control of their own destiny.

All that has changed: All things, but for one, have been made new. We are finally transfigured. It's amazing to see my Seconds kin again and, in their changed condition, to still recognize them. I'm still trying to comprehend my own body, since the change. What kind of a being have I become? I'm told that we are not *angelics*. That fairytale (our somehow evolving after physical death into one of God's other creations) is ridiculous. He said very clearly that we are created in His image.

I don't have wings like the angelics—I don't need them. I have hands and feet, arms, legs, a torso, a head, eyes, ears, a mouth, just as before, but I am also able to be outside of these things. My appearance is neither young nor old, such concepts don't exist here. Beyond that I am Blue. That is sufficient.

Angelics were built to serve as our protectors and God's warriors. They have no free will to lose, nor is that concept important to them. I know, we've had the conversation. We are very different indeed. My question to the heavenly hosts was this, "How could Lucifer and his legions have thought to rebel?"

The answer defines the essence of our unique separation from the angelics. Their struggle was one of pride and pure power, not a pursuit of knowledge or choice of allegiance. Lucifer truly was beautiful, and as such, why not think oneself more important? Why not prove oneself better than your Designer? Whereas humankind perceived themselves as independent from the spiritual realm, the angelics are well aware that power is held within the vibrations of the atoms, molecules and smaller things of the cosmos. Where we strove to define and manipulate such matter, the angelics possessed the means of bending, even adjusting elements to their purpose.

The authority to do so was given in trust, and when that trust was broken by the third of those who sided with Satan, that group could not be forgiven.

Even so, God would not end even such a despicable portion of His genesis. They were imprisoned on the very world where we were invited to dwell in free relationship with the Almighty.

And that is how we were nabbed. It was a whisper in our ear, not even our own thought, but a choice of whom was the better master. How easily we failed to consider the consequences.

All of this, YHWH knew would unfold. All of this was His to redeem, and so, He built into His creation, before it was even created, the victory of pure love—ours for the choosing—a gift exclusive to humans over all other creatures.

So now we Blue Ones are not sleeping, nor dead, nor whatever term you would try to use to explain our ancient divorce from our Deity. He has brought us back, re-married us with His own physical sacrifice. Our bodies have been (the scriptural word is *kabed*) glorified. There is no earthly way of explaining it, unless you have yourself been glorified. To participate in new-worldly things, I have the physical ability to materialize. I also do not need to be physically present to exist. You in the world who still refuse the love of God struggle to see me, complain of a bright blue light around me. It is the way of all encounters between God's kin and the unholy.

You who refuse His supremacy have one other downfall. You are refused entry through the gates into New Jerusalem. The city and its King cannot coexist with you. I'm sure this frustrates you all the more. We, however can pass through the gates to interact with you. Our mission is first, one of witness; to share with as many of you Last Ones as possible the love of your Savior. Additionally, we must administrate. This would be a frustrating duty, but Yeshua the Savior is also Bronzeman the King, and he has provided us with wisdom to redirect any who remain confused. By his guidance, we offer improved ways to work your land and to seek out a higher quality of life. Most of you resent the structure of the new society and I mingle your irritation. You perceive yourselves as second class citizens, and to be blunt, it's worse than that. You're not citizens at all. The only hope offered to you is to search your heart for repentance and sincerely seek His love. Your circumstance will change immediately.

Regardless of whether or not you confess to him, do not resist what is provided now. It may be the last gift you ever receive prior to your complete separation from Light. The hardest of truths for you to understand doesn't change your options. That truth is that you have only three choices to realize: Accept the better secular existence now offered; or claim Yeshua in your spiritual heart; or abandon all, escaping by seclusion into the darkest regions of the world.

It's strange to us that some of you choose the latter. You are apparently so bitter that your hatred seeks to blame all others rather than confess your own sinful nature. Bronzeman is aware of regions throughout the earth that remain unhealed because of you who would still kill your Lord if given the opportunity—you *Dark Dwellers*. Our King is even benevolent to you offering a last chance of comfort if any return in repentance.

Though we believers now know eternal life, you Last Ones do not. Even so, by our efforts to assist, most of you will now realize healthy lives of 120 years or more. It seems an amazing feat, considering the lifetimes shortened previously by the suffering during the seven year tribulation period. But we have another harsh truth to share—such a span is a blink of the eye. We long so much for you to join us in joy beyond the decay of death. What apparently doesn't register with you is the alternative you face—eternal existence without the presence of God. As Danny Adamson now calls it, "the true black hole of life".

The world is healing. It has started with New Jerusalem, which is a paradise difficult to entail with mere words. The Apostle John's language approaches a fair description; but terms like *crystal sea* and *azure sky above* are only comparatives punctuated by the once dark blue called V4641 (now it is some kind of shining portal through which the angelics travel). Visions from that now nearby place bring us to trembling knees even in our perfected state. Just a glance toward the heavens now inspires intense worship of the sovereign, omnipotent ruler whose jewel-like qualities are beyond terrestrial definition. His emerald throne glistens as a rainbow. There are elders and creatures; descriptions of which my vocabulary fails to capture. Lightning there; rumbles that are either voices or thunder, I can't tell.

At first encounter I was sure I would vaporize into ash, as had the Pounders. Scripture, which I did not know I knew, flashed into my awareness,

NONE IS RIGHTEOUS, NOT ONE.

But a gentle hand touched me from within. How can that be? I knew and know and will know the hand, for it's my Savior's. He settles me and helps me up from my prostrate position. He walks with me by the sea of glass and fire and explains more of his Father's grandeur. This place is a Blue Haven, it is lit with peace. But where Yeshua walks, the Blue mingles with his Golden Bronze. The combination takes away any other thought, but to live in that moment forever. He gives me fresh words and a new name to learn. We laugh as he pretends to be stern in the moment, telling me the name is our secret, and that he may have to give me another name if I divulge this one to others. He comforts all that I am. In him I am able to peer at the face of YHWH. And I utter, "Holy, holy, holy," from my lips and from my heart.

We kneel together to dip our hands into the river that now flows through the city. The water is both hot and cold. It tickles both my desire to constantly remain here in worship, and concurrently travel outward seeking a soul to save by the telling of my story. As we stay and as we go, songs of joy swirl in the atmosphere and in our hearts

Here in Jerusalem, there is a particular whispering melody of praise that charms the air around. It is almost visible, a coral crown honoring the presence of the world's Redeemer:

It is done.
The Aleph and the Tov
The Before until Then
He has made you His love
Forever, forever, forever
The Before until Then
The Aleph and the Tov
He has made you His love
It is done.
Amen!

The rushing of the waters replies in harmony and I find myself frequently breaking out into my own song of adulation to My Lord who is somehow my constant companion. We sit and gaze upon the Tree of Life. I am astounded as he points out my new name written on one of the leaves entwined within its shimmering branches laced with fruit of indefinable variety. Stooping beneath the tree, the Lamb who paid my ransom reaches and picks up a small white stone which he then gives to me with a knowing smile. Another scripture from the book of Revelation is immediately in my mind and I begin to tear up. Yeshua lifts his hand to brush the moisture away and then he kisses my forehead. *Holy, holy, holy.*

I speak with the other human spirits who dwell here, spirits such as BJ, and it's the same with them: Yeshua is their constant chaperon as well. He travels with them and with me. We dwell—tabernacle—together in the vast landscape filled with color and growth, incomprehensible before these times. It encompasses an area larger than any country known before with a population eager to serve and fellowship with our Lord. There actually is one word that does describe it. A breathable word that YHWH taught us in the original garden, a word poorly understood and mistranslated by humanity until this moment:

SHALOM.

Again my heart sings again, *Holy, holy, holy.*

We are there, and we are here, living two parts of the mystery. "Why we be going instead of staying?" My brother persists.

"Because He tells us to," I finally answer Black Jackson.

"Solid Ground," he answers back. "It be time for ploughing His borders."

For a thousand years it will be and then we'll experience, in perfect and complete understanding, what only God has known beforehand—the future.*

The rest of the globe will be reclaimed as well. It will take time because of the eons of spiritual damage that scarred the place. To help with the transformation, Preacher Elijah and Brother Moses, along with Danny Adamson have been given power by Bronzeman's authority. Their understanding of the micro-physical and macro-physical realms will help them replenish what has been lost. Tau neutrinos are the catalyst for the rebuilding. Laminin protein bonds will be the glue. I have to laugh at my words, because, before our final change, I had no clue as to what these things were. Now I have been given a broader education with the help of YHWH's *semicha's*—those He has breathed knowledge into, that they may perfectly impart it to others. I have mentioned three of them already. Ilbani the Keeper of the Kin, Jende, Amos, Eleazar and Ayita BenMadai, Ki and Küllo have also had the hand of the Almighty laid on them

—and now I am told that this honor and responsibility is being offered to me as a calling. I'm not deserving of His gift, but I will devote my entire spirit to carry out His desire.

As we go, I feel compelled to write other things that are in metamorphosis. We don't travel in the same way as before. Yes, we can walk or use steam vehicles, or ride, but why? I now think of—mingle—a location and I am there. I desire to relate with kin or with a particular Last One and there I am. In unusual circumstances, we do travel in the ancient style—an effort to be polite to you Last Ones who are not able to spiritually shift.

Yet another change affects us all: Time, or the perceived passage of existence doesn't flow as it once did. Sometimes it is much quicker, sometimes a moment can last what once was considered a lifetime. There is no explaining—un-puzzling it better. I've learned to experience and wonder at it with my grandfather. Old Ben, as we jokingly call him; not a one of us is old in our new bodies, travels with us and still finds beautiful ways to teach me.

"When we are with the Last Ones, is it not convenient to measure our encounters using the Earth's rotation and the lunar changes as reference points?" Grandfather imparts wisdom in the way taught to him, and to all of YHWH's followers: through questioning the student. "Are not any Un-lit, after all, still tethered to time and so require rest and methods for tracking planting periods, seasonal passage and of course reproduction?"

Grandfather Ben has brought up other significant minglings of memory for me. For example: Reproduction, a God-gift of the highest order, is one which still astounds me. During my brief time as a tertiary being, I didn't conceive a child. As an eternal, I no longer have that capability. It was a regret that I confessed to my Savior, that I was not able to procreate. He understood and I believe it is one of the reasons why he has sent me out. I'm helping him in a magnificent but different way, to bring new life to the kingdom. Still, I'll never know the preciousness of motherhood; so I marvel when I watch the process in the unlit regions. There is pain and joy in birthing, bearing one from the passion of two. I am told it is the way YHWH feels when we testify with His Spirit's participation, bearing new life in the form of another Blue believer.

All of this sounds fantastical to you Un-lit, for you live in our midst and yet cannot see or hear or travel dimensionally as we do. Because of this, we sometimes disappear from your sight. Sometimes we appear as if from nowhere and I suspect you are intimidated by the spiritual physics of it all.

Bronzeman explained this as the reason he desired us to go out, and the reason that he has blessed me with Ilbani's and Küllo's gift of writing. In my new form, it seems odd now to grasp a pen and press it to paper, a tactile sense that should not generate such desire in me. How do I explain the sensation? It's as if a void exists within me when I'm without the stylus and parchment. It's as if I can't <u>not</u> write. There's no better way to tell it.

My Lord assures me, it is for his glory that my writing ambition exists. The unlit world must have the word in script, even if it no longer holds the same power for us. That same word is now etched upon our hearts. Brother Moses reminded me, prior to my going out, that, "In order for YHWH to have spoken the universe into being, He first had to create the Word to be spoken." I am astounded at the thought—what He has given me to do, which is reflected from the first thing He ever invented, even before matter itself.

So many other things have been reordered. It doesn't take much imagination to see why YHWH has set the time as a thousand years for the world's healing. It will take all of that for us to acclimate.

Electricity is still not present in this reality. It is simply not relevant (and I hear you Un-lit Last Ones mourning its absence constantly). Commerce and barter, as tribal rituals, placing personal value on items and produce continue to cause strife outside the shimmering walls of New Jerusalem. Everyone outside the gates is now capable of growing all the food they need. Clothing and resources are made available for all yet you still fixate on who is the better producer of what. You bicker over what amount each should have and ignore the fact that each receives everything without cost according to each one's need. We pray that as many as possible become aware of their blessed condition and that worship of YHWH is the result.

My own prayer, for you, and for His kin, is that His will be done in the now.

So it is in this state of now that I and my clan praise at his throne. Simultaneously, Bronzeman walks with each of us individually and sends each one on their mission. It is the way of the New Heaven and the New Earth. He reminded me before our sending-out, that He is changing all things, even the Un-lit and the unholy, making something different. And to that purpose, my writing, our words, are not for our benefit but for you who will know Him when you choose to. It will happen because it has happened. He created the Word and the Word is with YHWH and the word is YHWH.

Küllo has been asked to stay at the side of Lord Yeshua. With him, dwells Ilbani. They will also be writing. But their task is to scribe the history of New Jerusalem as it takes place. I can only imagine their excitement as they watch the interaction of heaven and earth through the eyes of their Monarch.

And Han Ko, whom I first met under such terrible circumstances in a treacherous time of another age, she has become my dearest spiritual sister. I pleaded with my blessed Redeemer to allow her to travel with us, but her spirit is crucial to the printing and sending out of new letters to the Un-lit. Ours was the saddest of partings even though we are actually not separated at all—like the air that surrounds the planet. All of it, all of us, touch though we may be far from one another in true location. I can't explain it in terms more easily understood, unless you are Blue. All I know is that I'm lonelier in her absence; in Küllo's and my grandfather's absence. Bronzeman assures me we will be more closely united soon enough. I trust him in that and in all things.

Jason, Betty, Luther and Rachel have been given a task as well. Though the Pretender and his Pounders have been put down, there are still those of the dark who desire influence. Serge Palmotic is but one. He knelt before Bronzeman on the battlefield but our King saw his heart and knows its duplicity. The failed general, and others like him, are watched closely by the Keepers. Their ongoing obedience will be demanded and they are as powerless as electricity to initiate any sort of revolt. Still, there are more subtle ways to sow the seeds of fresh dissent over the span of a millennium. Our soldiers will journey to the foulest regions most desperate for healing. Theirs will not be a mission of testimony. They will be given special talents to use in smelling out evil ways. Our kin are being asked to be in the waiting for the nittiest of deeds initiated by the outcast. On discovery, those vile ones will be escorted to a place so dark and removed that will make even the rankest environ seem a palace in the heavenlies by comparison. Küllo named the people living in these places, Dark Dwellers, the animal-like and most hope-lost of all.

Why doesn't our King preemptively eliminate the potential threat? Why give any remaining chance for ill intent? How much like the enemy that would be? In this age, every one of you Last Ones will have your last chance to accept Bronzeman as your personal Savior. Then finally, on The Day, there will be no further mercy from God's final judgement. The reality in difference between eternal life and eternal death will be, as Black Jackson would say, "solid ground".

Within the Kingdom, many others have Do's, that Bronzeman desires for them. Each Blue One, regents designated by his authority, receives the task with honor and humility. By our accomplishments blessed by our King, the millennium will see the new heaven and the new earth come together as one. Preacher Elijah once taught that, in the old ages, theocracy was viewed as corrupt; of course because of the nature of human dictators corrupting the rule. But now we have become the perfect servants to be ruled. A disturbing concept? Only to you unholy ones; only to you who refuse the benevolence of the Perfect Ruler.

I suggested earlier in this writing that all things, but for one, have changed. That one unchanging thing is not a thing at all, but the Creator of it all. His Shekinah Glory has been infinitely and perfectly present, before this universe and before the minutest particle was spoken into existence. He will be unchanged, when this universe and all other things cease. He orders shalom and chaos and shalom again of all things. He is life. We are life only with, and through, Him.

We may now dwell with Him in holiness. We might dream that we understand Him and His infinite love, but still and forever there is only one perfect truth:

YHWH is God and we are not.

What He has planned and makes and completes; Before until Then, we are able only to glimpse, even with our new awareness. Throughout time and scripture there has not yet been a moment where He, the Creator, has destroyed matter. Yes: He has ended life when necessary; He reorders chaos when rebellion arises; but in this macrocosm matter has not ever been completely destroyed. Perhaps that will change as well. We cannot know. He can. It was always meant to be this way. To know Him we have to choose, and to choose, we have to be transformed. We are a part of eternity, but He is—the Eternal.

I mentioned earlier the sad distinctions—those separated and those redeemed. But as I and my clan transport to our next destinations, I'm aware of another hope for you Last Ones. It appears as a faint blue stream, flowing past our current, heading toward New Jerusalem. It is another answer to Black Jackson as to, "why we be going out": Because we make ourselves available to shine the dazzling light of Yeshua's love within us—daily, eternally. Because Moses and the prophets of old; the early apostles; Matthew, Mark, Luke, John, Paul, James, Peter and the Watchmen; Danny, Fitzgerald Elijah, Pasha, Jason, Han Ko and Küllo, Ilbani…and me. Because of all who were and are obedient in scribing His inspiration, the ever deepening river of blue continues to swell. The Ruach of God continues to stir new and unexpected surprises, always to His glory.

There are those in the unholy and dark regions who read the words of Holy Scripture; or maybe they hear a simple news-tell about the Bronzeman: and they believe. Even now they confess and kneel in obedience and joy. These have become the most amazing Blue Ones of all, for they have had to overcome the greatest obstacles to faith, enduring the most severe persecution and overcoming the greatest doubt of any group throughout the history of mankind.

They flood forward in total obedience and eagerness, drawn by the love of their Ruler to his new city. They have become an offering of thanksgiving. As they pass, we see in each one's hand, five sticks wedged together to form the perfect unity that is our Bronzeman. We exchange warm greetings and let loose the song that can't be held within:

It is done.
The Aleph and the Tov
The Before until Then
He has made you His love
Forever, forever, forever
The Before until Then
The Aleph and the Tov
He has made you His love
It is done.
Amen!

In that perfect unity we are gathered in. In that perfect unity we are sent out. I look at BJ to get his attention and I point toward the blue stream, smiling and telling him, "That's why we go."

And to you who have yet to understand, yet you continue to read these words, I smile as well. And I say in the name of Bronzeman who loves you more than life itself, that's why you too should join us.

—The End?—

*For I know that my Redeemer lives,
and at the last he will stand upon the earth.*

—Job 19:25

AUTHOR

MARK A. CORNELIUS

MARK A. CORNELIUS has authored numerous books, video productions, a journal ministry, musicals, and several podcast series.

His works include *RUT Management—Discovering Adventure in the Routine of Life, Believement—Breaking Through the Belief Barrier, Welfare Christianity, Thunder Buffalo Goes Home, Tomorrow's Bread, Marginalized, UnMeasuring—What if we are ALL Wrong?* and the popular fiction series The Ruach Saga (*including The Singularity, The Book of Seconds, Bronzeman, and War of the Lost Song*).

His books can be purchased at https://quantumdiscovery.net/shop/, and at www.RUTmanagement.com.

Amos 3:6-8, The Bible

Mark has authored other insights and blogs, all of which can be obtained on his website. You can experience Mark's passion for writing at **www.MarkCornelius.me**.

Catch Mark's podcasts at:

Watchmen podcast:
https://www.youtube.com/channel/UC3fA03AhXRh RZNhNyrEhgA

Mark My Words (Critical Thinking) podcast:
https://www.youtube.com/channel/UCR8Csunh9mJMOZHj197NUZg

Travel with Mark at his blog: **www.DeepEndFaith.blogspot.com**, and dive into discussion on **E-mail: Markcwrites@gmail.com**, or **Facebook: https://www.facebook.com/Mark-My-Words-103741988034911**.

Join Mark in asking his ongoing journey question…

"WHAT IF?"

Looking forward to our journey together!

ILLUSTRATOR - Shay Cavender was born in Nashville, Tennessee. She began her drawing career at a young age doodling and writing short comic strips. Her unique style specializes in animals both real and fantastical. Currently she is a student at the University of Tennessee at Martin as a Graphic Design major. She plays Trombone in the UTM Marching Skyhawk Band and aims to continue playing her instrument later in life despite her art-oriented career direction. Drawing and illustrating are her passions along with her love of animals including dogs and reindeer. In the future, Shay hopes to secure a profession that will utilize her distinctive talents.

Favorite words from Küllo's New Place Dictionary

מָשִׁיחַ: 'Messiah' in the old letters.

Bad-sung: Not having any good to say about someone or something

Be raised: Living after dying.

Blubbertonguing: sticking out your tongue and blowing air. same as Raspberry but stronger.

Blue or the Blue: The blue glow that shines from a Second. Used sometimes by the *Un-lit* as a label for a group of Seconds.

Bose-Spooks (Wicked Ghosts): Mede's strange machine-people who have the dimmest light of all. Also called Pounders.

Brainer: someone who God has given solid ground (strong knowing).

Bricked: Getting people's attention in a big way, throwing a brick. The brick hits one and that one turns into a brick that God throws at the other people.

Bronzeman: Jesus, the King-coming.

Bronze Word: God's plan to mingle the world with His son.

Call: Something Bronzeman whispers to his kin that excites them to Do for him.

Called-Out: Telling a new word or idea. Also used when Bronzeman makes a new Second or gives a Do. Best be praying when Calling-Out. Calling-Out is against the Do Board.

Caller: Someone who tells the new word or idea.

Catch: Hearing or reading something new.

Danny-Sticks: The five sticks used in telling about God's love

Dark Blue: The space hole that Bronzeman brought to suck the electric out.

Dark Dwellers: The most Un-lit of all. Hope-lost and animal-like, they have the farthest to travel to get back to God.

Dark-Tell: Pretender Mede's lies being spread.

Do: An order to be obeyed. Bronzeman and Mede both call to Do.

Do Board: Everywhere rules from the Mede and the Do Brothers, posted on boards (pictures too for no-readers) in every town and village.

Do Brothers: The Mede's Law Makers for the Green Order Government.

Do-gooder: Sacrificing your own good to help people.

Do-point: Place where you are expected to Do what you are told to Do

Done-done: Dead acause you didn't Do Mede's Do.

Fact: Whatever the Do-Board says.

First Do: Always listed at top of Do Board: "If the Do Board isn't obeyed, snuffing happens".

Get-rich: Grow, improve.

Glue: Keeping something or someone close and precious.

Gone-things: Animals and things that can't be found no-more.

God Poking: God getting directly involved, using his Spirit to call his people to action.

Hope-lost: Them that cannot or will not look to Bronzeman to heal their hurt. Dark Dwellers are the saddest of them all.

Hopping the corner: Avoiding entering a town or territory, going around the edge to avoid confrontation.

Hurt: Punishment given by Peacers for not following the Pretender's Do's.

In-kin: The closest of friends. Almost as strong as Bronzeman being inside.

In-traveler: A stranger from outside the city of Jerusalem who is looking for shelter or trade.

Jacksoned: A word given new or different meaning so ye can mingle God better.

Keeping Kin: Serving and being served by yer closest ones.

King-coming: Bronzeman. Seconds know that he has been afore. Remnant People call him Soon-coming.

Leathers: Protective clothing worn by most people to keep off the bugs. Worn by Seconds to protect their Blue.

Lit-Ones: Seconds or New Followers.

Lowers: What Pretender Meade calls anyone else.

Low-selfing: Showing by bowing, doing or telling that Bronzeman is best

Make-big: Something that opens ears and eyes.

Mingle: 1. Mix together, make two things one. 2. Gluing yer Calling Out to yer Do.

No-Mores: People who disappeared either by Gathering-Up, cannibalism or mystery.

No-Readers: Can't read this, acause they can't read no-thing.

Peacer and Boss-Peacer: Worldwide Green Government secret police trained to find problems and make them go away.

Ploughing His Borders: Obeying the call of Bronzeman.

Pounders: also called Bose-Spooks (Wicked Ghosts).

Pounder-trains: Armies of Pounders.

Pretender Mede: Acause that's what he is.

Puzzle: To wonder about something that needs figuring out.

Puzzled-up: Too much unknown to un-puzzle in the now.

Readers: Them that can read.

Red-lit: Them that choose the Call and Do of the Mede over Bronzeman. Their only light is the Red Chem-light invention of the Mede.

Re-know: Remember something strongly from the past. Re-knowing: An older thing coming back in your brain.

Righting the Writing: Telling the difference between Do and Call.

Sad-enough: Bad news, cannot be worse.

Seeing: Bronzeman showing Himself to people or giving them a view of something new.

Shine: Letting the Blue show, Shining: mingling God's love to people.

Snuffed: Yer light being put out by yer earth-life being stopped.

Solid Ground: Strong Knowing / Most true of all.

Souling: Witnessing to be done by telling No-lits and Red-lits about Bronzeman. Sewing seeds into souls.

Sour-milk: Something bad that be happening.

The Change: When Blue shows up on someone. It covers their skin and shines out from inside them.

The Dark: When the electric wouldn't turn on any more. The Dark Blue in the sky sucked it dry.

The Others: Can't tell who they are acause of the secret.

Trade or No-Trade: Trade means something matters. No-Trade means it does not.

Un-lit: Them that are not Blue-lit or Red-lit. They have no mingling at all and don't believe in Bronzeman

Un-puzzle: Putting the pieces of the puzzle together right

Visioning: The sight and sound of the Spirit being given to the eyes and ears of a Second.

Watering the Garden: Crying tears Bronzeman will take to build his beautiful new place for us.

9 781959 314387